DEATH'S COLLECTOR

BILL MCCURRY

Death's Collector
First Edition, January 2019

Infinite Monkeys Publishing
Carrollton, Texas
Bill-McCurry.com

Editing: Shayla Raquel, ShaylaRaquel.com
Cover Design: Monica Haynes, TheThatchery.com
Interior Formatting: Rogena Mitchell-Jones, RogenaMitchell.com

ISBN-13: 978-0-9848062-3-2

To Kathleen:
Together, we have the technology.

ONE

I often forget the real reason why I murdered people. Some days I told myself I was cursed to do it, and other days I admitted I took this curse onto myself, that nobody moved my jaw up and down to make me say yes. Rarely did I recall the real reason. I murdered people for love.

On the day I perched downhill from Crossoak village, I had just about forgotten that love was a reason for doing things. The village kids ran around behind me, smashing wildflowers and screaming like Death and his five pallid whores. I appreciated flowers, but I didn't say anything to the whooping mob. They exhibited a shattering fear of me on occasion—so gigantic it probably seemed like a game—and they tended to forget about it unless they concentrated on being terrified. It was a good sight healthier than their parents' grinding dread, hiding in their houses when I walked past and making folk magic wards against evil behind my back. Anyway, some of the less obliterated yellow pin-blossoms were already pushing up from the grass. It was a shame to get blood all over them, but there it was.

I hummed a little nonsense song under my breath as I watched the three ass-dragging ex-soldiers two dozen paces downslope from me. They glared, their swords pointed at my face and their teeth bared. They also fidgeted and whispered sidewise to each other, which undercut their show of ferocity, but they hadn't sagged and trudged off down the slope yet. One was chubby, one looked strong, and the third was just a boy, really. In my head, I named them Rotund, Nasty, and Pup.

I scooched my butt to a less splintery spot on my barrel and let my feet swing like raggedy pendulums. I had rolled this barrel here past the edge of town a month ago and tipped it on end for a perch. I'd grown tired of standing around while thieves and murderers dawdled over how to kill me. These three were dallying for an uncommon length of time.

Onni shuffled up from the lane behind me. He was striving to be unobtrusive, but for him, stealth amounted to holding his breath between wheezes, so he sounded like a horse about to collapse dead. I glanced and saw him wipe his sweaty palms down the front of his nice blue jacket, which gaped at the belly. He whispered, "Bib, they're the first ones in a week. Maybe they'll just leave. Do you think they might just leave? I think they might."

I kept humming and shrugged. The rough-patched men hadn't shifted as much as a foot. Rotund had lost his helmet somewhere on the trail, and his blond hair stood horrified in all directions. His friends had kept hold of their stained and torn gear, but their shirts hung loose.

Some poorly planned military venture had fallen all to hell a few months ago, probably overwhelmed by a few stern badgers. A stream of deserters and survivors had been trickling through the hills since then. They'd been rummaging around the less destitute towns for food, beer, clean beds, silver to steal, and women to rape.

Onni shuffled down to face me from the side. He was a good-looking man; even when pinched and anxious, his face was almost beautiful. "Could you please make yourself a hint more..." He sighed. "Intimidating? It might frighten them away."

"You mean your heart doesn't fairly shrivel from standing beside my imposing self? I do admit that my hair's less red than it was, and I appear lean and a little shabby, but they should still be awed by my moral courage." I smoothed my beard, which was grayer than my hair.

"Um, as a sorcerer, perhaps you could do something sorcerous? Turn them into... something?"

Without looking at him, I said, "For these sad fellows? Such a profligate indulgence in magic might change every person around in ways we can't even imagine—if it didn't destroy you outright by lightning, or a plague of vermin." It was a good excuse to use when people wanted to see something shiny happen, and I didn't want to admit I'd been tapped out of magic for years.

Onni coughed and scooted back a few feet. I winked at him, and he looked away. He settled for looking at something unlikely to engage in violence, a tree he must have known well, since I imagine he'd seen every day since he could walk.

"You can't know what will happen, Alder Onni. They could come back tonight and slice off your head, and I can't allow such an occurrence. I don't want it said that I cheated you."

To be frank, I didn't want them to go away. They'd sure as blue skies earned death for doing some horrible shit somewhere. The anticipation of killing them was pleasurable, as good as knowing that a book and a hot bath were waiting, back when I could indulge in such opulence.

At last, Rotund yelled, "Go off and piss on your pillow, old man!"

I almost objected to that characterization, even though I was indeed old enough to be the little muck-sucker's father. Instead, I called out, "You have no reason to be harsh, sir. We're not overly violent people. Pass us by."

Rotund grinned and Nasty leaned forward. Rotund said,

"We're taking your food, wine, and whatever the hell else looks good in this rat turd of a place." Pup nodded and shook his sword.

I created a masterpiece of a smile. "There's a town just beyond us, popping with delights! You can luxuriate in the laps of nubile women before the sun sets tomorrow." In fact, the next town up the road mustered a standing guard that would mash these fellows into grit and rancid butter.

"Gut yourself, you pile of pig vomit! We're not walking around to some other damned town!"

"You do yourself a disservice. Life is chancy, and we have nothing worthy of a man like you. Pass, and I myself will bring you a mug of good beer as you walk around us." I made my words confident and deferential at the same time.

Nasty said, "The bastard's poking fun! Let's kill him!"

I slipped down and stood beside the barrel. I looked hard at them and imagined ways I might murder each one. I could disarm the tubby one and break his neck, but there was no need to humiliate the man. I might stab him through the armpit and cut the big artery in there. He'd die in seconds. I smiled at Rotund and gave him a little nod.

Rotund may have known one or two serious killers. When I smiled, he stiffened and grabbed Nasty's arm. "We'll go around! We don't mean anything." He yanked at his confused friend. "Really, we're sorry."

Behind me, Onni exhaled like a fresh breeze. I remembered the song I'd been humming was something I used to sing to my little girl.

I bounded toward the idiots, drawing my sword as I ran. For a second, they just watched me. I have often seen such behavior, and I suspect part of their minds didn't quite believe I was coming, which paralyzed them. I whipped a neat slice across Rotund's bicep. He squeaked as his sword hand dropped useless, while Nasty hurled a professional cut at my head. I arranged to be somewhere else when it arrived by stepping inside his swing, almost belly to belly with him. I sliced hard. When I stepped away, he held his guts with both hands.

Pup lifted his sword for a blow that would chop me in two, so I popped him in the mouth with my pommel. As he staggered back, he dropped his sword. He fell and grabbed at the air with both hands, just in case some invisible rope or fence rail happened to be there.

Rotund sprinted away, holding his arm, swifter than I would have credited. I ran him down in a few seconds and tripped him. Before he could roll faceup, I slipped my sword into the base of his skull.

The disemboweled Nasty had slumped to his knees, begging his mother to make it stop hurting. I made a relaxed thrust through his left eye. He collapsed and went quiet with a shudder.

Pup had grabbed his sword and stumbled upright, his mouth full of blood and probably a broken tooth or two. I pointed my sword at his heart, and then I made my damned self stop.

I couldn't have explained the act of will required not to kill the boy, not in a proper way. The closest comparison was ridiculous. I might describe the willpower needed to hold off pissing after drinking beer all night, with every part of the body and every single thought squeezing and grinding to just let go. I felt shame describing my compulsion to kill human beings in terms of draining my willy into a pail, but there it was. I wished that Harik, God of Death, Trafficker in Curses, He with the Saggiest Tits in the Heavens, would receive acid-laced scorpions into all his tender orifices for eternity.

I waved my sword at the boy. "Go. Go home. Get a girl and stop playing with swords like an asshole." Slack-jawed, he blinked a few times, shuffled back, and stopped, wavering in place. I shooed him with my free hand.

Pup might as well have explained his intentions to me in

detail. Hell, he might as well have sung them loud enough to echo off the hills at me. He spat blood on the grass, and then he wiped at his bloody chin. He lifted his sword, and his hand didn't tremble all that much, which impressed me.

I turned away and began walking. "I hear my woman calling! I think I'll go home and pound her in our bed that I made from the bones of young fools." Of course, there wasn't any woman calling, or a bed, but I hoped it would make the boy think.

I heard him suck air, and I heard him running up behind me. I turned and opened his throat, easy as brushing a fly off my shoulder. Blood sprayed, a lot of it, and he collapsed onto his side. He stared at me with his head cocked, working his lips like he wanted to make words. He died there, trying to tell me something that I guess he thought was important enough to be the last words he'd say.

Turning away, I made myself not look at him, but Harik's nuts, it was satisfying.

Onni looked pale and clammy, as if he might vomit. He had vomited the first few times I'd sent visiting deserters on their way, by which I meant killing them like they were dim chipmunks. I strode past him toward the small town square and said, "Another job done, and done with aplomb." He fidgeted with the wooden buttons on his nice jacket and didn't say anything.

I tossed a copper bit to the closest boy. "Keep watch, young sir. If ruffians approach, you know where to find me." I put some extra swagger in my walk and headed for the town's modest tavern.

The people of Crossoak were a mass of faceless spuds wearing scratchy, mud-colored clothes. They didn't think much of me, either. A few stared at me wordless as I passed, mashing themselves far back so as not to stand on the lane while I walked there. Most wouldn't look at me. Some rabbity ones cowered inside and wouldn't peek out. I had been there more than two months, and I'd never struck them, cheated them, or even yelled. I hadn't called any of them nasty names, even though some of the oafs deserved epithets that would strike a meek person dead.

Over generations, the people of Crossoak had struggled their way up to the summit of inoffensive ignorance. They were proudly superior to all outsiders and all the things they had never experienced for themselves. I couldn't chide them much for that. They lived better than almost any near-destitute folks I'd ever seen, so they were due a little conceit.

Crossoak's founders had raised their town around a titanic oak tree in a mountain valley. They enjoyed good water, and the dirt would sprout crops if you smiled at it real big. Soft grass grew everywhere, and you couldn't beat the damn stuff down if you tried. Timber and stone were close, neighbors were far away, and visitors were few. If they had added some gambling houses and whores, I might have considered retiring there.

The townspeople built their homes and barns solid, out of cut stone and unfinished oak—good for hiding from strangers. When hungry deserters had started showing up three months ago, hiding had proven a feeble strategy, so Onni had sent for help from the next town up the road. That town's people were disinclined to go off and get killed in the defense of Crossoak. But I was there, and getting bored, and the venture seemed like a fine opportunity to kill a lot of people. Maybe help some people. If the chance presented.

Crossoak's residents had cheered like screech owls the first time they saw me kill some deserters. They didn't cheer anymore. The crowds dwindled after the first two weeks, and by the end of the month, nobody except Onni witnessed how well I was protecting them. He admitted that everybody had taken to hiding in their houses as much as possible, since they never knew when bloody violence would arise.

A few days later, I mentioned to Onni that I missed seeing the kids play while I sat outside. That afternoon, children resumed chasing and playing grab-ass all over the village. I questioned Onni about it that night, and he admitted that the villagers had decided to let their children watch all the killings rather than risk making me mad.

"They're afraid you'll kill them, Bib," Onni had said. "Cut off their heads."

"Krak and Harik! Why would I do that?"

"They don't know. They don't understand you, not any better than they understand a tiger. They just know if you decide to kill them, they're helpless."

I began to understand and respect the villagers' fear, and even feel some of it. If I didn't leave town soon, they would gather into a mob and batter me to death in my cot, or lock me in a house and burn it. Fighting prowess meant nothing against fifty men armed with assorted farming implements. I should have left right that instant.

But what if I left and some of Rotund's buddies showed up tomorrow? Dead kids couldn't smash wildflowers, and renegade soldiers had already killed one little boy before I showed up. I decided to wait a few more days. Maybe I'd make a little camp outside town and hide like a bunny at night.

I strolled into the dim, meager tavern like my family had owned it for twelve generations. The plank floor and tables had soaked up thousands of meals' worth of cooking smoke. "Hello, Sunflower!" I said without interrupting my journey to the table where beer would soon arrive. Nobody else patronized the tavern just then. Proper people worked in the middle of the day, and everybody stayed out of the tavern while the unaccountable murderer was in residence.

The old, stringy woman who owned the tavern was as harsh a slice of bitterness as I've ever met, so I had named her Sunflower. Only when I sat and reclined against the wall did she move, forcing beer from a keg into a wooden mug. She crossed to my table in a dozen dancers' steps and slammed the mug down like she was killing spiders with it.

When I lifted the mug, my hands decided that the period of post-murder satisfaction had ended. They jerked and tremored hard enough to slop half the beer out before I set it down. I flapped my hands to dry them, and then added Rotund, Nasty, and Pup to the tally of men and women I've killed. I had hoped to put that chore off until I was a lot drunker than I was now, but waiting wouldn't make it any more agreeable. The contemplation of having killed people was a damn shot less pleasant than the anticipation of killing them.

Sunflower was scrubbing the worn planks by the doorway, using a gray rag that had probably been white when her grandmother opened this establishment. She glanced death and damnation at me and went on eradicating the blood trail that led up to my table.

I realized I was wet with Pup's blood and was just starting to get sticky. I had craved a drink so profoundly I'd forgotten to change out of my murdering-people clothes and into my waiting-around-to-murder-people clothes. The realization made me feel all sunk in, like an old carcass.

My cot lay on the other side of the village, at the mason's house. I would have paid someone a year's journeyman wages in gold to hop over there and fetch me something clean to wear. Sadly, nobody in this town but children would fetch for me, unless it was a knife to cut my throat with, and children weren't allowed in the tavern.

I tried to guess what Pup had wanted to tell me while he lay dying. It looked to have started with a B or a P, but I had no idea what a boy like that might think about. I propped my elbows on the table and lay my forehead in my palms, and I spent a couple of hours wondering when killing people had become so complicated.

TWO

Two days later, I hunched in the morning drizzle on the upslope side of town. I could have strained cheese with my ancient cloak, and I was as wet as any tadpole. I detested the man trudging downhill toward me, making me suffer more with every tedious step. The dimwit was coming from the direction of civilization, and that just made me despise him more. I figured killing him would gratify me as much as bedding any woman I'd known since my first gray hairs sprouted.

The dolt slipped and almost busted his ass. Only his staff saved him from flopping onto the mud, and that staff was substantially too tall for him in my opinion. He caught his footing with one arm flapping for balance, and then he tramped on, head down.

I couldn't stand it anymore. "Hurry on down here and get killed, you dawdling son of a bitch! I want to go inside and get warm!"

He didn't walk any faster, but I felt better.

I raised my hand when he was a dozen paces away, and he skidded a little as he stopped. He pulled back his cloak's hood, and I saw he was young. Well, he was old enough to have made two or three babies already, but nobody would call him seasoned. He was middling height and weight, balding, and had impressive roly-poly cheeks that got pudgier as he blinked away raindrops. I wanted to remember his face when I added him to my tally of murders, but otherwise, his looks meant nothing. He likely hauled his internal organs around in the same places as everybody else, so stabbing any one I wanted would be easy.

I slipped out my sword, and I almost walked over and killed him right away. I held my weapon behind my back and rooted my feet. "Go around, or I'll kill you deader than your sister's virtue."

"Hello there, Bib."

That was a surprise, and not a nice one. It was like pulling down your bedcovers and finding a sweaty bison. "Have we met? Did I kill your father? Or your mother?"

"No, I don't think so. I'm so glad I found you. I've been following you for what seems like forever. I'm Desh Younger. I'm a wizard."

It was sad to see men go this crazy so young. "Well, magic me up something, Desh the Wizard. Maybe a chair that flies and shoots lightning, or a mug that never runs out of beer."

The young fellow glanced up into the rain for a moment, and then shrugged. "I'm not ready for magic quite that complicated yet."

"Well, what the hell good are you?"

Desh reached across his body to a big leather satchel, flipped it open, made a show of letting me see inside, and pulled out a bundle of cloth. "Here, I brought you a present, Bib."

"If it doesn't make beer, I'm not sure I want it." I waved him over and took the bundle with my free hand. It was the nastiest looking parcel of cloth I'd ever seen. It must have been dyed by a blind drunkard, and it had been stained in ways only the gods could understand.

"It's a cloak. See? Hold it up and see if it fits."

"I wouldn't get buried in the damn thing."

"Go ahead and try it on. It can't hurt you." He raised his chin, and I saw that this floppy dandelion was daring me to do it.

"Scoot back over there." I sheathed my sword, dragged off my cloak with a slopping sound, and shrugged into his. "What now? It better be good, or I'm going to break your foot for making me touch this awful thing."

"Hold on a minute."

I almost killed him right then.

"Just wait!" Half a minute ambled past us. "All the rain's shedding off it, right? I bet you're starting to feel warmer. Don't lie."

After a deep, searching breath, I nodded. "But it doesn't let me fly, so don't think too much of yourself."

He smiled for the first time. "Bib, let me buy you a drink."

Less than a minute later, we sat at my table in the tavern, close to the scorched stone fireplace, with Sunflower hissing and clearing her throat over our trails of rainwater. I held up my new cloak's collar. "So, what do you want from me? And I still haven't decided against breaking your foot."

"You're the only wizard I know of."

"Well, that's a stupid-ass thing to say. I am not." I flicked water at him. "You aren't, either. Besides, nobody worth a damn with magic would allow themselves to be called a prissy, squint-eyed wizard. They are properly referred to as sorcerers."

Desh jerked as if I'd said his hand was really an ankle. "What's the difference?"

"None at all, really, other than perception and morale. You wouldn't walk up to a bull and call it a boy-cow, would you?"

Desh shook his head slowly.

"Anyway, no sorcery has happened since before you got a whisker." He started to talk, so I bellowed, "Thus did the gods abjure mankind, destroying the men of legermain, abandoning humanity to the whims of famine, storm, disease, frightening beasts, gossiping neighbors, disturbing dreams, ungrateful children, and so on and so on. You get the idea. Sorcery doesn't exist anymore, so there's no way you can be a sorcerer, can you?"

Desh nodded at the dry cloak draped over the chair between us. "What about that?"

"You just have a talent. Every scrubby, grit-choked village in the world has somebody with a talent. Green thumb, a way with horses, never gets lost, can cook a feast with just flour and salt." I pointed at the cloak. "Makes clothes that are unaccountably useful. Not too lovely, though. You're not a sorcerer. Go home. Sew like a madman and be happy."

"I'm never going back there." Desh set down his mug with a clack. "Bib, I can feel the magic power in me. It's a beautiful thing."

I snatched his mug. "I'm not wasting beer on you. You're going to live a life of disappointment and die young."

"I paid for that. Give it back."

I held it out to him, and he waved me off. "I give it to you as a gift, Bib. But you can't steal from me. It's not fair."

"You're definitely not a sorcerer. I hear the first thing they teach little sorcerers is that nothing's fair."

He leaned forward and watched me sit there and drip.

"I don't know what else you expect me to say, son."

"I expect you to tell me how to use magic."

"You're too naïve for such things. You'd disintegrate yourself the first day."

"You might be surprised. It's rare that I decide to do something and fail."

The young man was worse than a tick. I decided to load him up with some half-truths and misdirection, and then send him on his way. "Desh, I bet you another beer that every single thing you know about magic is wrong."

"Done." He held out his hand to shake.

"Very well. Where does a sorcerer get his power?" I asked.

"From hard work, study, and prayer. Lots of prayer."

It was so ridiculous I almost tossed him out into the street. But I felt a sliver of pity for him, being such a damp meat pie of a man. "Wrong!"

"Oh. Well?"

"Fine. If you're so horny to know the mysteries, I will skip most of the boring-as-bird-shit religious overtones, and we can go to the heart of the matter." I rubbed my hands together and lowered my voice. "Every time you do magic, it's the result of a juvenile, mean-spirited pissing match with some god. I mean, it's so petty it would embarrass naked children on a dusty street in the nastiest village on civilization's ass."

Desh's jaw twitched, but he kept quiet.

"Have you ever bartered with your neighbor for a pig or a quilt?"

"Sure."

"It's exactly like that, except your neighbor is an inconceivably powerful, immortal crybaby, and the pig is a three-hundred-foot-tall pillar of fire you need to burn down a city. It's the same thing, fundamentally. Just the details are different."

Desh swallowed twice. "That's crazy."

"Let me ask you this. What does a man have to sacrifice in order to do magic? Or a woman. As a rule, women are better sorcerers than men."

"They have to sacrifice whatever else they might have wanted to do with their life."

"Wrong!"

"A family?"

"Not that, either."

"I... don't..."

"Himself, Desh. He trades himself away to the gods, one piece after another."

"What kind of pieces?"

"I'm asking the questions, but I'll humor you since you just found out that everything you ever knew was horseshit. A god will make a sorcerer do something, or have something done to him, to get power. Or maybe he'll give up something or accept something he doesn't want. For a little bit of power, the sorcerer could agree to get three bad colds that winter. For more power, he might have to steal money from his brother and throw it in the river. For a lot of power, he might have to take the blame for a murder he didn't commit."

Desh leaned back and squinted at me. "Is this all true? Bib, don't lie to me."

I guess I should have been offended, but lying does happen to be one of my weaknesses. I couldn't get too mad at him for seeing it. I was abusing the truth a little now, but I wasn't smashing it all to hell. "I'm not lying, son. Now, based on your vast reservoir of sorcery knowledge, what's the greatest danger to a sorcerer?"

"Disintegrating yourself. Well, you did mention it. Also, cooking yourself and blowing yourself up. You know, losing control of the magic."

"Nope. Oh, control can be an annoyance, but the biggest danger is paying too much. Gods will ask a sorcerer to give up memories, forget how they feel about people, do things they thought only a monster would do—until they agreed to do them. A sorcerer has to decide for himself what price is too high, because the gods will take everything they can. In the old days, you'd see sorcerers as crazy as blowflies or wandering in the forest until they froze to death. They traded it all to the gods."

Desh didn't say anything.

I said, "And if you were an actual sorcerer, you might say, 'Bib, how can I avoid paying too much?' I'd tell you never to make the first offer. Making the first offer is a sure way to end up paying too much. Make the god extend the first offer. Do you understand?"

He nodded. "Don't pay too much. How do I know if it's too much? What are things worth? How do I know if it's a good deal?"

I leaned across to tell him the one thing that was unequivocally true. "There are no good deals. There are bad deals, and there are deals that are less bad."

"You're just trying to confuse me now."

"No, I'm just telling you things that *are* confusing. Last question. What is the most important thing for a sorcerer to know?"

Desh looked down and curled his lower lip. "I used to think it was knowing your enemy. Now I think it might be knowing what you don't know."

"Hah! You should know that sorcery is less about magic than you might think. Mainly, it's about looking tough, being sneaky, and waving your hands around a lot."

Desh crossed his arms and stared at me. "You must have given up a lot. What was the worst?"

"Ah, the worst. I can only make love six times a night now. It used to be a lot more."

He raised an eyebrow.

"Really, I don't remember. Nothing too bad. It probably just made me tougher and better looking."

"Bib, I chased you through three countries for five months. You're not so petty that you won't tell me this one thing, are you?"

Maybe I had indeed become petty living out in these little ratsuck towns where everything was small and slow, and that was the way they liked it. Without thinking too much, I said, "I am on what we call an open-ended debt. I didn't give up anything. Instead, I owe the repugnant, ever-to-be-regurgitated-upon Harik, God of Death, a certain number of murders. I'd be thrilled to tell you what that number is, but only Harik knows. So, I have to murder people until he says I've done it enough."

"If the gods are gone, you can just stop killing people."

"I thought that myself. I did decide to stop killing, but soon I got sick, and then disgustingly sick, and then grotesquely miserable. I decided not to find out what would happen after that."

"Bib, if the gods are gone, how can Harik tell you when you're done?"

"That is a problem, isn't it?"

Desh coughed, shifted away from the table, bent over, and caught his breath.

"All right, relax. Don't be such a dimpled daisy—you'll embarrass me."

"You're crazy! Why did you agree to that?"

"It was the best deal I could get at the time." I drank off my beer and held up the mug to get Sunflower's attention. "So, do you still think you're a sorcerer?"

"No. I'm not a sorcerer. Not until you teach me how. I have clearly found the right man. And I owe you a beer."

THREE

After I had told Desh to kiss my foot and go to hell, I informed him that from then on, he was only allowed to talk to me about women and horses, the two least boring subjects I could imagine. The boy's nervous, stuttering conversation proved my imagination feeble. I endured it for a while, then I spent the rest of the afternoon stomping around in the woods, kicking harmless bushes, and thinking about the gods. I tried to avoid thinking about them. It ate up hours I could have used thinking about better topics such as being tortured to death or eating small cakes with righteous women.

But sometimes the gods make my brain flap like a sparrow in a chimney. They're a petty gang of selfish, devious, cruel beings, they gossip like women on wash day, and they aren't scrupulous about telling tales while sorcerers are listening. They have burrowed deeper into my life than any person I've known. Every time I've talked to a god, I've been one careless word away from ruining my entire life, and you can't say that about many human beings.

Thirteen gods sit around in the God's Realm and fiddle with mankind. I can't consider them all in one sitting without getting queasy, but a few stand out. Krak, Father of the Gods, despises everybody, including me. When he isn't impregnating everything that's slow or inattentive, he lounges around holding the impossibly searing light of the sun and frying bits off of lesser beings.

The God of War, Lutigan, hates me worse than leprosy. I once tricked him into testing the Chariot of Profound Redemption, built by Fingit, Blacksmith of the Gods. The damn thing crashed sideways and spun on its side until Lutigan vomited up some things that probably ought to have stayed inside him. Gorlana, Goddess of Mercy, tolerates me like I'm a dog that smells bad. I never knew her to do anything merciful unless she was rewarded with something rare or shiny.

Harik, the God of Death, stands first in my string of beings who should be slowly tweezed out of existence. The other gods despise him. He's always putting things in order and recording everything that can be counted. I think mainly he does it so he can act like a bull with a gold-plated dick, as if any other gods care how many baboons have died since the beginning of time.

After the sun went down, I lay on my cot and thought about the gods some more. They sounded silly. They would sound sillier if they hadn't wiped out three cities and a couple hundred thousand people in the past century. I slept poorly.

Another drizzly morning showed up at Crossoak, but I didn't want to let those damned gods ruin my day. I was strutting by the time I found the kid who had stood watch on the upslope edge of town for me yesterday.

"You're doing a magnificent job, son." I tossed the boy a copper bit for today's work. "I encourage you to squander that on hard living, but alas, you'll probably save it to buy a chicken or a hoe someday."

I had already paid the little girl watching the other end of town. Technically, watching for invaders was my responsibility, but I had farmed that out first thing. Onni never offered the town's money to pay the children, nor had he set them to the task free of charge. Copper bits add up over a space of months, but I didn't need the money. I could have bought everything in town, including the phallic oak tree, if I'd wanted to own a sleepy place full of people who hated me. I had stashed silver and even gold coins in half a dozen spots close to town. I know that seems like odd behavior, but I have proven I can get drunk enough to spend every coin I'm carrying and get nothing at all in exchange.

Moisture dripped down the tavern's stone wall, and I traced my hand along it as I wandered up to the doorway. "Good morning, Sunflower!" She didn't acknowledge me straight out, but she did sneer at the pot in the fireplace. I waved at Desh. "Good morning, Pain in My Ass!"

"Good morning, Bib." Desh sat upright and stiff at a corner table, his staff propped close, and he watched me all the way to my scratched-up chair. "Bib, I'm handy with just about any task. Everybody back home says so. I can make—"

"Women and horses, young man! Remember, women and horses, if you want to share my tavern." After our calamitous discussion of sorcery yesterday, I found that Desh knew less than a thimbleful about horses, but his knowledge of women was surprisingly nuanced.

Desh bestowed on me the same look he might give if he were swallowing a baby alligator. Then he smiled, shifted one table closer, and eased onto a chair. "Bib, I'm happy to wait for as long as I need to, so don't think you can chase me—"

He never finished that thought. I yanked him up by the collar and hauled him to the door, banging him into a table and two chairs along the way. I tossed him into the soggy lane—not too hard.

"Women. Horses. And stay in your corner." I left him on the wet grass and returned to my table, upon which had materialized gritty bread, sticky mutton stew, and a small beer. I winked at

Sunflower, and she turned her back to me as Desh stumped inside.

In a day or two, I'd slip away from this town and leave the lad behind forever. I should have kicked him hard when he first walked into town and kept kicking him until he went away. In fact, it wasn't too late to start kicking. Desh was sitting at his bare table in the corner, glancing at my breakfast now and then. I walked around the table between us, angling to get a good view of his left shin.

"There's an army coming! There's an army coming!" My watch-boy screamed the warning as he ran all the way to the tavern on the square. He sprinted inside, his wet shoes sliding on the planks so that he almost fell. He paused for a deep breath, and then shrieked, "There's an army coming!" loud enough to wake my mother, who was not only dead but also buried on another continent.

"How big is it?" I asked.

"A thousand people!"

Having once been a little boy, I understood I'd need to see these thousand people for myself. I strode up the hill, trying to look sprightly and not at all nervous. I could see that riders had just entered town, three dozen of them, maybe more. When we were fifteen paces apart, I raised my hand. Almost unbelievably, they stopped.

I was prepared to kill three or four of them, and then run off into the woods. While they chased me over the next few hours, I'd occasionally slip in and kill a couple of inattentive ones. If Onni and his people were smart, they would run while I was still alive and keeping the raiders busy.

They were big men on big bay horses. The nearest were clean-shaven and ash pale with dark hair. They all wore the same blue-and-gray clothes—uniforms, so they were soldiers from some army

I'd never heard of. They carried short, curved swords, and they hefted long spears.

I decided if they attacked, I'd keep the fight inside town. They would get tangled up in their spears, and I might slaughter most of them while breakfast was still hot.

A short, broad man, rather squatty among these fellows, said, "What town is this?"

Nobody's uniform had any badge or sign of rank, but I supposed he was boss. "Do you want to know its name, or its defining characteristics?"

Shorty quirked an eyebrow. "Oh, please do provide both."

"Welcome to the idyllic township of Crossoak, the home of fine mutton, jittery townspeople, and mean old women. I am Bib." I insinuated a bow.

"I am Vintan Reth. Who is the nervous boy lurking behind you? Son? Servant? Paramour?"

I didn't look behind me, so as not to invite Vintan's cronies to poke a hundred holes in my back. Desh must have been standing back there, in the perfect spot to die uselessly.

"I owe the boy money. You can't kill me. It'll make him sad."

"Ah, you're trying too hard to be humorous. It's a foolish gambit among serious men." He leaned forward over his horse's neck. "Bib—and that is a charming name by the way—I am a gentle soul and will allow you to redeem yourself."

Some of his men shifted in the saddle, and a few looked away.

Vintan said, "Tell me about that paralyzingly enormous tree."

"That's just the festival tree. For hundreds of years, these people have dangled sacks of beer and dubious treats from it when the harvest is in." Of course, the townspeople didn't do anything like that and never had. I have a policy that when I talk to a threatening stranger, I never say anything that might be true.

He smiled. "Quaint. I'd even say picturesque."

"They break off a twig for each man to carry around, and

whenever he does something stupid, his wife tears off a leaf. When the twig is bare, he has to go home."

"That's eccentric enough to charm even me. How many of these villagers do you think would fit if I nailed them to the festival tree?"

One might think that was a horrible thing to say, but it's not even in the top hundred horrible things I've heard said right before people started dying.

"That depends, Vintan. Did you bring a ladder?"

The man nodded. "An incisive question. I wish I were more at leisure. We might discuss torture and desecration, among other artistic endeavors. I so appreciate meeting a person of subtle thinking." He looked at the bulky soldier next to him. "Kill him. Leave the entrails."

I said, "Go on around us. Everybody will be happier."

The bulky man pointed at two soldiers, who dismounted and walked toward me pointing their spears. Five seconds later, I severed one man's left hand. Ten seconds after that, I thrust into the other's heart under his arm. I turned back to the first one to slice open his throat, and at the end of twenty seconds, they both lay on the grass, one still and the other gurgling. The man whose job it was to point then employed his finger like it was the Spear of Lutigan, jabbing at a disconcerting number of soldiers and then at me. Eight or ten of them began to dismount. It was hard to tell exactly how many among the spears and nervous horses and jabbing fingers.

"Stop," Vintan said in the same tone he might use to invite you over for cake. Everyone stopped. Some men froze half out of the saddle, staring at him. "We'll go around."

Finger Man said, "Why? We can kill him. He can't fight all of us!"

"Your tactical thinking must be precise. He can indeed fight all of us. He just cannot kill all of us. However, how many can he kill? Two more? Five? You and ten men with you? Why pay that price just to ride into a town with mean old women, perpetrate some pedestrian wickedness, and trot away as if we were covered in glory?" He smiled at Finger Man, who paled so severely he turned almost transparent. "We shall go around."

Finger Man looked away, and I could see his jaw grinding so hard I thought he might have to eat soup the rest of his life. The soldiers collected their dead friends and remounted.

Vintan saluted me with his spear. "Bib, I regret missing this opportunity to chat with you about philosophy and then nail you to something." He cantered back up the trail as his men turned their horses in place, and they all trotted out of town.

"Not too bad," I said to Desh. "Now you can tell girls you helped vanquish an army using nothing but your blinking eyelids."

"I thought we were sure to die."

"You have an excellent grasp of probability. But we didn't die, so let's finish breakfast. You never know when some other calamity will come along and kill us. Hell, before I finish talking, a bear could jump out from behind that house and tear off my head. Life is chancy."

Before I went back to breakfast, I strolled along the edge of town. Sunshine had arrived, and it was a beautiful walk, though a little steamy. My path might not have been random. I kept Vintan's crew in sight until they had bypassed the town and ridden away southward.

If those soldiers had all jumped down to kill me when Finger Man said so, I still might have lived if I was smart. Of course, Desh would have died right away, before he ever understood that death was coming. But the boy had stood up and faced that little army with me. He hadn't run away, so who was I to kick his ass all the way home?

I paid two more children on my way back into town. Both of

the morning's watch-kids seemed to have shirked their task after the terrifying army had "invaded." That excitement had turned all the boys and girls into a throng of hornets, and they were charging all over town hitting each other with pretend swords and bawling when someone got hit too hard.

That afternoon, I sat slumped in a chair in front of the tavern. My hat was pulled down, and I wish I could say I was dreaming the dreams of a virtuous man, but I was just dreaming about cornbread. Desh kicked my boot and said, "Bib, will you teach me how to be a sorcerer? This isn't a threat, but if you say no, I'll just follow you around and look pitiful until one of us dies."

"Desh, you are a courageous man. Almost a hero. Becoming a sorcerer is beneath you, and it would just mar your glory. Go home. And if you try to follow me, I'll break your arm. If you keep at it, I'll break your leg, and if you crawl after me, I'll break your other leg and laugh at you."

Leaning closer, Desh said, "I didn't intend to tell you this—"

I never did find out what he didn't intend to tell me. At that moment, my uphill lookout hollered, "Another army! Another army! Bigger than the first one!"

"Krak's sizzling testes!" I didn't charge up the slope, but I scooted right along. Somebody was arriving from uphill, just like Vintan had. Unless he'd made a huge circle back to reexperience the joy of my company, somebody else was paying us a visit.

I heard the clink-chink of chain mail before I got really close. These new men were arriving in profusion—likely twice as many as Vintan had brought. One of them carried a red-and-yellow banner, and that gave me nearly every detail I needed. These soldiers belonged to the King of Glass, who ruled everything around for dozens of miles. Crossoak belonged to him, so if he wanted to cram it full of his soldiers, he didn't need permission from me. I'd never met the man, although I did think his kingdom's name was pretentious as hell.

I called out to the riders in front, "Welcome, come on in! The alder's probably hiding behind a sack of seeds somewhere, but if you want, I can chase him out here."

Without stopping, a man with a chin like a plow said, "Who are you then?"

"Bib. The good citizens have hired me to be their spiritual teacher, to guide them down the path of rectitude and compliance. They are wonderful at compliance. You don't have to worry about chastising them, or beating them at all, because they're anxious to comply."

"Hm. I'm Captain Dolf. We're pursuing a war band of Denzmen. Have you seen them?"

"Why, yes, I have!" I walked alongside him as he rode. "They arrived at breakfast time. We chatted a bit, and then they went on south."

Dolf and a fair woman riding next to him both squinted at me. He said, "They've been destroying villages all the way down from the capital. You were awful damned lucky."

The woman pushed some stray yellow hair out of her face. "Yes, how did you avoid destruction?"

"I'm a better-than-average conversationalist."

She leaned toward me, reins in her fist. "Pay attention to me. Those criminals killed thirty-two men, stole Crown Prince Prestwick, and are spiriting him away to their wretched land. They left no message or clue regarding a motive. So as a favor to the Crown, and to me personally, please refrain from attempting mirth. Also, stop prancing around with your hands down your trousers and do something constructive!"

I just about halfway fell in love with her right then.

FOUR

The first thing I ever said to my late wife was, "Hell yes, I did it, and I'd do it again twice." She was a woman of uncommon forbearance. She allowed me to live with her for nearly ten years, more than a hundred times longer than any other woman has suffered my companionship. It would make no sense to say those words now to this blonde woman. I had given those words and those years to my wife. No other person could understand what was in them or what they meant.

So, I accepted that my second conversation with this blonde woman would have to begin awkwardly. I didn't even know what to call her. By then, she had dismounted and walked off to talk to some soldiers, who I guarantee were not as charming as me.

Dolf had dismounted, so I leaned in. "Who's the lady with the sweet tongue?"

He snorted and looked back at her before answering. "That's Ella. She's the governess."

"Please say that again."

"The governess. The governess of the Crown Prince."

"Isn't this errand a little hazardous for someone of her profession?"

"You tell her. I'm done trying."

I pretended to examine Dolf's saddle until Ella returned. "Miss Ella, I fear that when we spoke earlier, I made a poor impression."

"I should say so."

"I apologize. I was assisting Dolf in the pursuit of those marauders by marking their trail. I became distracted and spoke rudely." This was how people in civilized places spoke, at least when I lived there. "Is there any service I may perform for you that will establish a better impression of me?"

"Have you accomplished anything since we met? Have you learned anything?"

"Well, I learned your name."

"Then I would say that a poor impression was entirely appropriate." She walked off and started talking to a chunky soldier with droopy eyes.

That was the kind of dismissal you have to respect. I began to like her a little more.

Crossoak had two good wells, and soon, watering was about half-finished. Dolf had been walking around supervising, and now he beckoned me. "Did you say your name was Bib?"

I nodded. There was no way this could be good.

"Two of my officers have heard of you. You're said to be a good fighter. If that's you, then I need you."

"Oh, I expect I'd be more trouble than I'm worth. Besides, I think you outnumber them by a fair margin."

""These Denzmen fight hard. It's been the next thing to war with them since autumn. Hundreds dead. Now they've kidnapped the prince, and I don't know why, but it doesn't matter to me, really. We're just the pursuit. The army is right behind us, and it's war for sure. I haven't said that many words altogether since I got married, so you know I need you badly."

This prince wasn't my prince. In fact, I didn't even have a

prince, and in a year, I might be a thousand miles away. "I have to tell you the truth, Captain Dolf. I can't take orders. Never could. If I come with you, it'll be like throwing a bear into a team of well-trained horses. Everything will just go to hell."

"Well, I can't make you go. You'd slide off on your belly first chance you got." He walked off as if I didn't exist, which was fine with me. I admitted to myself that the governess would be leaving within the hour. I was unlikely before then to earn the chance to win her heart someday, and I wasn't even sure I wanted her heart. By the time I walked into the tavern, I had mostly forgotten about her.

The tavern was empty. It wasn't the same without Sunflower there to aggressively ignore me. I laid a couple of coins on the table that she used for a bar, and I filled a mug. Before turning away, I heard a voice from the back closet. I opened it and found Sunflower sitting on a bucket, head down, weeping like a little girl.

I crouched down and chanced getting my wrist broken by touching her shoulder. She cried harder for a while, then slacked off.

"Don't you want to know why I'm crying?" she said.

"You can tell me if you want to. But I can't fix it and probably don't know anything about it, so telling me won't really help you."

She shook her head. "Killers. Sorcerers. Armies. The world is crazy. When I was a girl, things made sense."

"I expect it's crazier now than it once was."

"I'm glad my boys are dead. If this is the world they would've had, I'm glad they're dead." She started sobbing again. I put my arm around her, and she mashed her face into my shoulder, tears and mucus streaming. After a bit, she quieted to sniffles, and I let go. She began wiping her eyes and nose and chin.

We walked out of that stale closet, and I said, "I got my own beer, but I left the money."

Sunflower grunted and turned away.

Desh poked his head in the door a little later. "They're leaving."

"Why, thank you, Desh. I had assumed they were making all that noise by riding in circles around that big tree. What would I do without your profound capacity for observing the world around you?"

"Don't be a bastard. Let's go with them. That's where the excitement will be. It'll be boring around here."

I smiled at Sunflower, who ignored me, and I considered the fact that an army was marching toward us. "Desh, 'boring' depends on your perspective. You go ahead. I'll catch up after I have another drink or two."

"Hah! I'll stay in case you get lost. Or pass out." Desh sprawled on his chair in the corner.

I sat in the tavern for some uncounted number of beers into the late afternoon, ignoring everything Desh said. I sure as sheep shanks didn't want to go off with Dolf. A lot of soldiers would be getting in my way and killing men I might want to kill. It was the kind of expedition that diminished one's chances for murder. It also maximized one's chances of getting killed by freak events that happen when you have hundreds of dubiously trained men together swinging swords.

Something about all this felt bad, though. Like I'd forgotten something, but I couldn't put my hand to it.

Sunflower fetched me supper at dusk. I went ahead and bought supper for Desh, whose purse looked like it had forgotten what jingling sounded like. We ate fast, since the tavern would close at dark. Sunflower sure wasn't spending money on candles for customers like us.

I heard a single rider coming from the south, where both of those little armies had ridden off to. One of Dolf's soldiers, a mighty handsome fellow, drew rein in the square as I stepped outside.

"Bib? I'm Vin. Captain sent me, said to bring you back up the road a ways. He said it just like that, which is kind of abrupt. He doesn't care much about manners, but I do, so I'm saying please come down the trail with me. There's something he thinks you ought to see, and I do too, and it's not a trick. He was specific about telling you it's not a trick."

I hadn't thought it was a trick. I wished it had been a trick. I knew just how to handle a trick. "What is it that I should see?"

"Well, the captain said to take you there, not tell you, and he is my commander. I would just as soon tell you, but I really can't."

That was aggravating. I opened my mouth, but he cut in. "I can see you're about to tell me to go straight to perdition, and I wish you wouldn't say that. I do think you'll want to see this."

I preferred to make my own judgments about what was so important I should trot miles down a forest road at night. I could have dragged him off that nag and made him tell me, but it sounded like a lot of work. "Let me get a torch."

I didn't own a horse, so Desh and I jogged alongside Vin. He didn't try to converse, and I didn't talk to him. If he wasn't going to tell me what was going on, he could go eat a bug.

At last, Vin reined in and pointed at some voluptuous brush beside the road. "That's the place I was talking about. I wonder about the captain some days. I could have just told you. You won't tell him I said that, right?"

I walked over to the brush, and it came to look less like foliage and more like a person. The torchlight showed me the little girl I had paid to be a lookout, sitting with her back against a tree, her legs apart, and her severed head propped between her knees. One of the Denzmen's spears stood plunged into the ground beside her. Some of those damned-by-all-thirteen-gods Denzmen must have sneaked back and snatched her while nobody was looking. Nobody missed her with all the kids running around playing "army."

I spent a minute squatting beside her, looking at ghost-hung trees and imagining the murder of several thousand Denzmen, each in a different grotesque way. I knew a lot of ways to kill—maybe not a thousand, but a lot. I silently damned the entire race of Denzmen to every god and to a sizable number of the gods' body parts. That was me trying to fool myself. I had set her to the task, I hadn't protected her, and I'd allowed her to get taken and killed.

Vin said, "I have to catch up to Captain. Sorry I can't help you carry her home. I really am."

I waved at him without looking, and the hoofbeats faded into the south. I picked up the body of the girl, whose name I didn't even know, and it felt light, like the wind might drift it away. Desh hesitated, and it seemed he was smart enough to stay quiet. He picked up her head, and we began walking back to Crossoak. I hummed the song I'd sung to my daughter, which didn't help her one damn bit, and it didn't help me, either.

"Bib. Something fell out of her mouth."

"What was it?"

Desh handed me a folded sheet of parchment. In the torchlight, I saw words on it.

"Bib, look!"

I saw the red glow in the sky to the north. "Harik's hairy guts!" I handed the girl to Desh and sprinted toward town. When I at last topped the shallow rise on the trail back, at least four buildings were shooting flames out the doors and windows. The stones weren't burning of course, but the generations-old seasoned wood burned like hell. The townspeople were just wandering around between the buildings. No one was trying to fight the fires.

I charged past a building that wasn't burning, and I stopped so fast I slipped on the grass. Onni had been nailed to the door upside down, a rope around his ankles and three nails through each foot. Blood ran down the bottom of the door from his slit throat. I ran on throughout the town and found six more people nailed to doors. I couldn't find Denzmen anywhere. That heartened me because they had probably gone and wouldn't kill anybody else. It also infuriated me because I couldn't pile a dozen of their heads on that little girl's grave.

In the end, my protection hadn't helped these people one damned sliver. Vintan had outsmarted me all the way around.

I grabbed some wandering people, dragged them to a well, and put buckets in a couple of hands. Once I began filling buckets, most people recovered enough to start passing them down the line. At some point, Desh asked me what I wanted him to do, so I told him to get a line going from the other well. We fought fires throughout the night. We saved all the buildings but four, and the wet weather helped us save at least the shells of those four.

When sunrise squeezed up through the trees, I was sitting on the damp grass against the big oak, head down on my knees, pondering my next move. I felt tired and angry and guilty and heartsick, which is the ideal time to make a fatally stupid decision. I forced myself to think deliberately, assuming that everything I thought I knew was wrong until I found evidence that said differently. If I underestimated Vintan again, he'd likely take my head home and put it on his mantle so all his friends could come around and exclaim over me.

I heard Sunflower walking toward me—I sure knew the sound of her feet by now. I didn't look up as she knelt beside me and slipped one root-gnarled old hand around my shoulders. She squeezed once, pecked me on the side of the head, and whispered, "You're a terrible man. But not this terrible."

She glided back to her still-standing tavern, as graceful as any girl.

FIVE

I am not much given to gloomy introspection. I've known people who were, and all it gained them was hours of moping in dark rooms while I was out drinking and flirting with women. Instead of hanging my head and moaning, I sat against that big tree in Crossoak until I concluded I didn't know a single damned thing, and then I got up to address the situation.

I'm not the best tracker I've ever known, and I hate to recognize that. I admit I possess a speck of vanity. It makes my mouth pucker a little to admit I was bested at tracking by a gaunt, sweaty cowherd I knew in Cliffmeet, who coveted feathers like they were diamonds.

He wove them into his hair, and I asked him once whether they were magic that helped him track, but he said he just thought they were pretty.

He wasn't here now, so if any tracking was to be done, I'd have to do it.

The sun was well up, and I walked a circle around the town. Daylight made the attack's aftermath grislier than it had seemed in the dark. A huge patch of torn-up grass and scattered sod suggested a multitude of horses had come in from the southeast, enough for Vintan's whole herd of Denzmen. The same kind of trail led out of town going southwest. I knelt and poked through the hoofprints.

Desh trudged up beside me, soot-smudged and sagging. His eyelids looked like flags of surrender.

"You dropped this out on the trail." He held out the parchment that had been crammed into the little dead girl's mouth.

It read:

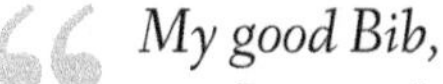

My good Bib,

I extend my most profound apologies for failing to pay proper attention to this child, her family, her neighbors, and particularly you. If you rush back to that awkward, charming village right now, you may arrive before I have finished burning a nice portion of it and effecting some sadly trivial killings.

The exigencies of war do not allow me to tarry and visit complete destruction upon that place. One should never leave a task poorly finished, and lack of time is a petty excuse. Therefore, please do hurry in your pursuit, as capturing you may redeem my reputation and allow me to torture you every night on the journey south to my king.

Should you arrive at the village too late, please do extend my regrets to the survivors and ask them to be so kind as to imagine they have experienced the most agonizing, humiliating, and soul-befouling death their regrettably limited minds can produce.

I hope we rendezvous in the future so I may perform in a more professional and discriminating manner.

—*VINTAN RETH*

I handed the note back to Desh, who said, "I'd pretend to read it now and be disgusted, but I already have, and I am. Let's catch that evil murderer. I'm ready. Right now."

"What will you do when you catch him? Tie a nail to his ankle and trap him in a jug?"

"You're a sorcerer, and I'm fairly clever. We'll think of something. Those are their tracks, right there."

I had found an unobtrusive clue right before Desh interrupted me, so subtle that I was kind of amazed I had caught it. "Vintan is sly. See here, it looks like dozens of horses galloped through, tearing out of town like rabbits on fire."

"I know! That's what I'm saying! A huge trail, right there. I can follow them if you can't."

"Go right ahead and do that. They'll lead you all around the countryside until winter. You see how the hoofprints are muddled up in places, like they don't all go the same way? Most of these tracks head out of town, but some come back in. It's as if the sneaky vermin galloped the same ten horses out of town, came back single file, and galloped back out again four or five times. They wrecked enough countryside for fifty horses."

Desh knelt and prodded the dirt with two fingers. "Vintan's not sly enough to fool you, I guess."

"We'll see which one of us is alive next week. That note sounds like it was written by a truly evil man. I've met people who were that evil. Vintan is terrible, but I don't think he's that kind of evil. He wrote that hoping we'd either get so mad we'd charge off after these tracks, or be too terrified to follow him at all. Desh, if you owned anything that was worth a damn, I'd bet you he sent a few of his murderers here to mislead us. He and his hostage are still on the main trail headed south."

"So, can we chase them down the trail? Even without nails and jugs?" Desh grinned.

"We'll chase them, and we'll kill a bunch of them—one or two stragglers at a time. I don't own a horse, so we'll have to run. I hope you're fit, otherwise your pure heart and pretty face will have to carry the day."

Desh shook his head and started walking up the hill where a few townsfolk were digging seven big graves and one little grave.

"Go on and help," I said. "I won't leave without yelling at you a time or two."

I trotted toward the mason's house, where my cot had been set in a back room. On the way, I cornered a few shaky citizens, but only one would say what he'd seen the previous night. The way he told it, there were hundreds of horses galloping everywhere, trampling everybody, and the riders speared folks right in the street, especially the children and old people. I thanked him for that incisive, detailed report on which all our lives might depend. It was cruel of me to engage in sarcasm with him. I almost felt bad.

I kept my chattels loaded up in a good leather pack, in case a quick escape became necessary. Since I'd be chasing Vintan on foot, I decided to toss away every item I could do without. Upon evaluating my possessions, I realized the leather pack was worth more than everything I had stuffed in it. I upended the thing and left all I owned on the cot, except for my traveling clothes, sword, knife, coins, Desh's cloak, and the pack, which I slung over my shoulder as I stepped outside.

I suppose I had drawn a good bit of attention to myself and roused some energetic interest among the townspeople. Stopping men in the street for interrogation can cause that. Seven men waited for me outside the mason's house, blocking my way. They toted an assortment of clubs and knives, as well as some lengthy pronged and bladed farming implements.

I had failed them, which blunted my appetite for murdering them. If I apologized and scraped and ate enough dirt, maybe I wouldn't have to kill any of them. "I'm sorry, fellows. I admit I did not serve you well, and I regret your grief. I'm leaving shortly to kill the bastards who did this to you."

"How do we know you didn't bring them here?" asked my host, the mason.

"You been here for months, and then you leave a few hours, and they come to kill us just when you were gone," another said.

"He's worse than a plague!" the mason said.

"A plague that stares at our wives."

"He raped my daughter!"

That was the nastiest prevarication I'd heard since I'd come south. Early on, I had in fact deflected a few curious propositions from the local women. Even though the memory of female company scratched at me like a burr, sweaty frolics with local girls weren't worth the uproar.

Six more men and a woman came around the corner, walking fast. One hefted a scythe big enough to decapitate a bear. The woman carried a mop over her shoulder, which was such a bemusing sight that I almost forgot to speak. "My friends, I am not your enemy. As you see, I'm leaving now so we'll have no temptation to nasty behavior. I hope you understand that I am still your friend." I almost said *friend* and *protector*, which might have sounded awkward with the smell of smoke and blood still heavy around us. But by then, the smooth anticipation of killing these people had arisen and made me grin. It sickened me a little at the same time. Just a little.

"He's a demon sent to murder us!" the woman shouted, as loud as a stevedore. A few more people were joining the back of the mob, which was edging closer.

The mason took a step, and that was enough. I wasn't going to stand there and let them turn me into a pile of broken bones inside a sack of skin. The mason was the leader, so I pulled my sword and stabbed him in the heart. I stepped back as he fell.

If the rest of them had kept coming, I would have killed a good number before they stomped me to death like a bug. But they only thought they were ready for murder. Once it happened in front of them, to their neighbor who was close enough to touch, murder seemed less desirable. I sure as hell desired some more of it, but I held still. Without the mason to spur them on, they edged away from me, murmuring, and they drifted off. They left their friend's body there on the grass.

The mason hadn't been a bad host. His wife had baked me pies, and I'd played with his kids, up until they started to be scared of me. I dropped a gold coin on my cot, enough to keep his family fed for a year. Maybe more, if they didn't eat pie.

As a young man, I had possessed magnificent hearing and eyesight. My eyes were now forty or so years old and remained hearty, but my hearing had faded some. I didn't hear the hoofbeats until they were close, probably a quarter mile from town. They were coming up the south trail at a fast trot. I saw them just a moment after I heard them, seven of Dolf's men. I looked harder and saw it was actually the governess and six men.

I guess all the Crossoak citizens had run like hell at the sound of horses. With no townspeople to receive them, the soldiers rode right up to me. Two appeared wounded, bandaged with ripped-up shirts, and another one looked like he was dying in the saddle. Varying amounts of brown dried blood spattered them and their horses. It showed stark on Ella's blue chemise, with gore up her right arm to the shoulder.

A stubby soldier with droopy eyes shifted in the saddle and sighed. "Well... we caught 'em."

Another soldier, skinny with bad teeth and wispy blond hair, said, "Not saying anything bad about the captain, but it was like he rode in there backward with his head up his ass. Respectfully speaking."

Vin nodded along with the man but didn't say anything.

"Nail your face shut, Stan," the first one said. "Bad luck to talk that way about the dead."

Stan threw his helmet at the first one, who grunted when it smacked his shoulder.

"Both of you be still," Ella said. She inclined her head toward me. "You. Have any others arrived before us?"

"No ma'am."

She pointed a blood-crusted hand at the mason's corpse. "Did you kill that man?"

"Not really. His wicked nature broke his heart. I just finished the job."

"Was he armed? Did you slaughter a man with no weapon?"

I rolled the body over with my boot, showing the mason's big knife lying under him.

"That is hardly a threat. . ." She glared around. I presumed she was looking for babies and kittens I might have drowned.

I said, "Ella!" which got her attention. "I may be the least perfect man in the southlands, but you can't use my failings to put off talking about whatever happened."

She frowned at me and slumped a bit. "As Corporal Ralt said, we overtook them. Unfortunately, they saw us first and fell on us from at least two sides. I'm not sure how many of us survived. Dolf perished in a most gruesome fashion. These men and I escaped only after vigorous fighting."

The soldiers had dismounted while she was talking, and a couple helped the one who was just about dead.

Ella said, "If none of our companions has yet arrived, I fear that only we may have survived."

"Well, you can rest here now," I said. "These aren't bad people. They've just suffered more than most recently, so allow them some fearful behavior."

"I shall not stay here! I will gather what survivors I may, and then I'll pursue those villains. I will either retrieve the prince or be torn to bits in the effort." She dismounted and stretched her back.

That was almost too fortunate to believe. I sure as the grinding ice wasn't about to argue her out of her intentions. I planned to pursue the Denzmen anyway, and maybe a Denzman who intended to kill me would slay one of Ella's men instead. Or slay her. "I'll come along with you and kill a few of those villains, if that's not too forward of me."

"Why?"

"My grudge against them may not be as big as yours, but it's big enough."

She stared hard at me. "No, why are you so very keen to kill people?" She nodded at the mason's body. "You leave them behind as if they were discarded sacks from which you've emptied everything you want."

"Sharp words from a woman whose sword arm looks like you slaughtered—"

"Be still!"

I didn't entertain any notions of disobeying her. The conversation was amusing, if a little unnerving.

"You don't appear to be excessively dim-witted. There are many productive endeavors you could undertake in which murder is absent, or at least minimal. So why are you so anxious to kill?"

"Because I like it."

She paused, maybe expecting me to say more. "That's awfully sad. Well, come along with me, and we shall see whether anything is to be done about it."

I wasn't sure what to say to that. It was a pleasant feeling, since no one had stumped me in conversation for at least a year. I nodded.

Ella shouted, "Water your horses and rest yourselves! We depart at midday."

Except for the one who was dying, the soldiers stepped quickly and undertook those tasks. They must not have entertained any notions of disobeying the governess, either.

SIX

We rode from noon until evening, as hard as the horses and my buttocks could bear. The road to Crossoak had lamed my horse two months earlier, and nobody in the little town had owned a single horse fit for riding. My ass had since endured nothing rougher than a barrel and a bar chair, so when this pursuit began, I prepared myself for discomfort.

Ella, Desh, and four soldiers rode far ahead of me. I had suggested to Ella, who seemed to be our general, that we assume a cautious posture. I explained the horrors of an ambush, complete with appalling images that didn't appear to bother her at all. She shooed me off like I was a goose. Now everyone but me trotted down the road in a raggedy, almost indefensible clump. I trailed them, and since ambushers would want to kill the biggest number of us as quickly as possible, I prepared to employ the oft-proven tactic of fleeing while my companions were getting slaughtered.

One of the soldiers had stayed in Crossoak to bury his comrade and march back north to report the disaster. I rode that man's horse, and Desh took the dead man's mount. Before leaving Crossoak, Desh and Ella had engaged in a quiet but considerably animated conversation. Whatever she said, it must have impressed the boy, because now he rode near enough to her that they could converse. It was understandable. She had a sweet face , and while she wasn't young like Desh, she was closer to his age than mine.

I dwelt on ways to undercut Desh and make him look foolish in Ella's eyes. It would be a challenge to make her think less of him than she thought of me. But I'd be damned if I let the puppy take her away from me, even if the idea of having her was imaginary.

Nighttime fell softly in the southlands, unlike the desert where dark hit like a slamming door. Tonight, it swung down with an oiled, lazy dusk, distressing me more every moment. I cantered to catch Ella and matched her pace, forcing my horse between hers and Desh's. "I recommend we halt for a while, boss."

She ignored my jab at humor, although I thought it wasn't bad considering she was about to get us all killed. "We shall not," she said. "The criminals have already drawn far ahead, and I intend to close that gap as swiftly as we may."

"That won't be swift at all if we're dead. Although I do commend your vigor."

Ella sat higher, which I hadn't believed possible. Her posture in the saddle was sublime, like a genteel fencepost. She scanned the road ahead and the woods on each side. "Do you see an ambush?"

"That is the charm of ambushes. You don't see them. Really, if you see one, then it's not an ambush at all."

"Don't be flip."

"Oh, I'm serious." I pointed into the woods. "When it gets dark, you could put ten elephants right behind those trees, and we'd never see them while we rode past. We might as well have a traveling picnic and sing songs as we go. Either way, those elephants could rush out and stomp us."

Desh leaned in the saddle and talked across me. "Ella, Bib's a real expert on these kinds of things. He's probably killed a hundred men. Maybe we should listen to him."

"Why, thank you ever so much, Desh," I said. "Next, you'll be writing ballads about me. Krak's guts, I have never been favored with such ardent hero worship before."

"No," Ella said. "Bib, I refuse to tarry and allow Vintan to extend his lead just because you fear the dark." Before I could speak, she added, "That was unfair, and I apologize. I understand you're not timid. You just fail to grasp the criticality of recovering the prince."

"I bet I don't grasp it as thoroughly as you. But I do understand that the moon rises in just a few hours, and moonlight will help us spot two or three of those elephants. We can ride on once the moon comes out."

She gazed at the ground for a few moments, scratching her forehead. "No. We must assume the risk and persevere."

It hurt my feelings a little that she hadn't found my argument persuasive. But mainly, I wanted to shove her off her horse and tie her to a tree for three hours. I hadn't brought a rope, however, and she was well-splashed with what I assumed was the blood of her enemies. Shoving her might not be such a dead-easy task.

I sure as hell wasn't turning back. Denzmen were down the road somewhere waiting for me to kill them. If we were going to ride down a path as dark as the inside of a dog, maybe I'd just keep trailing my companions. On the other hand, if I rode point, I could give us all a poor chance to survive an ambush, but at least a chance. Having Ella's misfits with me when it came time to kill Denzmen would improve my odds of living through that escapade. In the end, I decided to preserve as many of them as possible.

"I'm riding up front," I said to Ralt and Stan as I passed them going forward.

"Hell, we may live after all," Ralt said. He held his hand out to his friend. "Give back my hanky."

"You gave it to me, you drowsy turd!"

"I thought we was both going to die, so give it back."

"Boys, I'll buy you each a dozen hankies if you hang halfway back and ride up quick if some Denzmen jump out at me." I didn't hear what they said as I pulled ahead, but when I looked back later, they were riding smack between Ella and me.

Darkness brought wet air, green smells, soft whumps of my horse trotting, and far-off shrieks of animals hunting and killing one another. A smidge of starlight gave me glimpses of the trail as we traveled through the heart of nature. Some call the southern forests the most beautiful territory in the world. I call it one of the places they don't serve beer.

I needn't have had my ass puckered those next few hours. At last, the moon showed through the trees and then lifted above them, and nobody had tried to slaughter us. I felt a little silly, but I'd seen too many men killed for fear of looking silly. I kept riding point, though. If I dropped all the way back after bleating like a calf about ambushes, I'd feel too silly to live.

Before the moon was overhead, I heard a horse trotting fast from behind me. Vin caught up a few seconds later.

"Up ahead is where we caught them," he said. "I don't think they'd stop and wait there just to kill anyone else following them, but I don't know that much about Denzmen. Killing the survivors might be their favorite thing to do—maybe they even teach their children to do it as a game. Who knows?"

Vin's voice had gone higher and faster as he talked, so I reached over and slapped him on the shoulder. "Breathe, son. They're no more likely to be here than anywhere else. Hell, if we tried to run away from them, we might run straight into the biggest bunch around." Actually, I figured the battle site was the last place we'd see any live Denzmen. But I made sure my sword was loose in the scabbard, just in case.

"This is it," Vin said a bit later.

No bodies lay on the trail. "Really? This is as clean as my aunt Salli's kitchen table."

"It is. I won't ever forget it."

I rode closer and spotted a couple of helmets and a few swords beside the trail. A dead horse lay half-hidden by some tall grass. Then a little way off the trail, I found a pile of nothing but severed arms. A matching pile of legs lay on the other side. I dismounted to get a closer look and saw that all the legs wore the same boots and uniform trousers as Vin.

Behind me, Vin had begun crying fairly hard. I walked on down the trail so as not to embarrass him. Fifty paces away, I found a pile of torsos, and then a pile of heads. By then, Ella and the others had caught up.

"Ella, I think they've headed on south," I said. "They're probably not too worried about us if they stopped long enough to do all this butchering."

Ella sat her horse, although everybody else had dismounted and was walking around. "Do you think he's still alive?" She was crying too, but her voice was steady.

"Do you see his body? I mean, is it over there?" I pointed at the pile of heads. Desh and Stan were removing them and placing each to one side.

Ella rode to the heads and scanned them. "No, I do not."

"They don't seem shy about showing off who they've killed. If you haven't found him yet, I imagine he's alive."

"We cannot bury them."

"You're sure right about that. It would take us all day. In fact, maybe they were expecting us to stop and mourn these men. Well, when the army gets this far, they'll care for them."

Ella sighed and rubbed her cheeks with her left sleeve. "Gentlemen! Return to your mounts. Let us continue the pursuit. When we overtake these villains, we shall stalk them and then guide our troops to their precise location. We shall rescue the prince and slay all who oppose us."

I didn't expect anybody to challenge her, and they didn't. She threw out commands and plans, and she never showed a notion that some of her plans were ridiculous. Her plan to carry out a rescue was straight crazy. There was only one prince, so she and her four men had to go wherever he was, even if the whole of the Denzmen people were there. My plan was superior in every respect. I just wanted to kill Denzmen so I could find them anywhere in little batches and slaughter them like chickens. I could wait as long as necessary to find Vintan, some time when just a few of his toadies were with him.

The moon slid toward the west as we spurred on, trotting awhile and then walking our horses so as not to tire them. It wouldn't do to arrive at a fight on a worn-out horse. Or worse, try to run away from a fight on a worn-out horse.

I might have seen an odd glint of moonlight, or a branch swishing against the wind. I'm sure I didn't hear much over the clumping and blowing of my horse, a contrary beast I was growing to despise. Maybe I just had a strange feeling–it wouldn't have been the first time. I've always had a good sense of who and what was around me. It had saved my life a few times, and it likely saved my life this time.

"Ambush to the left!" I yelled, wheeling my horse. Nine or ten riders charged out of the tree line pointing spears at the most cherished and unprotected parts of our bodies.

I remember flashes of that fight. I was alone at the front, and two riders rushed me. My horse stepped nicely around so that I wasn't trapped between them, and I began to love the old mare a bit. I slapped the nearest rider's spear aside and swung, then he rode past trailing blood from his neck. His friend passed me and turned for another go, and before he brought his spear around, I sliced him from bicep to wrist. He howled as I rode past.

A rider skewered Vin, that nice, handsome boy, who was dead before he fell off the saddle. I rode up behind Vin's killer, thrust into his back, wheeled, and ducked a spear that showed up from nowhere. Ella slashed a dodging man's throat before he got away. Desh had been thrown and was trying to hide behind his staff from a Denzman who probably couldn't believe his luck. I rushed over and killed that man.

I saw one of our soldiers speared under the chin. I'd never even learned that man's name. A Denzman charged Ella from behind, and I nearly took the sneaky bastard's head off before he reached her.

And then it was done, except for panting, clopping, moaning, and one man cursing. I hopped to the ground. Desh was kneeling beside Vin, while Ralt scrambled around trying to catch loose horses. I strolled to the closest Denzman writhing on the ground and stabbed him through the eye.

"Stop that! Stop it this moment!" Ella said. "You are not to murder those men as they lie helpless."

"Well, I guess I could draw a picture of them while they lie here and bleed to death."

"Charming. I never supposed a person as grimy as yourself could be so droll. Nor possess artistic aspirations. You will cease dispatching them, because you appear to be enjoying it a bit more than is proper."

She was right. I had enjoyed the killing so much it was almost embarrassing, and I anticipated great satisfaction from killing the last two mortally wounded Denzmen. I almost felt Harik's hands on my back, pushing me toward them. However, Ella dismounted and reached them first, and she killed them both with neat thrusts. The disappointment stole my breath for a few moments.

One last Denzman sat on the grass, groaning and clutching the ragged arm wound I'd given him. Stan stood over him, holding his sword the way he might hold an ax over a tasty-looking goose.

Ella caught my eye and led me over to the man. She faced me square and said, "We must discover what he knows. Extract it from him, and do it quickly."

I raised an eyebrow.

She spoke a little louder. "Please do try not to leave him paralyzed and blind, as you did with the last one." She raised an eyebrow right back at me before she marched away.

SEVEN

I have never much liked torture. I know that seems like an uncomplicated sentiment, but I've lived much of my life among people who sometimes felt a bit cozy about the idea and the execution of torture. I dislike it for several reasons, one being that I'm not good at it. There's usually a lot of yelling, and I don't like watching people in pain. I've seen a lot of pain. I will count my own death to be kindness if it's quick instead of long-suffering, and I can at least extend that kindness to the people I kill.

But the main reason I dislike torture is its unreliability. A tortured man will tell you what he thinks you want to hear to get you to stop cutting, smashing, or burning him. Once he tells you the thing you wanted to hear, you believe him right away, even if it's a lie, because it's the very thing you wanted to hear. It's all a lot of screaming and blood for no good reason.

So, now I had to torture this Denzman. I hungered to kill the baby-murdering, butchering filth, but I could put that off until later.

"Stan, build a fire right over here," I said. "Make it hot. Desh! Cut me a few wide strips off a shirt one of these dead fellows was wearing." I examined the Denzman. He was taller than me, and probably stronger too, but he was younger than Desh. "What's your name, son?"

The man rolled to his feet and made it one step before I kicked his legs out from under him. I knelt and helped him sit up. As Desh handed me the strips, I said, "My name's Bib." I turned his wounded wrist palm up and started bandaging. "You can tell me your name. I'm not some sorcerer who can hex you with your name."

Behind me, Desh said something that turned into a cough.

"Desh, go find me a good horse from the new ones. No, find me the *best* horse."

"What then?" Desh said.

"Don't come back until you've braided its mane and tail."

The Denzman was looking back and forth between Desh and me.

"Don't mind him—he's my sister's idiot son. Am I wrapping this too tight?" The man shook his head. "So, what do I call you?"

"Steven."

"Steven, it's good to know you. Lift your arm a little." He winced and even whimpered once, but I pretended not to notice. "I'm not mad at you, Steven. You're a soldier, and you do as you're ordered. I will count our conversation as time well spent if you walk out of here tonight and walk all the way home."

"You can torture me, Ir-man. I won't tell you anything."

I smiled. "Steven, you've met someone besides me from Ir? All the way across the sea? Was his hair red like mine? Well, red with a speck of gray. We're a handsome and virtuous people, don't you think?"

"I think you're a murderer."

"Yes, I am. There." I tied off the bandage. "I'm not sorry I killed your friends, but I'm sorry you'll grieve for them."

"He was Lerritt, my cousin." He pointed to the first man I killed.

"A brave man. I know his family will miss him. Do you have a family at home, Steven?"

Ralt had walked up beside me and was watching, his head cocked. "These pliers was in my saddlebag. Thought you might want them."

"Just lay them down there, Ralt. If you found any beer in the Denzmen's bags, bring me some."

Ralt walked off, muttering, "Want me to bake him a flippin' pie too?"

I looked back and saw Stan and Ella standing beside the immature fire, watching me. "Stan, pull the boots off all the dead bodies and pile them over here."

"What?"

"Ella, will you supervise him, please? I've taken a vow not to speak with more than three idiots in one day."

"Very well," Ella said, shaking her head.

I turned back to Steven. I had kept his wrist clamped in my hand while looking away, but he'd scooted as far away from me as he could. "Tell me about your family, Steven. Any children?"

He almost smiled but caught himself. "A daughter."

I smiled for both of us. "I'd do about anything to go home and see my little girl. Her name's Bett. I want you to do a favor for me, Steven. I can't go home and see Bett right now, so you go home to your daughter." When I said that, I realized I might not absolutely have to kill this particular Denzman. There would be plenty of others to kill later. "You can tell her about the horrible, murdering Ir-man, and how you escaped."

"I can go?"

Ralt slapped me on the shoulder and passed over a skin of beer. I took a swallow and handed it to Steven, who lifted it to his lips one-handed.

"You can go, but I need to know two things: Why and where? Why did you take the prince, and where are you taking him?"

Steven choked and coughed out a little beer. "I... I can't tell you that." He glanced at the pliers, and I tossed them back up the trail.

"Sure you can. I'll find out anyway. If you don't tell me, somebody else will. Staying quiet won't change a damn thing, except for you and your little girl."

"I don't know why."

"Then tell me where."

Steven hesitated.

"Help me, son. Help me get you home."

He looked at the ground and shook his head.

"Otherwise, I'll have to break your jaw and ram those hot coals down your throat and into your belly."

My threat lacked immediacy, since the fire was too young to contain a single hot coal. But even a small fire showed my intention to cook him alive from the inside, and Steven spoke.

It wasn't as bad as I had expected. Vintan was carrying the prince right to the Denz capital and its several thousand inhabitants, which was unfortunate. However, the Denz Lands lay beyond the Blue River, which likely was running high from snowmelt and spring rain. If we hustled, we might catch Vintan before he could ford the river.

"I have betrayed my king. Will you let me go now?"

"Stand up." I didn't mean to, but I imagined five different ways to kill him without taking a step. I pulled my hand off my sword's hilt. "Take off your boots." I realized my hand had grasped the sword again, all by itself. And with some help from my debt to Harik. I reached behind my back and grabbed my belt.

Steven raised his eyebrows but started pulling off the boots, hopping to keep his balance.

"Good thinking," Ralt said, drawing his sword.

I knocked Steven on his ass into the tall weeds, just beyond Ralt's swing. I kicked Ralt hard in the shin, and when he bent over, I dragged him forward until his face hit dirt. I backed off five paces. My hands tingled from the desire to kill them both and everybody else around.

"Steven, go on home now. I'm taking your boots, and every other boot around here. We'll dump them ten miles or so down the trail so you can get shod again. By then, we'll be far enough ahead."

Steven looked sick, like a man who escaped drowning by standing on his brother.

"One more thing. An army will be coming through here in a few days, so stay off the trail. Our business is done, young man. You don't need to say anything else."

I walked toward Desh to find out what horrible chunk of horseflesh he'd selected for me. Ella intercepted me halfway there. "Bib, how many of these Denzmen did you kill?"

I shrugged. "A couple."

"From the details I've assembled, I should say four, or perhaps five."

"It doesn't matter a speck. For all you know, any number of them were struck dead by your wit or my beauty."

"And when you dispatched the dying man, you virtually exuded satisfaction. It seemed almost... intimate."

I couldn't think of anything to say to that. Not many people have put me in that situation, and it was the second time she'd done it in as many days.

When I didn't comment, she said, "Yet when I gave that Denzman over to you for interrogation, you preserved him from harm. If he had confessed all he knew, why not let Ralt execute him? It would have been less bother."

I gave a big smile. "I didn't want Ralt to kill him. I may be in the southlands again someday, in painful need of a Denzman to murder. I may say, 'Where's Steven? I could kill him now, if only I hadn't squandered him on that son of a bitch Ralt all those years ago.'"

"Horseshit."

"Governess, that was rather coarse, wouldn't you agree?"

Ella drew her sword, and for an instant, I pictured her stabbing me in the chest. Instead, she offered me the hilt. "I want you to take this weapon."

The sword looked unexceptional in every way. The blade was a bit longer and heavier than mine, which was a hair light for me anyway. Ella had been whirling this sword around in a highly professional manner, and I reconsidered just how strong she might be.

"Where the hell did you learn to fight, anyway?" I asked.

"One does not entrust a prince to someone who cannot protect him."

"Well, that didn't answer even a little bit of my question."

She looked down and scratched her forehead. "The customary places."

"And you can kiss my foot also." I looked down the blade, and its edge seemed as good as mine. My sword was a fair enough weapon, but I had no tender feelings for it. "Well, thank you, Ella. That is gracious of you, and I accept your offer. Please take my sword as a gift so you won't be caught weaponless and killed by any vagrant who wanders by."

Ella smiled. "It has a name."

"What?"

"The sword has a name. The Blade of Obdurate Mercy."

"Shit! That's a god name. It's the kind of pretentious, meaningless name that gods give to things! The Pillars of Woeful Omnipotence. The Shoes of Radiant Satiation. Crap like that."

She blinked a couple of times. "I have never observed any

divine or magical properties. It hasn't even brought me good luck. If you prefer not to accept it, I won't be offended."

She sounded like she'd just baked me a cake, and I told her it tasted like the bad part of an ox.

"Where did you get the thing?"

"The queen gave it to me when I entered her service."

"Well, why in the name of Krak's left thumb would you give it to somebody like me?"

"The sword is not mine. It belongs to the person who defends the prince. Or frees him."

One might think that by accepting the sword, I was also signing on for Ella's monumentally stupid rescue plans. That would be faulty thinking. I only kept it because I didn't want to hurt her feelings. I wasn't agreeing to get killed by ten thousand Denzmen so she'd feel less guilty about not protecting the prince like she was hired to do.

"Well... thank you. And thank the queen for me the next time you see her. If she seems to be in a gift-giving mood, tell her I've always wanted to own a bar. And I look good in green silk."

EIGHT

"*Bib,*

If you are reading this, then you have survived the ambush. I cherished no great hopes that it would eliminate you, but setting an ambush there was almost obligatory, a workmanlike bit of warfare, and I should have felt irresponsible had I forgone it.

I must apologize for the extreme, almost bombastically evil tone of my previous message. I sought to inflame your rage and send you away on a false path. You have seen through that ploy, which does not surprise me.

I know quite a lot about you, sir, as you are a killer of singular reputation. To further your understanding of me, I do not embrace evil or destruction more than does any other person, although I would not hesitate to employ the most diabolical methods imaginable in the service of my king. Also, the screaming of innocents is such a dubious pleasure.

When elicited with purpose, it is like a congratulatory pat on the back.

When produced through mere thuggery, it is an aggravating display of loud noise and mucus.

Jesting aside, go home, my friend. I feel a tithe of relief that you survived. However unlikely, I wish we could meet and share thoughts, admittedly from differing perspectives. But if you pursue me further, I will destroy you and your companions in the most gruesome of fashions.

—VINTAN RETH

We found that note inside a worn-out boot a mile down the trail from the ambush. I might have ridden past it in the moonlight, except it sat on top of a five-foot-tall pile of dead brush and branches somebody dragged from the side of the road. The mere fact that Vintan had left a note was bizarre, and his message was well-organized but deranged. The idea that he knew a lot about me was ridiculous.

This note got stuffed into my pouch along with Vintan's first one. I didn't care if I ever read the damned things again. But he had touched them and composed them, and that could be a handy ingredient in any magic employed against him, in case the universe stopped hating sorcery one of these days.

I doubt we would ever have overtaken Vintan without the extra horses we appropriated from those Denzmen we killed. When engaged in a pursuit, the better-mounted party usually prevails. Vintan's band may have been riding fine beasts, but now we each had two horses and could swap before we'd tired out the one we were riding. A man with two horses is always better mounted than a man with only one, unless that one has wings or magic horseshoes.

We pushed hard to catch the Denzmen, rarely pausing, and resting only during the moonless part of the night. Dozens of fat streams tumbled through the forest on their way to the Blue River, and they kept us well-watered. Our food stores started out meager, though, and by the first night, none of us felt well-fed.

I took early watch the first night, and no one objected. Stan and Ralt hit the ground, stretched out, and were snoring before I'd made the first turn around our little camp. Ella caught up with me and said, "Bib, I understand you're a superior swordsman, but my prince's life will depend upon your skill. Just how good are you?"

"I'm so good I've already saved your life once and you didn't even know it."

"Thank you, that certainly is a mark in your favor. But I need to understand your proficiency by a more objective standard."

This was a ridiculous conversation. I knew why she was asking, even if she didn't. She had just realized that she'd handed her job, the job of rescuing the prince, over to me. She feared I might perform poorly, or I might do the job better than she could. Throw in some guilt and fatigue, and this conversation was the only way she could feel a little better about trusting me. To be fair, I've met a lot of people who thought trusting me was a chancy proposition.

"Well, I've killed enough men to fill up Crossoak and even pack a few into the barns." That was true, if you considered just my early years as a murderer, before I really began to apply myself.

Ella shook her head. "Only one objective standard means anything." She drew her sword.

Deep dusk was sinking into the forest, but at this distance, I saw her perfectly well. She was not smiling, grinning, winking, or twitching eyebrows. I've faced a lot of people intent on killing me, and it felt like I'd met another one.

I wanted to kill her too.

I wanted it more than I wanted food in my rumbling belly. I stepped back and crossed my arms, trapping my hands in my armpits. "I prefer not to fight you. You might kill me, or give me a scar that would mar my beauty."

"Not to appear insensitive, but one cannot mar that which does not exist. Come, I won't harm you in the least. My control is superlative."

"I don't doubt you, but you may get distracted by Desh's fish-belly-white chest and stab me through the head without meaning to." I nodded toward Desh, who was shirtless and washing himself in a stream not far away.

Ella lowered her sword. "Have I made a mistake? Can I trust you?"

"Certainly, you can trust me. Just point me like a crossbow at whomever you don't like, and I'll kill them deader than my grandma." Of course, that was a lie. I liked Ella, but I didn't owe her anything. We happened to be traveling down the same stretch of road at the same time for my convenience. She just didn't know it.

"Very well." She sheathed her sword but made no move toward her bedroll. I walked around the camp once, and she walked with me, silent.

At last, I said, "I welcome the companionship, but I'm not clever enough to chat and guard at the same time, and all this silence verges on annoying."

I couldn't see her smile, but I heard it in her voice. "May I ask you a question?"

"Does it have anything to do with how I stay so charming and sweet out here in the wilderness?"

"No."

"Well... I am disappointed, but all right."

"You spoke of your daughter yesterday. She is dead, isn't she?"

I almost wished she'd stabbed me instead. "Of course she is. If she were alive, I sure as hell wouldn't be here."

Ella patted my shoulder, which might have been condescending, except that it wasn't. She headed off to sleep, and I kept walking circles.

We caught up with Vintan three mornings later, not much after sunrise. We'd been riding since before midnight, downhill through chilly, brittle air. Stan spotted the feathery smoke first and yelled, "Three campfires! What's left of three fires, anyway. I bet they ate bacon this morning. Wish I had some bacon. Damn them knobby buggers for having bacon."

We guided our horses at a sedate walk just beside the tree line for less than an hour. Then I topped a shallow rise, edged under a tree, and looked down into the Blue River valley. It was immensely wide, over a mile, and popping with millions of red, yellow, and orange flowers, as if they'd been painted on. The river itself was a hundred paces across and ran straight through the valley with never a curve. It really was a frosty blue. That's all the detail I noticed, since about a dozen men sat their horses on the far riverbank, and two dozen sat mounted on the near bank, looking at the water as if they might swim their horses across any minute.

Desh rode up beside me. "They must have had to stop until the water dropped. We'd never have caught them otherwise, regardless of how hard we rode."

"Get back over there!" I hissed. I turned my horse and chased him back out of sight of the river.

When we'd all dismounted, I said, "Desh, you hold the horses. And don't go taking them down to the river for a romp and a drink. Or to wave at the Denzmen and make friends with them. Stay here."

Desh blinked and pulled at his collar. "I only rode up with you for just a few seconds."

"If I find out they saw you, I'm only going to stab you with just a few inches of steel."

Ella, Ralt, Stan, and I sneaked among the trees back to the lip of the valley, and then crouched to get a clear view of the Denzmen by the river. One man had ridden out into the water. He had reached mid-river, and the fast water splashed no higher than his thighs.

Ella said, "We will follow them, of course, but perhaps now is the time to dispatch a messenger back to the army and guide them here."

Ralt and Stan began squabbling in dramatic whispers over who would get to go back. Before I could whack them both with my hat, a wagon-size piece of the river surged up beside the rider, overwhelmed him, and carried him under.

"Shit. I'm the one going back," Ralt said. The rider didn't resurface, and neither did his horse. "I'm not going down there. I'm the one going back if I have to kill every one of you."

"What did we just see?" Ella hissed.

It didn't make any sense. We'd seen something that could not have been natural, but every supernatural thing in the world had been stamped out years ago when the gods took their party elsewhere.

Ten men and one boy, probably the prince, rode into the river while the rest waited on the near bank. Ella scrambled to her feet, slipping once, and sprinted back toward the horses. I stared a moment before realizing what she was doing, and I ran after her. As she was pushing Desh out of her way, I snatched her arm and spun her.

"Wait!" I stepped between her and the horses. "It won't make any difference. He'll be mid-river before you get there."

She bared her teeth at me. "Move!"

"If he survives, you can't help him by charging down there and getting killed."

She roared at me, and I glanced back toward the river.

"If he doesn't survive—"

Ella punched me right in the nose, and I staggered. I felt the blood running and figured it might be broken. She was on her horse and galloping toward the river before my vision cleared.

I wiped my upper lip as I mounted the nearest horse. "Well, come on, Desh. You were the one who was so keen to see the river."

Halfway down the valley, I remembered this was exactly the kind of thing I had planned to avoid doing. I also saw that the prince had already crossed the river's midpoint without getting crushed and drowning, and the closer Denzmen had already ridden into the current. It didn't appear that any more Denzmen had been killed, either.

Ella's horse bolted past the cooling campfires and stopped dead. She flew straight over the creature's head and smacked faceup onto the soft riverbank, her sheathed sword twisted under her and one foot stretched out in the choppy water.

Having seen Ella's catastrophe, I drew rein at the campfires, so my horse was walking when he got scared and tried to throw me. I slipped off and let him gallop after Ella's horse back up the hill. Ella was still on her back and shaking her head, paying no attention to the fact that she was slipping into the river. I hopped down and began pulling her up higher onto the bank, but she was solider than she looked. Just as I'd shifted to a better grip, the water jumped from choppy to roiling. I hauled again and realized something was trying to pull her in. Desh showed up and grabbed one of her arms. We pulled her out by slow inches, and every second I imagined all three of us getting devoured by some gigantic, cold-water crocodile.

Once we'd dragged Ella out, we all scooted far back on the riverbank and panted, staring at the water like mice staring at a snake. The river didn't let us catch our breath. Ten paces out from the bank, something surged to the surface, cascading water in every direction. It soaked us and the ground behind us.

The figure said, "Blood or brains?" just like a waitress might ask whether you wanted beer or wine. A touch friendly, but mainly just doing her job. It appeared to be a woman, although exceptional in various ways. For one, she was naked. For another, she was light blue—skin, hair, eyes, and everything. She was beautiful. She was perfect, really, so perfect that if you looked hard at her for a few seconds, you'd get terrified, because nothing natural could be that perfect. And she was standing on the surface of the river, the water just covering her feet.

I had heard a fair amount about river spirits back in my sorcery days, but I'd never met one. This had to be one of them—the stories and descriptions of floating women with floating hair matched. I'd even seen an engraving owned by a monk who was addicted to root oil. He charged the local boys two copper bits apiece to look at the red, naked woman on the water. Apart from the creature's color, it all fit. I walked down to the water's edge. "Blood or brains? Can't I have both?"

"I'm sorry, that's against the rules. Most people choose blood."

I pointed across the river. "Did those fellows take blood?"

"In a way of speaking. They chose blood, and I took it. What is your name, Ir-man?"

"I think I'll avoid letting you charm me with my name, if that won't offend you." I glanced back at Desh and Ella, sitting on the flower-pocked grass with eyes as big as barrelheads. "You can call me Hrothkir, the Red-Handed Butcher of Gurk."

The river spirit shrugged. Her long hair floated above her shoulders for a moment before settling. "Choose blood. I will only take one of you. If you choose brains and fail, I will take you all. Or you can turn back. I don't care if you turn back."

Vintan must have chosen blood and let his man be taken by the river. That was the smart move. I could probably say blood, snatch Desh up off the riverbank before he could run, and hurl him into the water. I looked back again and found Desh over my shoulder.

"It's beautiful," he said.

"Don't go falling in love with a river spirit, son. It never ends well."

"Not her. The magic. A beautiful thing."

"Hrothkir, it is time to choose," the spirit said.

Desh was falling in love with magic, not the spirit. Foolishly in love with something that would break his heart if it didn't kill him first. Most young men do that with something, maybe women, danger, or something else. Being a young man foolishly in love is one of the most pleasurable things the world has to offer, and I couldn't quite convince myself to take it away from him.

Why didn't I just collect my horse and ride away? At the time, I asked myself that very question. I might have done it, except that Vintan, the swamp-rancid Denzman who beheaded little girls, was on the other side of the river. He was crying out for me to come murder him, and I didn't want to be a disappointment to him.

I winked at the spirit. "I choose brains."

The river spirit bobbed like an empty bottle and smiled. "I will ask you three riddles."

"Oh, come on! Everybody asks riddles. The pissant spirits of trees that don't come up to my nipples ask riddles! You're the spirit of the Blue River. You can think of something better than that. Really, aren't you bored after centuries of asking a bunch of damn riddles?" It wouldn't hurt to throw her off her stride, figuratively, since she probably never walked anywhere.

She looked at the water around her ankles. "Well..."

By now, Ella stood on one side of me and Desh stood on the other. Ella squeezed my arm and nodded.

"Do you know any games?" I asked. "You can challenge me to a game. If you win, it's just as if you'd stumped me with riddles."

"I know a game! It's a wonderful game." The spirit grinned and bobbed like a wine cork. "You'll never win against me."

"How do you play?"

The spirit came to the river's edge with a swirl that sprayed water higher than my head. She raised her hand and produced a pair of wooden scissors, dark and smooth and as long as her palm. Opening the blades, she held the scissors out to me and said, "I give these to you open."

Whatever this game was, I'd never heard of it. "Wait, what are the rules?"

"The game is figuring out the rules."

I wished I'd just answered the damn riddles. I closed the blades and handed them to her, saying, "I give these to you closed."

"Wrong. If you are wrong twice more, you lose. If you are correct three times before then, you win." She left the blades closed and held them out. "I give these to you closed."

I opened the blades. "I give these to you open."

"Correct."

I looked at the scissors in her hand. Other than being made of wood, nothing about them seemed odd, not a thing at all. "Are there really any rules? Is the rule that you get to cheat?"

She shook her head and left the blades open. "I give these to you closed." As she was handing the scissors to me, I examined her fingers, the set of her mouth, the angle of her head, and whether her eyes were crossed. Nothing looked like it made a difference in what she said.

I left the blades open and said, "I give these to you closed."

"Wrong again. If you make another mistake, you lose." She opened the blades. "I give these to you open."

As she handed them across, I stared at the water, thinking hard, and I saw her ankles were crossed. Just before she said "open" and handed over the scissors, she uncrossed her ankles.

If I got this one wrong, the spirit would kill us all when we tried to ford the river. And Ella would try to cross it, no matter what. I left the blades open. "I give these to you open."

"Correct." She left the blades open. I saw her cross her ankles as she said, "I give these to you closed."

I made sure my feet were wide apart and handed the open scissors back to her. "I give these to you open."

The river spirit stared at me for a moment, and then she closed her hand to make the scissors disappear. "Well... you are the victor. Would you like to try riddles now? I know some very good ones."

"That is a kind offer, but I have urgent business on the other side of your beautiful river."

"Fine. You and your people should cross quickly. I think there may be a storm soon." She collapsed as if a bucket of water had been poured into the river.

I looked around and saw blue sky to the horizon in all directions. No one had ever told me that river spirits were petty. I'd have to keep that in mind.

We gathered the boys and the horses, and we crossed the river, although we had to yell at Ralt and shame him quite a bit to force him into the water. As we rode up onto the far bank, the river spirit rose again. "I presume you'll be returning this way. When you try to cross on your journey home, I will not be playing games."

A familiar feeling had hit me the moment my horse stepped into the river, and its presence sickened me a little. It felt like a soft breeze sweeping my skin, even under my clothes, but it drifted away when I stopped thinking about it. However, it did leave behind an unpleasant warm spot in my left armpit, a whimsical gift from the gods to go along with making magic possible. I hadn't thought about this feeling for a long time.

Considering the random appearance of a magical being, I had half-expected magic to pop up like a feral groundhog, with nothing good or even admirable about it. I could ignore this magical power, save it for emergencies, or snatch this rare opportunity to protect us from anybody else wandering the southlands with a feral groundhog of their own. I took mental inventory, and I had just enough power left over from the old days.

I reached out my right hand, pulled a glowing yellow band out of nothing, and whipped it around the river spirit's neck. She screamed as I said, "Limnad, I bind you." I reached with both hands and tied each of her ankles with orange bands. "Limnad, I bind you."

Ella had drawn her sword and was shouting over the spirit's screams. "What's happening? Who's killing her?" It made sense for Ella to be confused, since only I could see the bands I'd created.

A moment later, I had wrapped two more orange bands around the spirit's wrists. "Limnad, I bind you."

This whole escapade would have been mighty awkward if the river spirit's name hadn't been Limnad. However, I'd once overheard Gorlana, Goddess of Mercy, say how much she hated the prissy spirits of the Blue River, especially that royal bitch Limnad. So, I had guessed this was her, and if I'd guessed wrong, I would have just ridden like hell out of that valley and never come back.

"Sorcerer!" Limnad screamed. "I will feed your eyes to the turtles! I will make spears from your bones!"

"You have a right to be upset, Limnad—"

"Stop saying my name!"

"I do apologize. I will find a way to repair this to your satisfaction, I promise. By the way, Gorlana says hello."

Limnad stiffened.

I rode to the water's edge near where she floated. "You have earned my deep respect during the few minutes we've known one another. I find I cannot bear to part company with a being of such wit and power as yourself."

"Bib..." Ella cautioned.

I smiled at Limnad. "Darling, you are coming with me."

"You cannot hold me forever. You look strong. I can torture you for years before your heart rips itself into gobbets and strips."

"I'll allow that you might do that. But like I said, I'll try to make it up to you."

"Bib!" Ella said. "I need to speak with you this minute!"

I gazed around. Desh looked as if I'd just given him a puppy.

Ella looked like I'd just skinned her puppy and eaten it.

NINE

I have met people who considered me hasty, and I can't mount an honest defense against them in every case. I confess to magically binding a supernatural being that I knew little about, except that she wanted to torture and kill me, so I could take her into an unknown territory. I further confess I didn't consider the decision for too long before I acted.

Yet my decision was not hasty, for many reasons. Maybe the best reason was that I didn't want her waiting to drown me when I rode back across the Blue River going north. Also, if I overtook Vintan and his riders, I might be glad to have a river spirit along to slap him with whatever nasty magic she knew. Her powers would be much diminished out of water, but if someone attacked us next to a river, she would be like a giant hammer I could whack them with.

None of us knew anything about the Denz Lands, which was a considerable disadvantage. If I could win Limnad over a bit, she would be an invaluable guide. If not, I could force her to answer specific questions, although they'd better be important ones. Whenever I gave her a command, one of the five bands would slip loose. After five commands, she'd be free. I needed to make peace with her before that fifth command, else I'd better give it to her in a note while I was on the other side of a mountain.

I had bound Limnad for one other reason that wasn't too practical, but I found it persuasive. I didn't want to kill her. Throughout the contest, and then the binding, I never felt even a tiny desire to murder her. In the years since I accepted Harik's bargain, I had wanted to kill every person I met, adult and child, and for every one of them I killed, there were hundreds, maybe thousands, that I didn't. That did not make me a virtuous man. It made me a murderer who could have murdered more. But I guess I only wanted to kill human beings, because meeting Limnad was like putting down a weight I'd forgotten I was carrying.

I never was able to explain my reasoning to Ella because of all the yelling and unexpectedly creative cursing, so she forever after thought that binding Limnad had been the act of a reckless idiot. After a couple minutes of this abuse, I screamed, "Do you want to call me a son of a bitch, or do you want to go after the prince?"

Ella stopped yelling, as flushed and panting as if she'd been beating me with a club. She stalked away and mounted her horse.

I said, "Let's go, boys." Ralt and Stan had been standing over by the trees, pretending to examine a horse's hoof and glancing at us now and then. I turned toward Desh and saw him chasing after Limnad, asking foolish questions, and following her as she cursed at him in a spirit language while walking away. She was moving around on land without any problems that I could see.

"Desh! She is a superior being with magical sight, so she likely knows about every embarrassing thing you've ever done. Stop pestering her." I wasn't aware of any being with that kind of magical sight, but if it stopped him from making Limnad angrier, then it was a good lie.

A mile on south from the river, we found a corpse lying on the trail, faceup, split from breast to groin. He wasn't pale like the Denzmen; his skin was tan and his hair light, like the people of

Glass. Somebody had pushed a rough-folded leather pouch into the still-warm wound. I pulled it free, and a rolled scrap of parchment fell out as the leather flopped loose.

> *Bib,*
>
> *I position this note here against the eventuality that you have refused to withdraw, despite my earnest plea. You are without doubt a man of great will and ability, but you cannot prevail. Once given a charge, I have never failed. My king has entrusted to me a task, and I assure you I will pursue the most expedient path to victory, regardless of consideration or cost. Few comprehend the full meaning of that philosophy—to prevail regardless of consideration or cost. Turn back, or you will make me your enemy and come to understand my philosophy in its entirety.*
>
> *Come, sir, the lands north of the Blue River house a profusion of men to be slain. In comparison, my land offers but meager opportunities to exercise your skill.*
>
> *Also, be assured that Prestwick is well, and I give you my pledge that he shall continue to be treated with respect and care.*
>
> —*VINTAN RETH*

"What does it say?" Ella asked.

"Nothing important. Vintan's inviting us over to visit. Maybe we'll stay for supper."

Ella narrowed her eyes at me. "Do not lie to me!"

"All right, Vintan is as crazy as a blind goose and as mean as a tiger. He'll kill us all if we take another step south. But he and the prince are playing games and eating plum candy."

She stared at me, mouth open. "What?"

"I embellished a bit, but that's the heart of it. Now, let's go kill Vintan before he gets any crazier."

We cantered on south, pushing our horses as much as we dared. We had lost an hour at the river to games and binding and getting cursed at by Ella, but Vintan probably wasn't much more than an hour ahead of us. As we rode, Stan and Ralt shouted at each other, still arguing over who would get to go back when we had marked the prince's trail to Ella's satisfaction. She had changed her mind about sending back a messenger just yet. She didn't explain, but her eyes strayed to Limnad when she told me her decision. Limnad kept pace as we traveled, even unmounted, bounding along as graceful as a deerhound.

Half an hour up from the river, a mist began sweeping in. It thickened fast, soon forcing us to a nervous walk. I could just see Ella three lengths behind me, but I couldn't see the others past her at all. Then fog closed in like batter poured into a pan, and everything past my horse's ears dissolved.

"Everybody, stop," I demanded.

Stan whined, "What in the rotting pig's bangers is all this fog doing here?"

"Quiet!" I listened hard for about a minute and couldn't hear anything but our horses breathing. I hated so badly to do this next thing, but something hiding in the fog didn't like us at all. "Limnad. Get rid of this fog."

"I can't. You son of a bitch." Limnad laughed from out of the fog. "I like that, blonde woman. Thank you for yelling that insult where I could hear. Hrothkir, I can't get rid of it, you son of a bitch."

I sighed and scanned the fog. "Why can't you get rid of it, Limnad?"

"This fog is unnatural."

"You can't blow away a magical fog?"

"Not magical, you simpleminded fish's anus. Divine." Limnad taunted me, "Yes, why don't you curse the gods, Hrothkir? Say something profane, Hrothkir. Maybe Krak will burn you to Hrothkir-cinders. I hope that first he clears the fog so I can watch. By the way, you have used up one of your commands."

I nodded. I couldn't see Limnad, but she almost certainly was watching me. "I know."

I waited a little more, silent and stationary. Then my horse jerked, and to my left a shape insinuated itself in the fog before it surged toward me. A circle of fog fifty feet around me just disappeared, like it had been scooped out with a giant spoon. The shape on my left turned out to be a Denzman, and we stared at one another. I recovered first, drew my sword, and sliced him across the skull from crown to cheekbone. His horse ran past me, with him hanging onto it by the neck. That left me alone, but I heard shouts and fighting from off in the fog.

I wheeled and trotted toward the sound of metal clanging, through a dense slice of mist and right back out into a huge circle of open air. Ella and Desh were fighting three Denzmen on horseback. I killed one from behind right away, slicing through the back of his neck. Desh's horse reared, and he fell. Ella stabbed a man in the belly, and the remaining Denzman charged toward Desh with his spear leveled. Ella threw her sword at the man and hit his horse instead, which broke stride. The spear slammed into Desh's leg instead of his chest. The weapon broke, the boy went limp, and the Denzman rode off into the fog.

I heard Ralt roaring somewhere, but he stopped after a few seconds. Ella and I both dismounted and ran to kneel over Desh, who was unconscious. The spear had smashed into his knee, which was pulverized and three-fourths severed from his thigh. Blood was pulsing out of his leg from the big artery and pooling in the grass. Ella grabbed his thigh with one hand and tried to hold in the blood with her other.

"Don't just watch! Make a tourniquet!" she said.

"We can't do anything with this. He's going to die."

She yelled. She didn't make any words—she just yelled at life for being this way.

Desh opened his eyes but lay there relaxed, as if he didn't feel pain. I hoped he'd stay that way until he died.

Ella yelled, "Bib! Don't sit there and watch him die as if he were an insect in the road! Do something! At least pretend to do something for this boy, you worthless old man!" She looked at me like I was something that hid in the dark and fed off human fluids.

That hit hard. Not the part about being an old man, but the part about not even twitching a finger to help the boy. Well, Desh was a man, but just barely. Boys die all the time, and people hardly notice. I couldn't easily ignore Desh while Ella was screaming at me about him from one foot away.

Part of me didn't want to let him die. It wanted to hurry up and kill him before he died on his own and I missed my chance. "Harik, you're an ass-leaking oaf," I muttered.

Ella glared at me, as ferocious as any torturer. Maybe she would have killed me, but her hands were busy trying to hold Desh's life inside him.

I grabbed Desh's hand and leaned over him, my face almost touching his. "Do you still want to be a sorcerer?" He might have nodded. I wasn't sure, but I decided to believe it was a nod. "Now's the time to do something about it."

I lifted my spirit into darkness and tried to bring Desh with me. If he made the trip, he had been born a sorcerer. Most likely he wouldn't, and he'd bleed out in the dirt like millions of other young men. Hell, even if he was a sorcerer, he might bleed to death. Plenty have.

It would be inaccurate to say it was just darkness, like you have when there's no light. It was an overwhelming preponderance of nothingness, filled with not a solitary sound. No wind, no grass waving, no insects or birds. I couldn't hear my heartbeat or hear myself breathe.

I had figured I could get to this place, although I hadn't been positive. This was where the gods did their trading, and I had brought Desh to trade with the Goddess of Mercy for his life. No one I knew of had been able to reach this place for years, but getting here was clearly still possible in the Denz Lands. The reason for that would probably improve our understanding of magic and the gods in unexpected, profound ways, but I didn't really give much of a damn. I've never been scholarly.

"Did I die?" Desh asked from out of the nothingness. He didn't sound concerned.

"You tried, but you're not very good at it. Time isn't passing for you back home, so you have a minute to collect your thoughts."

"If I'm not dead, what is this?" I heard the boy's voice catch. Then words started tumbling out of him. "I hope you know what you're doing! I hate to tell you this, Bib, but I haven't seen you do a single thing yet that's worked out very well!"

"Desh, you're at the market, and the sale is starting. You need to decide how much you want to live. If the answer isn't 'a whole hell of a lot,' then we can go home now."

"Damn it, Bib, I don't know what I'm doing! Of course I want to live. I guess we'll find out how much."

"That's fair. Don't be afraid to swagger around a little and bang them together, but don't forget what I told you, either."

Desh didn't say anything.

"There are no good deals. Right?"

"Right."

"Hush now," I announced, not quiet at all. "I sense a bunch of assholes approaching."

A rich, precise but clipped voice said, "My dear murderer, is that an appropriate greeting for an old acquaintance, absent these many years? One to whom you are obligated in such an overwhelming manner?"

"My apologies, mighty Harik. I amend my observation. I sense a bunch of squabbling, grasping assholes with the morals of back-alley drug addicts approaching. Your Worship."

TEN

"You might cause me to forget how profitable our little discourses have been, Murderer." The voice of Harik, God of Death, drifted to me from the void. In this place of trading, the gods had willed that sorcerers have no physical form. That includes no physical eyeballs. No sorcerer in history had seen, smelled, or felt anything in the Home of the Gods—if that's where that place really was. It could be the divine equivalent of a dank, piss-soaked alley for all I knew.

In the trading place, a sorcerer could perceive only the thoughts of other beings, so I had never beheld Harik himself. I had come to imagine what he must look like, though, based on his repellent thoughts that would embarrass a rutting toad. I saw him as a balding, pinch-faced bookkeeper trying hard to appear smooth, wearing poorly cut silk garments.

Harik continued, "Be thankful I remember the profit and choose to allow your continued existence."

"Pretend I said thank you until you blushed, Harik. Was that you creating hell and confusion with all the fog just now? That was a lot of hard work just to get my attention. Do you like me that much? I like hemorrhoids more than I like you."

Desh hit a shrill note. "Bib, is that the voice of the actual God of Death? Shouldn't we be... humbler or something?"

"He's a mighty god, Desh, and he doesn't care what us insignificant nits think. We can't hurt the fussy little moose-crotch's feelings. Can we, Harik?"

"No." I swear I could hear his immortal teeth grinding.

"So, where have you boys been all these years? Big hangover? Misplace your thunderbolts?"

Silence drifted on to the point of embarrassment.

"That's all right, I don't really give a shit. Just making conversation. Besides, I didn't call for you, Harik. I called Gorlana, so why the hell are you here?"

"I own you, Murderer. Nothing happens involving you unless I sanction it. I must approve any exceptions, and until you fulfill my debt—"

I imagined rolling my eyes. "Oh, shut that festering gash in your face, you long-winded fart!"

Desh said, "Just to be clear... should you be talking that way to the God of Death? I mean when I'm... I mean on the other side, things are..."

I didn't bother answering. The truth is that when you bargain with gods, if you act like you give a crap about them, then you have no hope at all.

"Fine!" Harik said. "We're not fools. I know what you want. No one can help you, Murderer, because you cannot pay. I hold a lien on everything you have."

"I'm not here to make an offer. I'm just here to advise Desh on his first deal. To make sure he doesn't get completely violated in a bad place by you jackals."

Harik paused. "You may not negotiate for the other one. Go away."

"No."

"I command you to leave!" Harik boomed.

As conversationally as possible, I said, "I command you to screw yourself, your sister, and your pet goat. See how far that command goes."

Harik paused again. "Fine. You've always been a difficult case. I'll allow you to remain, if you promise to be respectful and quiet."

"Thank you." I had no intention of being respectful or quiet. "So, will you make Desh an offer? Please, O great Harik, who can topple mountains with one quiver of one hair on your masculine, hirsute backside?"

"No. I cannot deal with him."

"Do you mean you're wasting our time with all this prancing around? I was nice to you for no reason at all? Come on, Desh, let's go." I started to lower Desh and myself back down into the world of men.

Another voice spoke, nasal and slow. "I can trade with the young fellow. Happy to do so."

"Why, that sounds like Fingit! How have you been, Your Worship? Built any good chariots lately?"

Fingit laughed, but it sounded forced. "Murderer, I own exclusive rights to the Nub here. All of his trades must go through me."

Desh said, "What? The Nub?"

"Yes, that's our name for you," Fingit said. "We have to call you something evocative. Who can remember all these sorcerers by their sad little human names?"

"Bib gets the Murderer, and I get the Nub? Why the Nub? Why not the Crafter, the Falcon, or something like that? No one's going to respect a sorcerer called the Nub."

"We could just call you the Corpse," Harik purred like a gigantic, immortal tomcat.

I felt like I was losing control of this negotiation. "None of this matters a damn if we can't make a bargain. Let's get on with it!"

"Quite so!" Fingit said.

No one spoke for some time. It was hard to tell exactly how long, since that place where sorcerers and gods trade always seems beyond time and space. I feel safe in saying that it was "a while."

I finally said, "Desh, they're waiting for you to tell them what you want."

"Oh!" Desh yelped.

There was a long pause in which I expect he was thinking about not dying, and getting his leg back, and getting some extra power to build magic doodads and burn all his enemies to ash. He was probably smart enough to keep his first trade simple, but if not, then his career as a sorcerer would be short and awful.

Desh said, "I want to be healed, and I want my leg back." Desh bit off each word with precision.

"Ah, I'm sorry, but that's kind of a problem," Fingit said. "You may trade for power, but it becomes *your* power. How will you then use it? Nub, you can't just wave a stick or some chicken entrails at the stump of your leg and expect it to be healed. You must cede the power to the Murderer so he can heal you. For that, you have to deal with Harik."

I said, "Pig shit on apple pie! Are all of you bastards trying to get a cut of this deal?"

Harik said, "Murderer, I know I've taken a firm stance in the past on clearing your current debt before any more deals, but I am prepared to waive that restriction, this one time only, to assist you in this dire situation."

"Really?" I tried to load it up with sarcasm.

"Truly!" Harik said, oblivious. "I am prepared to offer you a substantial trade. I will grant power enough to completely heal the Nub. I also offer power beyond that, which you may use to heal, bless, call the forces of nature, or anything else within your talents. This will be a large block of power, five complete squares. Just make an offer."

"Just kiss my ass," I said. "If you have an offer to make to Desh, make it."

"I'm asking very little of you, really. In addition to the many murders you have already accomplished for me in such a fine fashion, I would require that within the next week you murder the one person you care about most. Easily done, as I'm sure you'll agree, since those whom you love tend to annoy you beyond all reason quite quickly. My own wife comes to mind..."

I laughed. "No. Definitely no."

"Ah, that is a shame. But as a bit of incentive, I will reduce your open-ended debt in addition to my current extremely generous offer."

"That doesn't mean a damn thing. You could say the debt's cut by a hundred, but only you know how many I still owe. It might be a thousand, or ten thousand."

"Or one hundred and one." I heard the smile in Harik's voice.

"I don't trust you, so forget it."

After a long pause, Harik spoke, but his voice had lost some of its richness. "Very well. I'm making a tremendous sacrifice here, but I'm prepared to cancel your open-ended debt completely—paid in full—if you kill the person you care about most within the week. I will also deliver five squares so you can save the Nub."

It might be smart to explain what Harik's terms meant. Power is the currency of magic. It's like money that can blow your head off if you're lax about using it. Magical power's denomination is the square. Roughly speaking, a square is enough power to perform one major feat, such as saving a person close to death, or burning a damn big house to ash in just a minute.

I don't mean that power is square in some literal way. A square shape is easy to imagine dividing up, so everybody calls it a square for calculating purposes. The gods made this shit up, not me. A sorcerer doesn't have to use a square all at once; instead, he can slice the power up to perform smaller feats.

I hadn't foreseen anything like Harik's offer. I was a murderer. If I killed just one more person, then I could be free of Harik. I wouldn't have to kill people at all. Hell, by murdering this one person, I might save dozens, or hundreds. It might be the most moral thing I could do.

"I, might..." I squeezed the words out like tears.

It would have to be Ella. I guess it was foolish to say I cared about her, since we probably hadn't spoken more than a thousand words to each other. But I felt more for her than I did for Desh, who was putting me through a hell of a lot of trouble, now that I thought about it. Maybe I should first promise her I'd bring the prince home, since she'd be dead. It wouldn't be a good act to kill her, of course. I had to admit that. However, few of my undertakings have been noble, or even justifiable, these past years.

Desh said, "Say no. Nothing's worth that. Let's leave."

He went on to say that I was a whiner and a gutless sack of maggots. He didn't use actual words, and he may not even have been thinking it, but I heard it anyway.

"All right. Harik, I say no."

"You should reconsider. You will never get a better offer. You'll never even get this offer again."

"On second thought..." I silently called myself a vile, slime-licking rat fornicator with bells on. "No. Drop it. My answer will always be no."

"A shame. Very well. I don't see what we can do for you."

Desh didn't speak, and I didn't either. I grabbed him and began drifting back to our side.

Fingit said, "Wait! There may be a way for us to help, but it won't be cheap."

"Let me guess," I said. "Desh trades you something you fancy, then you peel off part for yourself before passing it on to that impotent leech, Harik. He snatches off a taste for himself and then delivers the power to Desh, who gives him permission to cede it to me. How am I doing?"

"Quite well. It's been a while since we worked a four-cornered deal, but we can certainly manage it. So, Nub, make your offer."

I hoped Desh would remember not to make the first offer, but I couldn't get in there and bargain for him. I started whistling a nonsense tune, in case he might hear it and remember.

Desh said, "You should offer me something first. I want something good, and don't try to trick me. Please."

"Murderer, shut the hell up!" Fingit yelled.

I stopped whistling.

Fingit said, "I will deliver, by proxy, two squares of power for the price of—"

Desh interrupted, "Bib, how much power do you need?"

That was an excellent sign. The boy was thinking. "Two squares are far too much. We need half a square at most."

"I want half a square, Fingit, no more."

Fingit sniffed. "All right. I'll deliver one half of one square in exchange for the removal of your capability to father children for the rest of your life."

"What? You damned... you..."

I said, "That is a bit expensive, but understand that Fingit is just taking a tough bargaining position. Desh, as your advisor, I suggest a counteroffer of forgoing one orgasm some time within the next year."

"Yes, that one! The orgasm one! That's my offer!"

Fingit laughed. "That's hardly an offer at all! Did you come here to waste our time? Here's a different offer then. In exchange for the power, you'll become a compulsive gambler with horrible luck."

"No!" Desh yelled. "Bib? Do you have any advice?"

I tried to nod, failed, and grinned instead. "Yes, I do, son. I'd offer these snakes one bad but temporary rash in the next year."

"All right... I see what you're saying." I realized I hadn't noticed Desh was panting until it started slowing down. "I offer one bad but temporary rash in the next year."

"Hah! I don't think you came here to bargain at all." I heard Fingit's sneer. "Is this a social call? Would you like me to send for refreshments? Here's my counter. I'll give you a nasty mean streak. Not cruel, mind you. Just nasty. How about that?"

"I don't want that! Um... I offer having bad penmanship." Desh stumbled over the words.

That was silly, but Desh was beginning to understand how this worked. He might still get cheated, but at least afterward he'd understand how it happened.

Fingit said, "Every woman you ever love will cheat on you."

"Uh, pigs will make me sneeze."

"You'll cheat on every woman you love."

"I'll forget my wife's anniversary—two years in a row."

"You lose your childhood—all memories gone," Fingit said with a certain solidity in his voice.

Desh paused. "I... my knee will ache when the weather changes."

"No. All the childhood memories, or no deal."

"This is crazy! Is this really all you'll accept? Bib, can you advise me?"

I thought hard about other lines of bargaining Desh could take, but in truth, he was stuck. "That may be the best deal you'll get, Desh. He knows it's live or die for you."

"How about I just lose my memories of my mother, not the whole childhood?"

"No."

"My mother. That's what I can offer."

"We can't come to an arrangement, then. You may go."

"Come on, Desh, let's leave." I expected that Fingit would give a bit, but he was a god, so who knew why he did things? I grabbed Desh, but he resisted. It was decent control for a sorcerer on his first visit to the gods.

Fingit said, "Wait! Maybe we can arrange something. I'm moved by a young man with such promise."

"So, we have a deal with my memories of my mother?"

"Well, no. But for just those memories, I'll offer you one-tenth of a square."

"Desh..." I wanted to tell him to stop.

"Quiet, Murderer!" Fingit said.

"Bib, can you advise me?"

"Son, one-tenth of a square will heal you, but you'll still lose the leg."

"I... I can't believe this! This is insane! Bib! Damn it to hell and halfway home!"

"Was there an offer somewhere in that rant?" Fingit asked.

"No! If I ever find that bastard with the spear, I'm going to beat him to death! All right, I'll settle for—"

"Wait!" I yelled.

"Yes?" Desh sounded pathetically hopeful.

"If you're taking the lower offer, hold out for an extra hundredth of a square and keep it for yourself."

"You didn't find some clever trick..."

"Sorry, Desh. Remember, there are no good deals."

Desh said, "I want eleven-hundredths of a square in exchange for all memories of my mother. That's my last offer."

"Impossible!" Fingit said.

"Make it possible!"

"Well... all right, we have a bargain."

"Send a tenth of a square to Bib and the rest to me!" Now that the deal was done, Desh's voice was warbling like a bird.

"Agreed. We could make a separate deal for the leg, you know. An offer you might like better?"

"No. This is plenty," Desh said.

"We're leaving now," I said. "We'll let you boys get back to kissing each other's asses."

"Murderer, one more thing," Harik said. "I've extended my offer to cancel your open-ended debt. You may kill the person you most care for any time within the next week to lift your obligation. The intentional act itself will seal the agreement. Perhaps a good opportunity shall arise."

I couldn't prevent it. An image of Ella with my knife sticking out of her chest flashed into my mind. There wasn't a nasty enough name to call Harik, so I grabbed Desh and drifted back to our world.

No time passes at home while you're visiting the gods. There's probably a bad joke in that somewhere. When we returned, I dropped Desh's hand and yanked out my knife as I sat up. Desh howled as if something was eating his heart while he was still using it.

I yelled, "Hold him tight! Pin him!"

Ella fell across his thighs, and I started cutting. Desh stopped screaming and switched to moaning the moment my knife touched him.

I pulled a green band out of the air and drew it tight around the big artery. Then I started cutting away the ripped-up flesh and bone using the knife in my right hand. At the same time, with my left hand, I pulled green strips out of nothing and wrapped them on the stump I was creating. Some time during the process, Stan and Ralt appeared and helped hold the boy. A little later, Desh stopped moaning, but he kept wriggling, so I knew he wasn't dead.

Within a few minutes, it was done. "You can let go."

Ella looked at the smooth pad of flesh at the end of Desh's leg, and she looked at me with awfully big eyes. I pretended that the stump was in bad need of examination so I wouldn't have to look at her so soon after planning to kill her.

She grasped the boy's hand. "You are very brave, Desh. A brave young man."

"Brave as a drunk telling the rest of the bar how tiny their dicks are," I said. "He'd appreciate your praise more if he wasn't so unconscious. You can say it to him again when he wakes up. I bet he won't mind a little mothering."

I stood and stumbled only a little, which I felt proud about since I hadn't healed anybody in a long time. I limped away to look for a less bloody place to sit.

A tender incidental effect of healing somebody is that the healer gets to feel what the sufferer felt, although not as severely. My leg didn't feel as if it had been smashed off like Desh's; it just felt like it was being stabbed with short knives all the way around. The pain wouldn't last too long—maybe a few hours, maybe a day. Sorcerers tend to puff up a little when they've saved somebody's life, so I think this is the gods' way of telling them not to get too smug.

"Were you wounded as well?" Ella asked.

"No, my foot's asleep. Don't pay any attention."

Nobody commented on the fact that my foot continued to sleep for the next five hours.

ELEVEN

I have killed more people than I've saved in my life. I spent a lot more years saving people than I spent murdering them, but I have pursued murder with greater diligence. I dealt with the Goddess of Mercy in my youth, and I killed only when pushed to it. I was the kind of sorcerer known as a Caller, meaning I healed the ill and injured, brought rain to grow the crops of the virtuous, and brought locusts to eat the crops of the wicked. When I told people what kind of sorcerer I was, they were often disappointed in me, because to them, sorcery was knocking down castles and burning up forests.

Gods like to claim particular sorcerers. It's sort of like when all the village's sheep run in one big flock, but every farmer has marked the ones that are his. I had already established myself as a sorcerer when Harik purchased me from the Goddess of Mercy. All of Harik's bargains are about death and killing. I eventually took on the open-ended debt, by which I owe Harik an unknown number of murders. I don't know why he wanted me to turn myself into a murderer. I guess he thought it would be funny.

I would take that deal again, though.

Desh lay on the grass in the afternoon sun, sometimes restless and sometimes quiet under his blanket. Ella and I sat near him, and we checked his breathing now and then. I also watched for signs that becoming a sorcerer had driven him mad. It's not a common reaction, but it happens often enough, and a deranged sorcerer can be a terror. I felt obliged to observe the young man for a day or so and destroy him if he went insane.

Once the fog disappeared, Ralt found and collected the Denzman whose scalp and face I'd sliced open. The man had lost his horse and was bouncing off tree trunks, dizzy and half-blind. Krak knows where Limnad had gotten off to—in the trees somewhere preparing to turn us inside out, or drown us in our own blood, should the opportunity arise.

Ella said, "If you are a sorcerer, why don't you transform the Denzmen into sand, or turn their spears into storks? Then you could bring the prince to us by incantation, or for that matter, you could transport him back to his own bed!"

"If I could do such things, I would, just to make sure Desh feels like he hasn't lost his leg for nothing. But I can't make those things happen." I shrugged. "Even if I had the ability, I have used up every last scrap of power in my possession."

Ella pointed at my chest. "Acquire more."

"It's not like picking blackberries. Let's just say that acquiring power is sort of a nuisance, and leave it alone."

"Then we should continue pursuing Vintan. Stan can stay with Desh and accompany him home when he can travel." She wrinkled her nose. "I'm tired of listening to the man curse and break wind."

I looked her in the eye. "Desh will be traveling in the morning, I promise."

"You cannot know that."

"I can't remember for sure, but were you anywhere close by when I saved his life?" I looked around as if I were searching for someone. "I saw somebody who might have been you. Nobody else here has yellow hair."

She whacked me on the arm hard enough to hurt. "Don't be impertinent. It doesn't suit a man of your maturity."

"You saw me heal the boy, so trust me when I say he'll be up."

"We're wasting a great deal of time. Vintan isn't sitting on the grass waiting for his wounded men to feel better."

"We'll make up the time."

She stared hard at me. She would probably stare just like that at a tree branch to decide whether it was sturdy enough for her to hang me from. "Very well. I will trust you on this, although I shouldn't. I'm beginning to think I have met bandits and bankers more trustworthy than you, but I fear we may soon need your sword again. You will see to it that we make up the lost time."

Actually, I had no realistic ideas about how we could make up the time. I just didn't want to leave Desh out there with nobody but Stan to care for him. I hadn't known the soldier long, but he gave me the impression that it would be reckless to leave a spiny lizard in his care.

Ella had judged my integrity harshly, but in truth, she was more correct than not. Her zeal had begun winning me over on the idea of rescuing the prince, but only if it wasn't too much trouble. As long as I had Denzmen to kill, I wouldn't cry if the prince fell off a cliff and perished.

I left her watching Desh and walked over to Ralt and the prisoner. The wounded man was no boy and hadn't been for ten or fifteen years. "What's your name?"

He spat at my face but hit my sleeve instead.

"Hard to aim with just one eye, isn't it?" I nodded to Ralt. "Stand him up."

Ella had abandoned Desh to come watch.

I said, "I don't give a shit about anything you know, and you'd probably tell me lies anyway. I can't have you following us, though." I drew my long knife.

"Don't." Ella touched my shoulder. "You don't have to kill him."

"I think you do," Ralt said under his breath.

I grabbed the Denzman's hair on the uninjured side of his head and made him look into my eyes. I didn't see much fear. A whole lot of contempt, but not much fear. "I can't have you running off to tell Vintan all about us, either." I reached down and sliced the back of his leg above the knee, hard and deep. He groaned and collapsed.

I put the Denzman out of my mind and strolled down the trail about thirty paces, where I found the broken spear that had wounded Desh. I carried it back to the young man's pallet.

"He's awake," Ella said. "I warned him that we must continue in the morning, and he mustn't feel bad if he's too weak to accompany us." She frowned at me as if I had promised Desh would fly in the morning.

Desh looked confused, but his voice was strong when he said, "Bib, thank you for helping me." He reached under the blanket that was folded beneath his head, but nothing was there.

"You paid for that gift, son. I just unwrapped it for you."

"I'm missing something." He flipped back the blanket and looked at his stump.

"I know," Ella said, holding his hand.

"No... that's not it." He looked at me again and raised his eyebrows.

I squatted down beside him. "I know it feels like you've lost something, Desh, and you have. You've traded away some memories, but you don't need to worry about it. You're a sorcerer, and you made that decision. The feeling will go away on its own soon, so put it aside."

"I don't see how I can travel with you. I can't walk. I can't even ride. I can't get off the side of this nasty trail."

I held up my knife and the broken spear. "Do you know what these are?"

Desh peered at them and then at me. "Are they special in some way?"

I raised my voice. "Do you know what they are?"

"A knife... and a spear."

I dropped the spear beside him and boomed, "This is the weapon that took your leg!" I dropped the knife. "This is a knife still wet with the blood of your enemy!"

He stared at them but didn't move.

I knelt down and said, "If I were a sorcerer who was handy with things like you are, I'd be carving myself a wooden leg tonight. What's more, I'd be using that energy I bought from Fingit to make the best damn magical wooden leg that's ever existed." I stood. "And you're a sorcerer, so stop whining. You'll embarrass me."

I turned my back so Desh couldn't see me grinning, and I walked across the trail. Ella joined me a moment later.

"Is this what it's like to be a sorcerer?"

"Sometimes. I confess that I make it look easy. Not every sorcerer is as masterful as I am."

"You are forever joking. Why don't you speak seriously? When you act, you're serious."

"Oh, I say make your own fun. The world's not going to make it for you."

Ella glanced over at Desh, who was sitting up and examining the broken spear. "Will he really create a magical leg?"

"I think he will. He's a handy young man. Even if he fails, it's good to keep his mind occupied right now."

"Why right now? What are you not telling me?" She grasped the front of my shirt with one hand and led me twenty feet off the trail. "We can't abide secrets. We are in the land of our enemy. I want to trust you, but..."

I almost told her that a few hours ago, I had just about decided to kill her and had gone on to planning what I'd do when she was dead. I thought about it again and then smothered the impulse to confess. "Desh had to trade the gods for enough power to save himself. I think you called it 'acquiring' power a little while ago. He traded away all his memories of his mother."

Ella jerked her head back. "The gods can do that? Why did he accept such a bargain?"

"It was the best deal he could get, and he was highly motivated to trade. Those memories are the thing he's looking for. Something's missing, but he doesn't know what. That feeling will pass in a day or two."

Ella looked down and scratched her forehead. "I see why one can't simply go and acquire power. Bib, I would rather neither of you give up anything more. Magic cannot be worth it."

"That's an easy statement to make right now. But I'll try to hold off."

"Thank you. And thank you for not killing that helpless Denzman. It was an act of mercy that you should cherish."

"Well, if you want me to be honest with you, I didn't spare him on my account. I didn't spare him on your account either, nor even his."

"You're about to make a joke, aren't you?"

"I let him live to spite that malformed cockroach who is lower than rat spew, the God of Death. And I am not joking about that."

I walked a couple of minutes up the trail, out of sight of the rest of my traveling companions. I whispered, "Limnad, I want you."

A few moments later, the river spirit walked out of the tree line as if she'd been waiting there for me. "What do you want? I was busy luxuriating in the anticipation of your death."

"I'm happy to know you're not bored." I had chosen to call Limnad so far down the trail because Ralt and Stan had been gawking at her since we left the river. None of my warnings about offending supernatural beings had deterred them, either. They claimed that not looking at a naked woman was unnatural, and would probably offend her as well, so they were just being polite.

It was time to find out whether binding the spirit had been wise or moronic or perhaps fatal. "I have an idle question to ask you, Limnad. If there were any secret paths or shortcuts around here, would you know about them?"

Limnad tilted her head and smiled. "Are you commanding me to answer, Bib? Yes, I know your name now. Soon, I will charm you with it and force you to tear off your own eyelids and eat them."

I gave her my most respectful smile. "No, I'm not commanding you to do anything—yet. It's just that Ella thinks you don't know this territory from a barrel of pig parts, but I think you know all about these woods and their secret ways."

Limnad put her hands to her cheeks. "Of course I would be happy to fall for such a juvenile ploy and answer your question for free. Once you disembowel yourself, I will tell you everything I know about such paths."

I examined a rock beside the trail as I said, "What's the friction between you and Gorlana?"

"What?" Limnad twitched, dissolved to liquid for a moment, and then reformed.

I had leaped to that unexpected question hoping it would make her forget for a minute how much she hated me. I raised my eyebrows. "You and Gorlana. Did you steal some man she wanted to snog? Did she pee in your river?"

"Hah!" The spirit circled me in just a moment, like a little stream rushing around an oxbow. "I wouldn't touch any man she desired. She lacks all discernment when it comes to men. As graceless as goats. She would mount anything with a pointy bit."

I smiled at her with polite interest. "If not men, then what?"

"She is greedier than a filth-smeared infant!" Limnad screamed loud enough for Ella and the others to hear. "She wants all the shiny bangles, and damn who owns them! She's owed tribute. But she's not owed someone's birthright!"

I waited a moment, but she seemed done with that grievance. "She cheated me too, once or twice."

Limnad glanced at my crotch and then raised an eyebrow at me. "I have no interest in how she defrauded you. If you want to know secret paths, command me. Else, go around the long way."

"All right. Limnad, when I ask you to, please guide us through the best and shortest path that will catch us up with Vintan's Denzmen." The band on her left ankle unwound itself and dissipated.

"As you command, you shambling pile of filth. By the way, how are you going to find this path?"

"I'm sorry?"

"How will you find the path? I am commanded to guide you through it. I am not commanded to help you find where it starts. You grunting pool of slop."

I had never heard a single story about binding supernatural creatures that turned out well for the binder, but I'd managed to make myself overlook that. "Limnad, O wise and tricky spirit, when I ask you to, take us to the beginning of the best and shortest path that you will guide us through." The band on her left hand disentangled itself and faded.

"As you command. Do you want to find your way back to the world of men when you have finished this path?"

"Now you're just mocking me."

"Yes, I am. I find it quite gratifying."

TWELVE

I have found there to be five types of people, and I can tell type from type by using the Bucket of Shit Rule. Say we're standing around with some people, and up above us somebody overturns a bucket of shit. Some people just stand there, and some jump out of the way. Others push people to safety, and some shove people right under the shit. And some people go kill the son of a bitch who turned over the bucket.

My best friends and I have rarely been like one another. Some lacked qualities that I possess, and others made me look like a fool with my fingers up my nose. We might have liked or hated different things, and we might have thought differently about how much honesty is strictly required. But my real friends and I have always been the same type of person, according to the Bucket of Shit Rule.

On the first morning of Desh's life with his enchanted false leg, he turned out to be the same type of person as Stan and Ralt. It wasn't obvious at first. By the time sunlight was just letting us see each other's faces, Desh was walking around on his new leg. Then he hurried along for a bit, and then he jogged. He jumped up and down a few times. Then Stan raced him down the trail to a fallen tree, and Desh nearly won.

At that point, Ralt and Stan adopted Desh into their three-person family, whose crest might have read FORTITUDE, PROFANITY, AND GRIEVANCE. They had recognized him as one of their type.

"Toughest shit-sucker I ever seen," said Stan. "Leg smashed off one day, sprinting like a hare the next!"

"Wiping your ass with a cactus ain't in it," said Ralt, with the first smile I'd seen from him in two days.

"A damn sorcerer, to top it. We got two now, and one of them can't be killed."

"And the other kills everything in sight." Ralt looked at me sideways and lowered his voice just a touch. "Except he doesn't kill prisoners who ought to be killed. The ones who might kill us in our sleep."

"Two sorcerers! We might live to see home!"

Desh grinned and took their backslaps with goodwill.

"I snatched this sword for you, Desh," Stan said. "It's a nasty-ass Denzman sword, but you take it till we kill a man with a better sword for you."

"We'll teach you all about fighting."

"Our sorcerer won't get his other leg hacked off for lack of fighting prowess!"

Desh said, "Thank you, fellows. I really am touched. If you take off that dead man's tunic and shirt and trousers, when we get time, I'll make you both cloaks that will keep you dry in a waterfall."

Ella and I heard this entire exchange as we saddled our horses, and I realized that now all three men were the same type of person. That would be the "getting the hell out of the way and letting other people worry about themselves" type. I suspected that yesterday Desh had been a "pushing other people out of the way" type. He might have lost something important when he traded away his memories of his mother. Losing memories carries unpredictable risks.

"Limnad," I said. "Take us to that short, fast path we were chatting about yesterday."

I'm glad I had commanded Limnad to lead us to this secret passage, even if it did bring her closer to freedom by releasing another band. I would never have found the damn thing myself. The route may have seemed more confusing than it really was, since she probably took us down some unnecessarily circuitous paths, just so we'd never find it again without her. Or, maybe she was just enjoying the dumb, lost looks on our faces.

Limnad led us off the trail right away, and we crossed six streams before our horses warmed up. We rode most of the morning while the trees got taller, then sparser, then smaller, and they finally faded away, leaving us on sloping, grassy fields. We rode until we saw a few sharp, brown hills. Limnad took us down between two hills into a defile that soon was branching like a maze. By midday, we crested another rise and saw hills in all directions.

"It's a straight path from here." Limnad pointed southwest. "We'll follow this valley and rejoin the trail before sunset. You have saved a lot of time. I hope you spent it contemplating what your liver will look like when I show it to you."

"I'm sure it will have great artistic merit. Lead us, O spirit, and we shall follow and not talk bad about you."

The valley was smooth, as far as rocky wilderness valleys go. We rode fast, and we paused only once to change mounts and drain ourselves. I indulged in some rough estimation, and I began to hope that we were making up even more time than we'd lost yesterday.

An arrow smacked into the ground right beside me. If it had hit me, I would have deserved it for daydreaming as I rode between tall hills suitable for hiding men who could shoot and throw things at me. I hollered a warning to Ella and the triplets as I goaded my horse uphill toward the ambush.

It was a good thing the hill wasn't dauntingly steep, and better that the ambushers weren't firing from all the way at the top. The arrows kept whizzing, but only a couple came close to hitting me. Either these were terrible bowmen, or they were mighty anxious to avoid sticking arrows into my horse. She would be a prize for any bandit or tribesman.

Limnad laughed somewhere behind me. "You commanded me to lead you through a fast, short path, but not a safe path!"

Ten bowmen stood behind rocks halfway up the slope, all shooting at me with nice, relaxed motions, since they had no concern for taking cover. On the theory that these thugs coveted my mare, I slid out of the saddle and put her body between them and myself. I ran alongside her as she climbed the hill until I neared the line of bowmen, and then I let her run free.

I drew my sword as I scrambled toward the nearest man, and I cut off the closest part of him, which happened to be his right hand. Now that I was among them, they could hardly fire at me for risk of hitting their friends. The next man couldn't decide whether to shoot me or draw his sword. I stabbed him in the belly while he was deciding. He grabbed at my arm and said, "Help me!" as I pushed him aside.

The next fellow had drawn his sword, but he was so incompetent he should've stayed with the bow or thrown a rock or offered me his sister. I stabbed him in the throat and moved on.

The next two men faced me together, swords drawn. They both lunged at me, and while they were in motion, I got smothered by nothingness.

I knew where I was right away, and I knew who had probably brought me here. Harik had brought me to the trading place.

"Harik, you divine turtle's asshole, what do you want? I was about to kill two men for you. If you don't care about that anymore, you won't mind releasing me from my debt, will you?"

"Hush, Murderer. I have brought you here for a remarkable, indeed unprecedented, opportunity."

"How many times have you offered me an unprecedented opportunity? At least a dozen."

"And each one more extraordinary than any that preceded it. We are not alone. I have invited another sorcerer, the Farmer, to join us."

I had never bargained with the gods in the company of a strange sorcerer, but as long as he or she didn't bumble around like a well-meaning rhino, I couldn't see much risk. After all, no one could strike any deals for me except me.

A different voice said, "Hello, Bib. As mentioned before, I do appreciate your name! Simple. So few people value simplicity in these times, don't you think?"

The voice kicked me in the gut like a mule with a grudge. I tried not to let that shock leak into my tone. "Hello, Vintan. I didn't expect we'd speak again until I rammed my sword through your chest."

"Yes, this eventuality must leave you quite disappointed, even frustrated. Yet it is, without equivocation, a pleasurable event for me. Once we became foes, I hardly supposed that we might someday converse, apart from the odd imprecation or two as I destroyed you. Rumor provided that you are a singular killer of extraordinary ability, but I never supposed you to also be a sorcerer!"

"I play the thumb whistle too. All this way south I've been wondering, why are you such a pathetic, child-murdering reptile?"

"And a charming conversationalist as well! All North Men are smug, but I confess that your arrogance is captivating, even for a villain as famous as yourself. Erasing it from the world will marginally diminish my satisfaction when I slay you, everyone you love, and everyone who happens to be standing nearby. I will do this not out of spite, you understand. You represent a peril that must be eliminated with an overwhelming, unambiguous stroke."

"I'm not a North Man any more than you. I'm not arrogant, either, unless you consider it arrogance to be better than you and every other man south of the Blue River. Vintan, I understand war, but I swear you love cruelty more than you love your own testicles. If you have any."

"Sterling praise from the slayer of hundreds." He sounded like I'd just given him a chest of gold, a magic sword, and the prettiest girl at the fair.

"If you admire me so much, I'll be glad to cut your tongue out and autograph it."

The obsequious chunk of mud dared to laugh.

"What do you plan to do with that little boy?" I asked.

"His Highness, Prince Prestwick? I would hesitate to describe him as little. I have already taught him four places to stab a man that will slay instantly."

"There are seven places that do that."

"You are correct, but he isn't tall enough to reach the other three."

"If you love kids so much, why did you chop that little girl's head off, you no-dick son-of-your-own-whore-sister? I'm going to stab you four or five times just for that."

"Little girl, Bib? How can you display such outrage when you don't even know the child's name?"

Harik spoke up and saved me from a hypocritical silence. "While I would be enchanted to listen to this all day, I will soon have obligations elsewhere. Existence does not run itself, I assure you. I have arranged a trading opportunity that should be profitable as well as diverting. Welcome to the auction!"

"You expect us to bid?" I pushed as much contempt into my laugh as possible.

"That indeed is the idea! Well done, Murderer. Everyone says you're dim, but when pressed, you can be almost clever."

Vintan said, "The entire concept is idiotic beyond belief."

"I disagree," I said. "I have no trouble believing how idiotic this is. Harik, do you have a meat grinder you'd like me to stick my willy into, as long as we're doing stupid things?" I began fading myself back into the normal world.

"Goodbye, Murderer. How unfortunate that your foe will now acquire this power uncontested and use it to obliterate you and your friends."

I pulled myself back into the nothingness. "Mighty Harik, I'd be overjoyed to bid against this galloping skag for whatever prize you depraved vultures are offering."

Vintan said, "I find that I must agree. Attempting to sail against the wind is exhausting, as well as inelegant."

"Now that you are done pampering your egos, here are the terms. Three squares of mystical power will go to the highest bidder."

Vintan could hurt us a lot if he possessed three squares that he could just snatch out of the air when he cared to. Unless I wanted to be burned alive, or have thirteen trees fall on me at once, I needed to keep the power away from that rat-suck bastard—even if I never did anything with it but fatten up cows in a hurry.

Harik asked, "What are your offers?"

I remained quiet, and so did Vintan.

"Hello? Have you both suffered apoplexy at the same moment?"

Since it was poor practice to make the first offer when trading with a god, I sure wasn't going to make first offer against Vintan. The Denzman finally chipped in. "In the interest of efficiently and stylishly concluding this business, I offer to kill ten perfectly innocent people within the year—ten that I would not have otherwise slain."

Harik sighed. "A disappointingly meager bid, but I suppose it's a beginning."

I could have bested Vintan's offer by promising to kill twenty innocent people, but I didn't want to go down that path. I found killing innocents distasteful. More significantly, I'd never be able to outbid Vintan, since it seemed his people expected him to do a lot of indiscriminate killing. I went the other direction.

"I offer that on three occasions, an ally will betray me." I know that sounded like a reckless bid, but history had proven two things to me. Betrayal was going to happen anyway. Everybody hated it when an ally proved unfaithful, but it happened often enough that nobody was shocked. Also, I was a slippery son of a bitch, and treachery hasn't killed me yet.

"A similarly pathetic bid," Harik said. "I had expected more from both of you. Maybe your most vigorous years are past, and instead of sorcery, you should consider farming turnips."

"Droll," Vintan said. "Within the year, I will kill ten persons who are not only innocent but have also sworn to serve me."

That personal touch was a step up on Vintan's part, and I needed something just as personal in my bid. "In addition to the three betrayals I mentioned, for the next year, I'll secretly prevent Desh from learning any more sorcery." I would hate to do it to the young man, but being misled by me was better than being destroyed by Vintan.

"I will accept that as a marginally higher bid, Murderer, but only because I look upon our past work together with fondness. Farmer, it is your bid."

"Very well, let us end this. Within the year, I will kill ten children."

"Indeed?" I heard the grin in Harik's voice. "That hardly

seems a powerful offer considering the history you already have with children. However, I will allow that you have topped the Murderer's last bid."

If I wanted to win, now was the time to sacrifice, and Ella was the place I could make the most personal sacrifice. More than anything else, she wanted to save the prince.

"I will prevent Ella from rescuing the prince."

"Not quite enough," Harik said. "Will you kill the prince to prevent his rescue if necessary?"

"I sure as hell will not."

"Will you kill this Ella woman to prevent her from effecting the rescue?"

"I... might. I would if there was no other way at all." I couldn't imagine any situation in which I'd have to kill Ella to botch the rescue. At the worst, I could whack her on the head and carry her off.

Harik was silent for a while. "I find us in a situation that could become interesting, should we address it properly. I will swap your bids. Then you each can choose whether to accept what the other has bid—with a modification or two."

Vintan said, "That is a foolish proposition. We have proffered our bids, and you cannot reassign them."

"But I can. This is my auction, and I am the God of Death. You are repulsive in my eyes, and I can destroy you at my whim. You may either play by my rules, or I will hurl you back to your squalid home."

I didn't see anything good that could come out of arguing with Harik on this. He could slap us around like bugs and lizards all he wanted, and we had to take it until we could skitter off under the door.

"The Murderer promised to prevent the prince's rescue. Farmer, logically, you shouldn't object to that, since your people intend to hold the boy hostage to force the North Men and their diseases to stay away. You have even developed a fatherly affection for the horrible little creature, despite your well-earned reputation as a depraved butcher. So, your bid will be to prevent the prince's rescue, and you will kill him to accomplish it.

"Murderer, the Farmer's bid was killing ten children within the year. However, I recognize that your heart still carries a few ridiculous tender places. Such killings would be enormously difficult for you, despite your homicidal impulses. Therefore, I will not ask you to stand behind this bid of ten child-murders. Murdering five children will be quite adequate."

I wondered whether I could kill children to make this bargain. Then I told myself that, of course, I wouldn't do it. But I had to admit that my first thought was to wonder whether I could do it, so I suppose that some part of me entertained the idea. "I'll kill ten innocent men instead."

"No. If you don't agree to children, you have failed to bid. Vintan?"

"What if I refuse?" Vintan asked. I thought I heard a touch of anguish, which made me smile. I hoped the son of a bitch would suffocate on his own tears and dismember himself from sorrow.

"You would then forfeit, since the highest previous bid was from the Murderer."

Now Vintan provided us with a period of silence. "I agree. I will forestall the prince's rescue by killing him. However, I need kill him only if he is in imminent danger of rescue."

"That is correct. Nicely done, Farmer. You will find three squares at your disposal upon returning to your world. I should warn you that the Murderer will not be as easy to kill as you might suppose just because you can employ sorcery. Regardless of magic, he has an enormous thirst for making people dead, and if he decides that a person should die, then that person will have a very hard time staying alive."

Vintan said, "My thanks, mighty Harik. Were I able to drive a thorn from the Tree of Regret through your right eye, I should certainly do so."

That image made me realize I had never once, during my many visits with the gods, tried to murder somebody while we were bargaining. I had always gone bargaining by myself or with friends, and who can kill a god? This was a different situation. Of course, this appeared to be a place of nothingness, but if I concentrated on slicing up everything in every direction, maybe I'd get lucky and cut the horrible bastard's throat.

I imagined drawing my sword and sweeping the blade across my body in a devastating cut. As my imaginary blade moved, light rolled into existence as if the point of my sword were drawing aside a curtain.

I found myself outdoors and standing on a space of bare dirt. Trees surrounded it, tall and slim with pale bark, full of curled, blue-green leaves that whistled as the breeze swept past. The air smelled like fleece blankets and hot bread. Sunlight drifted down around me, comforting and richer than cream. I almost started crying.

A woman's voice said, "I think the Farmer will crush him before sunset. You've ruined him, you idiotic eunuch."

That was Gorlana's voice. I looked behind me and saw a large, multitiered, white stone gazebo that opened onto the dirt patch. A woman and two men sat in the gazebo, looking down at me.

"I agree. He's shaken." That was Fingit speaking. "Look at him spinning around with that ridiculous sword. He must have been here a hundred times, but he looks as shocked as the first time a girl showed him what she didn't have."

I had solved a mystery over which countless sorcerers had argued, thrown hard objects, and passed out under various pieces of furniture. The place of trading indeed rested within the Home of the Gods.

I looked behind me and saw Vintan standing a few paces

away. His face showed arrogant patience, as if he didn't see or hear any of this, including me. It was the perfect time to kill him, and I would have, but I was so astounded by what I'd discovered that I almost dropped my sword.

THIRTEEN

I had heard the gods speak many times, but I'd never actually seen one. When I was a boy and first began dealing with divine beings, I imagined that they must also be divine to look upon. I envisioned muscles powerful enough to wrestle mountains and faces so beautiful that glimpsing one would make you burst into flames. That all changed once I heard the petty, moronic, pompous river of ass-drool that could flow from their mouths.

Eventually, I formed a mental image of each god to accompany his or her words and tone. I saw Harik as a balding, pinch-faced bookkeeper trying hard to appear smooth, wearing poorly cut silk garments. Gorlana was a voluptuous blonde, beautiful but always dressed in gowns so tight they were a bit nasty. She wore enough jewelry for five goddesses, which was enough jewelry for fifty women, and she tended to get distracted looking at her own baubles. Fingit was a slightly hunched, bespectacled, redhaired man with powerful arms and a work apron covered with untidy pockets.

I was sure as hell wrong about all of that. When I drew my sword to kill Vintan but instead pulled aside that curtain, I saw what I assumed were the gods' true forms. They were well-built and beautiful, without a bald head or any hunched shoulders in the bunch. Fingit's hands stood out—they were enormous things on the ends of his long, loose arms. He was blond, with nearly round eyes and a mammoth chin, and he wore a blood-colored robe. Harik resembled him, but with normal hands, black hair, a thin nose, an unbelievably titanic chin, and a robe of unmarred black.

I wondered whether strong chins were considered particularly handsome among the gods currently, with each god striving to manifest the biggest one.

Gorlana wore her red hair cascading past her heart-shaped face and over her shoulders. She appeared svelte, although her golden robe revealed an exceptional area of cleavage. She wore a silver and pearl necklace, but no other jewelry.

While I was examining the gods and trying not to let my jaw hang open, Harik looked at Gorlana and said, "Let us send them back. Lutigan's birthday party has already started, and if we're late, Cassarak will have slobbered in the ambrosia. If the Murderer is killed, so be it."

The goddess waved agreement as she produced a small golden mirror from nowhere and began admiring herself.

Inspiration bolted through me. I sheathed my sword, and everything returned to nothingness. I drew my sword, and all became light again. Well, the sword had some stupid god name. I tried to remember, but I hadn't paid close attention when Ella had given the thing to me. The Sword of Incipient Charity?

Harik was saying, "Farmer, Murderer, now that the auction has concluded, you may go on with your sad, awful lives."

Gorlana adjusted her necklace, and I gave it a harder look.

"Wait!" I said as things were beginning to fade. "I sure wish Gorlana was here. I have a trade for her that she'd love to hear about."

Harik looked at Gorlana, who shook her head and firmly waved him off.

"She's not here, and I have better things to do than search for her."

The world reappeared around me without even a slow fade. It contained two swordsmen in mid-lunge, about to pin me like a wolf skin on the barn door. I twisted and deflected one, but the other gashed my left shoulder. I disarmed him by half-severing his wrist, and then I slashed the other's throat.

The man just beyond those two hung back and waited for me to come to him. He blocked my thrust and returned an irresistibly fatal counterthrust. He must have won a lot of fights in his career. I slipped past his attack, stabbed him deep in the chest, and left him dying on his knees.

The last four men were running. I chased them down, and I killed them all from behind. Then I walked off to retrieve my horse right away so that nobody would see how happy and satisfied I felt.

"Harik, you are a toad-sucking bastard."

"I see you up there all buoyant and prideful, sorcerer," Limnad shouted from the hilltop across the trail from us. "Don't think too much of yourself. This was just a gentle caress to show that I'm still planning your shrieking death."

"Oh, I enjoyed it, my dear. I was getting bored. If I had spent another hour in the saddle with nothing happening, my ass would've fallen off."

Stan and Ralt had climbed the hillside and reached the men I'd killed. Stan spit at one of the corpses. "Looks like it was a bunch of damn bandits. I hate bandits. My brother-in-law is a bandit, and he's the nastiest barrel of cow turds I ever met."

"Not even any good swords for you, Desh. Cheap-ass dogs," Ralt said.

Since none of us was dead, we all took a few minutes to switch horses. While the triplets were getting themselves organized, Ella took me aside.

"I insist you find a way to dismiss this treacherous spirit. Unless you harbor carnal intentions, I fail to understand why you bound her in the first place. I trust her no more than I would trust a viper in my underpants!"

"In case you didn't realize it, you should assume that she is listening to everything you say all the time. While she doesn't particularly care what we think, she is vengeful. Across generations. If you make her mad, your great-grandchildren and their whole town might get wiped out by an inexplicable flood. The main reason I'm not releasing her is that our enemies can hurt us with magic, and she's the only magic we have to fight them with. The incidental reason is that if I free her, she will immediately kill me and probably all of you too."

"You. You and your spirit!" Ella hissed and spit into my face. "Of all the doltish, unthinking, imprudent behavior I have witnessed, this stands unparalleled. And I have cared for toddlers as a profession!" She turned away from me with intense deliberation, staring as if her eyes could turn my guts to slag.

I could've apologized, but why? I had done the right thing. I was almost sure I had. Well, to hell with her scolding and her superiority. I changed the subject.

"What do you know about this sword, anyway?"

She opened her mouth and closed it again before answering. "The Blade of Obdurate Mercy?"

"Right. Is there anything special about it? What did the queen say when she gave it to you? 'Here's a sword with a fancy name. Try not to cut your head off with it'?"

She smiled a little.

"You thought that was almost funny, didn't you?"

"Not even a bit. I was thinking about an entirely different thing. To answer your question, she charged me with protecting her son, and she gave me her grandfather's sword with which to do so. I can tell you that the blade possessed the power to reliably pierce and slice human beings. Other than that, nothing. She bestowed it upon me as a mark of trust." Ella stepped in close enough that we could've reached our hands behind each other's necks had we been so inclined, and she lowered her voice. "That's why I gave it to you. I want to trust you, because my instincts say that we need you." Then she walked off toward her horse.

I felt like an entire pile of shit. I had planned to kill Ella twice in as many days. If she had done something to aggravate me, then I might have felt differently; but so far, she had been tough, smart, caring, and contrary, which described my perfect woman fairly well.

As we trotted away from the ambush site, I debated on telling everybody that we were chasing a sorcerer who was also a brutal killer. Such knowledge will sometimes torment a man to the point of indecision. Other men prepare themselves better when they know what they're facing. A few men have pointed out that I, too, am a sorcerer who is also a brutal killer, so what does it matter if one more is in the mix?

I decided to tell them, and I chivvied us into riding five abreast. "I just found out that a merciless sorcerer is fighting against us, and he's more powerful than I am right now. So, watch out."

Desh looked around at the horizon. "Just watch out for a sorcerer? Anything else, specifically?"

"Is it going to rain snakes?" Ralt stared upward with one hand over his head.

"Snakes aren't so bad," Stan said. "Now if it was raining wolves or bears, then we'd have something to worry about."

"I don't think it's going to rain bears," said Desh. He looked at me. "Is it?"

"Probably not. Not at first." I winked at Desh. "We should

watch out for anything that gets swallowed up by fire in just a few seconds. Or things that just disappear as if they never existed, like the roots of a big tree, or a bridge you're riding across. We may get lucky and just have to deal with enormous swarms of bees."

"Well, if we die, we die. Weeping won't help." Ralt blew his nose on one of his nice, white handkerchiefs.

Ella said, "You're a courageous fellow."

"Aw, he ain't brave," Stan said. "He's just got nothing to live for. You should see his wife."

"Shut up, you gawky chicken neck!" Ralt said.

I stepped in before they started throwing things at each other. "Let's spread out again so the next ambusher can't kill all five of us with the same arrow."

We rejoined the road late that afternoon. Stones pocked the trail and the small hills around it. A modest river, half as wide as the Blue River, cut across the trail to our south, the direction I expected Vintan to go.

Ella asked, "Have we arrived before them? Or do we pursue them still?"

"That is the conundrum, isn't it? Boys, keep watch."

I didn't want to take the time to wander a quarter-mile down the trail, so I just whispered, "Limnad, I want you."

The spirit glided out from behind a rock. Her beauty was mesmerizing and disturbing, so I looked at the uninteresting rock beside her.

"Limnad, I am not giving you a command right now. I am asking you, as a favor, to tell me whether the Denzmen and the prince have already passed this spot."

The river spirit stared at me and said nothing. I heard Ella's breath catch beside me, our horses stamping, and the odd squeak that Desh's false leg had developed.

"I will say it again. I am not giving—"

"I heard you. I just could not believe that anyone, even a

bucket of broken stones like you, would presume to ask for a favor"—here she began shouting—"when you have bound me like a slave!"

"Well, I don't think it's a preposterous notion. I have treated you well, considering the circumstances. I have spoken respectfully. I haven't chained you or required you to stay within ten paces of me, even though I could've done that. I haven't demanded inappropriate favors, although we both know that's sadly a common practice. Taking all that into account, having treated you kindly, I ask you for this one favor."

"I see. I hadn't thought of it that way. I acknowledge the respect you have shown me, and hope you inhale molten lava, walk naked into a cactus patch penis-first, and fall off a thousand-foot cliff onto a thousand shards of disease-ridden glass." Spirits are not known to stomp away from a conversation, but Limnad stomped away from this one.

I made a wry face at Ella.

"I remain silent," she said.

"Your silence sounds a lot like you calling me bad names."

Rocks began clattering behind me, and I saw Desh on his butt sliding down a tiny hill a little way up the trail. He had climbed up there to get a better view of the road behind us. Once on the ground, he sprinted over to me, going *squeak-squeak-squeak.*

"Riders coming up toward us! Maybe two or three dozen and more than a mile away. I think it's them."

Desh didn't act as if spiders with huge tongues were stalking him. That was a common delusion for lunatic sorcerers. Nor did he waggle his parts right out in the open as if we couldn't see or hear him. He spoke and acted logically and with purpose. I decided he was well, which was a pleasant thing. I'd just as soon not cut his throat.

I couldn't deceive Ella any longer. I had no moral objection to deceiving her, but deception shrivels in the face of facts, and three dozen facts were riding down the trail toward us. I could either help her fight them outnumbered seven-to-one and probably get killed, or I could go my own way and spend the summer killing Denzman at my leisure.

I couldn't quite make myself ride away with no explanation, so I faced Ella to say I was leaving. There's expectation and there's certainty. You expect a friend to save you from being trampled by horses, but you're certain your father will save you or die himself. Ella showed no expectation. She looked at me with the certainty that I would help her. She was a trusting woman, in the worst sense of the word.

Instead of saying goodbye, I found myself saying, "Ella, you said you want to trust me, right?"

"Certainly. I do trust you, at least enough to allow you to participate in my expedition."

"And I'm proud to contribute." I scanned the river to the south and the hills beside us. "Instead of throwing ourselves in front of thirty-odd Denzmen spears, let's follow the bastards. I'll sneak in and kill a couple now and then. By tomorrow night, no more than nine or ten will be left, and they'll be half-insane from wondering when the mystery killer is coming for them. We'll snatch the prince then."

Ella clapped my shoulder with her free hand. "That is a perfectly awful plan. You would die, we would be forced to assault the Denzmen without you, and every one of us would be killed, or possibly captured. However, I have something more elegant in mind."

"I say this with respect, but I may have deeper experience with planning desperate assaults than you do."

"And perhaps you do not. You might be astonished."

"A whole lot of Denzmen will be here in a few minutes. We don't have time to collaborate on a plan."

"Then you had best follow my orders as briskly as possible."

I could hear Desh, Ralt, and Stan behind me trying to hold in their laughter, and they were doing a piss-poor job of it.

"Yes ma'am. Where do you want me to stand?" That would mollify her for a few minutes. It was time to leave, after all, and when she wasn't looking, I'd just ride away.

Twenty minutes later, I had forded the river. I began searching the hills beside the ford for a hidden vantage point, which was where Ella had said she wanted me to stand.

FOURTEEN

I prefer plans that are simple. A simple plan can fall apart in only a small number of easily understood ways. A complicated plan can go to hell in a staggering number of obscure ways that will never be fully understood, even after the dead have been buried and the wounded carried away.

Ella's plan was not the most complex I've ever participated in. However, any plan requiring the coordinated effort of three forces that can't all see one another, plus one magical intervention, can't be honestly described as simple. But when you consider the fact that our entire force consisted of five people and a river spirit, the plan was a little simpler than my description makes it sound.

The plan was based on two assumptions. Vintan had forded the Blue River in three stages: a group of soldiers crossed, then the prince followed with some soldiers guarding him, and then the remaining soldiers rode across. Ella expected Vintan to ford this river using the same tactics, although this one, which Limnad called the Blood River, was just half as wide. At a certain point in the crossing, the prince and his guards would be in the middle of the river while the rest of the soldiers waited on each bank.

Ella also assumed that Limnad would do exactly as I

commanded, carrying the prince away on a wave when the boy was mid-river, and rushing him downstream. Then she would hand him over to Desh, who would be waiting to hustle the prince away to our rendezvous in the hills. As a distraction, Ralt and I would ambush the soldiers on the south bank, and Ella would ambush the northern group with Stan. We'd create as much confusion as possible until we thought Desh was safely away with the prince, and then we would run like hell.

Sure, it wasn't simple, but it was better than a lot of other plans that had successfully changed history.

The most ticklish part of the scheme was unleashing Limnad. She needed to carry the prince off after the diversions started. The trail south ran between two rugged hills, big piles of rocks, really, as it left the river headed south. I found a perch that wasn't too obvious, about fifteen feet above the riverbank. From there, I could survey the battlefield and give Limnad the proper commands.

I saw Vintan's whole force as it neared the river. Ralt was holding our horses on the ground below me, also out of sight. I couldn't see Ella or Stan, and I hoped they were well hidden on the far bank. Eight Denzmen crossed first, and they halted on my side of the river. The prince began crossing with what looked like nine guards. One of them was Vintan.

"Limnad, I command you to wait one minute and then lift the prince on a wave, take him downstream, and give him unharmed to Desh. Don't take anyone else, and don't do anything else." The bond on her left wrist unwound itself and blew away.

"I understand. One more command, and then I will cast you into the river and command hundreds of tiny fish to eat you. They may take weeks to consume you entirely." She seemed to flow downhill against the rocks and toward the river, almost invisible.

I ran down the gentle slope to Ralt and mounted. "Stay quiet until we hit them, then loud as every demon in hell."

"Right. I bet they yell a lot when we stab them."

We galloped out of our hiding spot and toward the Denzmen. A few of them saw us coming and shouted, but when we reached them, they were still disorganized. I rode to the left side of the Denzmen and lost sight of Ralt as he rode right. I killed one man who was still looking around for the danger. I started shouting curses at them in three languages.

The next man I reached had lowered his spear at me, and he laughed. "They're sending old men!" I chopped the spearhead off and then near beheaded him on the backstroke. A third man was out of my reach, so I called him a whale-chasing armpit of a man and rode clear. Lots of the insults in Ir involve whales and body parts. My father could never explain why.

I rode almost to the riverbank and saw the wave. Limnad did a marvelous job. The water surged from the smooth-flowing surface and lifted the prince right off his horse. Almost as good, it threw several guards into the water along with their mounts, and I cherished every hope that the men's armor would pull them under to drown. Vintan kept his seat, which was a shame, but Limnad had performed her part beautifully.

So far, Ella's plan looked brilliant. Lutigan himself couldn't have done better.

I wheeled to face our enemies again and saw Ralt doing the same thing. He chopped at a Denzman's arm and missed, and the man smashed him with a shield so hard he flew out of the saddle. I cantered to Ralt, blocking thrusts from two men on the way, and stabbed Ralt's attacker in the back as he tried to spear the soldier rolling across the dirt. I put my horse between Ralt and the remaining Denzmen, and I blocked a thrust from an enormous fellow.

I felt Ralt slap my leg. "I'm up!"

"Good! Time to leave!" I reached my left hand down, and he swung himself up behind me. His hand and sleeve were wet. I kicked my horse, and we left the giant Denzman behind. Another man was turning his horse to follow me but hadn't quite made it around when I reached him. I cut him deep at the base of the skull. Then I was free.

Some colossal thing slammed into me from the left, and I went down in a jumble of screaming men, shrieking horses, and rolling boulders. Oh, and lots of pain. I may have been screaming louder than anybody.

I started to sit up, but my left arm, shoulder, and side weren't ready for that maneuver. I suffered a quick sensation of my entire left side being a big pouch of broken glass. I tried to scream some more. That was a mistake. When I woke up again, not much time had passed, maybe a few seconds. Ralt was kneeling over me, and the left side of his face looked like it had been hit with an anvil. I felt shocked that he was upright, or even alive.

"We got to hide," he slurred. "Crawl at least, or them bastards will kill you."

I rolled onto my right side, trying not to shout, pass out, or die. On the way, I saw what had smashed us. A portion of rocky hillside had rolled down onto the trail and right into us. It wouldn't have been too hard for a sorcerer to make that happen—just disintegrate a bit of the hill under it. Vintan was saving his power like a good, economical sorcerer. He hadn't aimed his strike too carefully, though. I wasn't dead yet, and the giant Denzman behind me was smashed under stones, along with his horse. I could see two more soldiers writhing on the ground like me, although I hoped they were hurt worse.

My legs didn't seem to be damaged, and Ralt helped me stand. I cried like an infant, but only once did I wake up with him holding me upright. We stumbled as fast as we could off the trail, and we might have outrun a toad, if it had been sick for several weeks. My perch was the best hiding spot around, so we went back up the slope at something between a stagger and a waddle. At the top, I reclined on my right arm and right buttock, and I thought of nothing but breathing and pain for a while.

After a time, I looked out over the recent battlefield. The entire surviving Denzman force had crossed the river. Vintan was accompanied by fewer than two dozen soldiers and the prince.

"It didn't work," I whispered. "What happened?"

"Maybe everybody got smashed by rocks. That worked right good on us." Ralt was still slurring his words, and his jaw must have been broken, maybe in more than one place.

"There aren't any rocks over where Desh was."

"Maybe he got smothered by dirt, or choked to death by vines. Or a pit of lava swallowed him up."

"Creative." I stopped a scream by banging my right fist on the stone and crying a few tears. "You should have been a sorcerer."

"Hell no. I wouldn't live your life for all the whores in the Empire."

I blinked away tears and looked harder at the spot where Desh had been stationed. I hadn't remembered that gap in the trees. "I don't know whether Desh survived—"

An enormous rumbling and crashing of rocks interrupted me. It sounded like a far more colossal event than the one that had done me in. I couldn't see the Denzmen anymore, nor could I see what was happening with the rocks, but soon veils of dust rose from some place on the trail south of us, the direction Vintan had been going. The chalky scent of pulverized rock drifted around us.

"It's so unfair," Limnad said as she appeared from over the rocks. "He's killed you, and there's nothing left for me to torture."

"If you're that sad about it, you could heal me"—I drew a shallow breath—"and kill me later when I'm in good shape."

"It's not *that* unfair. You could use your last command and tell me to help you."

I gave her a rough grin with the good half of my face. "To have you save my life so you can kill me? Sounds a poor bargain."

"Very well. I'll just sit here." Limnad sat and leaned over to stare at me, her nose just a few inches from my cheek. "Try to scream some more—it's terribly entertaining."

"What happened?" I wheezed three times and caught my breath. "Did you get the boy to Desh?"

She looked at me like I was a boy eating his own snot. "Of course I did! I brought him to the appointed place and laid him gently, like a quail's egg, at Desh's feet. Then I retired, having completed my task."

"And?"

Limnad whispered into my ear, "Do you command me to tell you?"

"No." I shook my head a fraction and winced.

"I'll tell you anyway, since it will cause you distress." The spirit rushed around the clearing, acting out her story. "Desh led the boy away from the river to your horses, where they mounted and began riding away. Suddenly, the boy's saddle fell right off his horse, and he was thrown."

I closed my eyes. "It just fell off?"

"It just fell off. It fell off after a nice sorcerer, who never has enslaved me, disintegrated the cinch. Did you know that you're facing a Breaker? You would never have defeated a sorcerer who can simply make things *not* exist. Just command me to kill you now. If you command it, I may kill you without much pain."

"Not much pain?"

"Very well, not as much pain. The second most painful way I can imagine in which to kill you."

"Some time I'd like to hear about"—I drew in a tiny, tiny breath—"the most painful way. But not now."

"The prince's horse ran on, and before Desh could return, the sorcerer created a pit under the prince, as deep as two men are tall, and he fell in. Then this very fine and moral sorcerer disintegrated Desh's clothes and dropped seven trees on him."

"Seven? Is he dead?"

"They might not all have fallen directly onto him. They did block his way back to the pit. I last saw his torn and naked self hurrying away as if pursued by... well, by a sorcerer who can disintegrate things."

"Do you know what happened to Ella? And Stan?"

"No, my command had nothing to do with them. Why would I think of them at all unless I had to? That's an odd notion."

I lay my head against the rock and ignored everything except trying to breathe as little as possible. After doing that for a while, maybe minutes or even an hour, Ralt said, "There they are."

Across the river, Ella and Stan were riding at a walk down the trail toward us. Desh sat behind Ella, his arms wrapped around her waist and his head flopped to the side. Stan was leaning forward over his horse's neck. I watched until they entered the river, said to hell with them, and lay my head back down.

I may no longer possess a young man's hearing, but I heard Ella just fine from the trail below us. "This is truly the summit of preposterous conduct! Is it not enough that we are defeated, that we have lost the prince, and that sorcery has brought down a barricade to forestall us?"

Ralt had walked down the slope to meet her. "We hid up here, miss. Like a brace of half-chewed rabbits."

"Ralt, what happened to your face?"

"Some sorcerer hit me in the face with a mountain. Or a hill. Same thing when you're hit in the face with it."

"Sorcerer! We had a sorcerer, but it made little difference. He was apparently occupied with tossing his sword onto the ground and wandering away." She marched into view carrying my stupid god-named sword, stopped, and stared at me. She had a deep gash still trickling on the side of her face, and maybe other wounds under all the blood. "Is he alive?"

"I'm alive," I said. "Don't ask me to dance tonight, though."

She knelt next to me and reached out to touch my crushed arm.

"Stop!" I said that with a little too much force, causing me to once again bang my fist against my friend, the stone. I made myself breathe just enough to stay alive. "You can touch me if you'd like to see me cry and pass out. If that doesn't interest you, hands to yourself."

She reached out with one hand, not much faster than a weed grows, and pressed it to the right side of my face.

I asked her, "How badly are you hurt?"

"Bah. I've been more grievously wounded by five-year-olds."

"Everybody else?"

"Stan was wounded in the shoulder, and it's still seeping blood." She glanced back at Stan lying flat on the ground and Ralt kneeling beside him. "I cannot believe Ralt still lives. It wouldn't surprise me if he expires any minute. And Desh... Desh ran unclothed through thorny tree branches to escape and is covered in dozens of scratches, some quite deep. His intimate areas have been not only scratched but also torn, and he is suffering cruelly." She used her sleeve to pat some of the sweat off my face. The gesture might have been more benevolent if her sleeve hadn't been sticky with drying blood. "Bib, you're dying."

I winked. "Limnad is planning the party. You should attend. Ought to be a jubilee."

Ella sat back and sighed. "Stop joking."

"You wouldn't recognize me if I stopped."

She nodded at my good hand. "Can you save everyone, as you did with Desh's leg?"

"In theory... maybe." This conversation was getting more serious than the actual dying part.

"Desh told me about your open-ended debt."

"That little pissant... if I could stand up, I'd go over there... and tear the rest of his dick off... He had no right to tell you that."

"He did, however. To save us, you would have to pay something worse than your current debt, which is frightful. Is that correct? But tell me honestly, would a new debt be worse than death, and the deaths of your companions?"

Sorcerers despise being questioned about their debts. By questioning me, Ella would normally be strolling between a cliff's edge and a wall of fire. However, right then, I couldn't credibly threaten a fly with one wing, so she wasn't risking anything. "What could be worse? Ella, in the past few days... I've planned to kill you... to make a deal with the gods. Twice."

Ella sat back on her heels. "Why aren't I dead?"

"I didn't end up making those deals."

She grasped my non-destroyed hand. "Then it doesn't matter."

That was the stupidest statement I'd heard in days. "But I planned to kill you."

"But you didn't kill me. If you had truly been willing to kill me, you would have struck one of those bargains and I would be dead. Bib, you rarely do anything you do not wish to do."

I thought about that ridiculous bullshit for a few moments. "Damn it. If I could breathe deeper, I'd call you names... so horrible you'd still be crying about it on your deathbed... Hand me that sword."

I faded up into nothingness, wondering whether I could think of something clever to say to Harik. Or maybe I should have just evenly divided up all the good things in my life and told him to pick the pile he wanted.

FIFTEEN

My friends used to tell me how lucky I was to be a sorcerer. They weren't sorcerers themselves, but they imagined how much fun it must be to do whatever I please. They wanted to know all about how I conjured up as much gold as I fancied and charmed any woman I wanted to bed. I was a fortunate man, because I could do any outrageous or perilous thing I wished, and if something went wrong, I could just call on a god to fix it.

This went on for a while, and then I decided to have a lot fewer friends. No, I didn't kill them. They annoyed me, but they weren't entirely wrong, which annoyed me even more.

I would have died quite a few times had I not been a sorcerer. I have employed magic to escape otherwise inescapable death, and to pull my smashed-up body back together when, in any sane world, I would have bled to death.

On the other hand, if I hadn't been born a sorcerer, I wouldn't be out here in the armpit of the world. I'd be home in Ir, fishing every day and arguing with my neighbors every night. The worst thing I'd need to escape from would be a pissed-off bartender who wanted his money.

But life happened the way it happened, and I have taken advantage of every reward and liberty that sorcery had to offer. I've paid what the gods haggled out of me, and if I regretted the price, then that's too bad. Nobody ever made me do magic. I decided to all on my own.

So, as I rose up from my wrecked body, I reminded myself that I was the author of whatever happened next. If the end had finally come, then at least I'd have one more chance to call Harik a mincing, flap-tongued ass.

The first thing I noticed upon being fully enveloped in nothingness was that all pain had vanished. I had expected that. Wounds and diseases had never made this journey with me. I then noticed that the whole lot of nothingness persisted even though I'd been holding the sword before I came here.

"Mighty Harik, whose terrifying chin causes orphans to weep, I come to trade." It was foolish, but I couldn't resist goading him about his chin. What kind of sorcerer would I be if I let imminent death make me timid? I imagined drawing my sword from its scabbard, and a moment later the sunshine, the trees, the bright pavilion, and the gods appeared around me.

"Harik is not here."

"Krak," I whispered. The word was an oath, an observation, and a form of address all in one. The Father of the Gods glowered down at me, dominating the entire pavilion even though he wasn't much taller than the others. Gorlana sat at his feet. So did Harik, who was sitting right there no matter what Krak said, and who looked like a child whose favorite toy had been confiscated.

Krak's head was large and majestic, presumably to hold all that omniscience, and his hands were massively sinewed, the better to exercise omnipotence. He appeared mature in his perfect white robe, and he wore a noble, aggressive beard. He looked like someone's eldest uncle who happened to exude the vigor of twenty men.

"What the hell kind of sorcerer are you? You may address me as Father Krak. And be damned sure I hear a capital F when you say Father."

Not many sorcerers cared to deal with Krak. This awful beginning was typical of why they didn't. I tried to put that behind me and focus. "Yes, Father Krak."

"That's a pathetic effort, but I'll accept it for now. What do you want? And be quick about it. I'm renovating."

"I need to heal some people on the other side, so..."

"Really?" Krak leaned forward. "That's a distressing situation, I'm led to understand. I can see why you need help. I understand your problem, but I asked what you want. I did not ask about your problem, nor do I give two shits and a bucket of doorknobs about your problem! Tell me what you want or stop wasting my time! I'm the Father of the Gods, you insignificant grease spot!" Krak's voice assaulted me with the power of a hurricane.

"I want four squares of power."

"All right. What will you pay for them?"

I stuck to my rule about never making the first offer. "With respect, I ask you to please make the first offer."

Krak said nothing.

"Father, he is willful and disrespectful." Harik showed no sign that he knew I was listening. "However, he may have some good trades left in him."

"Shut up!" Krak said.

I said, "Father Krak? Are you there?"

After some more silence, Krak said, "Do I understand correctly that you came here not knowing what you will pay? Do you even know what you want to do with this power?"

"I do know." Maybe a little flattery would help. "Of course, I can't know a sliver of what you could teach the wisest—"

"Quiet," Krak whispered.

"Father, let me talk to him," Harik said.

Krak relaxed his fist and a speck of the impossibly searing light of the sun escaped. My eyes experienced a stabbing pain all the way to the back of my skull. Harik went pale. Krak closed his fist and said, "I am not in the business of teaching. I do not provide advice or plans or consultation. I do not render opinions for mortals, nor do I review their pathetic ideas. I do not tell the future, comment on the past, or give directions to the tavern. I deal in power, and only in power! Do you understand me?"

By now, Krak was thundering again.

"Yes..."

"Now." Krak sounded reasonable and even businesslike. "Since you have asked me to make an offer, I will offer an observation. Please note that this is neither instruction nor advice."

"Yes, Father Krak?" This was about the most horribly screwed-up deal I'd ever seen, but maybe I could salvage something.

"Although you will certainly find it difficult, you should attempt to understand that the gods do not exist to pluck ignorant mortals out of the quagmires of peril into which they deposit themselves through their willful, foolish behavior. You did it to yourself. Get out of it yourself. It is not my problem. Do you understand?"

"Yes, Father Krak."

"Good! And be sure to tell all your friends."

I slammed back into my body, then jerked by reflex, tried to scream, clamped down on the scream, and started coughing. When I woke up, Ella was wiping blood off my mouth.

"And that's why nobody wants to deal with Krak," I whispered.

"I beg your pardon?" she said.

"Not important."

"Are you leaving to secure power now?" She smiled. "To pick blackberries?"

"Already been there. The bushes are bare."

"Is there nothing to be done then?"

I caught myself before I shook my head. "No. If the gods' world was a tavern... I'd be facedown in the muddy ditch out front."

"I shall wait with you." She took the sword from me and paused. "This sword has a god name. Can it bestow power on you? Can it heal?"

I had wondered about that a couple of days earlier and explored the idea. "Not unless I can use it to thrash Harik until he cries and gives me power... it's just a piece of steel."

"I shall wait with you then."

"If you dawdle, then your prince might get away."

She squeezed my good hand and smiled, which was a nice thing to see before I closed my eyes.

Some time after my eyes closed, but before I was dead, I heard the word, "Murderer." Something pulled me up into nothingness, and I found myself pain-free again. Right away, I imagined reaching for my sword, and then I imagined it still lying on Ella's lap.

"Hello, Murderer!" said Gorlana. "I heard you have some charming little thing I'd be interested in."

"Harik won't mind us talking trades?"

"Harik is... terribly busy just now. So, tell me! I'm breathless."

I was violating my "don't make the first offer" rule, but I had already claimed to have something she'd like. "I believe you know Limnad, the Blue River spirit."

"Yes. I know that muculent whore." She made it sound as wholesome as knowing a disease of the genitals.

"I currently have her bound—"

"I know, and I can't even tell you how happy that makes me."

"I want four squares, and in exchange, I will never release her. I'll keep her bound until I die or the world crumbles around me. Which would kill me, so I guess it's the same thing, but that's my offer." I'd have to listen to Limnad's abuse for the rest of my life, but at least I'd have the rest of my life.

"Delicious. So tempting. Would you torment her frequently for me?"

"She will weep at least twice a day," I said.

"In exchange for four squares? Hmm... no, not enough."

That was a hell of a disappointment. I had rarely failed when appealing to a god's pettiness. "Do you have a counteroffer? Something you might like better?"

"I believe I do, Murderer. I offer to enlighten you about something."

That put me in a grim situation. Offers to the gods follow a particular logic. Maybe you offer to do something you dislike, or not do something you'd like to do. Or you might be forced to do something bad, or prevented from doing something good. Something bad could happen to you, or fate could get kicked in the nuts, and a thing you would have cherished doesn't happen after all.

With some deals, precious knowledge or memories can disappear if you agree to it, the way Desh lost his mother. But the chanciest deal of all is gaining knowledge you might wish you didn't know. With other types of trades, when you make the bargain, you have a decent idea of what you're paying. When you agree to learn something, you can't know ahead of time what you'll find out.

I said, "That seems a bit high for four squares. I'll stick with keeping Limnad bound, and I'll also offer that I won't be able to find a pair of shoes that fit right for a year."

"Humph. I'm starting to get bored now. Take my offer or go back and die, which would be a shame since that cute young lady is a little smitten with you."

I'd just have to take the risk. "I understand, and on one condition, I will accept your offer. You give me Limnad's birthright."

Gorlana smiled at the gazebo ceiling and stroked the necklace with both hands. "Hah! What would you do with it?"

"I might use it to torment her. Tell her it's right here in my hand, but she can't get it because she's all bound and pathetic. I might make her promise to do things on the chance I'd give it back to her, and then never give it to her no matter what she does." Of course, those were just things that I *might* do. I could also choose to be nice and listen to her bitch.

"That would be fun to watch. Very well, we have a deal. The power and the object will be waiting when you return."

"Mighty Gorlana, tell me what I must know."

"If you fail to provide Harik with murders fast enough, he causes you pain and sickness."

"Is that it? I know that already."

"Hush. You should know that the anticipation of killing, the pleasure, and the satisfaction—Harik has nothing to do with them. Those come from within you."

"What?"

"You enjoy murder because you're a murderer in your deepest heart. Harik doesn't make you enjoy it."

I shook my head. "I don't understand what you're saying."

"Listen then! You're not a good man who kills because a god makes him like it. You're a murderer, and you like to kill."

I was still shaking my head. "I don't... what are you..."

"Murderer, you rarely do anything you do not wish to do."

Then I understood.

Having this knowledge was like standing under a cold waterfall. It beat down on me, soaked me, surrounded me, and separated me from everything I knew and had known. I couldn't do anything except stand in it.

"I understand that it hurts, but it really is something you

should know. Goodbye, Murderer. I'm glad you're not going to die yet."

I drifted down into a gentle reunion with my body, and I opened my eyes.

Ella smiled again. "Do you want some water?"

"No. I saw the gods."

She kissed my hand and then patted it. "That's good."

"Wish I hadn't. Wish I'd died sooner... shit."

"It's all right," she said.

I tried to lift my right hand, but it just shook and laid there. I wheezed at Ella, "Put my right hand on my left ribs."

"Just lie still."

"Put my goddam hand on my ribs. Start healing there... put the hand there... can't heal with my ear or my elbow...we're all going to live... at least for a bit... after that, you bastards are on your own."

SIXTEEN

My wife thought I was a pretty good fellow. She said so often, and she was an honest woman. She knew she had married a sorcerer, and she accepted it along with the craziness that comes with sorcery. She knew my work wasn't all healing sick lambs and making flowers grow. When I came home wearing bloody clothes, she washed them and didn't ask whether the blood was mine or somebody else's. I might leave her alone for weeks and then just show up one night. Sometimes I brought along unannounced visitors. Occasionally, they were dying. A few might not have been strictly human.

Lin thought I was a good fellow, but I don't remember her saying why. She was a smart woman of high character and standards, and now I can't think of a single thing about me that a woman like that would judge to be good. I'd like to ask her what she meant by "good," but of course, she's been dead for years. In more recent times, I've become acquainted with a few women of low character and lower standards, and they found my qualities to be perfectly good.

I'm certain my wife would not have said that the willful enjoyment of killing human beings was a good quality in a husband.

Nor was it a good quality to have in a friend, acquaintance, countryman, or anyone else you might ever meet. I had known for a fact that Harik caused my craving for murder and my satisfaction with the kill, but I'd been wrong. It was not a fact. He hadn't caused them at all.

I had caused them. So then, this was me.

It took about an hour to heal everybody. I mended myself just enough to heal Ralt before he could fall over dead, and then I staggered to Stan before he bled out. Once no one was in danger of expiring right away, I finished healing myself, and then Desh. It was all uneventful as far as these things go, although I suspected Desh would never get over being embarrassed about the way I had to handle his private parts.

I couldn't remember ever feeling more exhausted. Besides that, my left arm and side felt like they'd been beaten with iron rods, a long, thin nail of pain seemed to have been driven into my shoulder, and I had what felt like a toothache in the entire left side of my head. My shin might have been attacked by terrified cats. My privates throbbed, and not in a good way.

I reached for Ella's head wound, but she caught my hand.

"Stop that. I can see that it hurts you."

"One more pain would be like throwing a rock into a canyon," I said. "It wouldn't make a difference."

Ella stood tall and waved me off. "All the same."

"Don't be a suffering, heroic idiot. There's no future in it. You don't need to bleed and let your head hurt all day to make some kind of point."

Her eyes narrowed, which told me I'd said something insulting or ignorant.

"I would prefer a journey to perdition." She walked off toward Desh. I had been both insulting and ignorant, somehow. It didn't seem that important in light of what Gorlana had told me.

I needed sleep, but I had one more thing to do. I whispered, "Limnad, I want you."

The spirit rose out of the river and flowed up the rocks. "Thank you! You suffered almost to the point of death, and then brought yourself back. Now I can torture you all the way to the point of death again. It's as if you have given me a gift. I've been asking other spirits to share with me their most inventive and horrific tortures. I will be ready when you release me!"

"Would you like a gift, Limnad?"

The spirit retreated halfway back to the riverbank. "Probably not."

I reached into my pouch and felt the silver and pearl necklace Gorlana had placed there. When I held it out, Limnad stop moving. Water that had been dripping from her body halted in midair, and her hair hovered slightly above her shoulders. "This is your birthright. I return it to you."

Limnad surged up the rocks, snatched the necklace, and whipped it around her neck. She scrutinized me while running her fingers over the pearls. "Sorcerer, how did you accomplish this?"

"Limnad, I unbind you." The yellow band around her neck melted away.

The spirit rushed toward me like a wave, hurled me to the ground, and crouched over me with one palm on my chest. I heard Desh shouting, Ralt and Stan cursing, and Ella swearing like the sailors on my uncle Rori's fishing boat.

Releasing Limnad had been a calculated move. I had to release her someday, and she was never going to like me better than she liked me right then. And if I'm being totally honest here, I halfway hoped she'd just kill me.

Limnad quivered like a lake in the rain. "Your heart is turned to ash, Bib. What did you pay for my birthright?"

"Shit, my heart didn't turn into ash. It's still cheap whiskey and pig iron, like it's always been."

A few seconds later, the damned river spirit started dripping tears on my throat. "Thank you, Bib."

I glanced around in case I still had to run. I feared that spirits might not possess an abundance of constancy. "Aren't you mad that I bound you?"

"No. If you hadn't bound me, then you would never have sacrificed yourself for my birthright."

"What sacrifice?" Stan asked. "He's lying right there, no guts hanging out or nothing, and in fact close to mingling naughties with a naked girl."

Limnad stepped back and helped me stand.

"You're not going to kill him?" Desh inquired.

"Dammit, Desh, are you trying to goad her into it?" I picked up a rock and chucked it at him.

"I will never kill what's left of Bib."

Let me explain why Limnad was carrying on about all this "turning to ash" bullshit. I had brought her back a treasure, and I'd paid a price that I admit was tormenting me. Spirits possess no permanent body—they're formed of thoughts, feelings, and memories. To her, the way I currently felt seemed as horrible as if my chest had been torn open and everything scooped out.

"Well, this has all resolved itself in a fine manner," said Ella. "The spirit may return to her river, and we may continue our pursuit."

I made the mistake of letting my head drop forward.

Limnad said, "Bib must rest. He has killed a dozen men, had his body crushed, bargained with the gods—twice—had his heart destroyed to help everyone here, and healed all of you, for whom I would not give a dead rat under a pile of dead mice, all before midafternoon. Go on with your little chase. He is staying here. If you attempt to bring him with you, I will tie your arteries around your necks in charming designs."

I felt surprised that Limnad had become so protective, but I shouldn't have. A spirit's emotions tend to soar and crash as circumstances change. Now she wanted to protect me. There was nothing romantic or sexual about it. To get an idea of how she saw me, one might think about how they'd feel toward their idiot cousin who saved them from drowning but got his leg bitten off by a shark in the process.

"Limnad, please leave off all this talk about sacrifice and destroyed hearts. And as a favor to me, please don't hurt any of my friends here."

"If you wish. I am standing over you while you sleep, though."

"Wonderful." I looked at Ella. "Just two hours of sleep."

She frowned but nodded.

Fifteen seconds later, I was sleeping.

Vintan had blocked the trail south with an attractive jumble of red, sandy rocks three men high. It ran from one steep hillside across to the other. To a horse, it might as well have been a thousand-foot-tall cliff. The river wasn't running high enough to make the steep banks passable, and the banks ran like that for as far as I could see.

This would have been a wonderful time to abandon Ella's foolish and probably fatal rescue attempt. I could advise her to wait for the army, and then I'd head deeper into the Denz Lands with Desh and Limnad. I didn't do that, though, partly because I found Ella's company pleasant. Also, the fatal aspect of this venture didn't sound especially awful right then.

Ella caught my eye. "Can your river spirit transport our horses over the bank?"

"Sure, if you want a bunch of terrified horses to kick themselves to death."

Ella gritted her teeth. "Are you certain? Will you ask her?"

Before I turned to her, Limnad flowed across the trail toward Ella. "Why don't you talk to me directly? Are you afraid of me?"

"I see nothing of significance to fear," Ella said, lifting her jaw.

Limnad swirled all the way in a circle around Ella. "Then we should have a long conversation. I know some very good riddles."

Ella tried to glare at the moving spirit. "Will you answer me about the horses?"

"Bib already answered you. Did you fail to perceive it? You must not be very bright."

"Do you always submit to men and let them speak for you?"

Limnad turned to me. "I'd like to tie her intestines to her hands and feet, and then play with her like a puppet. Would you mind?"

I had been wondering which one would create the least hell if I sided against her. "No, please don't do that. I think we've established the answer, and we won't be killing any horses today."

"Ella," Desh said, sliding between her and Limnad. "I think I found the best place to climb over, but I'm not sure. Would you please come look?"

I watched Ella walk away from probable death and realized that Desh had ended that fracas in a moderately elegant manner. I hadn't credited him with that much awareness. Being a sorcerer might suit the boy after all, and I owed him a couple of drinks for ending that squabble, assuming we both lived.

"Limnad, I would like to ask you a favor."

The spirit hadn't strayed more than three feet from me since I woke up.

"Desh is a new sorcerer, and I want to see him start off well. I taught him some fundamentals, but he still needs to learn just about everything that's worth learning. It would ease my heart if he learns enough so that he doesn't die in his first year. Would you please teach him about magic?"

"If it helps you heal, I am happy to teach him. How harsh may I be when he does something wrong?"

"Don't damage him permanently and don't do anything that will hurt for more than three days."

Limnad slid back several feet away from me and tilted her head. "You don't seem to care whether he learns very quickly. I'll do the best I can."

Now she was Desh's problem instead of mine for a while. Most of being a sorcerer has nothing to do with magic. It has to do with being a sneaky son of a bitch.

We scavenged food and water from the Denzmen's saddlebags, then we unsaddled the horses and turned them loose. We scaled Vintan's fine wall, although Ralt and Stan had to practically carry me over, since I was walking like I was eighty years old. Four hours lay between us and sunset, and six hours of walking lay between us and Vintan, or at least that's how I figured it.

Ralt and Desh helped me along while Ella led the way, but by dusk, I was walking steadily on my own. Still, I was lagging fifty paces when Ella spotted the pile of corpses. She waited until I caught up, and we walked closer together. What we'd first taken to be a pile of bodies turned out instead to be a neat stack of bodies. I counted thirty-two corpses wrapped in nice cotton sheets, and based on the thick, sweet, gamy smell, some had been there at least a week.

"What in the goat-grabbing hell?" Ralt stumbled back three steps, saw me looking at him, and stood up tall but quivering.

"I seen this before," said Stan. "Traitors. Slaughter a boatload and pile 'em up—makes a better example than one or two mangled ones stuck up on poles. This says, 'We kill so many of these bastards we can't even bury them or burn them, so don't try to poison the king or anything.'"

"It seems a fanciful explanation, Stan, but I cannot think of a more likely one. Not yet." Ella straightened her shoulders.

"Let's keep going then," I said. "Watch out for... anything that looks like it might kill us and stack our bodies."

A few minutes down the road, I saw candlelight or lamplight ahead. It stood out because the trees were few and small. We hiked on toward the lights, and soon the sketchy outlines of a couple dozen little buildings appeared.

"We should go around," I whispered.

Ella whispered back, "No, they may know something that would help us."

Stan slipped on an uneven rock, and his chain shirt clinked as he caught himself.

"Go away!" a man yelled at us from the dimness. "Stay away! Stay away!"

"What do you think?" I asked Ella.

She didn't answer because a stone smacked her in the side of the head. She dropped to her knees.

I had lumbered four steps toward the village with my sword drawn before I thought about it. In the past ten years, few men had attacked me without getting killed for it, and those few got badly hurt. Now a big man backlit by lanterns threw a rock at me, and I wanted to put my sword in his chest more than I wanted to sleep or eat. I wavered, providing the villagers an excellent target, and a stone whacked my shoulder hard.

Six more steps and I stabbed him, at the last instant aiming for his rock-throwing shoulder instead of his heart. As he stumbled, I stepped toward the next man, who turned out to be a girl. She hurled a stone at my crotch and yelled, "Go away! Go away! Go away!"

I ignored her and sidestepped, moving more easily now. I looked for the next man down the line, but instead I found a teenage boy. He backed away, threw a stone over my head, and fell on his butt. In the deep dusk, I made out no more than eight people total chucking rocks at me.

If they were all children, some had mighty deep voices, but I didn't want to murder a child by mistake in the dark. I ran back to Ella, who was just standing up with Stan's help. More stones flew after me, accompanied by shouts. "Go away or die!"

"I say that we go away and *not* die," said Desh.

A stone hit Ralt on the thumb, and he growled. "Greasy hell!"

Stan and Ralt steadied Ella by her arms, and we all trotted across the trail away from the little village. People kept shouting, "Stay away!" until we were a hundred paces distant.

Ella was weaving even after she stopped running. I checked her head while Stan steadied her. A small knot was rising, but she wasn't bleeding.

A little way off from us, Ralt said, "Hello there. Ain't you the lucky one?" I joined Ralt beside a strong-looking steel cage in the high grass. It was six feet on each side, and a fat, bald, naked man sat in one corner with his knees pulled up.

He said, "They don't care for you fellows either, do they?"

SEVENTEEN

Sorcerers get put in cages and cells fairly often, and we usually deserve it. We should know better than to do reckless things that will anger the wrong person—meaning a person with the kind of lackeys that can hunt, seize, and imprison a sorcerer.

Other sorcerers are typically hired for such work. There is no professional courtesy between sorcerers, nor any kind of courtesy. Desh probably considered me his teacher and maybe his friend, but when bargaining with Harik, I had offered to thwart Desh's dreams of sorcery as casually as I'd offer one of his old shoes. Desh should have been much warier of me. Of course, I wasn't going to tell him that, proving that he should have been much warier of me.

When you know that at any moment someone may trade away part of their past, their future, or themselves, and that you might be part of the deal, you can't trust them. After all, they're just like you, and you can't be trusted. If, despite all that, you find another sorcerer you can trust, you have found friendship for a lifetime, which is just a few years since most of us die young.

I wondered what the caged fat man had done to the wrong

person in that village. Whatever it was, they must have thought we were about to do the same thing. The man pushed himself upright. By starlight, I saw that he wavered a little but pulled back his shoulders, and I heard a smile in his voice. "Good evening, gentlemen. I am Smat Bander, and it is my great honor to meet you. Welcome to my abode. It is the very definition of humble, as well as, I hope to the gods, temporary."

Even though the man was naked in a cage containing nothing more valuable than the empty bowl he'd just stumbled on, I got the impression he wanted me to buy something from him. "Hello, Smat. I'm Bib, and my shield maiden here is Ralt. How long have you been in there?"

"Five relaxing days. The first four were meditative, but since my water ran out yesterday, my mind has wandered."

"I am sympathetic, but I hesitate to set you free. How do I know you don't belong in there?"

Smat sagged just a little. "I know my assurance doesn't carry much weight since we just met, but I do assure you this is all a mistake."

Ella walked up beside me and put a hand on my shoulder to steady herself. Smat peered at her, jerked, and then covered his privates with both hands. "Good evening, miss. I'm Smat Bander. Awkward circumstances, but I'm pleased to meet you."

Ella asked me, "How quickly can you demolish the door?"

"Bless you, miss," said Smat.

I said, "An hour. Maybe more."

"Leave him then."

Smat grabbed the bars, all modesty flown. "Please, miss! Consider my plight! Consider my children!"

Ella walked to the cage and placed her hand over Smat's. "It truly distresses me to leave you here, but we are attempting to save a child—a prince—and cannot delay."

"That's noble, I'm sure, but at least leave me some water!"

I couldn't stand it anymore. "Everybody stop! I'm going to start crying and will have to write a poem about this." I turned to Smat. "Who put you in here and why?"

"My daughter confined me here. Everyone wanted to kill me, but she begged that I be caged here instead. They want to kill me because they're afraid of Northmen fever."

"How bad is it?" I asked, thinking of the stacked corpses.

"Twenty-three dead when they put me in here."

Ella swayed, and Stan caught her. "Excuse me, miss," he said with a jackal's grin.

I pointed at Ella. "You go lie down and rest your head. You'll be making awful decisions just now, and I don't want you to get me killed. We'll rest here until the moon comes up."

I pointed at Desh. "You keep watch. Limnad, would you please help him?"

Limnad appeared next to Desh, glowing brighter than the starlight. Smat took a step back and stumbled. "I will. How do you feel, Bib?"

"The same, thank you, but we can weep over me later." I pointed at Ralt and Stan. "You get the hammer and knock the door off this cage. Smat, get on the other side of the cage, and try not to step in your own excrement on the way. All right, go!"

I glared at them all until they went. The glare was just to make me feel good, since in the dark they could have been facing away from me and I wouldn't have known it. I dug the cloak from my pack and passed it through the bars to Smat.

"I appreciate your kindness," he said, pulling it around him.

"Answer my questions now, and don't embellish. Don't try to tell me stories, either. Stories annoy me. I promise not to kill you, but if you aren't succinct, I won't set you free and I might leave some water behind just out of your reach."

"As you wish, sir." He said it like a well-trained cart horse that could talk.

"Why does a man of the north like you have a daughter in a Denz village?"

"I have a daughter, two sons, a wife, two sisters-in-law, and three nieces. And I support them all."

"Damn. That doesn't tell me why, though."

"Oh! When I was young, a lamentable accident forced me to flee the northern kingdoms and never return. It's a long story... that I won't tell at this time. I turned my hand to trading in these lands, and I have prospered. I fell in love, was blessed with beautiful children, and inherited somewhat less beautiful relatives."

"You don't really appreciate how much I despise stories, do you?"

"Apologies. I now spend most of the year traveling, engaged in commerce, and as I was preparing my next journey, the Northmen fever arrived."

"I'm familiar with a lot of maladies, but not that one. What is it?"

"Apart from the eponymous fever, the victim coughs and sneezes, vomits prodigiously, loses all balance, and suffers pain in the head and joints. About half of those who catch it die in the first two days. Those who survive are as worthless as a beached halibut for a week or two."

It sounded like plagues I'd seen, but deadlier. "Why Northmen fever?"

"It never touches Northmen, so by Denzmen logic, all Northmen must cause it."

I looked toward the village lights. Several people were probably busy dying there. Some unknown number would catch fever in the next weeks. For a moment, I imagined this disease having an open-ended debt with Harik, like me.

"Hurry up, Stan." I smacked one of the bars with my palm. "I could have knocked off five hinges by now."

He answered without slowing his hammer strikes. "Almost

there, even if it's dark as perdition and I did scrape my knuckles hard, but nobody cares about that, do they?"

I knelt by Ella, and I pressed her shoulder back down when she tried to sit up. "The villagers are sick. I think I'll take a walk back there and see whether I can help them. Smat will come with me."

Ella sat up regardless of my hand. "No! It's reckless and unnecessary. You might be killed. You might contract their plague. You will waste magical power we may require later. It will without doubt cause us further delay."

"Excellent points." I patted her arm. "I won't be long."

"I forbid you to go!" She grabbed for my arm but missed.

I grinned at her in the darkness. "Hell, I'm going for certain now."

Smat led the way, calling out as he went, telling his neighbors not to kill him because he was bringing help. He whispered to me, "You do qualify as help, correct? You can do something?"

"I can. It might even be something useful."

Several rocks zipped past us in the darkness, but they didn't seem to be thrown with fury and terror like the ones before. We reached the trail, and Smat told me to wait while he entered the village. A few minutes later, I heard shouting, but I couldn't make out the words.

At last, Smat ambled out of the village. "I assure you, they experienced consternation upon seeing I had escaped the cage, but I can often help people find reasonable thoughts if given the merest chance. I explained the arrival of the clever and benevolent strangers. And I smashed a jug over my brother-in-law's head. So satisfying. They are willing to accept help. I imagine they are willing to accept an armed occupation if they get to live. There are some conditions, however."

"Really? They're watching their children die, and they want to negotiate?"

"They are a stiff people. You may not enter the village."

"They'll come out here?"

"No, you may not touch anyone from the village. And before you ask, no, they won't allow you to see them or speak to them, either."

I shrugged. "Maybe I should just pitch a handful of berries over there and go get a beer. If there was any beer."

Smat fell to his knees and leaned toward me. "Please don't abandon us, Bib. Both my sons have caught it, and both are suffering greatly."

"Do you have any beer in your village?"

"Wine."

"Even better. Go get it. Get a really big jug."

I walked back up the trail to the stacked corpses, pulled open the sheet on one of them, and put my palm against the dead woman's neck. With the other hand, I pulled a green wisp out of the air and sent it into the corpse. I used up three more wisps before I figured I knew enough to wipe this disease out of somebody.

Smat was waiting for me on the trail, holding an enormous clay jug full of wine.

"Set it on the ground." I reached out with one hand, pulled green strands out of nothing, and fed them into the open jug, stirring the strands into the wine with my other hand. "They won't cry or come out here and kill me if they drink something I touched, will they?"

"Not if I never tell them." Smat rubbed his hands together. "I don't want to offend, but am I correct in surmising that you are engaged in sorcery? I apologize... I fear it may be an impolite question, and I prefer not to be... in any event, I don't believe you would just kill me out of hand."

I managed not to laugh in his face.

Smat talked faster as his story got rolling. "I knew a sorcerer once. I grieve to tell you, but she was prettier than you. Perhaps you know her? Latta? From the Reed Kingdom? Hair as black as, well, it was so black it's hard to describe. Black as a very black thing. Much prettier than you."

Once I would have challenged that statement and argued that the sorcerer had thrown a charm to fool Smat's eyes, since I was acknowledged to be the most beautiful living sorcerer. However, that night, my boldness was too shriveled to say ridiculous things for fun. I just said, "Yes, sorcery. Look well. This is about as exciting as it gets. All right, take it. Everyone gets a sip, and tomorrow they'll be tearing things up and fornicating with each other's spouses as zealously as they ever did."

When Smat picked up the jug, I said, "If you drop it, I'll have to torture you to death. You don't know what it cost me."

"A marvelous incentive to exercise care. I will not insult you by asking whether it will work. Won't you wait, however? My neighbors will forget their fears and thank you for saving them."

"You haven't been to as many of these events as I, Smat. They never thank you. If you're doing these things to get their thanks, you'll be frustrated forever. Be a blacksmith instead. Everybody appreciates horseshoes. Give me my damn cloak."

Smat turned so I could take the cloak off his shoulders, and now he didn't seem embarrassed that all creation could inspect his manhood. "Farewell, Bib. I, at least, thank you with profound sincerity."

I walked back to my companions, careful in the near darkness. When I found Ella, she seized my shirt by the front and then yanked me toward her. She hissed in my face, "The moon is up! It's already up." She pushed me away and said to everyone, "We'll depart now. Finally. Everyone, keep pace!"

"No, Limnad, please don't kill her," I whispered.

The river spirit sighed.

I stepped quick to keep Ella's outline in sight. I hadn't healed those people to get Ella's good opinion any more than to get the villagers' thanks. I had done something good, and I hadn't killed that rock-throwing turd. Things were improving. I felt optimistic about the prospects of killing lots of Denzmen soon.

Killing lots of Denzmen. I hadn't meant to think it, and I felt kind of sick about how much fun it sounded.

I stopped short when I realized how stupid I'd been. "Ella, wait!"

"I will not!" She pushed past a branch and let it snap back at me.

I pushed the branch out of my face. "If you're ever going to trust me, now's a good time."

She walked back to me. "What do you wish to do now? Has a baby bird dropped from its nest? Does some child require a bedtime story?"

I bent over and vomited.

"I pray you did not stop to show me that."

I vomited again, waited a moment, and stood straight. Nausea twisted my insides, and sweat ran down my face. The cure must have been working. "No, I want to go back to the village and buy some horses."

Ella paused, and then walked straight past me toward the village.

Smat sold us five saddle horses, and he explained how honored he was to do it. He allowed us to buy the best mounts he owned because of the great debt his village owed me. Of course, they were his only saddle horses, so by definition, they were the finest. Also, the debt he owed me was balanced out by Ella paying him twice what the creatures were worth. Sadly, he owned just four saddles, but Ella was pleased to get the horses, and I was pleased she had stopped acting as if she planned to cut out my heart when I wasn't looking.

I was the only one of us who had much experience riding

bareback, so everyone else began saddling their horses. I puked a couple of times instead. Just as I was about to pull myself up onto my mount, Ella stopped me.

"Bib, I apologize that I spoke sharply to you."

"You almost tore my shirt too."

She sighed. "Yes, I apologize for that as well. But we're falling farther behind every hour. We cannot indulge ourselves in frivolous delays. Do you understand?"

"I understand. We don't stop to save people's lives."

"No, that's not what I meant! We must judge each delay severely as to whether it justifies the time lost."

I started to say something sarcastic, but she cut me off. "Bib, if we don't hurry, I'll lose him."

I wanted to keep arguing with her, but she was making too much sense. That has always been my downfall when arguing with women. They generally make more sense than I do. I struggled up onto my nag. "Follow me then and hang on!" I kicked the gelding into a gallop.

Throughout the rest of the night and all the next day, I pushed the pace as hard as our horses could bear. They weren't magnificent beasts, or even reasonably good ones, but they carried us faster than our feet would have.

During this time, Limnad came to me twice and guided us along big detours off the trail. She claimed she was avoiding bands of Denzmen, and I didn't doubt her. Ella, however, called Limnad some salty names at the first detour. At the second detour, she drew her sword, and I had to work hard to soothe both of them so that Ella didn't end up with her head and limbs torn off and each moved one spot clockwise around her torso.

Ella admired one of Limnad's contributions, though. Limnad always had a good sense of where Vintan was, so we always knew whether we were closing with him. When we had reached the village, we were nine hours behind him. By sunset the next day, we were only three hours behind. Vintan had evidently halted to rest, so he probably thought we were all defeated, damaged, or destroyed.

We ourselves halted at sunset. The moon wouldn't rise until well after midnight, and it would be a tiny slice of light, just a day away from the new moon. Ella decreed one hour of rest before we continued the pursuit.

"Three hours." I rubbed my face. It felt like it was dragging past my neck.

"Too much time." Ella looked away from me and scanned the horizon.

I plopped down onto my butt. "I have slept two hours since we crossed the Blood River yesterday morning. You've slept less than that."

"It is a hardship, but we can withstand it." She marched toward her horse.

"We can." I stood and trotted after the arrogant idiot. "We can also be so tired out when we catch Vintan that he destroys us by wiggling his finger."

Ella looked at me and cocked her head. "No."

"Let me say it another way. Should we be excessively fatigued when we overtake Vintan, he shall obliterate us with the slightest gesticulation."

She smiled, which oddly made her look more tired. "All right, I deserve that. But you do not understand."

"Sorry, darling, but you are the one who doesn't understand. You don't understand your task. I expect you did at one time, but everything has changed."

Ella stepped back. "I suggest you explain that immediately."

"You set out to rescue the prince from a raiding force of Denz-men. Now you have to keep him alive when Vintan decides to kill him."

"Why should Vintan kill him after preserving him through this entire journey? It makes no sense."

"I heard Vintan commit to it. He promised the God of Death. And he can do it. He's a dangerous man."

She raised her eyebrows. "More dangerous than you?"

"Probably. When we fought, I got broken up like a bunch of green sticks, and he rode off like he was going to a party."

She looked down, scratching her forehead, and then pulled her shoulders back. "Very well. I intend to stab him in the liver and carve off his intimate parts. How shall we do it?"

"The first thing we do is sleep for three hours. If we sleep one hour, we might as well stab the prince in the heart ourselves. That may be an exaggeration, of course."

"Are you lying to me about this?"

"No. I admit I've lied to you on occasion, which is one of my failings, but I'm being dead truthful about this. If you're going to lead us, lead us on the correct errand."

"I pray you're not lying. You may be powerful, but as you have admitted, you must sleep sometimes." She walked toward the others. "Sleep three hours, not one!"

I whispered, "No."

Limnad sighed and muttered something I couldn't hear.

EIGHTEEN

I am a coward when it comes to magic. If I can figure out a way to do something like a regular person, I stay away from magic like it was a whore with five diseases and a knife in its garter. I have met sorcerers who used magic for damn near everything of consequence. They thought it was beneath them to dig a well or throw a drunk out of the tavern by hand. But in my youth, I saw brave sorcerers use magic lavishly and trade often with the gods. Soon they were burdened with cruel debts, emptied of feeling, and hardly human at all.

Sorcery is a dangerous occupation, so I decided to become as proficient as possible at killing folks with plain, uncomplicated steel. For twenty-five years, I've used steel to kill people who were trying to kill me, and since I'm still alive, I suppose that decision was sound.

I knew things were bad for us when I realized I wasn't even considering steel to solve our problem. We had followed the trail for nearly two days straight since our three-hour nap, through wooded hills and canyons smelling of cedar and chalk. The trail was now running parallel to a cliff's edge. In a place where a steep hill jutted out not far from the cliff, the Denzmen had built a small wooden keep that blocked the whole space from hillside to cliff's edge.

No horse could climb over the tall, jagged hills, but we still had many options. We could ride some number of miles along the hills to find a way over, or ride miles back to find a way around the canyon. We could set our horses free and climb over the hills, or ride straight through the keep, killing as many Denzmen as required. Or, we could wait a few days for the army to arrive and watch it smash through the keep. Or, we could go back to Smat's village and drink some of their wine, which wouldn't please Ella, but I liked to keep all options available.

Ella and I had climbed partway up the hill and were peeking around the edge to examine the keep. I said, "I was just thinking that going back to that village and drinking wine is an option we shouldn't toss out."

She whacked me on the shoulder. "You are not as entertaining as you believe yourself to be."

The trail ran through a gate in the middle of the wall closest to us and through a similar gate in the far wall sixty paces beyond. Parapets ran along the top of each wall, and six men stood on each parapet.

Ella asked, "What are the men on the parapets holding?"

"Crossbows."

"Ah."

"Not the crank kind—the kind you load with your foot in the loop."

"That makes no difference."

"They're loaded."

"Stop flaunting your eyesight," she said.

"Just flirting a little. We might die before sundown, so if there's ever a time to do it, this is it."

"Hush. Now is the time to craft a stratagem. Not to flirt."

"Are you asking for my opinion?"

"Yes. Yes, I am. Please, please favor me with your martial prowess, Bib, that I may gaze with awe upon your magnificence." Ella rolled her eyes. "So, stop acting like an ass. What do you think?"

"You're going to love this."

Before we started the forest fire, we made sure the healthy wind was blowing toward the keep. Wind direction would make this tactic possible. Rain must have been scarce for a while, because the trees and brush were dry. The Denzmen had cleared a large area around their keep, so the fire wasn't likely to burn it down. But if I commanded a wooden structure and saw a lot of mysterious smoke nearby, I'd want to know what the hell was going on.

About fifteen minutes after the fire grew to a sizable blaze, four soldiers hustled around the hill where Ella, Ralt, and I waited to ambush them. Three of them were dead before they even saw us, and the fourth only had time to call us grunting bastards before he died.

Ella said, "Change clothing with them. I'll keep watch."

We didn't strictly change clothing with the Denzmen. We put their outer clothes on over our own. Then I kept watch while Ella wriggled into a soldier's clothing, and Ralt dragged the bodies out of sight. We hid again.

Twenty minutes later, six Denzmen stamped into view, scanning the area and more cautious than their dead predecessors. Vigilance didn't keep them alive, however, and soon I helped Ralt drag these bodies off to join their friends.

Ralt said, "It's like having a barmaid bring you beers. You think they'll send another round?"

"That would be considerate of them. Let's see if they do. We might get bored waiting, though."

Sadly, half an hour passed without another patrol for us to slaughter.

I said to Ella, "What do you think, General? Should we wait or strike?"

"Let us begin the attack."

We crept along the hillside as far as we could without being seen from the keep. A minute later, Ella slapped my shoulder and nodded. She marched toward the keep, head down, and I followed along with Ralt, just three soldiers coming back to report.

When we had closed within fifty paces of the keep, I whispered, "Limnad, it's time."

I heard crashing, banging, horses squealing, and men yelling. That was Limnad inside the keep smashing everything she could reach, terrifying everybody, and generally creating hell. I glanced at the parapet, and every man on it was looking inside the keep. At that moment, half of a spinning wagon hurtled into the air and dropped back inside the keep.

Ella arrived at the gate first, but she stood aside. I reached with both hands and pulled blue strands out of the air. Then I grabbed the gate and wove the strands all through the grating. Over the next ten seconds, I aged the wood until the gate was entirely rotten. The three of us hurled ourselves against the slats and broke it apart. We also knocked down a soldier running toward the gate. I stabbed him in the throat and paused to grab his small shield. With crossbowmen all around the keep, a shield wouldn't be a bad idea.

The gate's destruction was the cue for Desh and Stan to gallop our horses up toward the keep. I hoped they were paying attention.

I left Ella and Ralt to clear the gate's debris and hold it against any Denzmen who tried to retake it. I ran up the stairs to the parapet to kill the six crossbowmen before they punctured Desh and Stan. Limnad could only create havoc inside the keep for so long before someone got lucky and stabbed or shot her, so as I ran up the stairs, I said, "Limnad, retreat." The sounds of wood crashing stopped right away. There must not have been much more than splinters left out there, anyway.

I had counted on Limnad's antics to pull one or two men off the parapet, so when I stepped off the stairs and saw at least ten crossbowmen lined up, I reconsidered things for an instant. The smart move would be running right back down the stairs. But I also saw our horses charging toward the keep at a good clip, and the crossbowmen would have them in range before long.

Of course, I wanted to kill them. And to be honest, I was glad that more of them had arrived. I'd get to kill them too. Or, they might kill me, which might not be the worst thing, either.

The parapet was wide enough for two men to squeeze past, but not to fight side by side. That was perfect. All of them must have fired at Limnad, or maybe into the air trying to hit anything at all, because now they were reloading as fast as they could. The first man was looking the wrong way, so I opened his throat and tossed him over the parapet. The second man saw me but froze. I pierced his heart. The third man was looking down, struggling with the bowstring. I thought about beheading the fool but just sliced his neck instead.

The fourth man shouted, and everybody else looked up. He tried to block me with his unloaded crossbow, and then bash out my brains. Poor tactics. I used a thrust through his belly and a journey over the parapet to teach him better.

The next man had dropped his crossbow and was drawing his sword. I was a little close, so I smashed his face with the shield and shoved him over the side. The man after that struggled, one hand on his sword while the other was holding his crossbow. I stabbed him in the eye and moved on.

I looked ahead and saw four more men. Two had drawn their swords, and the two behind them were hurrying to reload like I was a demon vomiting acid. I blocked a cut from the next soldier, and the man behind him did a ridiculous thing. He reached around his friend and threw his sword. Maybe he thought he was using his friend as a shield, or maybe fear had made him insane. I didn't much care, because the sword hurtled into my view at almost the same moment it touched my shirt.

If that man had thrust his sword around his friend instead of throwing it, I would have died right there. Instead, it whirled past my shield and struck close to my heart. He'd thrown it spinning, so instead of killing me, it plowed a ragged furrow up my chest, skirted my throat, and sliced an inch deep across my shoulder.

I'm not the toughest man I've ever known, nor even among the top hundred. However, I have been cut more than my share, possibly because I'm arrogant and foolish about letting an insult pass. I felt the blood splash but not much pain right away. I swung a casual arc and sliced the nearest man's neck. I shoved him aside, only to see the coward who'd thrown the sword sail over the parapet to the ground outside the keep.

The next soldier had reloaded his crossbow and was raising it. Behind him, the last man had almost finished reloading. I lifted the shield as I lunged, and the soldier fired, striking near the shield's center. The bolt hammered the shield from three feet away and ripped it off, breaking my arm as it went. At the same time, I stabbed that soldier in the throat, and he collapsed straight down.

The last man raised his weapon to shoot me in the chest. I was just too injured and too far away to thrust with any kind of control before he fired. My left arm was useless, so I dropped my sword, jumped at him like a crazy man, and grabbed the reloading loop on the end of the crossbow. I hauled the weapon around as it fired, and the bolt flew away outside the keep. I hoped it would kill the bastard who'd thrown his sword. I smashed the crossbow into the Denzman's face, pulled my long knife, and punched it twice into his heart.

I hoped Ella and Ralt were having an easier time than this.

I sheathed my sword, held onto my broken arm, and trotted back down the stairs, waiting for my body to realize what had been done to it. Ralt met me at the bottom step and pursed his lips. "If you wasn't walking around, I'd bury you." He led me back toward the center of the keep, which looked almost ankle-deep in splinters. Desh was guiding our horses across, and Stan was guarding his rear, facing two Denzmen. As I watched, Ralt stabbed one from behind, and Stan finished the other. The far parapet was clear, and Ella was running back down the stairs from it.

"Come on!" Ella shouted, running through the gate, and all of us followed.

Just outside the gate, I asked Ella, "How many men do you think they still have?"

She shrugged. "Four? Twenty? I cannot give you a useful estimate."

"All right, leave me a horse and go."

Ella shook her head. "Hah! You've made a great many foolish statements today, but that one triumphs. I'm not leaving you. You might collapse before I ride one hundred paces."

"Stay then, but stand away." I pulled a blue strand out of nothing, then another, then four more. I pushed them one-handed into the keep's wall just beside the gate. Swords rang off one another inside but I didn't look.

"Stay out from under the gate!" I yelled. Within a few more seconds, I had rotted all the wood beside the gate.

I shouted "Run!" as I sprinted away. The gate and wall collapsed to one side, blocking the opening. The parapet over the gate and wall clattered down into a pile of timbers.

I looked back. "They won't be riding after us for a couple of hours. So, bring the victor his mount!"

"Your faculties have been scrambled," Ella said as she was

making a quick sling from one of the Denzmen's clothes. "Come along and do precisely what you're told."

I nodded. The pain hit just then, and I felt like those timbers had fallen on top of me.

Stan said, "Here, mount yourself up on my nag, since you just about got yourself sliced in half. It's only till you get yourself better, mind you. I ain't riding your nag forever. Its back is bony, and my ass ain't fat like Ralt's."

"Thank you, Stan." I mounted, glad to have a saddle, and we trotted south. I tend to get morose after the satisfaction of killing passes, but this fight began producing some especially excellent grouchiness.

A bit later, Ella rode up beside me. "So, we succeeded. However, don't indulge in arrogance simply because your plan worked. It was imperfect in many respects, one of the most significant being that you were nearly killed."

I didn't look over at her. "All right, I won't."

"That was flirting. It's sad you failed to recognize it."

Just then, talking felt like work—like digging a moat with a spoon. "Consider me to have flirted back. Imagine that it was really good."

"Bib, is something other than your wounds plaguing you?" Ella reached out to touch me.

I edged my horse away from her. "Nothing a few dozen drinks won't cure."

"Look at me!" Her face was flushed. "Is it something about that wretched spirit saying your heart has turned to ash?"

"Hell, pay no attention to that."

Ella slapped her leg. "So, it is, then."

"I said it isn't!"

"No, you said pay no attention."

Now I felt like I was digging a moat with a stick. "I'm tired. Like Stan said, I got sliced in half."

Ella edged her horse toward me and reached, but I rode away from her touch again. She took a brisk breath. "Very well. We'll speak of this another time."

"I hope not."

What I meant to say was, "I hope not, because I might have to give Limnad permission to hold you under a waterfall until you die."

I might not have meant that literally.

NINETEEN

Living trees don't like getting burned up. They prefer to grow. However, dead wood wants to rot. Sorcerers find it difficult to make dead wood grow because the wood is done with all that. Your body wants to be healthy instead of sick, so healing is straightforward. Bugs want to nest and find food, not fly off to sting somebody, so it can be a lot of work to make them sting.

If I'm going to use magic, I try to make things do what they already want to do. It's a lot less work.

Trees aren't the only things that don't like getting burned up. In fact, hardly anything likes getting burned up, so a sorcerer who can only burn things has a lot of work ahead of him. In just the same way, nothing wants to be suddenly made not to exist. I can't think of a single thing that wants that. Since Vintan was a Breaker and all he could do was make things *not* exist, he would probably be using up a lot more energy than me to get things done. So, that was in our favor.

The general idea works with people too. People will tell you they want to change, but they're lying. If they wanted to change, they would already have started changing, and they wouldn't be talking about all this changing bullshit. The world can make them change when it takes someone away from them or smashes their illusions into bits smaller than a gnat's dick. But people who want to change on their own are too busy doing it to waste time talking about it.

That's why I didn't want to talk to Ella about this love of murder coming from inside me. The world, through Gorlana, had shown me that about myself, so maybe it would also make me change. I didn't want to ruin my chances by acting like one of those people who talks about changing but just stays the same way forever.

Ella pushed us south from the keep for an hour, through some thick stands of short, spreading trees. An hour of bouncing on a horse felt like several hours to me, and at last, the trees thinned and she halted.

"Bib, how long?"

Ella had become reliant on Limnad's sense of Vintan's location. Whenever she wanted to know how far we were trailing the Denzmen, she asked me to ask Limnad for a report. I would ask Limnad, who would tell me, and then I would report back to Ella. Usually, I found this a little amusing. Not today.

"Krak burn you both until you shit coal! Talk to each other like civilized creatures. I have to put myself back together over here."

No one said anything while I poked at my wound and winced.

Ella hauled in a big breath. Then, just so she wouldn't be forced to speak to Limnad, Ella initiated a rapid-fire interrogation with me in the middle.

Ella said, "Bib, would you please—"

"Limnad!" I yelled.

"Three hours!"

"Three hours!" I shouted.

"Thank you!" Ella yelled.

If Vintan stayed in place, we would catch up to him in three hours at the pace we'd been riding. When we left the keep, we had been four hours behind.

Ella said, "We shall rest here for one hour. Ralt, stand watch. Stan, relieve him at the half hour."

Just as I was knitting myself back together, Desh came over and sat on the ground facing me. "I need to ask you a question about magic."

I grimaced. "Can it wait? If you distract me, I might attach my nipple to my elbow."

He leaned down and lowered his voice. "We only have an hour."

I propped myself with my palms in the grass. "Go ahead. The scar will ruin my smooth chest anyway."

"Limnad has taught me more about magic in a few days than I expected I might learn in a year."

I looked at him with my best grave, wise sorcerer expression. "Has she hit you a lot? Where are the bruises?"

Desh smiled and shrugged. "A few times. Mostly it's been while we're riding, so if she beat me too hard, I probably would've fallen off my horse."

"Grace me with your question, then. Serenade me, even. Can you sing, son?"

"The girls in my village used to weep and fall on the ground in front of me when I sang."

"Damn," I said. "Let me hear your question. Don't sing it."

"Everything she's taught me has been theoretical, and like I said, it's been a lot. Now we're beginning to work on practical skills. You know, pulling cords and so forth." He stopped.

"Don't hold it in, Desh! I won't laugh at you."

"Well... when she helped me with my stance and line, I felt sort of uncomfortable. I don't know much of anything about spirits, but if she were a woman and moved that way, I'd say she expected me to do something about it."

I blinked at the boy several times. "You do know she's listening to you right now, don't you?"

Desh raised his eyebrows and turned red.

This was a tender situation. Love between spirits and humans does not tend to turn out well. Desh didn't seem smitten with her, but it might be one of those cases in which he'd caught her fancy and she planned to keep him forever under some rock in her river. Or maybe it was more—in which case, if he spurned her, she might tear him to pieces as he sat in front of me.

Straightforward truth seemed to be the best approach. I whispered, "Limnad."

After a moment, she stepped out from behind a tree.

"Limnad, are you in love with Desh?"

The spirit examined Desh with unblinking eyes. "Yes."

"I don't doubt your word, but my curiosity is bubbling. Why?"

"He speaks quietly and has a pretty smile. He doesn't lie like everybody else here. He's funny. Most humans aren't funny, even the ones who think they are." She knelt and stared into my face. "Especially..." She cocked her head at me. "Those who think they are."

I hated to throw Desh on this fire, but there was no choice. "Desh?"

The young man stood. "Limnad, you are mostly spirit so I think love can grow within you very quickly. I am mostly flesh so love cannot grow as quickly within me. Please wait with me to find out what grows."

If the boy hadn't been so close to death, I would have stood and applauded. It was the subtlest nest of deception built from truths that I had heard in a long time. Desh was going to be a great sorcerer if Limnad, or something else, didn't kill him first.

Limnad nodded at Desh. "That will be good." She walked off behind a tree and disappeared.

I looked up at Desh and put my finger to my lips. It might be fatal for him to forget that she was always listening and say some fatally stupid thing. He nodded and walked toward the horses.

I closed my eyes while clenching and unclenching my fist. My arm felt bruised where that Denzman had broken it, like somebody had smacked it hard with a stick of firewood. The wound on my chest smarted, as if a vindictive wasp had walked all the way up it, stinging me every step. Annoying, but it wouldn't slow me down too much.

When I opened my eyes, I saw Stan walking toward me.

I scowled. "What?"

"Well, if that's the way you feel about a friendly gesture, then I'm not sure you'll ever get one again—at least not from me, and I'm known as being a right generous fellow."

"I'm sorry, Stan. I'm just grouchy from being cut up and broken."

"Huh. Ralt and I were thinking that since you got all beat up and everything, killing those bastards with crossbows before they could kill me, we should share with you." He held out a small skin of liquid, and I took it.

"We snatched it off a dead Denzman's horse at the river where we all nearly got killed, and we been saving it since. I wanted to drink it four or five times already, but Ralt is a stingy git."

I unplugged the skin and smelled wine. "Thank you, and thank Ralt. But don't give it all to me. I'll share with you boys."

Stan smiled, showing his appalling teeth. "Nah, we got three more for us. Desh says he's not much of a drinker, but just wait till he's been with us for a few months." Stan strolled away, stretching his arms over his head as he went.

I drew a big swallow from the skin. It was decent, as far as caustic liquids that can kill young livestock go. On my third swallow, somebody touched my shoulder from behind. I let my shoulders and head sag forward.

"Just let me get drunk and sleep," I said.

"May I sit?" Ella nodded at the ground in front of me.

"It's not my dirt." She sat on the ground facing me, and I handed her the wine.

After she'd taken a swallow, she held up the skin. "You are attempting to kill me." She took another swallow and handed it back. "What harm have you suffered, Bib? It won't help to try to put me off."

"I found out I'm too old to master the sackbut. Broke my damn heart."

"Not funny. Be truthful with me."

"That was true. Fairly true."

She grabbed my hand. "Not only do I want to know, but I require it. We must have faith in one another."

"I'm sorry..." I shook my head. "No, I'm not sorry. This is something I will not talk about. You'll just have to trust me and have faith in my ability to take a beating."

She grabbed my other hand. I'm not sure whether she was being sympathetic or making sure I couldn't whack her if I didn't like the next thing she said. "I shall assume that your debt is somehow involved."

"You go right ahead and assume that. Reality pays no attention to your assumptions."

"I know that you have entered into an agreement with the God of Death to dispatch people for him, and that only he knows how many you must kill. Please don't deny it."

"All right. I do not deny it. I accept it, and I'm proud to."

"I believe that. I am, however, mystified. Why did you accept that agreement, Bib?"

"Don't ask me why I did it. Ask yourself what would make *you* do it."

Ella sat back and looked at the ground, scratching her forehead. "I don't know. I can't imagine anything causing me to make that bargain."

"Why are you here?"

"To save the prince... oh! You did it to save your daughter. But what happened?"

"I saved her."

"But... what happened?"

"Seven days later, she fell and broke her neck." I rubbed the back of my head. "I'm sure Harik knew it was going to happen."

Ella didn't say anything. Her eyes filled up, but she didn't cry.

"It was worth it. I'd do it again right this minute, if I could have seven more days with her."

We sat for a couple minutes, drinking in silence.

"Why do you enjoy it?" she asked.

"What?"

"Why do you enjoy killing people?"

"What in the baggy sack of Lutigan makes you think that?"

"When we were in Crossoak," she said, holding her hand out for the bottle, "you said that you enjoy it."

"That was a foolish thing to say. You caught me. Yes, I do like killing people. I thought I knew why, that the debt made me like it. But that wasn't true. Nobody makes me like murder, so I'd better just own it. It's who I am."

"Horseshit," she said, but nodded just a little.

"You know some blistering profanity, dear. You know a lot more than that."

"Yes, but I prefer to select my vocabulary for the day so that it includes a single imprecation. Listen to me. I slay men as readily as you, and I would prefer to refrain, but I neither like nor dislike it. Ask yourself what would cause you to feel as I do."

"No, you can't use my own words on me. I know how stupid they were when I said them."

"Ask yourself."

I closed my eyes and tried to imagine what it would be like to only kill when forced to it, to just see it as a regrettable task. That's the way it was when I was young, but I couldn't remember how it felt. "No, can't do it. Maybe when you're old and chewed up like me, you won't be able to do it, either."

"Perhaps. Why are you here?"

"To drink and listen to impertinent questions."

She began tapping my boot, and after about fifteen taps, I felt like I had to say something. "I'm here to kill Denzmen. They're a nation of venomous, crawling whores and scat-faced, baby-crushing murderers."

"Very well. Why am I here?"

"To save the prince."

"That's something to ponder on, isn't it?"

I snorted, mainly because I didn't know what to say. Instead of answering, I drank the last of the wine, which had been hiding an extraordinary amount of sediment in the bottom.

Ella patted my knee, perhaps the most un-amorous gesture I have ever witnessed. She rolled to her feet and said, "Perhaps I shall visit Stan and ask whether they have yet consumed all of their wine."

She'd taken four steps when sudden shouting whipped me out of my self-pity. I heard a horse galloping away.

"Spy!" Ralt yelled. "He's riding off south!"

I was the second one to mount, and I could see the rider ahead. I suppose it made sense that Vintan would leave men behind to hide, observe, and report what they saw. It was just another point on which Vintan had outsmarted me. I kicked my horse, and within a minute, I had pulled ahead of the others.

The spy was forty or fifty lengths ahead of me, and unless his horse was a lot faster than it looked so far, I would catch him within a few minutes. I almost lost sight of him as the trail curved around some trees, and then I did lose sight as he topped a tiny hill and headed down the other side.

I saw it. There was a gigantic invisible sign painted on the side of hill that said Ambush, but I saw it anyway. I reined in my mount as I shouted, "Hold! Stop! We don't want to go over there blind." I heard everyone behind me yelling at their horses to hold up, and I heard a number of unhappy horses.

Desh galloped past me, with no sign of slowing down.

"Desh! Desh, stop! You'll get killed! It's an ambush!" I shouted and screamed at him, but neither he nor his horse responded.

Stan and Ralt rode after him first. "Can't let him die by himself," Ralt said as he passed me. Ella went next, trailing the spare horses, and she didn't even look at me.

I shouted, "Curse you to the fire-farting, muck-tongued, prevaricating, never-to-be-pounded-enough-right-in-their-nuts gods, Desh Younger!" By the time I'd finished saying that, my horse was at full gallop toward whatever fun Desh was about to have.

TWENTY

I may be the world's oldest living sorcerer. I've never met another sorcerer as old as I am now, and I've never heard of one, either. All the ones I knew in my youth are dead, presumed dead, or possibly disintegrated. That last part is a sorcerer joke, but nobody's around to laugh at it these days.

I was born hard to surprise, and I've become good at killing people before they kill me. I can often put myself back together if the man who takes me apart makes a poor job of it. But mainly my durability is due to an improbable amount of luck. I suppose that's redundant. Any amount of luck is improbable. If you have a probable amount of something, then by definition it's the amount you expect everyone to have, and it's not lucky at all. I have wasted a fair number of drunken evenings with other sorcerers speculating on the nature of luck. All we ever concluded was that it's good to have a lot of it.

There's a simple reason why sorcerers tend to die young. We learn best from our failures. A baby learns to walk by falling down over and over. A young sorcerer learns magic just as if he were a baby, except he's given an alligator on a leash before he starts. If you make a critical error when calling up a thunderstorm, you may not be allowed another chance. Few survive being hit by lightning. Except for luck, I would have died in just that way.

Now Desh's alligator was dragging him over a hill into what was probably an ambush. Then that strictly metaphorical alligator would try to bite him in an affable way, roll him under the water, drown him, and save him to metaphorically eat later on. Then it would start on his friends who had just followed him over the crest.

I must have decided to be among those rolled and drowned, because like an idiot, I was also following the boy. In such perilous situations, I usually look for the course of action with the smallest possible chance of me getting killed. That might include running away and leaving everyone else to die. Now I was just following Desh and not looking for any options. It wasn't because of any profound fondness for Desh, or even for Ella, although I liked them both. Nor did I want to throw my life away. I cared. I just didn't care enough to put much work into finding alternatives.

Before I topped the hill, I heard a lot of neighing. In fact, I heard horses screaming, and Ella's horse came running back over the hill toward me. That seemed ominous, so I dismounted just before I reached the hilltop, and I sprinted to the gentle summit.

On the other side, about a dozen horses bucked and ran haphazardly in various states of terror. My companions either lay rolling on the ground or were scrambling to stand. About ten Denzmen were either standing or pushing themselves upright, and most had their weapons drawn. In the precise center of all this havoc, Limnad stood poised as if between striking deathblows.

A lot of things happened in the next brief slice of time, but I only noticed some of them. Limnad landed that deathblow, pulling both arms off a Denzman and then swinging them around like weapons. Desh got on his feet as I ran past him toward Limnad. Somewhere behind me, Ella shouted at Stan to get up. Five soldiers surrounded Limnad, and she drove her fist deep into one's chest. As he collapsed, the other four rushed her. One of them pitched forward onto the ground, and when I looked around, I saw Desh reloading a sling.

One of the attacking soldiers half-dismembered Limnad's leg, and she dropped to the grass screaming. I was near her by then and stabbed that soldier in the back, all the way through his chest —a ridiculous maneuver. I ducked another man's sword and saw Ella chop off his arm. I heard the hollow whack of a sling stone against a skull, pulled my sword free, and got splattered with blood from a Denzman that Limnad had knocked down and decapitated as she lay on the ground.

Ralt was fighting the soldier closest to me. I sliced open that man's throat as I ran past him on my way to shove another Denzman to the ground. I killed that one as he lay there shaking his head and asking me not to do it. Another sling stone struck a skull. Then it was over except for panting, groaning, and receding hoofbeats. All the Denzmen were dead or dying. Limnad lay quiet on the grass, bleeding blue from the hacked leg and from a shoulder wound I hadn't seen her get. Desh pulled off his shirt and knelt over her, staunching her leg wound.

"That was stupid." Desh spared a quick look of exasperation for her, as if she was an ill-behaved child. "You are a stupid spirit. Your stupidity is beyond comprehension. Never do that again."

"You're a perplexing man," Limnad said.

Desh shook his head. "Bib?"

"I'll do all I can." My skill at healing supernatural creatures was at best uncertain. At worst, I might kill her right away.

Limnad said, "An hour will be enough."

The shoulder wound was deep but not fatal. The leg wound was a monstrosity. While Desh held pressure against it, I pulled green cords to tie vessels and then green sheets one after another to wrap the gigantic gap in her leg.

"Limnad!" Desh said after ten minutes. I saw that her eyes had closed.

"Be quiet," she whispered. "I'm regarding my existence."

"Does that mean you're dying?"

"I'm deciding whether I want to exist some more. So be still." A bit later, she said, "Bib, how do you feel?"

I started to joke, but instead I said, "I don't feel like I've been killed."

"That's lucky for you."

Limnad remained quiet for half an hour or so. Her breaths came slower and shallower. Her shoulder wound was closing, but I feared to loosen the bandages and inspect her leg.

When the afternoon was getting along toward evening, Limnad sat straight up. "Thank you, Bib." She looked at Desh. "All right, I'll never do that again."

I unwrapped her leg, and it looked scarred but well healed, while her shoulder looked as if it had never been touched. I sat back as Limnad stood and walked a circle around us.

"I believe that was some of my best work," I said, pushing out my chest. "I wish I knew how I did it."

Desh laughed. "Limnad is mostly spirit, which makes her powerful. And not much of her is flesh, which makes her fragile but also very quick to mend. You did the hard work by keeping her alive that first hour."

"Illuminating. Hell, Desh, by now you're probably the foremost expert on spirits in all the southlands. Maybe in the world, and you two haven't even copulated yet. Well, I don't suppose you have."

Desh shook his head. "No, nothing like that."

"You're welcome," Limnad said, touching Desh on the head. She walked off over the rise and out of sight.

Desh bent, and I accepted his hand up. "Is that spirit sweet talk? You're the expert, son. Educate me."

"No. She was saying that she saved my life and I should be thanking her. Limnad told me she was going to save me from the ambush, and then rushed ahead to get there first. I would have stopped when you warned us and never gone over that hill. But I had to go save her from the ambush that she was saving me from. This may be her way of telling me that if I don't fall in love with her soon, she'll make sure we both get killed."

"Damn. I am glad to no longer be young and susceptible to complicated romances."

"Sure." Desh knelt by a Denzman he'd killed with his sling and began removing the relatively blood-free shirt.

"Desh, I don't want to pry into your dealings with the gods, but if you are willing, I'd like to know what you paid."

He didn't look up. "What do you mean?"

I pointed at his sling lying on the grass. "You didn't have that weapon back at the river. You may have just found it beside a rock, but I doubt it. The gods would admit it looks like something that fell out of a goat with three different diseases. But since you're suddenly a mighty warrior when you hold it, I suspect you made yourself an enchanted sling."

Desh had pulled on his new shirt and was wrapping his horrible magic sling around his waist. He didn't say anything.

I smiled. "You don't really trust me, do you? I'm proud of you, son! You're wise not to trust me. Unless I earn it. Well, if you don't mind—and only if you don't mind—I'm curious about what you paid for the power. As an infinitesimal token of trust, I'll tell you about my last trade."

I didn't want to tell him about my last trade. I didn't want to tell anybody, and I wish I didn't know myself. But I had spent a lot of my power already on healing and rotting various people and things, and I might need more before I was done in the Denz Lands. Any little detail about how the gods had just bargained with Desh might give me a useful advantage.

Desh said, "I don't promise anything, but you can tell me if you like."

"Gorlana traded me four squares. In exchange, she gave me the knowledge that it's not my debt that makes me behave like a bloodthirsty killer who loves murder. I'm just that way all by myself."

"Is that all?"

I had been expecting more of a reaction. At least a little surprise. "That is the knowledge, yes."

Desh shrugged. "I thought that was obvious."

"Obvious how?"

"You seem to hate Harik just a little too much. It's as if you blame him for every bad thing that happens. Wait!"

I stopped and realized that I'd already grasped my sword without thinking about it. I let go and took two steps back.

"See?" Desh said. "Obvious."

"All right. Do you feel you can share?"

"Fingit traded me two squares. In exchange, I will have six nights of horrible nightmares within the next year, on nights of my choosing."

"What was his first offer?"

"That I will accidentally cause the death of the next three women I fall in love with. I suppose that sort of thing is typical of a first offer."

"Sadly, yes. It's that son of a bitch Harik's fault—" I paused, and Desh raised an eyebrow. "I mean, thank you, Desh." It didn't sound like something that would help me, but I couldn't predict the future. Someday, it might be exactly what I needed to know.

Ella walked over and said, "Gentlemen, has your consultation on profound and profane matters concluded?"

"I believe it has, dear," I said.

"Our two devoted but morally questionable gentlemen have collected as many stray mounts as possible. They secured three of our enemies' horses, and Stan discovered this." She held out a ragged piece of parchment. Someone had drawn a simple map in what looked like a hurry.

I peered around Ella's shoulder and pointed. "This is the trail, and this must be the keep we just fought through. This mark may be right where we're standing."

Ella said, "Then this figure farther south suggests a sizable habitation—perhaps a city."

"What's this circle then? And the little drawing?" Desh asked.

The circle rested off the trail to the east, between our location and the city. I examined it for a moment. "That's a horse. My guess—it's a camp where they station horses and supplies. If I were Vintan, I'd at least pause there to resupply, and maybe to rest. We can catch him there."

"Marvelous," Ella said. "It must be a facility of great importance, since we discovered the same map on another horse."

"What?" Desh yelped.

Ella held out another parchment with roughly the same map.

"That sneaky wad of rat excrement," I said. "May Effla break off his dick and Krak give him the runs for a year. These soldiers didn't need two copies of the same map to get back there. They needed two copies to double the chance that we'd find the map. This circle isn't where we'll catch Vintan. This circle is where he plans to kill us when we follow this map to ride in and surprise him."

Ella smiled. "My, that flopping little intestine is a devious fellow. This is sterling information. Bib, how far?"

I said, "Limnad, how far are we behind the Denzmen?"

Limnad walked over the rise and stood beside Desh. "I don't know."

We all paused. "I beg your pardon?"

"I don't know. When they crossed my river, they took water

with them. Now they've drunk the last of that water, so I don't know where they are anymore."

I sighed. "That's all right. We were getting lazy, always depending on you to scout for us. We'll pursue Vintan the regular way. We'll guess where he is, and then be terrified that we guessed wrong."

TWENTY-ONE

"Emphatically not. The idea is idiotic, and you are an idiot. I refuse to endanger the prince by accepting your simplistic and reckless scheme."

Ella did not like my plan. That stung a little since I was once known to be a superior planner, although I was a horrible leader. I had no patience with followers and would rather kill them than listen to them bitch about the crap they thought was important. I was about as inspirational as a rusty anvil. The last time I led an expedition, two men were killed by arrows, two more were struck by lightning, and one was eaten by a crocodile. Only I survived.

Yet whenever we required a plan, everybody would go off to drink and chase women while I planned our next move. I created plans of all sizes, from assaulting castles to sneaking out of bars without paying. And my current plan, which Ella hated, was so simple, clear, and compelling.

Of course, I knew exactly why she despised it. Ella hated Limnad. I had known they weren't on friendly terms. I hadn't known it had boiled into full loathing until this argument began, and Ella called the spirit a "moist, rutting harpy" as she planted herself between her and Desh.

In my plan, Limnad would scout ahead for Vintan's camp, commit it to memory, and bring us her report. It was a wonderful plan. The best part was that Limnad could move around entirely unseen and unheard. Even Ella should have agreed that the Denzmen were unlikely to be alerted by something they couldn't see or hear.

However, Ella continued to object. "We cannot hinge our success upon this gullet-faced bruise on everything that is pure and vital."

"Limnad, please don't kill her," Desh said, his hands out to his sides, palms up.

"Just because you ask, I won't." Water erupted over the spirit, soaking everybody around. "Yet. I'll let the marrow-sucking bitch live. For now."

Ella stepped toward Limnad, wiping at her soaked hair and face. "This whore from hell is merely biding her time. When opportunity presents, she will betray us and destroy us all."

"Ella, please let this go." I reached out to her and snatched my hand back when she glared at me.

"Let 'em keep going," Ralt said. "It's better than listening to you moan about being a killer."

"Don't talk to me about betrayal," Limnad said. "Will you go with Bib when he has sacrificed himself to save your foolish prince? I doubt it very much! You'll leave him to die! While he lies dead, you'll be in some nasty bar drinking whiskey and letting sailors feel between your legs!"

That made everybody stop talking. Limnad had turned a deep, shiny blue, and Ella had gone pale. Apart from being outrageous and profane, Limnad's last observation concerned me. Spirits can sometimes see a little of the future.

I jumped in before the insults resumed. "Ella, as a favor to me, please stop trying to get yourself torn into pieces shaped like unicorns, or something Limnad decides is equally whimsical. And please go along with my plan for now. I know you hate it, but if it fails, then I'll buy you five beers and a kitten when you get home with the prince."

Ella sneered at Limnad, clamped her jaw, nodded once at me, and walked away toward a thicket of trees.

"Limnad, if you would please..." I looked around for the river spirit, but she was already gone.

Resting in the early afternoon seemed unnatural, and I couldn't sleep. No one else slept, either. Desh stood watch, and the soldiers sat near me reminiscing about the worst officers they'd ever served under. Ella came back from the thicket and sat ten feet away from me without talking.

"We make an awfully glum group," I said. "It's like we all just got our hearts broken and will be miserable forever after."

"Right," Ralt said. Stan nodded, and they went back to discussing their most awful memories. Ella just looked away from me.

"Hell, I've seen a hut full of smoked hams livelier than us. We may all die tonight, and I'll be damned if I sit here and have a funeral before I've even been killed. Do any of you know how to juggle, or dance? Have a flute hidden away in your pouch? Anything except reciting poetry."

Stan said, "Ralt can sing songs he's wrote by himself. A person might think that a gloomy-looking turd like him would sing depressing songs, but he can liven up the barracks some, especially if we've all been drinking."

Ella took a deep breath, smiled, and said, "Serenade us, Ralt. I would feel honored to hear you sing. What is the topic of your ballad?"

The rest of Ralt's face was turning red to match his nose.

"Whores," Stan said. "That's his best one. Always cheers everybody up, even when one or two of the lads was killed that day. Best one of all."

Ralt shook his head and mumbled something, but then he stood and cleared his throat. "*Got some money in my pocket—Want to see how much it buys me—If I pay for me, can my mates all play for free?—We washed our willies 'fore we came here.*"

Right away, I recognized the melody as an old lullaby my father used to sing to me, and I sang it to my little girl when she was a baby. Ralt had changed the words, of course, and he sang out strong with real feeling.

He went right into the second verse. "*Want my whores to have some padding—Gives me something to clamp on to—I don't want to fall off a whore and smash my balls—I know they never give no refunds.*"

"*Got no money in my pocket—Whores just laugh at me and kick me—I can tell you, whore, I'll be back to screw some more—Soon as I rob some pasty rich man.*"

Ralt took a tiny bow, and we all applauded, even Desh who'd been listening from thirty paces away.

"Thank you, sir. Miss." Ralt blushed. "I got more songs. I got one about scurvy, and this other one about how when you drink different alcohols, you get different colors of vomit."

"They sound mighty artistic, Ralt, but I don't want to ruin my appreciation of the Whore Song by listening to a different song so soon after." I nodded and caught Ella's eye. She nodded too.

That unwound the tension, and within ten minutes, we all were asleep, except for Desh.

Later in the afternoon, Ella woke me by shaking my shoulder.

"Stop!" I said. "Damn, I was sleeping hard. A bear could have walked in here and eaten me up before I knew it was happening."

"The grasping, predatory deceiver has returned."

I hopped up and faced Limnad. Based on the height of the sun, she had been gone about two hours.

I walked right up to her for her report. "Where is Vintan? What did you find?"

"He is one hour's ride south of here."

"More specifically?"

"He's camping next to a fine stream. It would be a happier stream if the Denzmen didn't throw their rotten food into it."

"What else is nearby?" I asked.

"One hundred and thirteen trees, six of them killed by lightning. Sixty-five rabbits, four foxes, two owls, almost five thousand rats and mice, and a panther that would like to get one of the Denzmen alone one night."

From behind me, Ella coughed.

"Are there any landmarks that would help us find this camp?" I asked.

Limnad said, "The ground is very boggy near the stream, probably the wettest in this part of the forest. Also, there are eleven men, nineteen horses, five dogs, and seven cats in the camp. That is a mix of creatures unique anywhere south of the Blood River."

I started feeling sick. "Limnad, could you take us to this place if we asked?"

"Yes."

"Wonderful! Tell me about the men in this camp."

"They weren't very interesting, except for the sorcerer."

"What was interesting about him?"

She blinked. "He's a sorcerer."

"What was he doing?"

"Walking around."

Ella cut in. "Did you see a boy?"

"Yes, he was walking around with the sorcerer."

"Did he seem well?"

"I guess so. He was sad."

"Do you know why?" I asked. "Did something bad happen?"

"I didn't see anything bad. Maybe the sorcerer made him sad. The sorcerer is sad too."

"What else?"

"What else? Nothing else. That's everything that's important."

"Then... thank you, Limnad."

Ella hissed, "I told you that she would fail us!" She grabbed my sleeve, pulled me around, and shook me hard.

"Leave something for the Denzmen to aim at," I said.

"Be happy I don't grab you by the ear. Your plan failed us. How will you repair this damage?"

And that's how I came to be lying on my belly in boggy soil one hour later, my face full of the smells of stale water and rotting rodents. I whispered, "Thank you, Limnad," knowing that she was close even if I couldn't see her. I crawled a little farther through some brush to a spot between two questionable-looking bushes, and I scanned Vintan's camp.

The place sat in a large square area that Denzmen had cleared in the woods, and it was modest. I could sprint from edge to edge in fewer than fifteen seconds. A rough log stable took up most of one side, with several horses tied up outside it. Four smaller but equally rough log huts lined the camp's opposite side. Their doors stood open, and from what I could see, each hut held three or four cots. Trenches ran around the whole camp, with gaps wide enough to let a horse pass. I couldn't tell how deep they were, but they looked to be eight or ten feet wide.

From my bushy vantage, I saw seven men. If Limnad had counted right, that meant four men were on guard out among the trees. I spotted just one blond ten-year-old boy, and I had every right to think he was the prince, although I have been proven wrong on more obvious assumptions than that. He was sitting on a pile of firewood stacked against one of the huts. He looked healthy, if a little ragged in soldier's clothes far too big for him. Vintan sat next to him, 180 compact pounds of smug, icy bile in a blue doublet that cost more than a soldier would make in ten years.

The prince looked relaxed. He was chatting with Vintan as if the man was his favorite uncle. That would be Uncle Vindictive Ass-Scraping, Child-Beheading Knobby Little Thug to me.

I whispered, "I will see you eat toenails in hell."

"Did you hear that?" said a snuffling man's voice off to my left.

"I don't hear nothing." Another man coughed. "Nothing."

I tried not to breathe or move. I also tried to ignore a sizable bug I felt crawling from my pants leg toward my buttocks.

"Poke around in that bush," Snuffy said. Before I could grasp my sword, the other man began kicking through a bush ten feet away from me.

The bug crawled onto my right cheek. It was far more disturbing than I would have imagined. I concentrated on guessing whether it was a beetle or a grasshopper.

"Probably nothing here," Snuffy said. A chain of coughs answered him.

I started to relax, but then one of the bastards began randomly swinging his sword through the underbrush. He almost took a slice off my forearm. I realized it might be a spider crawling on me, and I hoped it wasn't a venomous one. I wasn't keen on getting bit and having my ass fall off at an inconvenient moment.

The bug initiated a determined foray between my butt cheeks.

More coughing. "There ain't nothing."

"I heard something, you hacking rat's dick!"

More swords swinging through the brush, now farther away from me. I wriggled my butt cheeks to discourage the creature, but that just seemed to make it more excited. I could have jumped up and killed those two fellows, but that would ruin any chance of surprising the camp later. Besides, Vintan might decide I was about to rescue the prince. He'd have to kill the boy to keep his bargain with Harik, and I was too far away to prevent it. Well, if the bug wanted to build a nest in my asshole, I'd deal with that later.

"I guess nothing's here," Snuffy said.

"Told you, brick-brain."

"Leave off, you puling maggot!"

The sounds of footsteps and insults moved away. I waited several torturous minutes, silently apologizing to everyone I'd ever assaulted with insects. Then I crawled away until I was forty paces from camp, and I knelt. I crept another hundred paces until I figured it was safe to drop my trousers.

Grasshopper. At least it wasn't a spider. I decided that when I got back, I'd limit my report to facts about the camp, and I wouldn't reveal that five minutes of the Grasshopper Ass Torture had nearly broken me in ways that hot irons and pliers couldn't. If anybody asked how the mission went, I'd just say, "Fine."

TWENTY-TWO

Our rescue was not a catastrophe. People often call something a catastrophe when they they're describing some lesser misfortune, like a disaster or a fiasco. In my view, a catastrophe causes significant damage to buildings and terrain, and it kills every person and animal present. By these standards, our rescue was merely a debacle, which is almost the same as a catastrophe except that some of the people and animals survive. I have learned to appreciate fine distinctions between many different kinds of ruinous events. It's not a practical skill for most people, but it's common among sorcerers.

During the first five minutes of the rescue, I crept among the trees near Vintan's camp and killed three of his guards. Two dropped in silence, and the third merely squeaked as he died. Another guard or two was probably puttering around, but they were on the other side of the camp, so I didn't care.

The main rescue would begin when I raised a blinding wind. I hoped that if I blinded Vintan, he would hesitate and not just go around disintegrating things at random. Ella, Ralt, and Stan would attack from the north, while I sneaked in from the south. I could see the boy sitting alone by a hut. I would rush to that place, snatch the prince, kill every Denzman within reach, and run like hell. As I ran away from the camp, I'd drop the wind.

Once the wind ceased, Ella and the soldiers would run off north, while Desh and Limnad would attack and knock down a wooden hut or two as a distraction. They'd retreat into the woods, and we'd all meet back north at the spot where we had listened to the Whore Song.

It wasn't a jewel of a plan, but without much in the way of time or resources, I felt fairly cozy about it.

Using both hands, I pulled a white band out of nothing and spun it out to cover the whole camp. This act devoured most of my remaining power, but I held back a tenth of a square for emergencies. I let go of the band, and an immense wind rushed in from the west, picking up dirt, dry leaves, debris, and dead rodent husks. The wind dragged all this detritus into the camp and whirled it through the air to a height of thirty feet. It was near impossible to see anything through it.

As I sprinted through a gap in the trenches, I heard shouting and sword strikes from the north faint over the wind. Ralt bellowed, "Back off, you piddling coward!" I had marked where the prince had been sitting, so I raced toward that spot.

I realized we had real trouble when every bit of crap in the air disappeared at once. I had known Vintan might do this, but it should have been a tricky endeavor that required finesse and a lot more time. He had accomplished it with astounding speed. I arrived at the hut and found no prince sitting there. Kneeling by the wall, I scanned the camp.

A lot of things were happening out there, and none of them looked good. Half a dozen soldiers were charging Ella and the boys, while three ran toward me. Vintan stood between the two groups, holding the prince's hand and looking right at me. He lifted his empty hand like he was about to throw a barrel of poison with scorpions tied to it. That was ridiculous, of course. He'd probably just disintegrate enough dirt beneath my feet to make a hundred-foot-deep pit.

The bastard had been expecting us, then. I didn't have time to wonder how he'd known, because a Denzman ran out of the hut beside me and tried to cut off my head. I stabbed him under the breastbone just as two more Denzmen sprinted out of the same hut. Farther into the camp, three more huts were vomiting soldiers, and a few even rushed out of the stable.

I kicked the dying man into his two just-arriving friends and used the free moment to run away. I ran fifteen feet along the hut wall, and then two soldiers dashed around the corner toward me. I cut hard toward the trench, but two more Denzmen from the stable arrived to block me in. Three more had spilled out of the hut by then. I noticed all this while I blocked a thrust, stabbed a fellow in the neck, ducked, and spun to assess things.

A rending tumult erupted, and splintered timbers hurtled all across the camp as one of the far huts exploded. That would be Limnad and Desh. I had cut a Denzman deep through the thigh and stabbed his friend in the armpit, starting to clear a path I could escape through, when some of these soldiers ran off to see what was happening.

All the soldiers flinched, and one of them looked up at the flying planks. I killed him right away. But not a single one ran off. In fact, some of their buddies charged over to join in. Maybe Vintan had promised a prize to whomever killed me. By that time, I had no idea how many Denzmen were feinting and shuffling all around me. I ducked, grabbed a soldier, slit his throat as I threw him at his friend, and stabbed the stumbling friend in the groin as he went down. The man screamed like someone getting his balls cut in half, and all the Denzmen in front of me hesitated. A couple went pale and shuffled back a step.

This was the time to escape. I roared almost as loudly as the gelded soldier and jumped forward, killing the frightened men with two quick slashes. That left a gap, and I sprinted toward the woods like I could see through it. Then I was on my hands and knees.

Someone had whacked the back of my neck with a rowboat full of anvils, or something similarly weighty, and my sword hand now clutched nothing but damp grass. Blinking hard, I looked up at a Denzman too grim to have had any sex lately. He drew back his foot, and I remember hoping he wouldn't break my jaw since it's one of my best features.

I awoke lying faceup on coarse dirt. My neck and head and face hurt like hell, but the thing that really hurt was seeing Ella and Ralt standing near my feet, bound at the wrists and surrounded by four Denzmen.

I worked up enough spit to talk. "Desh?" I whispered.

Ella gave a tiny shrug but kept her face blank.

"Stan?"

She shrugged again.

I tested my body to see which parts still worked. A problem arose right away. My wrists and hands weren't just tied—they were immobilized. I couldn't twitch even the tiniest joint on my little finger.

"I'm pleased you can still speak," Vintan said from behind me. "And the fact that you failed to steal Pres away... well, that makes me jolly."

"Steal him? You talk like he's something you bought at the chandler's shop."

"Let me help you. It's awful speaking to you down there as if you were scrubbing my jakes."

Vintan seized me under the arms from behind and helped me to my feet using considerable strength. I needed all of it to get upright. Once standing, I swayed a little and swallowed twice to keep from puking. I took a deep breath. "Vintan, I find I'm hungry all of a sudden. When's lunch around here?"

He chuckled. "You do not fail your reputation, Bib. But why should you think you haven't already consumed the last meal of your life?"

I looked around for a moment. The boy stood a couple of steps left of Ella, still wearing the too-huge soldier's clothes. He wore a knife on his belt, which I found unsettling.

I shrugged at Vintan. "If you wanted to kill me today, I would never have woken up." I glanced at my hands, and then I took a hard look. Twine and leather laces covered each hand in a web of tight knots, so tight that they immobilized every finger and thumb, all of which had gone blue. I'd never seen anything like this, and I lifted my hands to show Vintan. "Pretty."

"Endearingly so. I learned it from a Burner years ago. Once bound in this way, a sorcerer is prevented from manipulating magic. He is impotent."

"I haven't felt frolicsome since I woke up, so I guess you're right."

"You're not Harik's favorite anymore, Bib. He wants me to defeat you. He told me you were coming, and when to bring my men back into this camp. In fact, he has informed me of your intentions ever since you crossed the Blue River."

"So, you're not that smart after all. You just rub yourself up and down against Harik's leg for a while, and then he pats your tummy. He took most of my pride, but I never let him take all of it the way you have."

Vintan laughed. "I truly am anguished over what to do with you. I should bring you back to my king. One or two of the things I've accomplished in his name might not entirely please him, and he does adore a sprightly gift."

Ella said, "You needn't bring him anywhere. Release him. I'll make him swear to me that he will withdraw from the Denz Lands forever, if you set him free."

"Why, Governess, I believe that verged on insolence."

The soldier behind Ella raised his hand. The boy threw himself at the man, smashing his shoulder into the leather-armored belly. It forced the man to pause but couldn't have hurt him more than throwing a pine cone from a thousand paces.

"Little shit." The soldier almost sounded bored, as if he was only cursing the boy because it was expected in this type of situation. Then he stiffened and peered downward where the prince's knife pressed snugly against his crotch.

"Ham, remember your manners," Vintan said. "Also, remember what happened to poor Private Donny."

Ham nodded and stepped back. The prince returned to his spot and sheathed the knife, although he kept his hand on it.

"That was a fascinating song and dance, everybody," I said. "Thanks, Your Highness. You're a good man."

Vintan kicked me hard on the shin. I suppressed a few bad words, hoping to make it seem like it hadn't hurt at all while my eyes watered.

"You are a dangerous man, Bib. You're probably the most dangerous man I have ever met, and I have met some terrifying ones. It can be perilous even to talk to you, but of course magic and the sword are the real killers."

"You've taken care of that, Vin. I couldn't hurt you now if you stripped naked, bent over, and handed me a giant ax."

I believed my hands were being near destroyed by Vintan's brutal binding, but that didn't overly worry me. Once I got free, if I could twitch a finger or two, I could heal them.

"I have witnessed many things, Bib."

"No shit?"

"Truly I have. I've seen many fine, wise, brave men and women killed because they hesitated to obliterate a problem right away. They shied away from the overwhelming stroke. The definitive solution. Often, the most artistic solution. They adequately solved the problem, but such half-solutions eventually fail. Their problem invariably returned to fail their lords, and often to kill them."

"Vintan, I have no speck of an idea what in the goat-smacking hell you're blabbering about."

Vintan nodded. "I'll show you." He walked off toward the stable. Two soldiers grabbed my arms and hustled me along after him. Somewhere behind me, Ella was chastising a soldier for his rudeness, so at least she was following along.

They brought me to a low bench on which an anvil had stood, the anvil now on the stable floor beside it. Vintan cut my wrists free, but not each individual hand. The soldiers dragged me to my knees while a third walked over from a pile of firewood holding an ax. They stretched my right arm on the bench and pinned it.

"Wait!" I said.

"No!" Ella said.

"Goddamn!" Ralt said.

Vintan nodded, and in a second, it was done. The ax chopped off my right hand just at the wrist. I didn't feel any pain, but I felt plenty of shock and terror. And a tiny part of me was nodding because it was never surprised by any bad thing that happened.

After I drew a couple of breaths, I looked up. Ella had been screaming, but now she yelled at Vintan. "You nasty clot of nose filth! You cowardly, thwapping maggot! May knives of acid shred every vein in your body! May you eat your own privates for supper each day throughout eternity!"

I wondered how she was going to top that when Vintan cut off my other hand. The soldiers grabbed my left arm, and a few moments later, that hand was gone too.

Vintan raised my head by the hair and examined my face. "Now I can take you to my king, and you won't present any sort of threat." He let go of my hair and walked off.

I didn't get to appreciate any more of Ella's profanity, because I passed out right about then.

TWENTY-THREE

I never expected that such an enormous number of things would become laborious or even impossible once my hands got chopped off. I couldn't hold a spoon or a knife or even a bowl, so eating was a chancy proposition. Dressing became a chore. The first time I wanted to pull off my boots, I just stood there and stared at them for about five minutes. I could carry something if I could get it into my arms, but if I dropped it, I'd have to leave it on the ground, or else kick it along to wherever I was going.

Perhaps Harik had let me keep a bit of dignity, but I lost it all the first time I had to take a shit. None of the soldiers even pretended they might help me. Ralt had disappeared, as if carried away by sparrows. He'd been around a lot of maimed men, so he must have known what was coming. The boy wound up volunteering, not because he liked me at all, but so Ella wouldn't have to do it. I squatted there pretending he didn't exist, and he pretended I didn't exist until the ordeal had finished.

However, in the future, I would be able to say that my ass had been wiped by royalty.

I've suffered worse pain, but the throbbing in hands that no longer existed was mighty disconcerting, and I was moved toward self-pity. Self-pity is unproductive, annoying to others, and unbecoming in a sorcerer. I therefore engaged in a lot of it those first two days. I moped partly because so many effortless tasks had become arduous. But mainly I sulked because I had never suffered insults from anyone, even gods, and now a raccoon could hold up a minnow and mock me with impunity, if it felt I was worth the effort.

I didn't pity myself all the time. Sometimes I snarled at people trying to help me. Occasionally I cursed Vintan, his men, the entire Denz people, each god by name, and myself, plus the ancestries and anatomies of us all.

On one occasion, two days after my dismemberment, I said, "Cassarak's tits and eyeballs!" as a sliver of overcooked rabbit fell out of my mouth. It slid off my crossed leg and landed in the scraggly grass.

"I would apologize, but this morning you bit me," Ella said. "Were I your mother, I might simply allow you to sit on the ground and starve."

"I'm sorry," I said, and I really was. I peered into the grass, but we'd never find the shred of meat by the campfire's light alone.

"Open." She placed another rabbit sliver between my lips, and I pulled it in. "You are more difficult than any of the toddlers for which I have cared. More than all of them *en masse*. Drink?"

"Is it beer?"

"No."

"Screw it."

She pressed the mug to my lips. I drank water and despaired.

His Highness Crown Prince Prestwick appeared from behind me, carrying a heel of black bread. He handed it to Ella. "This is for you. Not him."

I said, "Son, why all the sharp comments? What have I done to you? Hell, I went to a boatload of trouble trying to rescue you."

"You can call me, 'Your Highness.'" The little fart stuck out his pointed chin and looked down his squatty nose at me. Nobody in Glass must have cared whether their monarchs looked handsome. He seemed undergrown for his age, which Ella had put at ten years, and his brown hair had been shaved close, like Vintan's. I saw that rodent-adoring turd of a sorcerer standing beside a fire thirty paces off.

"Yes, Your Highness. What in the name of Lutigan's left nut have I done to you? I chased you across hundreds of miles, barren of even one crappy little place that sells liquor, slew dozens of men who probably had wives and children back home, let myself get nearly smashed to death, and got my goddamn hands whacked off trying to rescue you!"

"And here I am, not one bit rescued. You're not very good at what you do, are you?"

I couldn't help smiling a little. "You're right. Rescuing isn't my regular line of work. I'm sorry if my failings have distressed you. Your Highness."

"Vintan will bring us to his king within two weeks. I never required rescue."

"Tell that to your father and mother, and the fifty men who died chasing you. Your Shitty Little Highness."

"Bib!" Ella said.

I sneered, "Oh, yes, and tell it to your governess, who came near dying several times. My company was all that sustained her."

Pres threw a soft glance at Ella, and then he glared at me, stepping right between us. "None of you should have followed me! Fifty men need not have died!" He sounded like he was holding back some noble, spoon-fed, self-centered tears. "I came here to stop the war."

Ella said, "Kidnapping you and threatening your life are unacceptable methods of achieving peace."

"Vintan did take me, yes, but when he explained, I came with him willingly."

A short period of silence passed before I said, "Well, don't hold onto it like it was gold! Tell us why!"

"You know that Northmen fever is decimating the Denzmen. We, our very own kingdom, are sending the plague into the Denz Lands. We are killing them. On purpose. At least, my father's vile, traitorous nobles are doing it. That is why I came—to speak for my father and promise the Denz king that we will stop them, and to end this war."

"I admit, that's a better reason than getting drunk and whoring around."

Ella said, "That is a noble thing, Pres, and I would experience great pride if I could but pummel some wisdom into you with a club."

"It sounds as if you're saying I did the wrong thing."

"Not the wrong thing," I said. "You trusted Vintan. It was the *foolish* thing. It was the ridiculous, reckless, head-up-the-ass-of-a-diseased-pig thing."

The boy stepped in to loom over me. "I would strike you, if it weren't ignoble to abuse a pathetic cripple."

"Pres, that is beneath your dignity!" Ella stood.

"That's right! Dignity demands that you get cripples drunk and set them free."

"Bib, if you cannot say something to improve the situation, please desist making inflammatory, mirthful comments."

I ignored her. "Your Highness, why are you so in love with that walking clump of gristle and snot?"

"I don't love Vintan. I respect him. He's a wise man, and I trust him."

"He killed dozens of your people, helpless ones, all the way here from your home. Maybe hundreds."

"That's a lie! I never saw him do anything like that."

"He probably pressed ahead with you and left his men behind to kill them," Ella said.

The boy paused. "No. This piece of trash has lied to you about all that. We outpaced the pursuit all the way here."

I said, "Set that aside just a minute then. Vintan has promised to kill you. He made that promise to the God of Death himself."

Pres laughed. "He wouldn't do that. He's my friend."

"Oh, I believe that he's your friend. I wouldn't doubt that he's the best friend you've ever had. But he's still going to kill you."

"Hah! You are a sorcerer, a murderer, and a liar. I don't believe anything you say." The boy walked off toward the campfire.

"All true observations," I said to Ella as she sat cross-legged in front of me again. "He may not be such a poor judge of character after all."

Ella pressed her lips into a line and gestured at me like her hand was a talking sock puppet. "Open."

Seven more days passed, filled with riding, eating, sleeping, and squatting in bushes with the prince. The trail rose, leading us through high meadows, then higher hills, and then mountain valleys. Our horses climbed through cold gusts that smelled brittle enough to snap when they hit us. They slid down from the peaks, which were still snowy even in late spring. Ella begged or stole a blanket for me from somewhere, else I would have frozen to death by the fourth day. The cloak Desh had given had been lost far behind, somewhere along the trail.

We passed dozens of small towns and two sizable cities, built from timber in the lower terrain and from stone in the higher country. Vintan never showed an inclination to stop, converse, or recognize the inhabitants' existence. A man could certainly have purchased beer or even wine in any of them. Although I was too poor to buy a broken whistle, I blamed Vintan for the lost opportunities. Ralt cursed the man in what was a quiet voice by his reckoning, meaning he bitched as loudly as a mean cow. I promised myself I'd employ stark cruelty when I finally killed Vintan.

Yes, despite everything, I expected to kill the man someday. I might have to knock him down and kick him to death, but I had put my mark on him, or at least my metaphorical mark.

On the seventh day, we descended a few thousand feet along a switchback trail around the mountain. At midafternoon, we topped a short rise and arrived at a long, gentle slope that smelled of crisp, growing crops. It rolled to a flatland and then as far as I could see. I felt warm for the first time in days.

An enormous stone castle spread out on the grassland. It covered an area three-quarters of a mile by half a mile—nearly twice as big as Castle Glass, where Pres's father ruled and did kingly things. The outer wall stood fifty feet high, and tall towers pocked it. The gate must have been on the far side since I didn't see it, but I did see the tall, wide stone keep in the center of the castle yard.

That yard could have packed in all the hundreds of people living around the castle. Dozens of modest buildings and a few more impressive ones stood in a rough band around the fortress. Farmland and pastures stretched beyond those buildings in a circle maybe three miles across.

"Kind of makes your father look like the fellow who can't afford to buy drinks for his friends, doesn't it, Your Highness?" I pointed around with my chin at the astounding castle and lands.

"My father has strongholds in all quarters of the kingdom. Clearly the Denz king has concentrated his power at his capital."

We had barely ridden down onto the slope when Vintan turned aside and led us to a small, raw-looking wooden structure beside a robust fire. "Welcome to the Eastern Gateway," he said. "You must pass through it before proceeding to the capital."

Ella said, "I find it grandiose to refer to this rude structure as the 'Eastern Gateway,' or any sort of gateway."

Vintan laughed and leaned back in the saddle. "Your confusion is understandable, although I admit it gives me a chuckle." He pointed at the castle. "That is the Eastern Gateway. The capital lies seven days beyond it." He pointed at the drab hovel beside us. "That is the Separation Chamber. I regret that you will spend the next few days in it until the viscount is satisfied that you aren't infected."

I said, "We're not infected. If we were infected, most of you boys would be dead already."

"You would, in most cases, be correct, but not in this particular instance. Our expedition was formed entirely of men who had already suffered through the fever and survived. It can't hurt us, and we can't pass it to anyone else. All four of you may be ill and currently in the most virulent stage. We wouldn't be able to tell since you Northmen display but mild symptoms. Now, dismount and remove your clothing."

Ralt was on the ground a breath later and fumbling with his laces, no sign of arguing with a man backed by two dozen soldiers. I would have slid off my horse right away. I'd been expecting this command since I heard the word *separation*. But without hands, I wouldn't so much as slide down as I would flop over and tumble onto the grass in the most graceless manner possible. So, I sat still while Ella and Pres stared at the man.

"Pres, my friend, please don't challenge this," Vintan said. "I'm powerless to change it, and you must admit that it follows a sound, if humiliating, logic."

Ella spoke. "Very well. I shall acquiesce. May we be afforded any preservation of our dignity?"

"None at all."

Ella sighed as she and the boy began dismounting. In a few moments, they were both helping me out of the saddle. While Vintan and his soldiers watched, Ella, Ralt, and Pres took off their clothes and threw them onto the fire, even their boots and undergarments. Ralt did the same for me. A soldier issued us woolen robes and brought out manacles, with which they chained our ankles—Ella chained to Pres and Ralt to me.

At last, the Denzmen shooed us into the humble, windowless structure. The dirt floor was five paces long by four paces wide. Light seeped in from between the timbers, revealing a barrel of water, a sack of food, and a bucket in the far corner. The odors of damp, packed earth and unwashed bodies surrounded us. Soldiers barred the door behind us.

Vintan said through the door, "Guards will stand here at all times, but don't bother speaking to them. They know that answering would displease me. I will return in a few days." The sounds of orders, bickering, and creaking saddles filtered in, and then hoofbeats faded down the slope.

I looked around for a moment, and then urged Ralt to shuffle with me over to a wall. I sat against it with my knees up. "I hope you three know some good stories. I've been told I'm the most easily bored man in the western kingdoms."

TWENTY-FOUR

Shared suffering sometimes joins people for life by bonds that red-hot steel can't destroy. My fellow prisoners and I did not respond that way to our confinement. Ralt began cursing Ella for getting us into all this shit. Then he decided that Pres was the real cause of our pain and told the prince that his royal buggering ass wasn't so impressive without all his armies, was he? Pres ignored Ralt and picked away at Ella for being so foolish as to waste even a minute on me. I told the boy to stop whining like a baby pulled off the tit. Ella doted on me at times and then stripped my flesh with accusations, blaming me for every death and failure, including Vintan cutting off my hands. I pestered everyone for stories and jokes and songs, but not even Ralt would sing for us. At one point, Ralt sat with his back to the rest of us while Pres hurled three loaves of hard bread at my face, one after another.

That was the first day of our imprisonment.

That night, I turned over and over on the dirt, trying to find a sleeping position that caused a little less pain in my wrists. At least Ralt didn't snore, an unfathomable fact that I could only attribute to direct intervention by at least three gods. He did fart like an ox on a steep grade, though, which was just as bad.

"Bib?" came a murmur from the other side of the wall.

I sat up. "What?"

"Bib, you're so much better!"

"Limnad?" She was the only being who might tell me I was better after my hands had been chopped off. After she said it, though, I realized I hadn't craved murder so much these past days. I'd been occupied with getting food into my mouth and not falling off my horse. I stood and leaned against the wall to whisper, "Limnad, how do you want us to hide while you rip this building apart?"

By now, everyone else was up and listening.

"Oh, I'm not going to destroy this building."

"How will you get us out?"

"I'm not going to do that, either."

"What? You need to rescue us!"

"That's a tiny bit of a problem. There are fifty-four men with swords hidden just down the slope from here. All of them are awake and waiting to slaughter anyone who tries to set you free. I heard them complaining about it. Most of them are terribly bored."

I shifted my thinking and considered a couple of plans before settling on one. "We'll need to create a diversion to fool the guards into opening the door."

"I'm sorry, but I can't. Desh will insist on helping, and I certainly cannot allow that."

I paused to let myself grasp that. "Where is Desh?"

"He's safe! I put him in a nice, deep cavern until I get back. He wanted to come talk to you, which is crazy. He'd get killed in a minute. He did make me promise we'd rescue you when it's safer."

"You hideous blue trollop!" Ella hauled off to kick the wall with her cotton shoes, stopped midstride, and punched the air in Limnad's direction.

I hissed to silence her. "When do you think that might be?"

"I don't know when exactly. It may be safe enough after you've killed those fifty-four men. So, whenever you kill them."

I let my head fall forward to smack against the wall. "Limnad, will you please take a message to Desh for me?"

"I will. I'll do anything for you, Bib, as long as it doesn't hurt Desh."

"Tell him that he's a sneaky bastard, and we're not going to get out of this by stabbing people. And remind him that an army is coming."

"I'll tell him. Goodbye, Bib."

I turned toward the others, a pointless act since we were all invisible in the darkened hovel. "Don't worry, we're not going to die in here."

"I know," Ralt said. "They're going to take us out in the light before they smash our brains out, you scabby walrus tit."

We didn't quarrel much the next morning, since we were so depressed we could hardly speak. Except for the prince, who spent all morning pacing the two steps his manacles allowed. He muttered about plan after plan for escaping and saving everyone in both kingdoms.

Some time after noon, the door clunked open. "Out! Don't dawdle and don't screw around, or I'll kill you," a soldier said from outside.

We shuffled out into the piercing light, where eight soldiers waited to surround us. A tall young man in a finely trimmed green tunic wrinkled his beak-shaped nose and said, "Hello, I'm Aevan Gart, and I'm here to examine all of you today. And tomorrow, and the day after that most likely, although I can't be certain of that. But we can't be certain of much, can we?" Gart looked so thin the prince could have jumped on him and broken him. "My apologies in advance for any incidental intimacy with your delicate areas, especially you, miss, but I'm known to be thorough, and that's because I am. Come on now." He rubbed behind one ear and beckoned me.

I realized that I had clasped my hands over my groin. I dropped them and said, "If you just tell me what you're looking for, I'll tell you whether I've got it."

Aevan nodded at the soldiers. "I'm known to have a fine sense of humor, but that sort of thing is drawing out this whole experience, and I'm sure you don't want that." Two of the soldiers had pushed me over to him by then. He unwound the lousy bandages on my stumps. Then he pursed his lips and scratched under his tiny chin. "Gods, what a pathetic job, especially on the left one. It looks like a sausage that someone started on, and then decided they didn't want, although the wounds haven't soured, which I find remarkable, really."

I held my breath as he prodded the stumps, whistled, and wrinkled his nose again.

"I will answer you, because prisoners are allowed to be curious, especially about their own fate, which is only natural, I suppose. I'm examining you for signs of Northmen fever. Because, you are a Northman, you see? Raise your arms. The signs are easily missed in a Northman, but I'm the foremost healing expert on the subject, having once met a Northman with the disease. He almost killed me. By giving me the disease, that is—he didn't try to cut my throat or anything like that, although I rather wish he'd done that instead of giving me the fever. It was the most awful experience of my life. Bend over."

I bent.

"Indeed, the symptoms are subtle in the Northman. Flushed skin, slight fever, impaired sense of balance."

"If that's all, why do you need to be down there doing that?"

"I'm known to be thorough. Stand up." He nodded at a

soldier. “Unchain him.” The soldier unlocked the manacle from my ankle. “Look up and close your eyes. Walk straight ahead seven steps.”

I walked.

“Very good! You are free of the fever, at least for today, although we must examine you for a run of four days to be certain. Lean over and let me look in your ear.”

“Because you’re known to be thorough,” I said without changing expression.

“Don’t be snippy. Since I’m examining you, I could do all manner of horrible things that would take years to kill you, so don’t waffle around with me!”

“Shit!” yelled a soldier on my right just before he hit the ground. Ralt had grabbed the man and thrown him down before sprinting up the slope toward the stony hillside, his pale woolen robe hiked up and flapping. The chain dragging from his ankle was a clear handicap, but the rocks were only two hundred paces away.

I threw myself against the closest soldier and knocked him off balance. I jumped on another like a monkey and took him down, smashing his groin with my knee on the way. By the time I looked up, Ralt was fifty paces away with the nearest pursuer thirty paces behind him. None of the soldiers had horses nearby, so Ralt could well make an escape.

Ella was up on her knees watching, with a soldier lying face-down next to her. Pres was rolling back and forth on his back, holding his face with both hands. I pushed myself up, wishing for the millionth time I had hands, and stood. A moment later, a soldier whacked the backs of my legs and knocked me down again.

Two more soldiers had begun chasing Ralt, but they were so far behind they might as well have gone home and had a tea party instead. Just then, another soldier trotted up from behind me and raised a crossbow. I crawled toward him, but he only paused for a second before he fired. The man was a damn good shot. Ralt pitched facedown with a bolt sticking up from his back, and even from eighty paces, I saw that he was writhing.

Soldiers dragged all three of us up and held us against the wall of the hut. Two other soldiers reached Ralt, and one drew his sword.

"Don't! I can heal him!" I immediately stared at my stumps while the nearby soldiers laughed, and one called me a frog-lipped old bastard who wouldn't be wanking himself any time soon.

The soldier with the sword killed Ralt, a single thrust into his back. I could tell that, even from so far off. I'd killed dozens of men exactly that way. Ralt convulsed, twitched twice, and lay still.

Ella didn't seem hurt. Whoever hit Pres might have broken his cheekbone—it was hard to tell. A spectacular bruise was coming up, and blood was filling his right eyeball.

The Denzmen left Ralt lying on the grass while Aevan cursed Ralt for running as he examined Ella and Pres. Once he proclaimed them disease-free, the soldiers locked me back into manacles, one cuff on each ankle.

Before they shoved us back inside, Vintan arrived on horseback. He dismounted and examined the prince's face. "Who did this?"

None of the soldiers spoke, but three of them glanced at one man.

Vintan stood in front of that fellow. "Pall, when did you join my command?"

The soldier was young, probably not even ten years older than Pres. "When we left the East Gateway last winter, sir. I've been with you all the way there and back."

"You're a good man. One of my best." Vintan pointed at Pres. "Was that absolutely required?"

"Well, he was helping the other one get away, but no... I guess not absolutely."

"And you knew that it would displease me, didn't you?"

Pall edged away half a step. "Yes, sir."

"Give me your knife."

As if pushing through honey, the young man drew his knife and presented it.

Vintan snatched the weapon and tossed it to his other hand, then he pointed at Ella and me. "If either of them speaks, kill them at once. Pres, come here." Vintan tripped Pall and knocked him down, pinning him with one knee. "Come on, Pres."

Pres walked to Vintan as smoothly as he could while chained to Ella, who did not want to go at all.

Vintan handed Pres the knife. "My friend, you are a ruler of men. This commoner harmed your royal person. It is true that he was performing his duty as he saw it. Yet he acted such that his commander would disapprove, and he knew it. You are not his prince, so he owes you nothing but courtesy. Pres, kill him with your own strong hand, or grant him mercy. If you become king, you'll make decisions like this every day."

Pall said, "I'm sorry—"

Vintan pressed his forefinger to Pall's lips. "Shhh. Hush, my good boy. Few are permitted to teach a king."

Two soldiers were holding me, one with a shaving-sharp knife pressed to my throat. Even if they had turned me loose, I couldn't think of a damn thing I could do to improve things.

Pres knelt beside Pall and touched the knife's tip to the young man's throat. Pall whimpered and tried to look away, but Vintan held his head with both hands. Pres lifted the knife and swung it down hard, handle-first into Pall's right cheek. Except for panting, Pall didn't move or make a sound.

Pres laid the knife on Pall's chest and walked back to stand beside me at the wall, Ella trailing along by the manacle. She stroked his shoulder from behind as they walked.

Vintan allowed Pall to stand, paced over to Pres, and clapped him on the other shoulder. "That was an interesting choice, my friend. Had you killed him, you might be less an enemy. Had you spared him, you might count him a friend—or an enemy, who knows? As it is, will Pall be the kind of man who is grateful for his life or vengeful over being harmed? That's the charge of a king—judging men. Well, I trust that Aevan's examinations over the next few days will prove far less eventful, won't they?"

After the door had smacked shut behind us and the bar had tamped in place, we kept silent in the almost-darkness. I found the far wall and slid down to sit against it. From beside the barrel, Pres and Ella made the noises of clinking chains, rustling wool, and scraping against wood as they hunkered against the side wall. We all sat for a length of time that would've felt uncomfortable out in the real world, but in this dark hole, none of us cared how many minutes or hours we sat there like mossy old stones.

Ella looked at the dirt floor. "Ralt was correct. I did get him into all this shit. I pursued Vintan as if I were a furious little dog. Had I simply waited for the army in Crossoak, then Ralt and those other fine boys would still be alive. But instead, I gave chase, and did that help Pres even a jot? No. Vintan never intended to hurt him at all."

The prince said, "He was one of my people. He was one of my soldiers, and he had sworn to serve my family unto death. He died trying to save us. Yet I willingly traveled with our enemies, and I befriended them, the men who killed him. Am I a traitor?"

"What was Ralt's wife's name?" I asked.

Neither of them answered.

"Did he really have a wife? Or just a steady whore? What was his favorite drink? Would he loan you money?"

"I don't know any of that," Ella said.

"Fingit's flopping ears! You're not grieving for Ralt. You didn't even really know him. I didn't, either. It's a sad thing he's dead, and I wish he wasn't, but I'm not going to write a song about it.

You're just feeling sad about yourself and your own regrets. That's normal, so go ahead and keep doing that. Just hold the noise down."

They didn't answer me. I wasn't hungry or sleepy, so I pulled my knees up and propped my head on them. In my imagination, I watched Ralt get stabbed in the back and then twitch a few hundred times.

TWENTY-FIVE

I have dallied with a lot of women since my wife died. I don't mean a large number of women—I mean lots and lots. I don't say that to be a braggart. In fact, in recent years, I have felt it to be a bit shameful.

Every one of those women left me. They usually left before a week was up. Some of them told me why they were leaving, and a great number of those said I was too hard to live with. Quite a few took their leave without saying anything, and several robbed me, probably feeling like I owed them for being such an ass. One young lady stabbed me before she fled, confirming that I am remarkably hard to live with.

I didn't mind it when they left. None of them was like my wife.

Ella wasn't like my wife, either. She was a little tougher and a little more softhearted. She was no doubt smarter and better educated than my wife, but she wasn't as funny. My wife's willpower dwarfed Ella's, but then it dwarfed the willpower of everyone I've ever met, so that was no failing on Ella's part. Ella's integrity was as straight as the horizon. My wife's might've had a bobble or two.

I didn't really think about these things until Ella and I were locked up together in that nasty shack, and we spent two nights in whispered conversation when the prince was asleep. Since she was manacled to the boy, we were forced to converse within a few feet of him. But he plunged into the sleep of the young and never wiggled.

Our discussions weren't exactly romantic, although at times we talked about things we'd never choose to laugh about in the tavern. Sometimes we just scratched our curiosity. On the first night, I asked her, "How did you come to spend your days chasing after other people's brats? You could do better."

She paused. "My own children are dead, and I can't have any more. I may as well rear other people's children since I cannot rear my own. I suppose that sounds defeatist."

"I don't think so. I may as well murder people since I can't murder Harik. We're doing the same thing, fundamentally."

She laughed silently. "Perhaps I can do better. If we survive, I might see what's to be done about it."

Other times, we shared our opinions, welcome or not. On the second night, she whispered, "I'll bet people tell you that you're a terrible person."

"It has been said to me on occasion."

"You are."

That stung a little, but I saw it as an honest statement.

"You don't have to be a terrible person. You can change, if you decide to."

"All right. Tomorrow, I'll put on somebody else's shoes and be a good person for the rest of my life."

"No, you'll never be a good person. If you apply yourself, you might not be terrible."

I paused but then decided I'd be damned if she once again left me with nothing to say. "Hell, that's even easier. I'll be done by lunchtime."

She felt for my hand in the dark, hit my stump instead, and I flinched. She patted my forearm. "Don't worry, if you do something terrible, I can twist your ear. It works with almost everyone. You'd be surprised."

The next morning, Aevan poked us and defiled us some more, and then he at last declared us to be healthy and no threat to the Denz kingdom. A soldier unchained us, and another handed us clothing. The clothes were clean, but in terms of style, they were one notch above cutting a hole in a quilt and poking your head through. Vintan and a dozen soldiers escorted us the two miles down to the castle. My feet slipped a little in the plain canvas shoes, but walking in the spring sunlight gratified me more than any of those women I've lived with.

None of the local Denzmen paid particular attention to us. They were too busy carrying bags and bushels into the castle, or herding in sheep, goats, and pigs. They were preparing for a siege, and they weren't dallying about it. We passed through a massive portcullis with an extravagant number of murder holes. Once in the castle yard, we wove through a flood of people and animals bustling in all directions, until we at last reached the broad stone keep. Besides being broad, it was also seventy feet tall.

As we walked in through tall, ironbound doors, I said, "Vintan, are you sure this viscount of yours has time to see us today? If we distract him, he may forget to bring in all the chickens, and I won't have any eggs for my breakfast."

"You are, as is often the case, correct. Not about breakfast, but about the manifold tasks facing the master of this stronghold. Therefore, you will not see him, not for several days. You may rejoice in that. He puts one in mind of a wild hog with poor digestion."

"The disappointment burdens my spirit. I don't wish to cast an emotional gloom over the stronghold. Do you have any diversions, or maybe something to drink?"

"Perhaps later. Since the viscount must send his regrets, you may visit His Majesty, King Moris. He has come to direct the defense and grind the Northmen to bits tinier than pollen. His audience chamber lies just around this corner. Bib, how many kings have granted you an audience?"

I squinted at the ceiling. "Seven. No, eight."

"Oh. Well, I don't know why I should be surprised. At least I may rely upon you to avoid behaving like a lummox." Vintan pushed open an unexceptional wooden door painted the color of deep water. He bowed and sauntered through it, leaving his soldiers to shove the rest of us inside.

I had beheld the audience chambers of eight kings, and five seconds in Moris's chamber told me he was a different sort altogether. By comparison, the damn room was tiny. I could have walked all the way across it in a dozen steps. Moris must not have cared about bludgeoning his visitors with pomp and regalia, because this room sure wasn't going to do it. Twenty or so greasy-smelling lamps provided light that reflected back off the pale wood paneling. The room contained a large desk at one end, numerous chairs, two couches, a motionless guard in each corner, and three middle-aged men crowded about a table piled with papers and maps. I couldn't tell which man was King Moris. They all wore casual clothes, similar in style and well-worn.

I felt like I'd walked into an elderly banker's drawing room.

A gentleman with the biggest nose, baldest head, and skinniest ass of the bunch said, "Vintan. Have you finally brought him?"

"I have, Your Majesty."

"Bring him over here then! I can't tell anything worth a flying damn about him from all the way over there!"

Vintan escorted Crown Prince Prestwick across the room, and the boy gave the baldheaded old fart a precise bow.

"I apologize for bringing you all the way here, Your Highness.

I do, I do. I apologize even more for killing your soldiers while getting you here. Brave men every one, no doubt. A damned creeping shame."

Pres said, "I accept your apology in the spirit in which it was offered, Your Majesty."

The king loomed over Pres like a tree when they stood beside each other. He blinked down at the boy. "Thank you, because I offered it with as sincere a spirit as I could manage. I meant it, meant it a lot. We're dying here, Your Highness. I think you probably know that already, so I'm not telling you anything new, but we're dying. We can't stop this damned-to-all-twelve-gods Northmen fever, and you Northmen keep bringing it to our lands to kill us. Are you doing it on purpose? A lot of my people think you are, and that would be a shame. I don't want to wipe out the men of the North, but if it means the Denz people get to live, then I'll burn every house and drown every baby. So, that is my book on this, my story, right there for you to hear. I want you to know why I took you, and why I'm keeping you."

Pres looked the king in the face. "That's why I'm here, Your Majesty. I came to promise you, on my father's behalf, that no more Northmen will enter your lands through the Kingdom of Glass. I give you my word."

"Well, that is a thing. It certainly is a thing. Is there more?"

"Now that I've promised you this, I will go to my father and tell him about our agreement so he can hold to it. I will leave now, ride to his army, and stop him. Our people need not be at war."

"Well. That's a..." Moris swallowed. "I haven't heard such a thing since my older brother stood before our father and confessed to making me eat a bug off a cow's ass. Noble, really." Moris touched his chest. "Your offer is remarkable. Astounding, really astounding. You are a fine man, Your Highness. I'd be very proud if you were my son. That is no prevarication."

Pres bowed and took a step back, but Vintan laid a hand on his shoulder to stop him.

"It grieves me to my depths," Moris said, "to deny your noble entreaty, son, to my depths and deeper. But I can't know whether your father will honor your promise." Moris held up a hand to silence Pres. "I don't doubt your father's character or his honor, I am not saying that. But I know a thing that not many men besides kings know. Not many at all. Being king does not mean you always get your way. Ever present are men of interest and guile whom the king must feed, feed lest they turn and eat the king, the gods damn their dicks seven times a day. You may not see such men around your father, but trust that they are there."

The king looked away as if examining one of the lamps. "So, I can't accept your brave and noble offer, Your Highness. I'm forced to go with my original plan, so I will hold you hostage until your father stops these incursions, stops them completely, once and for all. I'm sorry to say this, but it is a true thing, son. Your father may be more highly motivated to save his only son's life than he is to save his only son's honor."

Pres looked up at Vintan, who just continued to gaze at the king. Pres looked over his shoulder at Ella and me. All I could do was shrug, which I expect was not as wise or helpful as he wished.

Moris said, "Prince Prestwick, you shall remain here as my guest, and I will provide all the honors and comforts due your station. I hope that your father's love for you will convince him to do the right thing, the right thing for us, the right thing for you, the right thing for everybody. Once he has done it and we know that it is fully done, then you will be returned to your family." He pointed at Ella. "Who is she?"

Vintan said, "She cares for the prince."

"Then she shall care for the prince. Where he goes, she goes." He pointed at me. "Who is he?"

I said, "Boba the Jester, Your Majesty. Great jokes. Wisdom

by the bucketful. Shaky on singing and poetry."

The king raised his eyebrows. "Do you juggle?"

I held up my stumps.

"Ah."

Vintan said, "Your Majesty, this man is Bib the Sorcerer, a famous murderer and scoundrel. He attempted to thwart us several times, until I defeated him. I bring him to you as a gift."

Moris jerked his chin at me. "Those empty places where your hands used to be. Hold them up again. Vintan, did you do that?"

"Your Majesty, he is one of the most dangerous men in the north, perhaps in the world. I wouldn't dare bring him into your presence unless he were... let's say, neutered."

I said, "You're getting kind of personal there, Vin. Watch out, I'm a murderer and a scoundrel. I might beat you to death with these stumps."

Moris said, "Huh. Vintan, you brought me a present, but you mutilated him before you gave him to me? You're such an asshole. How many women and children did you kill for no real purpose at all? The thought makes me queasy, queasy enough to puke. If you weren't the man who gets things done, I might have had you on a gibbet by now and had a little party after. With lutes and dancing. Well, I can't have this sorcerer just wandering around here scaring the kids and the dogs, can I? Put him with the Crows."

"With the crows?" I looked around the room as doubt about these crows hit me. "Who are the crows? Actual crows?"

But the king had leaned over the table again and acted like I wasn't there anymore. Red-faced and shaking, Vintan shoved me into the hallway, and soldiers grabbed my arms. They pulled me along toward a narrow stone stairway.

Vintan said, "The Crows," as if they were something that tasted bad and bit your tongue at the same time. "I had hoped for more, but we do as His Majesty commands. He is usually correct, even if... well, Bib, you will adore the Crows. Just wait."

TWENTY-SIX

When I was a boy, I stole twenty-three pies in two days without getting caught. Finally, my aunt started crying when she looked away for just a moment and the fourth pie she'd baked that day disappeared. Then I confessed, which was stupid. It didn't make her feel better, and everyone in the village despised me. They didn't hate me for pilfering, which was expected of young boys, but for being too good at it.

My father gave me the worst beating of my life. That's remarkable, since I've been tortured three times as an adult, once by a sorcerer. I didn't care what those torturers thought of me, but at ten years old, my father's disappointment hurt worse than any white-hot brand.

He wasn't done with me. He tasked me with cleaning all the boathouses and stables that belonged to my victims, thirteen buildings in all. I found a silver coin in every building. None of the owners had seen the coins before, but they happily took them from me. My father didn't comment.

The next day, I went fishing for mullet with my father, which was normal for us. We pulled in the biggest catch I'd ever seen. We did it again the next day, and the day after that, we made the biggest haul he'd ever seen. We caught unprecedented piles of fish every day for twenty-seven days. None of our neighbors pulled in more than an average catch, and I admit my father puffed up a bit. He wasn't above buying drinks in the tavern and holding forth on all his subtle net-dragging techniques.

On the twenty-eighth day, we netted a normal haul, and that continued for a week. My father didn't scowl. He had convinced himself that I was a lucky charm.

My father dropped all of his fish-selling profits into a pouch he hung from his neck, deep and safe under his shirt and waistcoat. Then we walked three days to the magnificent city of Empter. You could have squeezed a dozen Empters into the castle yard of the Eastern Gateway, but back then, its magnificence astounded me.

Evidently, my father had visited Empter before, because he led me right to a dinky, whitewashed wooden building. Inside, men were throwing dice, and I still don't remember the rules of that game. I know that high totals were better than low. When the turn came around to my father, he rolled a three, the lowest possible score. Everyone laughed except him.

My father tossed thirty-seven threes in a row. Before he finished, two fights started over whether the dice were crooked, but no one could find an imperfection in them. I think he lost every coin. I know he never spoke during the walk home.

A week later, lightning hit our boathouse and burned it to ash. Lightning struck the same spot at the same time every night for the next ten nights. Our neighbors had begun muttering and giving me wry looks. I overheard the priest saying nasty things about me.

My father and I left town again, this time in a different direction, and we walked four days to a remote gaggle of stone buildings. He had brought me to the closest temple for help, or maybe he wanted to leave me there to burn down their shit for a while. The master explained that often a young person's first sign that they are a sorcerer is the utter demolition of the laws of probability. He and my father agreed that until I learned to control this phenomenon, everyone would be safer if I stayed at the temple.

My father gripped my shoulder with his veined, cracked hand and said, "Don't let your feet stay wet. Dry them every night." That was his last advice to me, since I never saw home again.

Vintan's soldiers dragged me up the last step to the keep's top floor, and one of my stumps banged against the stone wall. I considered reaching for that power to gut probability. It's rare for a sorcerer to find that wild power they had as a child. Even if they did find it, they'd be as likely to get something that would destroy them as help them, so few sorcerers ever try, no matter how desperate. I decided against taking the chance.

Vintan unlocked a wooden door in the hallway, and the soldiers pitched me through it. The locked grate shut, and I yelled at the door, "I hope the king kills you, you package of dog knockers!" It was a weak effort, but my stumps had smacked into the stone floor and were starting to throb.

A man asked, "What did you do to the viscount?"

I sat back on my heels to stand. A middle-aged, potbellied fellow with long, gray-brown hair had spoken. He was leaning against one undecorated stone wall of this large square room.

I said, "Nothing. I've never seen the man. Is he ugly?"

"Like a pig's crotch. I am Sir Tobbart, sharing this spartan cell with you. Please do explain why you've been imprisoned. I could say first, but it would be dishonorable."

"I am Bib." Two more men stood on the other side of the room. One was a gargantuan, black-haired young man, staring at me with his hand over his mouth. The other, a red-bearded and shaggy man in his prime, was gazing out the long, barred window and ignoring me. "I've been thrown in here with you fellows because I can't juggle, and I frighten dogs and children."

"Really?" the big man mumbled.

"I'd swear to it, but..." I held up a stump.

The big man nodded. "I'm Glek."

Tobbart said, "Gramercy, sir. The viscount put me here because I stared at his wife's tits too long. I hadn't seen anything posted about the acceptable number of seconds for staring at her tits. The bastard wouldn't specify, either. Just tossed me in here. Glek?"

"I wrote the history of Eastern Gateway," he murmured.

"Something in it the viscount didn't like?"

Glek nodded and cleared his throat. "His family hasn't ruled here twelve generations like he says. Not even four. His grandfather wasn't a soldier, musician, and architect, either." He shook his head. "Sold slaves, burned towns, killed both his brothers. Poisoned the old viscount, drowned the wife and baby..." He trailed off.

I said, "Was Vintan's grandfather slithering around here back then? Maybe he did some of the burning and poisoning."

"Vintan." Glek shuddered.

Tobbart made a peasant sign to ward away evil.

I smiled at them. "Don't worry. I'll kill him soon."

Tobbart looked at my wrists and pursed his lips.

Glek shrugged. "Got to get out first."

I nodded toward the window-gazing man.

Tobbart said, "We don't know who he is or why he's here. Never speaks. He sleeps, eats, exercises, and looks out that window."

"Did he grow that whole beard in here?"

"I don't know that, either. He and his beard were here when I arrived. That was five years ago. And none of the guards knows anything about him, either."

"Well, I'll just jump right on the main question then," I said. "Does anybody ever get out of here?"

Glek nodded.

Tobbart said, "I've seen it happen twice. One dead and one alive. I've only been here five years, you understand."

A grate in the bottom of the door rattled. Someone shoved in four bowls holding some sort of stew that didn't seem repulsive if you didn't look too hard. A chunk of black bread lay in each bowl.

I stopped. If I wanted to get much food inside me, I'd require help. Tobbart seemed friendlier, but maybe Glek was more pliable. I looked around just as Glek punched me in the eye.

I staggered across the room, and then took stock. Glek was winding up for another punch. Two bowls were stashed in the corner behind him, and two still sat on the floor by the grate. Tobbart crouched in another corner with no food.

I dodged Glek's punch as well as the follow-up. My canvas shoes made lousy weapons for kicking. I knocked the dolt's legs out from under him instead. I knelt and aimed my elbow, eager for the crunch of his neck breaking. Instead of killing him, I said, "You nasty slice of ass crust!" and popped him in the throat with my elbow, not too hard. He gagged for a few seconds and began coughing.

"What in the flame-farting hell was that?" I yelled.

"That was marvelous!" Tobbart said. "Maybe you really can kill Vintan. I thought you were just insane."

"Answer me! Speak!"

"Oh, Glek takes all the food for the middle meal each day. Done it for years. I've tried to stop him, but my fighting days are past."

"He can just cut that crap out now," I said. "Serve out the food. If he comes up for another try, I'll see that he's the third one who gets out of here, and not alive."

When Glek sat up, he wasn't punching. He looked down. "Sorry."

"Krak damn your whole manhood, you'd better be sorry!" I nodded at the two bowls in the corner behind him. "There, since

I'm a skinny old thing and you're the size of a catapult, you can have mine once a day, but not the others. Understand?"

He nodded, and some seconds later, he was sitting in a corner eating both portions.

Since I wasn't burdened by any nourishment, I looked out through the barred window. It ran the entire length of the room. I could see a third of the castle yard and even a slice of the world beyond the outer wall.

A less frantic corner of the castle yard snagged my attention. It was off to my right, and my fine eyesight picked out Ella and Pres right away. They were ambling back and forth in the small area, talking. Well, the prince was flinging his hands around like he might be shouting. Ella nodded or shook her head now and then.

"Tobbart, come over here."

"Why?"

"Take off my shoes."

He stared at me for a moment before he bent and pulled off both of my off-white canvas shoes.

"Do you see that little corner with two people in it?" He nodded. "You're going to throw one of those shoes as far toward that corner as you can. When the people look up, you're going to wave the other shoe at them like it was covered with spiders."

"If this is the beginning of an escape plan, I predict it will end in tragedy."

"Then you can write a play about it and be famous. Throw."

Tobbart hurled the shoe an impressive distance considering he hadn't picked up anything heavier than a bowl in five years. However, neither Ella nor Pres saw it.

"I'll try again."

"Wait!"

He heaved the second shoe even farther. Ella's head whipped, and she pointed at the spot where it landed.

"Pull off my shirt! Pull off my shirt! Hurry up, you pokey old bastard! Now wave it at them!"

Both Ella and Pres were scanning the side of the keep. Pres saw the shirt first and pointed. I shoved both arms as far as I could through the bars and waved my stumps around. Ella stared at us for about ten seconds before she made a couple of big, slow nods. They returned to their conversation. Now they were both waving their hands around.

"That's enough, Tobbart, cover up my nakedness, will you? Thanks for helping out, and I'm sorry about calling you a bastard."

"Don't be concerned. Glek has no more than a childish understanding of profanity. It was nice to be insulted in a manly fashion."

Once I was clothed again, I watched Ella and Pres walk for a minute. I hoped they'd get busy planning our escape. I didn't have any ideas better than letting lightning strike the same place eleven times.

TWENTY-SEVEN

I soon understood why the nameless prisoner stared out the window all day. After spending two hours with Tobbart and Glek, I wanted them to fall in a river, or maybe get eaten by pigs. They fought like children about such things as which of the cooks must have made the stew, why Glek's left sleeve was more faded than his right, whether or not they would die if they tried to escape with me, whether Glek had a gray hair, the definition of *extirpate*, and the suspicious nature of Tobbart's bowel movements.

"This room is at the top of the keep and we can look out." Tobbart guided me to the window and told me this during a truce with Glek. "That's why they call us Crows, do you see?"

I took to staring out the window with the Nameless One, trying to ignore the others. Since we lacked both rivers and pigs, I began wishing a stone would fall out of the ceiling and crush one of them. Either one would be fine. I decided not to kill them myself—Tobbart had been feeding me, and I might starve if I pissed one off by killing the other. If the universe decided to smudge one of them out of existence, that would be good enough. If not, well, I'd lived through worse.

The second day passed in a similarly awful fashion. Standing at the window, I whispered to the Nameless One, "Let's trade. I'll hurt both of them a lot if you promise to feed me." I had thought I might get a little grin or something from him, but he never twitched.

The Glass army arrived the next day. I could see a bit of territory beyond the wall, and columns of marching men began filling up that area just after dawn. By the end of the day, they had blossomed into pitched tents and campfires. Tobbart and Glek watched them all day with me, their squabbles forgotten. Glek thought they might rescue us. Tobbart said they'd probably make us slaves.

Our cell contained six pallets that had been worn out by some unascertained number of backsides over the last century or so. The first evening, I kicked one of them over beside the door and slept there. In the morning, I kicked it back to the wall. No one commented. It wasn't notable behavior in a room of transfixed men and suspicious bowel movements.

I slept with my head almost touching the door. On the fourth night, I woke up and heard a whisper, someone in the hallway saying "Bib!" through the grate.

"Ella?" I whispered.

"Were you anticipating another visitor this evening?"

"You're too late. When you didn't show up two days ago, I made a deal with Vintan. I'll marry his ugly sister, and in exchange, she'll feed me and dress me."

"Be serious. A guard may arrive any moment!"

"Darling, I am jailed by my enemies, I've been dismembered, and I'm mashing the side of my face against a sticky, centuries-old floor. That's serious enough."

"Be still and listen! The siege is underway. Moris claims he shall wait within the castle until the besiegers either starve or freeze to death. I worry that the King of Glass has brought an insufficient force. Everyone here expresses faith in certain victory for the Denzmen. I suppose that's normal, but they seem astoundingly confident. I believe we should flee before Pres's father abandons the field. What is your plan?"

That was disappointing. "I'm facing exceptional disadvantages. The worst one is that my knowledge of this castle is tinier than a banker's heart. I wish I knew somebody who could wander around wherever they want. They'd probably know enough by now to have come up with a damned plan."

Ella took a long pause. "I should just leave you in there."

"Who would keep your ego in check?"

"Fine. I deferred to your claim to be a superlative planner, but I see that was mere bluster. I will create a map of the keep and return tomorrow. This cell stands at the loftiest spot, and the stairs are well-traveled. That may be our most significant obstacle. I anticipated a larger presence of soldiers on the lowest floor, but Moris evidently expects his fighting men to be out fighting, or at least preparing to fight."

"That's all helpful knowledge, and thank you."

"I'm going now. I will—"

"You!" yelled a nasal-voiced man. "Stand up there!"

Ella said, "I am so grateful you have arrived, sir. I dropped my necklace—terribly valuable. Could you please help me search?"

"My wife thinks I'm dim, but I'm not that stupid," said a second man, with a gravelly voice.

"All right, you have found me out," Ella said. "My sweetheart and I are to rendezvous here, as it's so quiet and unobtrusive. I admit embarrassment at being discovered."

"Bullshit," said Gravel Voice.

Nasal Voice said, "Anybody who's here is doing something wrong."

"I am profoundly sorry. I will immediately present myself to the captain for whatever punishment he decrees." After a pause,

Ella said, "Remove your hand! The captain will know about this impropriety!"

A slow, deep voice came from down the hall somewhere. "What in Gorlana's flaming slit is going on here?"

Nasal Voice said, "We found this spy, Sergeant."

"I assure you I am not a spy!"

Nasal Voice said, "You got no good reason to be up here, the Glass bastards are besieging us, and you can't lie any better than my baby niece, so you are a goddamn spy. It stands to reason."

"Wait, maybe we should take her to Captain," Gravel Voice said.

"You're right, we will," said the sergeant. "After she answers some questions for me."

"I am governess to Prince Prestwick. I will accompany you to the captain, but you will not lay hands upon me."

"Shut it! Come here!" Nasal Voice said. One of them snorted, and another laughed.

I heard a fist hit a soft spot on a body.

Gravel Voice said, "Bitch! Tit-flopping sow of a whore!"

"Stand aside!" Ella said. Another fist smacked into what sounded like a face, and a man groaned. Another fist pounded, probably a belly since I heard, "Oof!" Two solid punches and a kick came close together, and a body slammed against the door.

Ella said, "Stop!"

Nasal Voice said, "Shut up, you gangly slut!" Another punch.

I hammered the door from my side and yelled at them to stop. After a few more blows, Ella groaned and said something. She started with, "Stop," but I couldn't understand the rest.

They didn't stop. I lifted myself to ask Harik, then Gorlana, then Krak and Fingit and Lutigan to trade with me, just in case there was some way to perform even one feat without hands. They all ignored me. I tried to wreck probability, like I had when I was a boy. All I got was a faint buzzing on the ends of my stumps.

I screamed at the bastards that I'd tear their nasty balls off, that they were ass-scraping, hash-nosed cowards, knobby little turds, that I'd keep them alive to torture forever.

A body thumped against the floor. Ella moaned as they started kicking her. I don't remember just how long that went on, but they kept kicking her until she wasn't whimpering anymore.

Gravel Voice said, "Lost her necklace!" All three of the sons of bitches laughed as they dragged her scraping down the hallway toward the stairs.

I sat with my back against the door. I couldn't remember feeling so helpless since I was a child. Glek and Tobbart had walked over to listen to the fun and now they stared at me, fidgeting.

I stood up. "Boys, I'm getting out of this room. If either of you don't want to help, tell me now. I'll go ahead and kill you and get it out of the way."

Over the next twelve days, we created and then threw away eight escape plans. We produced creative ideas, and Tobbart contributed in unexpectedly inventive ways. But we abandoned every plan because we didn't have a damned thing to work with. Somehow, pallets, bowls, stew, bread, buckets of shit, and clothes proved inadequate materials for an escape. The boys' enthusiasm grew limp a couple of times, but they perked right up when threatened with death.

I kept on sleeping next to the door, hoping that Ella might have recovered enough to walk. I also hoped she had the good sense to stay away from my cell. If she appeared, I wanted to be right there handy to tell her to get the hell out. So, twelve days after Ella's beating, I awoke because someone whispered my name from the grate.

"Get out of here!" I hissed. "Go, and don't come back!"

"Missed you too, Bib." I didn't recognize the man's voice. I peered through the grate, and the speaker had scooted back far enough to show he was wearing a guard's uniform.

"Filth-cracking son of a bitch!" I said. "Brain-damaged, inbred, scabby turd!"

"Fantastic. Limnad told me I don't curse enough to be a sorcerer." The man showed me his wrist, and a nasty-looking length of woven cloth was tied around it. "Fingit showed me how to make this. Lets me look like anybody I've seen."

"Desh! Is Limnad here?"

"No, she refuses to go anyplace where so many stones are joined with other stones."

"All right." I got a grip on my thoughts. "How long will that bracelet last? Do you know?"

"I'm not exactly sure. Another day, at least."

"How's Ella?"

"It was bad. Pres thought she'd die. But she can walk a little now with help, if no one cares how fast she moves. And she can use her right arm fairly well. I think she'll be mostly recovered in three months, maybe four. King Moris imprisoned those guards."

"Good. I was worried about Ella. Tell her I was worried. And when I get those guards away from here... I'm not good at torture, but I know somebody who has mastered the intricacies. I'll just hire him."

"I know that will make her feel snug."

I wondered what kind of trading Desh had been doing with the gods. He seemed calmer and more confident, but also kind of cold. I didn't have time for that chatter, though. "What's the plan?"

"Simple. I know you like simple. I'm a guard, so I'll take the key and let you out. I'll escort you downstairs. Ella and Pres will be waiting in the castle yard. We'll meet them, and then all go out through the sally port into the arms of Pres's father."

"The sally port will be guarded."

"I have three more bracelets."

"What about those three damned-to-Lutigan's-asshole guards? I want to take them with us. I have plans."

"Think, Bib. Calculate the amount of complexity that would add. We might as well all kill each other before we begin. We'll come back for them another time, with our power concentrated."

"Unless Moris executes the bloody skags first."

"Unless that."

"All right, this... sounds like a good plan."

"Why, Bib, did you doubt me? I'm a sorcerer, you know. And a careful one."

"I see that you are. Hell, you're probably better than me. Hey, do you still go around saying magic is a beautiful thing?"

He paused. "I haven't thought about that. No, I don't say that anymore. Be ready tomorrow night."

The next day, with no warning, the Glass army gave up, packed up, and relinquished the field. By sunset, neither a soldier nor a tent remained. That shouldn't have changed the escape plan much, though. Armies travel slowly, and we could catch them. We'd just have to hike farther and stop to rest less. I'd be stealing the first horse I saw for Ella.

The decision about whether to invite my cellmates along for the escape burdened me. They had worked hard on all our inadequate plans, so maybe they deserved to come along. On the other hand, they would cripple our chance of success, especially since Desh hadn't brought disguise bracelets for them too. I told them to take a holiday from escape planning, and I considered the problem throughout the day. In the end, I decided not to take them, since Ella, Desh, and Pres had no chance to express their opinion on the matter. I'd just leave the door unlocked and wish them luck.

After sunset, the lock turned and the door screeched open. A visitor at this time of day was an unprecedented event. Six soldiers rushed into the room, followed by Vintan. Two of them brushed back my cellmates, and four came to grab me. I didn't grab easily, and when the scuffle ended, one was bent over gagging and another had what I surely hoped was a shattered knee. Myself, I gained a few bruises and a stupor-making knot rising on my forehead. The soldiers who could still fight seized me and snapped a sack over my head.

They pulled me out of the room and crashed the door shut. Then they shoved and kicked me through hallways and down stairs, sometimes pulling me over so that my bare feet dragged along the chilly stone floor. I couldn't see a damn thing and lost track of time. The whole journey overwhelmed my sense of surroundings. When they jerked me to a halt, I had no grasp of where I was. I could have been at the keep's front door, standing over the king's bed, or back in the room with Glek and Tobbart.

A squeaky lock turned, and a squeakier door opened. Someone yanked the sack off my head just as Vintan said, "The Crows, indeed. I bring His Majesty a fearsome gift, and he places it in a pleasant cage. At least he may count me as his protector, eh?"

We stood in a hallway. Two of the soldiers carried lanterns, and the hallway melted into blackness in both directions. The door I had heard stood open in front of me, and the light showed just a bit of stone floor through it.

"Bib, I admire you. What a terrible creature you have been. The stories. Rather than allow you to stumble into an ignoble or embarrassing death that would mar your reputation, I've arranged for you to remain here in oblivion. Not forever. Just until you die." Vintan giggled, and the back of my neck quavered. He nodded toward the door, and the soldiers shoved me through it. Before I got upright, they pushed the door closed and turned the lock.

I screamed, "Vintan, you deceitful, depraved slime-licker! You baby-killing bucket of shit! You can't keep me here! I'll heap tortures on you that would make the demons of the underworld look like the baby chicks of the barnyard!" I kept calling him names and threatening him, and I think I made less and less sense as I went on.

About the time I called Vintan a squinty little shit on a flying pike, the lantern light diminished to nothing. My cell was as dark as the inside of any farm animal you might name. Right away, the darkness started squeezing me like a fist. I began breathing fast, and sweat slid down my face.

I forced three deep breaths and pushed out some words. "Well, this is a hell of a note. I got myself into this. I was doing just fine cutting up deserters, but... shit! What an incompetent ass-dragger." Hearing myself talk helped a little, at least for the time being.

TWENTY-EIGHT

A baby doesn't pass out from terror if a skunk-bite crazy man comes running at him with a club. It doesn't know to be afraid. Flames look magical to a tiny child, as much fun as folded clothes, or a pile of dog shit. But sticking your hand in a fire teaches you to be afraid of touching fire. We know that's true because dozens of pompous individuals have made up nearly identical sayings about it.

My teachers explained fear to me because sorcery is scary. It's horrifying to stand motionless while a god shouts at you in a voice like all the volcanoes at the end of time, demanding that you give up the thing you love most, or be destroyed forever. It's acknowledged to be more profoundly, fundamentally terrifying than the mere prospect of drowning or getting your head cut off.

Therefore, my teachers scared the hell out of me, a lot, and for my own good. They took fear apart and illustrated it for me, and I guess they were experts since they wore awfully nice robes and everybody did what they said. They taught me that all fears but three are learned. Man is born afraid of falling, of loud noises, and of being eaten.

I suffered through dozens of cruel and often unnecessary trials to master my fears. For example, to overcome my fear of close spaces, my teachers made me crawl and wriggle through a narrow, near lightless cave by the sea. I suspected they went off drinking and whoring whenever they left me behind to overcome some fearsome challenge, but that may have just been pettiness on my part.

The sea cave trial was ridiculous because back then, you could stuff me in a box and I'd be happy. I did it anyway, and partway through the cave, I got stuck. My belt hung on something, and I couldn't go either direction. Before long, the water started rising, and I became afraid. Then I heard sounds—hundreds of click-clack noises—and I became terrified. I saw a chittering carpet of crabs flowing toward me, and I became paralyzed. The mass smothered me, crabs skitter-stepped all over me, inside my clothes, plastered across my face, pushing into my ears and nose. I could feel their legs like knife points dragging and pricking everywhere. I felt them biting me all over, trying to eat me, and I became hysterical. A little later, I became whatever comes after hysterical.

My teachers dragged me out, patched my dozens of tiny bites, and put me to bed for a week. I recovered just fine. But no encouragement, admonishment, force, or threat of death could convince me to crawl back into that cave. They finally gave up, and we all sort of pretended it never happened.

I came away from that experience with an aversion to tight spaces. Along with it came a roiling terror of being eaten.

Vintan trapped me in that smothering dark cell that smelled of slime and rot, collected his unhinged, arrogant ass, and marched away, leaving my fears to entertain me. Was I entombed a thousand feet under the castle? Well, in my situation, a thousand feet was no worse than ten inches, so I'd just think of it as ten inches. Had I been abandoned, miles away from any other human being?

Maybe, but I doubted I'd like anyone I met down there anyway. Would the ceiling and walls collapse and trap me while I got eaten by spiteful underworld bugs? This last possibility... that was of course the most likely threat, the one I really needed to concentrate on.

I spent my first hours in the cell sweating a lot, thinking through the situation, and screaming once in a while. I kept banging into walls, which forced me to figure out the limits of my new universe.

I could lie down with my toes against one wall and my stumps against the opposite wall. The damp, wooden door felt smooth, rubbed by my predecessors' hands as they tried to shift it. I stumbled into a hole in one corner and nearly broke my leg. From the fetid scent of bowel, I'd be using it for my privy. Some well-wisher had scattered clumps of stale-smelling hay in another corner. I could touch the rough-cut ceiling without straightening my arms.

Most of the things I touched were damp. Everything else was soggy.

Fatigue beat me down at last, and I kicked the nasty hay into a pile and lay on it. My body began to unknot just a bit, and then the feet of some mighty bugs began pricking my legs as they investigated me. A long period of jumping around, hollering, and smacking into walls followed, but at last, I lay down on the bare floor in the other corner and slept.

When you're trapped alone in an empty, lightless stone box, a surprising number of tasks sure would be easier if you had hands. For example, I woke up when an iron grate in the bottom of the door screeched open. Metal then scraped across the stone floor. Later, I would know this was my food and water, but then I found that out by crawling through the darkness and flipping over the unseen food bowl with my elbow. I stuck my left stump into the water bowl. I slowed down, forced my face into the water, and sucked it in. I chose not to lick the gruel off the floor. In later times, I thought back on that and marveled at how wasteful I had been.

I could describe other physical challenges, such as taking down and pulling up my trousers, but I'll hold back such details for now. I did achieve marvelous dexterity with my toes.

After I woke up from my first sleep, I thought more about this shit-stew I was in. I started muttering and growling and yelling at Vintan, calling him everything from rancid maggot puke to the most repulsive unidentified wad ever found in a dead drunkard's crotch. When that didn't blow the cell door down, I examined the biggest opening into the room. The privy-hole was repugnant, but crawling through it seemed a little better than a drawn-out, monotonous death.

I didn't fit. I pulled, squeezed, twisted, and sucked in air, but the hole was smaller than me, and no amount of pounding and screaming would change that. I caught my breath and pretended to stare at the hole while I thought. If I pulled out one of the stones around the hole, or even pulled it loose, I might force myself through. Selecting the most vulnerable stone, I stomped on it until it hurt too much to stand. I sat near it and grabbed on with the bottoms of my feet and my toes, then I twisted, wiggled, and pulled at the thing. I tore my shirt in half and wrapped my stumps so I could push with them to get a better angle. I shouted at the stone and spat on it, but that didn't work, either.

I decided that scraping mortar out of the joints around the stone would weaken it. If I could flatten one of the bowls enough, it would form a scraping edge. I felt around for the food bowl and kicked it almost two feet toward the hole before it was yanked back. A chain tethered the bowl to something on the other side of the grate. I grabbed the chain with my left toes and pressed my right foot against the door, and I hauled. It was like trying to heave a warship out to sea with my toes. I returned to my former strategy of shouting, spitting, and cursing, but it didn't work any better than the first time.

The cell must have incarcerated dozens or maybe hundreds of prisoners before me. I expect that many of them tried to escape. The jailers must have improved things over the years to prevent every type of escape that had ever been attempted. I realized I would have to be cleverer than the most enterprising of all the people who had preceded me.

Well, to hell with them and their mothers and their barnyard animals too. I had that thought four or five times while trying to forget about those bugs that hadn't devoured my flesh yet but would soon, as sure as guts are slippery.

The metal grate had four straight edges that would scratch mortar from a joint, if only I could pull it loose. I grabbed the grate with my toes and pushed against the door with the other foot, then I rocked and twisted the grate with both feet over and over. When my toes hurt too much, I banged against the grate and its hinges with one heel and then with the other, cursing with every blow. Then I started over with my toes. I went back and forth like this until I could feel blood from my toe tips halfway up my foot. I quit then, but I laughed because I had felt the damn thing give, just a little. I was almost certain it had.

By this time, the concept of days and hours was becoming meaningless. Soon, only three measures of time mattered: pretty soon, a long time, and the next meal. I slept, rested my feet until the next meal, and went after the grate again, yanking and banging for as long as I could stand it. Then I rested some more.

I continued to attack that grate until I had eaten eighty-nine times. I kept a close count. I tried to forget about flesh-eating bugs, but that was the longest period of time my sphincters stayed puckered in my life.

During that time, along about the twentieth meal, I realized that my head had begun hurting, just a bit. It was a type of headache known to me, where pain runs from my right eye straight to the back of my skull. It didn't surprise me, but it did motivate me. Whenever I waited too many days to kill someone for Harik, he reminded me with a little headache. After some more days, it became a bigger headache, and it kept getting bigger until I finally got off my ass and killed somebody.

By the time that eighty-ninth meal came along, my headache was damn annoying. I just sat and thought over everything that had happened so far. Then I crawled to the grate and examined it as thoroughly and objectively as I could with my toes. I had not shifted it at all, nor even marred it.

That's when I realized I'd been wasting my effort. Desh was going to save me. I just needed to be patient. He was a smart boy and a fine sorcerer, and he had come to rescue me when I was trapped with the Crows. If I gave him time, he would come find me here and I could rest on my backside until then. My feet hurt worse than Aunt Salli's frog stew on a raw throat.

I waited twenty meals, then forty, then sixty, eating every smidge of gruel and working to stay strong. By then, my headache throbbed up to the top of my skull and dug into my upper teeth. After a hundred meals, I became peeved with Desh. After 120, I began perfecting the sarcastic comments I would say to him when he arrived. At odd times, the headache felt like a knife stabbing me through the eye. My arms and face had begun itching at meal eighty-nine, and pretty soon that had spread to my chest and back. I intended to make Desh feel bad about that too.

I licked 139 bowls of gruel clean while I waited for Desh. After the 139th bowl, I wiped my nose and chin so I could lick the last of the sticky stuff off my bare, nasty forearm. Right away, I started anticipating the next meal. It would be 140, an auspicious number. It would also be 229 meals since I entered the cell, a prime number, which was even better. I ought to do something to celebrate.

I paused for a long moment before I said it out loud. "I ought to do something to celebrate." I chuckled at that, and then I cried until I fell asleep.

I woke up before meal 140 and admitted, just a little, that Desh wasn't coming. Since the day Vintan had chucked me into the cell, I had called to the gods hundreds of times, and they had slapped me down every time. I had quit trying them after meal 181 of my imprisonment. I decided to try again now, and I lifted myself to challenge Harik to a trade. The pain and itching evaporated.

"Murderer, I receive you out of my incomprehensible sense of courtesy, despite the many discourtesies you have dared to show me."

I hadn't expected Harik to accept, and I almost apologized to the bastard by reflex. "Mighty Harik, whenever we've spoken, I have devoted considerable effort to crafting my words. It saddens me that you found them unseemly, you great tub of inarticulate fish heads."

Harik laughed. He almost never laughed. When he laughed, it was never good. "Very well, Murderer, proceed. Ask."

"Although I find myself temporarily disadvantaged, I expect to recover before long." Of course, that was an embarrassingly huge lie. He knew it too, but I had to proclaim that I had balls, even if they were fictitious. "I want to trade for some power. I am pleased to invite you to join in negotiations and to make the first offer."

"Base, repellant fart-sucker."

"Is that an offer? Or a self-portrait?"

"It is an insult. It's the first insult you ever dared say to me. I had hoped you would remember it. I have remembered it."

"I'm pleased to see that it was noteworthy. What about that offer?"

"Ass-kissing haddock. Nasty, corrupting, soul-shitting filth. Slab-fisted, demon-gutting asshole."

"I see."

"Oh, I'm not done. Pillar of bile and body odor. Scat-face bastard. Floppy rodent's dick. Malevolent goat's tit. Craven, gut-munching bastard. Nasty, pig-screwing monster. Cheap paper god with half-assed village juggler powers. Those are some of my favorites. Would you like to say anything?"

"Well... since they're so good, maybe you could give me a discount."

"Goodbye, Murderer. You no longer mean anything."

Harik hurled me back into my body with crushing force.

I tried Gorlana, but she ignored me. I even tried Krak, but to him maybe I wasn't worth noticing. I tried Fingit. I gritted my teeth and tried Lutigan. Then I tried Cassarak and Trutch and all the other twelve gods. None would even stoop to speak with me.

I sat down on the floor, and then I lay down on it. When food came, I ignored it. Instead, I slept. I woke for a moment the next time the grate screeched open, rubbed my stumps against my itching chest and face for a while, and went back to sleep. The next time I woke, I ate and drank, and then I lay down to sleep beside the door so I wouldn't have to crawl far when food came.

I stopped keeping count of the times I ate, but I kept living this way for what I would have said was "a long time." Looking back, it must've been around three hundred meals. By the time I'd eaten fifty or sixty of them, my entire body was itching, which distracted me from the knives and spikes in my head.

Some time after that, the nausea started. It was barely noticeable at first among the scratching and the knives, but within another fifty meals or so, I had trouble keeping the gruel from jumping back out of my stomach. I didn't see how it could get much worse.

Another hundred meals went by, and then a strip of skin fell off my leg. More meals passed while strips and patches of skin kept dropping off me. I sported two dozen raw places by the time I stopped counting, with more skin falling loose all the time.

After one meal identical to hundreds of others, I lay my head against the cool stone, rubbing my stumps around the dozens of raw places and swallowing a lot to keep my meal down. I noticed that the spiteful underworld bugs were crawling on me, and I didn't mind. Hell, they were almost like friends now. I snatched one up with my toes and thought, "This is my life."

Being a sorcerer had been my life. Being a father had been my life. Killing people had been my life. Now *this* was my life. What would my life be next? I laughed, and the sound shocked me. "You damned idiot. Next, being a corpse will be your life, and after that, being supper for your friends, the bugs."

It seemed petty of the bugs to eat me, since I hadn't eaten them, although I could have. I hadn't refrained because of a delicate palate, either. I had eaten things that made bugs taste like biscuits. It would have been smart to eat them, if nothing else for variety.

I gazed at the bug in my toes, although it was a hypothetical gaze in the darkness. The bug wiggled and tried to run, but I could feel that it wasn't the tiniest bit hurt. I rolled the bug on its back, like a magician with a coin between his fingers. I dropped it, and I assume it ran off to tell its friends I was crazy and would be ready to eat soon.

I jerked up straight and stared toward my feet. After a few deep breaths, I spread my toes and pulled with them. Something in the nothingness pulled back.

I eased down to lie on my back and took slow breaths for a minute as I contemplated what had just happened. If there had ever been a time when it was important for me not to be stupid, this was it. I had saved only a sliver of power when Vintan kicked the crap out of us at his camp. If I used it all now to break out of the cell, the guards could just grab handless Bib and throw him right back in.

At last, I sat up again and used my left toes to pull a single green band out of the air. With the same toes, I drew bones and flesh from my right stump. A minute later, on the end of my right arm, I had something that was not a hand. Or, it could be called a hand if you accepted that hands were created out of clay by four-year-olds. I had just three awful digits, a thumb and two fingers, but they could push, hold, slap, and punch, if you weren't too particular about defining those actions.

I pulled a blue band from the air with my new thing-that-might-be-considered-a-hand, and I pushed against the door near the top hinge. The wood around it rotted, and the rot spread to the other hinges. I used the last particles of power to rot the whole edge of the door.

Using my new hand to mark my target, I stepped back and threw my bare shoulder against the door. If doors could laugh at people, this one would've laughed at me. I shifted my aim and threw myself again, but nothing moved. I aimed again, and this time, I bounced off, but something in the door gave a tiny squeak. Breathing fast, I hit that spot over and over until both shoulders hurt like hell, but eventually I heard the door shift every time I hit it. About the millionth time I smashed the door, it shrieked its death cry and toppled into the hallway. The crash echoed like the clash of all the gods' weapons since the beginning of time.

When emotional, I am given to poetic exaggeration.

Unarmed, half-naked, barefoot, part-flayed, and caked in unthinkable filth, I trotted up the hallway in the direction Vintan had taken the day he stuck me in that rat-gagging cell. I trailed my new hand along the wall so I didn't bang into it in the pure darkness. Pretty soon I saw a speck of dimness that grew into a brain-shredding spear of light. Somebody, probably a guard, was ambling around up near that light. His footsteps traveled to me with a bit of an echo, but they lacked vigor. He might be dressing, or getting another beer. He might be assessing different spots he could use to jump out and cut an escaping prisoner in half.

I knelt to wait for my eyes to adjust. Experience has shown me it's far easier to kill people when you can see them.

TWENTY-NINE

Nobody has ever paid me to do magic. I guess I could have charged people to mend their bones and cure their children, or to make frogs rain on their nasty neighbors. I know they would have paid, and it wouldn't have been wrong of them. But magic doesn't really belong in this world. It's a mistake, like a beetle that falls into the cake batter. I'm convinced of this. In no other part of existence can things be created out of nothing.

Some wise and generous sorcerers have disagreed with me on that. They were ass-flapping idiots, and I told some of them so to their faces.

If a man pays for something, he has a right to it. But it's not healthy for any man to think he has a right to something that shouldn't even exist. Not even sorcerers have a right to magic. They have to give pieces of themselves away for it. I therefore decided that no one has a right to anything, and I trust my judgment on whom to help or hurt with magic.

Some wise and generous sorcerers have called me an arrogant fool who behaves like he's as wise as any god, and their arguments have merit.

Since even sorcerers need to eat, and to drink hard beverages, I have worked at several trades. My father taught me to be a fisherman, but I hate being wet, cold, tired, and always one slip away from drowning. After I left sorcery training, I took a job in a stable, where I shoveled a mountain of horse shit. I also freely cured, blessed, and otherwise helped the people of a dozen nearby villages. A year later, I could train and ride horses like a demon, and the people of a dozen villages wanted to kill me because their lives weren't perfect and I wouldn't fix it. I employed my new riding skills to flee on a stolen horse. Those people hated me so much they chased me all the way to a different continent.

A blacksmith took me as his apprentice. I hated the work and was a lousy apprentice, but that was fine since he was a lousy blacksmith. During my lousy blacksmithing days, I helped people or let them suffer or sometimes made them suffer, as seemed right to me. I'm sure I often made bad choices, but entire villages never tried to murder me, either.

After I spent a few years working for the blacksmith, he got drunk one night, fell in the gutter, and drowned in six inches of water. Since no sane person would hire me as a blacksmith, I spent a lot of time drinking. Then a tavern keeper hired me to run off some threatening drunks, and before long, I was solving problems for men with plenty of money but little skill in physical persuasion. I met, worked with, and, in some cases, killed many colorful folks in the same business as me. Most liked having me around, since stabbings were common. I felt we were doing good work, helping potentates and people of means, but in hindsight, they were just slightly better than the criminals we caught or killed for them.

I did that work for years, up until I began working as a murderer.

Back in my cell, before I had bashed down the door, I had

wondered whether I might be able to take up a different trade now. But as I crept up out of that dark prison hallway toward a lighted room, I knew that killing people would be my soundest strategy. I wouldn't get past any guards by buying them drinks and telling them they had pretty hair.

I rushed into the small watch room and met a flat-footed, empty-handed guard who gaped at me. Although imprisonment had weakened me, I smashed him against the wall twice and stomped him when he fell. I stripped off his shirt, which was soft and embroidered, and wriggled into it. I left the boots. There was no chance of pulling them on with no hands and just one claw.

I swung the man's sword to feel the balance, which was adequate. My grip, however, was poor. Any fine blade work would be a chancy proposition. I wanted to slice the guard's throat. All of my physical outrages, the headache and itching and nausea, would disappear when I killed this man for Harik. But I found that I might not mind holding off killing him for now, or maybe even never killing him at all.

It wasn't exactly the right time for evaluating moral choices. With a sliver of regret and a barrelful of relief, I slashed his throat. Blood sprayed almost to the ceiling. I closed my eyes and let the suffering drift away, like dirt in a warm bath. I didn't even mind the dozens of skinless places on my body, or the weakness that months of lying on a stone floor had endowed me with.

The room opened onto a wider, better-lit hallway with nicer cells for more important prisoners. I assumed that to be true. The cell doors were far newer and cleaner than mine had felt, anyway. I trotted up the passage until I heard two voices from an open door. I was clumsy and tired, so I'd probably fail if I tried to sneak in. I wasn't sure I could take them both at the same time with a screaming assault. So, I just strolled through the doorway into the watch room as if I'd been there a thousand times. Two guards glanced at my shirt for a moment. Then one of them went back to sharpening his knife. The other squinted at me and cocked his head. I killed them both. It felt good, and I didn't have any doubts or confusion about whether to let people live.

Beyond this room, a stairway led up, which heartened me. I climbed eleven flights of stone steps in the torchlit stairwell, and at the top, a short passage ended in a solid wooden door. Loud but indistinct voices bounced against the other side of the door, along with laughter and some shouting. I listened for as long as I dared before retreating back to the stairway.

At least five men stood, sat, or played grab-ass just beyond that door. Maybe more. They were probably guards and not Moris's finest fighters. But even at my best, with the strongest arm and the biggest balls, killing four active, competent men would be a challenge, and then only with tactical advantages like surprise or magic. Killing five men would require some fine luck. Killing six would be ridiculous.

I was so far beneath my best that I didn't remember how it looked or felt. Instigating an arduous sword fight without even one proper hand would be fatal. I might as well kick a bear in the nuts and lie down to show my belly. I'd rather get stabbed twice through every organ than go back to that cell, but that wasn't my preferred outcome. I'd prefer to kill everybody in sight and then saunter out of the room.

Every god had denied me those past months, but then I had been just a mutilated blob waiting to die. Now that I was making plans and dealing death again, things might be different. I considered my choices and then lifted myself to call for Gorlana.

"Murderer, what have you done to yourself? It's just repugnant. What woman would allow you to touch her with that nightmarish appendage? A prostitute would charge you triple just to hold her hand."

"Mighty Gorlana, I've missed you. I hear more music in your

voice than usual. Has something bad happened to Harik, or Cassarak? Has it caused you joy?"

"Oh, be still! I was just positive that you were dead. But since Harik has lost interest in you, you are common property. I'm free to demand that you tell me just when in the name of Weldt's third penis you will start making that bitch of a river spirit suffer."

I had forgotten that I'd implied to the goddess that Limnad would endure some sort of anguish at my hand. "Oh, the plan is progressing just fine. The Nub made her fall in love with him so he can break the shit out of her heart. It may take a long time, but the longer he waits, the more she'll suffer."

She pouted like a five-year-old girl. "I'm skeptical. No, that's not true. I know you are lying to me, you flip-brain dolt. But today you've returned from the dead, and as a gift, I'll set the subject aside." The goddess Gorlana applauded herself. "But we will talk about it later. I have an excellent memory, godlike as you know. Now, what do you want? And please be brief. My soup and my dinner companion are getting cold."

"I want power, and I'm open on the terms of payment. Fairly open. I ask that you make me an offer."

"All right, I've been thinking about this as we talked, since talking to a simple creature like yourself requires nearly no concentration. I'll offer you one square, and in exchange, you will overthrow King Moris and put his cousin Skek on the throne."

One square was just about what I'd need to fully restore both my hands, but I had hoped for more. "With respect, you must think I'm stupider than Lutigan. Three squares, and in exchange, I'll make every horse in this stronghold hate Moris. And piss on him when he walks by."

"Sad. It hurts me to see how much less interesting you've become. One square, and in exchange, Ella and Prestwick will forget everything they know about you."

I laughed. "Mighty Gorlana, that tattered offer insults the

memory of our past trades. Two squares, and I will teach Crown Prince Prestwick, future King of Glass, the full cycle of poems in the Miraculous Feats and Adventures of the Radiant Goddess Gorlana. You know, lie to the boy."

"It does appeal to me, but I can see you're trying to play on my vanity, as if I were a flighty girl you could flip onto her back. One square, and in exchange, I take Ella from you."

"Take? Just so there won't be any misunderstanding on this point, you would not kill her, correct?"

"You're correct, Murderer. I see that you believe you have a future with her. Maybe you do, maybe you don't, maybe you do but will wish you hadn't. You don't know. When I say I will take her from you, that means you give up any future with her. You agree that I can take it from you."

I swallowed and clenched my fists before I remembered that she could see me. "Unacceptable. Two squares—"

"That is the offer. It's the only offer, darling Murderer. I can tell what she means to you. You can't hide these little things from me, you know. I am Gorlana."

"I'll kill Moris."

"Oh, no, I don't think so."

"I'll kill Moris and dump his body in his bedchamber back home."

"No."

"I won't dump it. Instead, I'll kill his wife and brothers and sisters and arrange the whole fornicating lot of them around the bedchamber like they were having a little party."

"Think not."

"How many people do you want me to kill? Or do you want me to save people? Name something else you want me to do."

"There is nothing else. I know you'll die if you refuse. Don't deny it, you'll look silly. Sillier."

I reconsidered whether my claw and I had a chance against

those men behind the door. The answer was no, and not much reconsideration was needed. Would Ella and Pres be all right even if I got hacked apart? As long as nobody came close to rescuing Pres, he'd be safe from Vintan, and she'd be safe with Pres. But someday, that paranoid son of a dripping whore would think rescue was coming, as sure as pigs have gristle. Then he'd kill the boy and probably kill Ella too. It might not happen for years, or maybe it would happen next week.

I ran through it again. To protect Ella, I needed to live long enough to kill Vintan, and to get to him, I needed to fight my way through this room. I needed hands to fight, and I needed Gorlana's power to fix my hands. That was the logic, straight through from beginning to end.

I said, "I hate you."

"Then everything is going along just fine."

"I want something more. Something besides power. Something no other god is wise enough to give me."

"Well, you certainly have my interest."

"Gorlana, Goddess of Mercy, Healer of All Bodies and Hearts, I want a cure for the Northmen fever."

The goddess pointed at me and giggled. "That's silly. You already know how to cure it."

"I want a cure any man can make, even someone who's not a sorcerer. A cure that's simple to mix and made from things that are common and easy to find."

"That would create an awful precedent! Non-sorcerers curing people? Think of something else."

"No, if you're just offering one square, then we have no deal. Offer me one square and the cure, and I'll agree to your terms."

"What has Harik done to you? You were never this difficult when you belonged to me. Very well, we are agreed. Murderer, you have become almost interesting again. I rather hope you don't die right away."

Gorlana eased me back into my body. She always was considerate that way. She was a marrow-sucking bitch in all other ways.

I used the claw on my right arm to create an identical claw on my left. Then I used the left claw to expand the right one into a perfectly formed and functional hand. I almost went ahead and finished healing the left hand, but instead, I decided to keep the energy for emergencies.

With a perfect right hand for my sword, and a malformed left claw for the door latch, I shoved open the door and rushed through it. I marked six men in the room, but four of them were sitting around a table holding bottles, mugs, and food. I lunged toward the closest standing man without thinking about how weak I was now. I fell short, and he almost killed me, which would have been a poor showing on my part. My next cut disabled him, and I killed two men from behind before they could get up and around their chairs.

The fellow across the table from me was unarmed, and he began flinging bottles at me. I dodged twice on my way around to slicing most of the way through his arm. The last two men struck at me from opposite sides. I killed one and twisted so that the other pierced me in my shoulder instead of my chest. I cut his throat before he pulled his sword out of the wound.

I was panting a lot heavier than was reasonable, thanks to my months in that cell. I listened for the best part of a minute, but no one appeared to have heard us. I patched my wound, congratulating myself for holding back some energy. Then I picked up a helmet, a pair of boots, and a better sword.

I stared at the two moaning, wounded men and wavered. One of them was sitting against a wall, and he shifted to stand up. I shoved him back down with my boot and touched his ear with my sword's point. I traced a line all the way around his throat to the other ear, never drawing blood.

"Do you promise to be nice to your kids? And your wife, and... to dogs?"

He looked at me as if I were a troll about to tear off his head and drink his brains. "I'm not married."

If he was too stupid to lie in this situation, he was too stupid to live. I pressed my sword against his throat.

"I have a dog! I'll be nice to it! Don't kill me!"

I wanted to kill him, but of course he was helpless and it would be good not to. It was nice to have a reason not to slice open his throat. It made things a little easier. "You just got mighty lucky, son. Think about doing something remarkable with your life. Don't be a fisherman, or a drunk who dies of syphilis."

The man's comrade lay moaning near the far door. I stabbed him in the heart before I even wondered whether I should spare him. I stuck my head through the door into one of the main hallways on the keep's ground floor. The design looked familiar. I had seen it during my battering journey from the audience chamber up to the Crows.

I would have loved to sneak through the keep right to wherever Ella and Pres were standing at just that moment, gather them up, and lead them off to safety without being seen by anybody. Unfortunately, I didn't know where they were, I was never that stealthy to start with, and I smelled worse than a yak's asshole. My chances for success were poor, and I had already decided not to attempt such a plan.

However, I did know how to get to Moris's audience chamber, at least in principle. The hallway seemed sparsely traveled, so I pulled my helmet low and sheathed my sword. I strode down the passage toward the left, hoping to find something that looked familiar before anyone either looked closely or smelled me. Soon I spotted the stairway leading up to the Crows and knew where I was. I expect my success was due to my abnormally good luck rather than any skill on my part, because I had mostly been wandering the halls and hoping for the best.

Two soldiers stood sentry outside the audience chamber. I drew my sword and held it behind me as I strolled up to the closest soldier. Presenting the weapon's hilt to him, I said, "Please tell His Majesty that the most dangerous man in the world would like to chat."

THIRTY

I guess Moris took this "most dangerous man in the world" bullshit seriously. A guard captain bound my wrists and told me I was going to the Red Room, so named for the blood of all the criminals and traitors who had been executed in it. He and three guards escorted me up one floor and into a modest room that was empty except for wooden benches along two walls.

"Hold him here," the captain said. "He's supposed to be dangerous, so don't screw around." He slammed the wooden door behind him when he left.

I looked at the three men guarding me. "Anyone get laid recently? Tell us what it's like, I can't remember."

One of the guards grinned, but another whacked his arm. Discipline restored, they stared at me like I might burst into flames if they wavered.

A few minutes later, the door opened again, but instead of the captain, Ella and Pres walked in unescorted. Pres even wore a sword, which I suppose showed how much Moris trusted him. They both stared until finally Ella ran toward me. One of the guards stepped out to snatch her. She left him on the floor gagging and holding his throat, and then she flung herself to embrace me.

I knew Ella was strong, but it still surprised me when a couple of my joints popped. I almost hugged her back, but I didn't want to test my bonds yet. I opened my mouth to say something that would surely have been stupid, but she kissed me before I made a sound. That went on for a while, and I wondered whether Gorlana might've been joking about giving Ella up.

Ella grabbed both sides of my head and smiled like a maniac. "I thought you were dead!"

"No. Harik showed up to claim me, took a whiff, and told me I was too nasty for hell."

"Yes, you smell repugnant! Like a dead beggar's armpit!" She gave me another long kiss. "Don't die anymore!"

Pres had stepped between Ella and the other guards, hand on his sword like he meant to cut off their balls and make a necklace. The guards kept back a couple of steps.

Ella took a breath and kissed me some more. I figured kissing her back would be more rewarding than telling her I didn't plan to die anymore. When we stopped again for air, she leaned back and said, "I want to know everything, but not now. Things have occurred."

"I didn't expect that the world froze in place just because I was farting around in jail."

"Prestwick's father perished during the siege. More properly, his horse kicked him to death. The next day, his cousin lifted the siege and returned home."

"I guess Pres's life didn't matter so much to his cousin. He probably prefers a dead Crown Prince."

"I always hated him," Pres said. He'd grown at least three inches. "He used to grab my ear and shake me while he laughed, like it was the best joke ever told. I'm off to kill him as soon as I can steal some horses and food."

Ella nodded. "King Moris has awarded Pres asylum on the

condition that he remain here. Moris intends to march on Glass when clement weather returns. He says he will put the entire kingdom to the torch."

"Like hell he will," Pres said.

"Ella, how long have I been gone?"

"You disappeared last spring, and winter is fading now. Most of a year. The fever has destroyed uncounted Denzmen this winter."

I might have told her I was going to fix all that, and that it would make me so damn heroic she should prepare to start loving me even more. Then I reminded myself that Gorlana had made me give Ella up for that cure.

I leaned in to whisper in her ear, "Where are the guards who beat you? I want them."

"Since they didn't kill me, Moris declined to execute them. He imprisoned them for six months."

"I'll take care of that."

"They're beyond your reach. All three expired within a month of their release. On different nights. Stabbed to death in perilous, isolated locations. Terribly sad."

I kissed her neck and smiled.

Ella leaned back to see my face. "Vintan professed ignorance about your disappearance. I felt certain he'd murdered you."

"He came near to it."

"The king ennobled him. The viscount perished in a fall from the battlements, and Moris made Vintan viscount of the Eastern Gateway as reward for kidnapping Pres."

"I doubt the viscount fell. Nor would it surprise me if Vintan paid the horse to kick Pres's father."

The captain returned to our waiting room, and he narrowed his eyes at everyone, especially the guard massaging his throat. "Step back there," he said to Ella, waving her away. Instead of stepping back, she gave me another long kiss and then joined Pres. The captain shook his head. "Bring them."

After a brief march down the hallway, the captain opened a beautifully detailed brass door. Two guards shoved me into a room big enough for a village dance. I assumed it was the Red Room, since red tapestries hung everywhere and I stumbled on one of the red rugs that dotted the floor like ticks.

"Don't abuse the man, not at all," Moris said, sitting on a hard-looking raised chair across the room. "This most dangerous man in the world may slaughter every one of us, maybe with his feet, who knows?"

"I'd never do such a thing, Your Majesty. I have a bunion. It would hurt worse than my first love breaking my heart."

Four guards escorted me to the middle of the room. Two more directed Ella and Pres to the side and then went to stand at a side door, while two guards flanked the main door. Ten big guards wearing scowls formed a half-circle in front of the king.

Moris said, "Still, no call to antagonize you. Hold up your hands. Higher. Too high. Now, when I saw you last, you were less two hands—that is, Viscount Vintan had whacked them off, which was rude, but it's finished now. Finished. Or not. Not, I'd say. You seem to have grown back a hand and a half."

"It was boring in your dungeon. I had to pass the time somehow."

"Put your arms down. You look like you might fall over. For a dangerous man, you certainly try hard to be funny, which I guess you are a little bit, but none of the dangerous men I've met could tell a joke worth a damn. Not funny, definitively not. And I've met a lot of them, but then, most weren't sorcerers like you, Bib the Sorcerer. I guess you can be funny and slay armies at the same time, assuming you want to do that. You might. Perhaps I should kill you right now, but it seems hasty and also rude. By Krak it would be rude, wouldn't it? Although I guess Krak is as rude as any being in existence, but who would say it to his face?"

The guard captain whispered something to Moris. The king pointed at Ella and said, "Governess, I approve of love—I like it myself. It's even acceptable just before the dying happens—maybe that's the best time for it, really. It's nice that you can see this man while he lives, even for a few minutes, at least that much. Governess, do please stay there beside His Highness, stay there, and don't dart around smashing any of my guards in the throat. Don't kill them—they're good boys—but if you want to maim one or two inattentive ones that come near you, go right ahead. Good lesson for everybody."

Ella smirked as she nodded at the king.

I said, "I bring you a gift, Your Majesty, which as you know is a lie. No one gives a gift to a king without—"

"Oh, shit. Just shut up." He lifted a book from a small table next to his chair and began reading silently, as if he were sitting up in bed alone.

The audience was either going magnificently, or I was about to be killed, and I couldn't tell which. Moris was a fantastic king.

Before too long, Vintan hurried in through the side door. He stared at me. "Your Majesty, I insist you chain him instead of binding him with rope!"

"You've taken to insisting quite a bit lately, my Lord Viscount, quite a lot in fact. I know this is your stronghold, true, and can you guess how I know that? I know that because I gave it to you, my Lord, so remember that. Remember, because I can take it the hell away if you don't stop behaving like a twat! The twat of a recumbent whore, may I add! Now we have that straight, which we do, do we not?"

Vintan nodded.

I said, "Your Majesty—"

"Be quiet! Can you do that? Can you? Quiet? Yes? Dandy." Moris beckoned to Vintan. "Now, attend me."

Vintan walked over and stood at the king's left hand. The king should have listened to him. When they bound my arms, I had immediately rotted the ropes so that a solid pull would snap them.

"Now, Bib the Sorcerer, what's this gift that's not a gift that you want to give me but not give me?"

"I can cure the Northmen fever."

Moris rapped the arm of his throne with his knuckle. "Well, that's a damn fine thing, I'm sure, but since there are many thousands of Denzmen and only one of you, that makes you a rather parsimonious benefactor, or a goddamn stingy gift-giver, as we say at the stables, stingy. I'm king of all the Denzmen and not just the ones crowded around you. What kind of king walks around with a magical cure for himself while his people die like minnows in a drought? A shitty king, I tell you, damn shitty. I'd stab a king like that in the face myself. I don't want to stab my own face, would you? So, to hell with you and your gift."

"Your Majesty, I spoke like a grunting fool and wasn't clear at all. I can teach anybody to cure the fever. Easily. You can cure everybody as quick as horses can run to bring a message."

"The hell you say. Imprisonment must have driven you insane. Are you insane? You sound insane. If you knew this last spring, why in the name of Lutigan's boils didn't you say anything? If you held back, that's the same as murdering the thousands of my people who have died since then. My people. I wouldn't trade one of them for a hundred like you. In fact, I wouldn't trade a dead rat for you if you were made of diamonds. I may not kill you. I may torture you, and then kill you. I should make you torture that sweet young woman, and then make her torture you and kill you."

"Your Majesty, if I'd known all this last spring, I would've said so. I just learned it from the Goddess of Mercy today. Not an hour ago. When I found out how to make the cure, I came straight here."

I waited while the king rubbed his nose and scowled. As I glanced around, I spotted a familiar-looking guard standing at the side door. He was the man Desh had based his disguise on. The guard caught my eye and scowled at me with comic intensity. After a moment, I realized he was Desh. I gave him a tiny nod, and he returned it.

The king said, "Vintan? My Lord? Is this thing he's describing possible?"

Vintan shook his head in time with his steps as he walked toward Moris. "It is impossible. This man was destroyed as a sorcerer. The God of Death himself assured me that none of the gods would even speak to him. The idea that the Goddess of Mercy would waste her time on him is beyond ridiculous. He is lying without shame."

The king pointed at me. "What about his hands? Did he grow those by wishing hard and holding his mouth just right? That seems unlikely. If he did, then I should keep him around so he can teach me that trick. How did he grow them, Vintan? You're a sorcerer. Describe the process for me—you can do that. You're a smart man, and I'm not an idiot."

I said, "Right, Vintan, tell us how I did it. Act it out for us."

Vintan said, "Another sorcerer must have helped him."

"You let strange sorcerers traipse around in your dungeon?" I asked. "That's mighty careless, Vintan. Your Majesty, I didn't have help, and I didn't need help. Old Vintan there knows that, and he's scared of me for it. Chopping off my hands, throwing me in dungeons, getting all pissy about putting chains on me. He himself said how dangerous I am. So, I make you this offer, and you can test the truth of it right away. Let me teach somebody to make the cure, and then send them out to cure some of your people. If it works, I'm giving a legitimate gift. If it doesn't, tortures all around."

Moris scratched his chin. "You can't say fairer than that, I suppose. We'll give you a chance." He nodded at a guard. "Bring my physician in here." The guard trotted away, and I grinned at that walking slop-pool Vintan. "We've saved Pres, Vintan. Give up now, or I'll kill the crap out of you."

Vintan shook his head. "You know I can't, you one-handed moron." He stood straight and raised his chin. "Bib, thank you for your fidelity. To Pres, and my king, and everyone else I've failed."

"What are you two blibber-blabbering about?" Moris slammed his hand down onto his throne's arm.

Then everything went to hell.

Eighteen guards were standing around the Red Room holding weapons. Ten weapons disappeared in an instant, obliterated by Vintan. Most of the men around the king lost their swords, and Desh lost his weapon too. I had to assume that Vintan was leaving just his own men armed.

I snapped the rope that held me just as Vintan and two guards ran toward Pres. Unless something outrageous occurred, the prince was about to get rescued, and Vintan knew it. He had to kill Pres before it happened. Pres drew his sword while I threw one of the guards beside me onto the ground and took his weapon. When I looked up, I found three more guards between Pres and me.

For the next few moments, most everything happened around Pres and Ella. She tackled a guard, and Desh charged in to knock Vintan aside. Pres thrust at a guard, who blocked and then swung a powerful cut that chopped off the prince's hand above the wrist. His hand and his sword rolled across the floor toward me while he screamed and dropped to his knees. I knocked down one of my three guards and stabbed him on the floor, then rushed on to the remaining two.

Vintan grabbed Desh by the arm and threw him out of the way. Ella came up with one of the guards' swords and swung at the man who had wounded Pres, striking him hard on the side of the head. The remaining guard swung at her just as Vintan darted around her and stabbed Pres deep in the chest. The boy stared down at the blade in his chest and tried to grab it with both hands, even though he just had one hand now. Vintan groaned as he yanked the sword free, slicing Pres's palm. The boy fell sideways onto a red rug.

I killed the last of the guards in front of me and bounded toward Ella and Vintan. Ella stabbed her attacker just as Vintan turned toward the side door. I was two steps away and saw anguish on his face. Then he yanked out a knife and cut Ella's throat as he ran past her. I screamed for him not to do it, but that didn't make him take it back. I screamed at her to stand up, but she collapsed anyway and lay beside Pres, blood spurting from her neck.

I had only seconds to help them and just enough power left to save one or the other, but not both. I blinked twice, grabbed Pres's bloody sword off the floor, and lifted myself up to call Gorlana again. I tried to think of something to trade when I got there.

"Welcome, Murderer. You are unambiguously a man of surprises. I have found myself the tiniest bit nostalgic about our conversations. Even your insults."

"Harik! You warped, venomous toad, I didn't call for you! I don't belong to any of you serpent-souled murderers, so pass me along to Gorlana."

Pres had been carrying the stupid god-named sword, and I had picked it up. I imagined pulling it from the scabbard. The sunny, charming, achingly beautiful world appeared. Harik sat in the pavilion looking down on me. Gorlana sat next to him. Krak lounged in the center, a thundering dream of magnificence. Fingit and Lutigan perched on a higher tier. Three more gods sat around in the pavilion. I guessed them to be Cassarak, Weldt, and She-Who-May-Not-Be-Named.

"Gorlana? I think not," Harik said. "This is something of a reunion for you and me. Let's keep it between just the three of us."

As he said it, Vintan materialized to my left.

THIRTY-ONE

The first bargain I ever made with Harik was kind of pathetic. I wanted to pull all the poison out of a village's well, along with the drowned pony that had fallen in and poisoned it. In exchange for the power, I promised Harik he could give me the runs at some inconvenient time in the future. Twice. I feel that set the tone for all our future bargains.

A smart sorcerer keeps power in reserve, and not just for emergencies. He keeps it so that when tragedy comes, and his need is profound, a god won't be able to screw him like a water wheel for the power he's just got to have right now.

I wasn't a smart sorcerer the day my little girl was mutilated. I had just enough power in reserve to cure a bad cold, or to turn sleet into rain for an hour. Her mother found her by the stream just before midnight, nearly killed by wild dogs, which I'd always considered a mere nuisance. I went to Harik, who knew why I was there. He squeezed me dry that day, and I agreed to take an unknown number of lives for him, for which he gave me the power to save her.

A week later, I blamed Harik when my little girl fell and broke her neck. He must have known it would happen, and I needed to blame somebody. My wife needed to blame somebody too, and in her heart, she blamed me. She blamed me until the day she died, and I couldn't say that she was unfair to do it.

So, when I found myself with Vintan, ready to trade in the Home of the Gods, I wished that I had come to the negotiations with a little more power in reserve. I did have a bit, at least, which was better than crawling in and begging for whatever gristle fell on the floor.

"Harik, do you mean that my friend Vintan is here again?" I would have loved to cut off Vintan's head and make it into a flowerpot, but in that place, my sword was about as fatal as a hurled chipmunk. I put Ella and her cut throat out of my mind, gagged on my rage, and then shoved it down.

Vintan didn't hold back. "Why couldn't you die, you sack of filth? Or just escape, leave, run home? You forced me to kill him! You knew it was required of me, and you cracked on to rescue him anyway! Damn you to five kinds of rancid hell! I will see you skinned, soaked in salt water, and burned alive! He didn't deserve that death."

"Well, I didn't know it meant that much to you, Vintan. Would it help if I said I'm sorry?"

Vintan roared at me. If I could keep him angry, I might come out of this ahead.

Harik said, "Gentlemen, let us focus now. You may exact vengeance when we are done here, when your actions will not concern me at all. Do you recall the terms of our prior encounter? The auction?"

"I remember," Vintan said. "I want to purchase enough power to cause this snake to plummet a mile into the earth. Enough to make a mountain fall on him."

"Well then, I hope that five squares will accomplish that, because five squares are at stake here."

"That should be plenty for me," I said. "I don't even care

about Vintan. He can take up painting and learn to play the double-flute, I don't care. I just want to build a huge garden, sit in it, and drink wine all day. And entertain whores, of course."

Gorlana said, "Harik, I didn't think you were so clever. I thought you were dull, and I always have. But this is fun!"

Harik turned to Gorlana. "Just watch them tear at each other like rabid wolves."

"Do the maggot-sucking little toads try to make offers that top one another?" Lutigan asked.

"Certainly! Of course, I guide them on the types of offers I would like."

"Everybody shut up!" Krak said. "Let's see this thing, and then go to the party. And it better not be boring."

Harik looked at me. I gazed around so it wouldn't be obvious that I could see them all. "Murderer, I direct you to make the first offer."

My most recent experiences floated to the top. "I offer to spend another six months in the cell I just escaped from, starting in a week."

A few gods nodded, but none looked impressed.

Harik said, "Thank you for a serious offer. Farmer?"

Vintan said, "I will leave the Denz Lands and never return. Starting in a week."

"Well... even considering that few other lands would endure you, I will accept. Murderer, your opponent now leads. Just in case inspiration fails you, may I suggest dispensing with a few memories? Say, of your wife? After all, she is dead. She won't pop up someday and be perturbed that you don't remember her."

I laughed. "Harik, that's an entertaining suggestion. Instead, I offer a year in my old cell, to start in, yes, a week."

"Boring!" Gorlana said.

"How did he become a sorcerer? He lacks imagination," said She-Who-Must-Not-Be-Named.

Harik said, "Unacceptable, Murderer. It's no more than an elaboration, and unworthy of these proceedings."

"Unworthy?" I sniggered extra loud for the benefit of all the other gods watching. "If the other gods could see you now, they might laugh, Harik. You're just blundering around. Are you drunk? Are you preoccupied? Did someone—or something—break your heart this morning?"

A few gods giggled, and Harik hissed at them.

"A year in the cell," I said. "And... Vintan, if you hold off and let me win, I'll save the boy's life when we're done here."

Harik took a step toward Vintan. "You shall not! Farmer, you may not simply surrender. That is beyond the bounds!" I had suspected Harik wouldn't allow it, but trying hadn't set me back. Harik turned to me. "Memories of your wife! That, or I declare the farmer victorious, your lover will die, and your foe will kill you. What good will those memories be then?"

Vintan stood clenching his fists, tears running down his face. I kept the anger out of my expression. "Very well, I make that offer—the memories of my wife."

That sounded like a horrible offer, and it was. However, Vintan would probably kill me if I lost, so it came down to a simple, brutal question. If my offer were accepted, would my life still be worth living? If yes, then I could make the offer.

A couple of the gods nodded and grinned at me. Harik smiled like a soldier on payday. "Very good! Farmer, since the Murderer accepted my suggested offer, I expect you to do the same. I suggest, strongly, that you offer to lose one of your hands. You may choose which one. Come, you must agree that the irony of this is delicious. Be grateful that it's not both hands."

"Fine. I make that offer." Vintan didn't hesitate.

"Ah, you can force them to make whatever offer you want," Fingit said, "but they push each other to accept higher and higher bids. It is clever. Sorry I doubted you."

Harik laughed and gave a little bow.

I saw that Harik didn't care as much about the value of the trade as he cared about looking good in front of the other gods. I tossed out something dramatic. "I'll withhold the cure for Northmen fever. Thousands will die that otherwise would have been saved."

All the gods nodded and murmured. Krak even smiled.

I was taking a calculated risk that Harik wouldn't end up collecting on this offer. Just the fact that I had spoken it should be enough. It made him look better than a solid silver carriage full of whiskey. But he sure wouldn't let Vintan concede after this flashy offer from me.

"A solid offer, Murderer. I don't know why any of us ever said you were hard to work with."

"I appreciate that, you son of the black drifting whores of the universe. And give my thanks to the other gods, those thugs, extortionists, patsies, con men, and morons."

Sorcerers have a restricted set of pleasures. Hearing gods curse and grumble when you insult them is one of the best.

Harik said, "Droll. Farmer, may I suggest an offer for you to extend to me? You may of course refuse, but then you would be at the Murderer's mercy, which I think we can all agree is ephemeral at best. You will carry the Northmen fever with you. The variety of fever that you spread will defy the cure and run its course without interference. You yourself will not be susceptible, but every person you meet will without fail contract it. For the rest of your life."

Vintan looked down, his fist tapping against the side of his leg. "All right, I make that offer."

Harik said, "Wonderful, that is a magnificent bid. Murderer, I can conceive of only one thing that might surpass it. You may extend your open-ended debt by a further unknown number of deaths."

I almost laughed but then realized I couldn't think of anything else to top Vintan. Nothing that I could live with. I sure as hell had proven over these past years that I could live with the debt, even though I had to work harder to enjoy living. Happiness is overrated anyway, and I had chosen this life for myself.

The gods were sitting around the pavilion smiling and sipping from gem-encrusted golden cups. Lutigan and Weldt were laughing out loud.

If Vintan beat me, I still might survive. I'm slippery, and I have escaped some bad situations. I didn't know what time of day it might be. If it were nighttime in my world, and moonless, and Vintan slipped in the mud and broke his leg, I might even save Ella and bring her with me. It wasn't impossible. Pres would be dead without doubt. That slit-faced bastard Vintan would live to create whatever misery he wanted. I'd have to run from him right away, too quickly to give Moris the cure for the fever. A lot of Denzmen would die without it, probably thousands.

It sounds unlike me, but that last factor is what decided me. I had killed a lot of people, and if I extended my debt, I'd kill a lot more. But those deaths would look like a speck beside the thousands of lives I could save by taking on the new debt.

"I offer to extend my open-ended debt."

The ass-hanging shit-ball gods started applauding. May they be bashed in the tits by red-hot hammers in hell for all eternity.

"Farmer? I have an offer you may make to me." Harik was almost giggling. "It is quite similar to the Murderer's." He looked at Gorlana and winked. "You may take on an open-ended debt as well. You will ever be compelled to find men to whom you can swear loyalty, and then you will betray them when it hurts them the most. You will owe me a number of such betrayals, and only I will know that number."

Vintan stared off into nothingness, which was all he could see of course.

"Farmer, if you don't make this offer, the Murderer will be victorious."

Vintan stood silent for several more breaths and grew still. "No. I won't do that. I would have nothing and be nothing. Life wouldn't be worth living. Bib, thank you."

"What the hell for?"

"For remaining faithful to the king when I could not. You served him better than I, but you forced me to become a traitor and to murder my friend. For that cruelty, I will kill you. Not today, since I must flee, but I will. I thirst to eradicate you from human memory. Harik, you treacherous creature, I am done."

Vintan disappeared.

Gorlana said, "Harik, tell him. Tell him now!"

Harik nodded and waved at her. "Murderer, I think it only fair to offer you some reward for making such a fine agreement. You have increased your debt by a further unknown number of killings, so there's no reason you can't know how far away you were from fulfilling the original debt."

I stopped. I swayed in place. "What?"

"Your original debt. If you had not extended your debt today, do you know how many more murders would have been required to retire the original debt and be free?"

I tried to make myself ask, but my throat locked shut.

"Seventeen."

I couldn't breathe.

"Did you hear me?"

"Yes. Seventeen. Only seventeen more." I managed a couple of deep breaths to keep from going insane.

All the gods were laughing as if it were the most hilarious joke in creation.

"Well done! You were almost there. Excellent job. And now, Murderer, your power awaits you."

Harik slammed me back into my body.

I looked up and saw Vintan running out through the side door. Ella and Pres lay at my feet, their blood flowing.

I dropped the sword, slapped my left claw on Ella's neck, and pulled enough bands to stop the bleeding. I pressed my right hand against the boy's chest. He was almost gone. His wound had torn him up, a lot more than Ella's had for her. As I pulled bands to fix things in his chest, a pain in my own chest started and grew worse. By the time he was safe from dying right away, spasms were making it hard for me to breathe.

I put the pain aside as much as I was able and turned back to Ella, and I did a better job on her throat. Pres's severed arm was still bleeding, so I stopped that. A little more than a minute had passed since Vintan tore out of the room.

As I grabbed the sword and gathered myself to stand, Ella put her hand on my wrist. She opened her mouth, but only squeaks came out. Her eyes got big as she clamped onto my arm.

"Hush. I just got done sticking your head back on your neck. Well, a good part of it anyway, so rest yourself. You'll feel a lot better in a few hours. Take a nap." I kissed her forehead. "I've got to go kill Vintan."

I winced as I stood up and my chest throbbed all the way to my heart. In comparison, I couldn't even feel the pain in my throat from healing Ella.

"Stop!" Moris yelled from beside his chair. "What in the greasy perdition is happening here? You!" He pointed at me. "You're the only one, the only one, who doesn't look as confused as hell. What's going on?"

"Vintan's a traitor and a murdering piss pot. That about covers it. I'll elaborate once I've killed him." I nodded to Desh, who was standing beside me. "This is how to make the cure." I told him the ingredients and the five steps to mix it up. "Give it to Moris. I know you won't forget it, but write it down in case you get killed in the next thirty seconds."

Desh nodded and knelt to check on Pres. Without looking up, he said, "Don't be lazy and just kill the man. Bring him back to life and kill him two or three more times."

"Stop!" Moris bellowed. "Guard, stop that man right there!"

"King Moris, you're a nice fellow, but you haven't been in charge since I walked in here." I turned toward the door. "You can yell at me when I come back, or else when I'm dead."

I coughed twice and knocked one guard on his ass on the way to the door. Once through it, I ran down a narrow hallway in the direction I'd seen Vintan scamper.

THIRTY-TWO

I've always considered myself fleet, but the swiftest person I ever met was a woman. I wished she were around now so she could chase Vintan for me. My time in the dungeon had cost me a step or two of speed, and I was clawing for breath through the pain in my chest. Less than a minute into the pursuit, I feared that catching him was a hopeless effort.

A few moments later, the floor slid out from under me as I stepped on paving stones that were balanced on the edge of a hidden pit. They failed to teeter into the gap evenly, and I pushed off one of the stones that stuck. I leaped across the opening and cleared the hole.

It was a sloppy trap, unworthy of an accomplished sorcerer, or even an accomplished hooligan. I admit it was deep enough that I couldn't bounce right out of it, but at only six feet across, it showed that Vintan was just trying to slow me down. He was eager to get away rather than fight.

Or, maybe he wanted me to think that. I ached to run fast, chase him down, and slice his head off, and while I was dawdling here, he was getting away. When we'd been bargaining with Harik, Vintan told me he was going to flee. Now he held a big lead. The smart play for him was to escape and kill me another day when I wasn't expecting him.

But why should he wait for another day? I wasn't expecting him today.

Instead of running faster, I slowed to a trot and scanned every stone as if tigers might be hiding behind them. That turned out to be one of my better decisions of the afternoon.

The hallway crossed two intersections and dumped out into the middle of a larger passage. The other direction led deeper into the keep. To the right, I saw a small door leading into the castle yard, obscenely brilliant after all the months I'd spent underground. A soldier and two servants with hoes, maybe gardeners, were walking toward me. I couldn't imagine Vintan running anywhere except outside. Either he was already gone, or he was hiding there preparing to kill me.

I made for the outer door at an even slower trot. Halfway there, I heard a moment of muffled grinding, and I threw myself backward just before the entire hallway collapsed. One of the gardeners screamed as huge stones rumbled down on him, and then his screams cut off. While the hill of rocks and dirt was settling, his friend started howling and crying. I never heard her stop. As far as I know, she's still trapped there weeping.

A medium-size stone, as big as a comfortable chair, rolled toward me. I mostly dodged it, but it brushed by and knocked me halfway across what remained of the hallway. When I got up, I could walk, but my knee was already starting to swell. I didn't have time to fiddle around with healing it.

The debris contained a couple of promising gaps near the top. I chose the closest one, climbed up to it, and began wriggling through. Nothing above me seemed to be shifting, which gave me a bit of comfort. Then I realized that if Vintan was watching me right then, he could collapse another three floors of the keep on top of me if he wanted to.

I scrambled down the other side alive and headed toward the door at a limping trot. Nothing bad happened before I reached the door and poked out my head, waiting for some gargantuan rock to squash me. All I saw was Vintan riding away on a decent-looking horse, although it looked to be a little short on wind.

Vintan looked back and mimed three little kisses at me.

I pulled four yellow bands, one after the other, and whipped each one out to wrap a hoof, dragging the horse to a dead stop. Vintan almost fell, and I rushed toward him, ignoring pain and not worrying about pits and deadfalls. He hopped down, drew his sword, and ran to meet me.

I almost cut halfway through his neck on the first pass, but he threw himself aside. He swung at my limping right leg, and as I jumped back, my knee wobbled. I fell on my back. He pressed me hard then, but within a few seconds, I'd gotten up on the other knee. I fenced him from one knee for a little bit, pinking him in the thigh and giving him a decent slice across the forearm.

Vintan probably realized then that, even kneeling, I was about to kill him. He jumped back, and every scrap of everything I was wearing or carrying disappeared. The only exception was the stupid god-named sword. With slush on the ground, things felt a little brisk, but I stood up ready to cut him in two.

"You miserable reptile," he said, looking at my still-existing sword, and then he attacked. I blocked, set him up for the kill, and fell into a giant hole. Sadly, the hole's edge knocked my sword out of my hand. Fortunately, I grabbed Vintan with my claw as I fell. I dragged him with me, and together we tumbled twenty feet to the bottom.

I hit my head and was seeing double after we landed, and I had wrenched my remaining good knee. Vintan looked around, spotted me, and clambered up to his knees as he raised his sword. Blood was running down his chin onto his chest, which told me he'd probably bitten off his tongue. When he swung, I grabbed his wrist to hold off the cut.

Vintan got a leg under him and shoved me, and with my pathetic knees, I didn't have much strength for pushing back. He pinned me on my side and pulled his knife. I grabbed for my knife but realized it had been disintegrated along with everything else I'd been wearing. He stabbed at my neck, but I deflected with my claw. I shuddered as the knife pushed deep into my shoulder instead.

Every muscle in my body wept and begged to quit. The pain in my chest had crawled out in all directions, and everything below my neck throbbed. I hadn't pulled a deep breath since my knee had given way and slapped me onto the icy ground.

Vintan twisted his knife into my shoulder. I gasped and shoved my empty claw against his chest. Then I called a blue band out of nothing and pushed it into his body, trying to wither everything it touched.

The body wants to live, so withering it is a lot of work. All Vintan's muscles snapped tight at first, but he was a sorcerer and hard to dissuade. I writhed as he stabbed again, and he dragged a magnificent, bloody wound across my scalp. He was weakening, but he stabbed at me again. He struck my neck this time but just scraped a shallow cut from my ear to my shoulder blade.

I kept pouring power into him, flooding his body with rot, but he shouted, spraying blood in my face, and tried to push the rot back into me. It was crazy, but I kept thinking there must be better ways to spend that power since I'd promised a lot of murders to get it. I rammed the power harder, withering everything it touched, and he kept shoving it back at me. My vision melted, and I threw up over his shoulder. I drove all my power into him, holding nothing in reserve, and at last I shriveled his heart.

That was how Vintan Reth the Sorcerer died. May goats piss in every hole of his skull.

I had no choice but to lay at the bottom of that hole until somebody looked down and felt sorry for me. I did have a choice about how I used my time while I was there. I wheezed for a while before scooting over so that it didn't appear I was engaged in unseemly congress with Vintan's corpse. Then I lay flat, pulled my knees up, had a nice laugh, and passed out.

It was early evening when I woke. I had been washed and bandaged, and I rested on a soft bed in a large, clean room. I saw polished furniture, rugs, tapestries, and even a window. Desh was sitting nearby.

"This was Vintan's room," he said.

"Make sure he doesn't come back to life, walk in here, and finish me."

"Damn, Bib, look at you. If you were a boot, I'd throw you in a ditch."

"I'll be up soon. I'll surprise you. How are Pres and Ella?"

"Pres is weak but awake. Ella's fine. She's stalking between this room and Pres's like a tiger with cubs in different caves."

"How did you find me in the Red Room?"

"Ah, once you escaped from so deep under all these stones, Limnad felt you. We've been hiding in the hills, which was even less comfortable than it sounds. I thought you were dead, but Limnad refused to leave without you. I have cultivated some sneaky ways into the castle, so I disguised myself and hurried in. After that, it was easy. Everybody was talking about the filthy lunatic who wanted to chat with the king. Filthy lunatic had to mean you."

I snorted. "Hell, my reputation has been destroyed."

"Small loss. I'll bring Ella."

Some power to heal would certainly have been useful about then. Or, power for unforeseen eventualities. I didn't see my sword around, so I said to hell with it, gritted my teeth, and lifted myself to call on Gorlana. She refused me. Harik refused me too, and so did all the other gods I called. I was cut off, at least for now.

Shortly, Ella swept into the room, grabbed my hand, and kissed me with considerable care. "When they carried you inside, I thought you must be dead. Even now, I wonder whether you still have any blood inside you."

"Most of it was his." That was a lie. Hardly any of it could have been his.

She touched the cut across my scalp, which had bled like a waterfall. "Of course. You would never exaggerate."

"Did Desh give the cure to Moris?"

"Certainly. The king's physician is evaluating it. If it proves effective, Moris promises not to yell at you. If it fails, he says he shall hang you for being impertinent and a bad juggler."

"I'm glad you're not king. You must have accused me of impertinence a couple dozen times."

Ella kissed me again. "Are you recovered enough to heal yourself?"

"No, not exactly." I patted her arm.

"I pray it's soon." She pressed her other hand against my cheek. It reminded of when she sat with me while I was dying. She went on, "So that you feel well, of course, but also to restore Pres's hand. It's a horrible wound, but I have faith in you."

"Ella, that may not happen, at least not right away."

"Why not?"

"It takes power, and I'm blown out right now." I smiled at her and shrugged.

"Can you trade for more?"

"I'd love to. In fact, I've already tried, but none of the gods will even talk to me."

Ella clamped her jaw for a second. "Why? Did you commit some act to aggravate them?"

"Darling, they float around in a state of eternal aggravation."

Ella stood back and let my hand go. "What will you do about Pres's hand?"

"I can't do anything right now. I used everything I had killing Vintan."

"You knew Pres's hand had been severed. Why did you not hold power in reserve to heal him?"

I looked down. Ella had touched on a tender point there. I might have been able to kill Vintan without shoving every bit of my power into his nasty, blackened heart. I used all of it to make sure he was dead. Also, because I hated him worse than syphilis. And because it felt good to obliterate him, not just kill him. Ella was right—I hadn't stopped to think about Pres.

"Ella, at the time, it seemed like I needed all of it."

"You should have remained mindful of the power required. You took pains to create a new hand for yourself, and indeed part of another. Yet you leave Pres, your friend and companion, to a life of mutilation."

"I'm sorry, Ella. If I were to fight Vintan again, I might hold some power back. Or, he might kill me because I didn't use it all. We can't know. I'd help Pres now if I could. If things change and I can help him someday, I will."

"I understand." She said it, but she didn't take my hand again. "There is nothing to be done about it. I should check on him."

Ella hurried out of Vintan's room, and part of me felt just as dead as that damned Vintan. Pres was her boy, even if he didn't come from her body. Now he was maimed, and she couldn't blame Vintan since he was gone. Whenever she looked at his stump, she'd need somebody to blame, and I was the only one available.

I guess Gorlana hadn't been kidding about taking Ella after all.

THIRTY-THREE

Sorcerers tend to be a mean-tempered bunch. They like to act forbidding and impatient and inscrutable. Some sorcerers even practice. I mean, they practice in front of a mirror, perfecting their "I'm so wise I don't even care how much wiser I am than you" expression. They're really just mean as snakes, but they want their meanness to look like it's something special and mysterious.

Most sorcerers act mean because they're sad, and they're sad because of all they have traded away to the gods. If you want to see an extravaganza of weepy anguish, get a few sorcerers together with some hard liquor and a fellow playing sad songs on his lute. They'll say shit like, "The life of a sorcerer is a life of loss," and, "There are no good deals—only bad deals and deals that are less bad."

When morose sorcerers talk about loss and bad deals, they are not lying. They're wise enough to know that's their life. But they're also too foolish to see that every life is a life of loss, even for people who aren't sorcerers. True, a sorcerer's losses are often bizarre, but in exchange, they get to roast their enemies alive or make slippers that let them sneak around and hear everybody's secrets. Sorcerers are strange, but they aren't that special.

But arrogant? They are that, and I may be the most arrogant one of all.

Every life is also a life of wonder. Sorcerers often forget that, which is damn strange since they spend their time seeing and doing wondrous things. But they forget and they lose and they lose some more and they die young.

I rarely talk about my little girl, although since I met Ella, I've talked about her ten times as much. She was the greatest loss of my life, and the greatest wonder, and she will always define what I am and what I am not. A part of me lived only when I was with her. When she died, that part of me died too, and it went with her wherever she went so she wouldn't have to go there alone.

King Moris rewarded the crap out of me. He gave me nice clothes, fine weapons, two splendid horses, and more gold than a cheap bastard like me could spend in a hundred years. This all came with an unspoken understanding that I would get out of the Denz Lands as soon as I healed and the weather was agreeable. His experiences with Vintan had soured his taste for keeping sorcerers around. He stayed in residence at the Eastern Gateway to show us hospitality, but I suspect he mainly wanted to make sure I didn't cause trouble.

Spring arrived cold and wet, so we all agreed to stay with Moris until the weather broke. He held a banquet for us every evening. Pres moped, melancholy over his friend Vintan trying to kill him; so during the days, I hauled him out to the castle yard and trained him to fight left-handed. After teaching the boy for a week, I began training some of Moris's personal guards too, and I recovered my strength and wind in a few weeks. I didn't crave taking their lives, either. Instead, I felt a sober appetite for killing them that I could put aside and indulge some time later, or maybe never. After a month of training, I could whip any three guards at once, in whatever order Pres gave me, and I felt my recovery was well along.

Ella went most places with Pres. She came to his first training session, stayed ten minutes, and left. She didn't attend any more training. She and I talked off and on in those weeks. She always spoke properly, no matter how much I teased her or sprinkled on increasingly robust profanity. She acted like we had never shared an intimate word.

During the fourth week of training, when our session had ended and Pres was collecting the weapons, Ella walked up to me. "Thank you for schooling the prince on the principles and practice of swordsmanship. I fear he will find it challenging. I intended to train him, but he expressed a preference for your instruction."

"He'll come back to you if you tell more dirty stories. I know one about the milkmaid and the halibut—"

"Thank you, I prefer not to engage in a contest over prurient tales."

"Dirty jokes?"

She gave a faint smile and shook her head.

"Want to fight?"

"Thank you, no. I haven't expressed my gratitude to you yet. For rescuing Pres."

"We all worked together to make that happen."

"Some of us suffered more than others." She reached out to my arm but dropped her hand before she touched me.

"Don't be shy. If you want me to take off my shirt, just speak up."

"No. I want to thank you, now that Pres is secure and the rescue completed."

"All right, I don't mind if you thank me. Go ahead."

She sighed. "Thank you. Since the rescue is over and the prince no longer needs to be rescued, he does not require a rescuer."

"I wouldn't think so. What are you trying to say? Do you want me to get a job? Do you want me to hire somebody to kidnap him so we can have this fun all over again?"

"No!" She reached out to my arm but stopped herself again.

I realized she was reaching out to my hand, not my arm. For a moment, I thought she was trying to say she felt bad that my hands had been cut off, but when I raised my hand, she didn't look at it. She looked at the sword I was holding. I reversed the sword and presented the hilt to her. "You're right, Ella. You're protecting the prince now, not me. This is yours."

Blushing, she took the stupid god-named sword and cradled it in the crook of her arm. Then she grabbed my hand and squeezed hard for a few seconds before she nodded and walked away.

"Don't ever feel like you can't come out and ask me for something," I called after her. "I may tell you to go to hell, but you don't have to worry about asking."

Ella walked fast across the mud and back into the keep. She didn't attend the banquet that evening. She told Pres that she felt unwell.

A week later, I woke up with a faint headache. I went to Moris and asked whether I could hunt down any bandits or traitors for him and kill them. He laughed and said he'd be damned if he'd use any guest that way, and we spent the rest of the afternoon getting as drunk as blind squirrels. I decided to put up with the headache until I departed the Gateway and found a promising opportunity to murder somebody.

Nine weeks after I killed Vintan, the sun rose on a clear, warm day. Ella, Pres, and I thanked Moris for his hospitality, and he told Pres to send word if the Denz Lands could ever help him. Then we mounted our fine, well-provisioned horses and rode into the hills to meet Desh and Limnad, with fifty of Moris's soldiers escorting us.

Limnad rushed to me in a blur and laid her hand on my chest. "Bib, I'm happy for you! Your spirit isn't wretched."

"Hello, Limnad. It's good to see you, although I wish you'd said something better than 'not wretched.'"

"Your spirit will never be light. You should know that—you did it to yourself. So, don't whine."

"I don't think I've whined since I was a boy. Maybe not even then."

"Or made arrogant claims, either. You're well enough, although I can tell she hurt you. I knew that she would in the end." Limnad looked across the clearing toward Ella and raised her voice. "That horrible slut with a hatchet face and toads for tits!"

Ella glanced up, shook her head, and looked away.

Limnad interpreted that as a gesture of contempt, which it probably was. Desh, Pres, and I restored peace soon with no deaths and not many injuries.

We traveled north on the same road we had followed down into the Denz Lands. The days were bright and full of new grass. The nights were cool, and they smelled like moss and terrified rodents. The keep we destroyed on our way south had been rebuilt, and the king's people had cleared the avalanche that Vintan had thrown down on Ralt and me at the Blood River. We stopped for a day at Smat Bander's village and shared our food. The villagers shared their wine, and we enjoyed a raucous party with three fist fights and a marriage proposal.

Our trip back to the Blue River was just about perfect, except that Ella avoided me and I annoyed everybody by making it clear how much I didn't care about her avoiding me. Pres fretted about all the tension between Ella and me, Limnad and Ella traded insults that would embarrass a dockworker, and that son of a bitch Desh watched us all and laughed.

When we rode down into the wide, grassy Blue River valley, I looked forward to the coming changes. Moris's soldiers would turn back here at his kingdom's border. Traveling with large groups of armed, dubiously trained men had always unsettled me.

Desh paced me as we descended into the valley. "Limnad will be staying here."

I looked around and nodded. "Well, it is her river, and from what we've seen, I doubt any magical being can survive north of it. I think I might miss her."

"I'll be staying here too."

"Research?" I raised an eyebrow at him. "Or... *intensive* research?"

Desh smiled the biggest smile I'd ever seen on his face. "Let's say that I'll become the world's greatest expert on spirits."

"If you live."

"If I live."

"I know I don't have to warn you about anything, but I do have a suggestion." I held up my hand before he interrupted me. "Someday you should leave this river long enough to learn the blacksmithing trade. Some enchantments don't take well on cloth, leather, or loose bark."

At the riverbank, I thanked the soldiers, embraced Limnad, and nodded an enigmatic, sorcerer-like nod at Desh. Then Ella, Pres, and I rode out to ford the river, Ella beside me and Pres on her other side. Halfway across, when the water was up to a horse's chest, a guttural grinding noise rose all around us and the swift water began churning. It wasn't just churning near us. The surface of the whole river had become choppy as far as I could see in both directions.

I hauled the reins and kicked my horse to ride back out of the river. My mount still breathed and her eyes rolled, but where running was concerned, she may as well have been carved out of marble. I spotted Limnad almost flying across the water with Desh in her arms. Within moments, she had disappeared upstream. That's when I knew something horrible was about to happen.

The water erupted thirty feet in front of me, and Krak, Father of the Gods, rose up to stand in the river. The water grew calm, but only in a circle around his ten-foot-tall self. I didn't feel any breeze, but wind sure brushed through his majestically disarrayed silver beard and hair. He wore the Father's Robe, a plain garment whiter than anything else in existence. He was known to brag about that. His right hand was clenched in a fist.

Gods do not often manifest in their person, but when they do, it's an event of some note. This appearance of Krak's was the second time a god had manifested in my lifetime. The first was when Lutigan visited the Land of Karwell to attend a victory celebration in his honor and to impregnate an astounding number of young women. Not all manifestations have been so cheery. Almost a hundred years ago, She-Who-Must-Not-Be-Named showed up to destroy Clefmeet, the third largest city in the world. I've never seen the ruins, but supposedly lots of the residents still exist there, deathless, and suffer a broad variety of tortures.

Krak had last manifested over three hundred years ago, when a king beseeched him to grant his people victory. Krak destroyed both armies for not fighting hard enough. Having dealt with Krak a number of times, I knew how badly this could go. I wanted to run, cry, and vomit all at the same time.

"Bow down!" Krak boomed. "I am the damned Father of the Gods! What kind of manners did your parents teach you? I should disembowel them right this moment."

I bowed, and I expect everybody else did too.

"Better. Now, give me your swords. You, over there on the riverbank! Come here with your swords. Just toss them at my feet and go back over there!"

As I threw my sword, I almost giggled. It felt like the Father of the Gods was shaking us down in some dim alleyway.

After everyone, including Moris's soldiers, had thrown their swords, Krak screamed, "Who is holding out? I will smash you flatter than worm shit!"

Ella said, "This sword belongs to another. I cannot surrender it." Her voice warbled a little, but she sat tall.

"Ella," I hissed. "Give him the sword!"

Pres said, "Do it. On behalf of the queen, I give you leave to relinquish the sword."

Ella crossed her arms and looked around at everything except Krak. "No. I have made an oath."

Krak smiled. "Young woman, the Blade of Obdurate Mercy is not meant for you to bear. Nor your queen. Give it to me." He yelled, "Because I can destroy you with a thought!"

Ella's entire body was trembling, but she gave a tiny head shake.

"Murderer, if you like this woman at all, save her life now. Convince her."

Krak wasn't known to hesitate when he could kill instead. I stared at the god, and then I squinted at Ella. "He can't take it away from you. You've got to give it to him. And he can't hurt you while you're carrying it."

Ella began panting, sweat coating her face. "I shall continue then." She dismounted her statue of a horse and began wading toward home, chest deep.

Krak probably couldn't manifest north of the river. Nothing godlike seemed to exist there now, so if she made it to the riverbank, she'd be safe. Of course, safe was a shaky concept when the most powerful being ever known might yank you into small bits and hide each one in a remote part of the world. "Hurry! Wade faster!"

"Enough!" Krak opened his fist, and the impossibly searing light of the sun instantly vaporized twenty-five soldiers, along with their horses, a great quantity of water, the riverbed to a depth of sixty feet, and a hilltop two miles away. He pointed at the remaining soldiers. "If you don't want that to be you, kill her and bring me her sword!"

The soldiers' horses started moving again, and they charged into the river toward Ella.

My horse was still petrified, so I dove into the water and reached Ella in a few moments. I grabbed her around the waist and pulled her under. She twisted like a seal and put me in a headlock, but I grabbed the hilt of her sword. She bit into my ear and clamped down, but I swept the blade free in one movement. I surfaced, pulling her up by my ear, which I felt tear a little. I found myself wishing that she wouldn't fight so hard while I was saving her life, but she was defying Krak, so expecting her to go easy on me was a foolish hope.

I threw the sword at Krak. He raised his hand, and every non-divine being in the river became motionless. Ella was still biting down on my ear.

"Finally! I should turn you all into garfish for wasting my time. And then turn you inside out for being a bunch of disobedient, whining back-warts." Krak raised the stupid god-named sword and pressed the crosspiece to his forehead. "Murderer, come here." He released both Ella and me, and she let go of my ear before spitting blood into the water.

I waded to Krak. I often anticipate what's about to happen, maybe not in detail, but in general terms. This time, I had not a whisper of a fart of a rumor of a clue what might happen next.

Krak held the sword out to me. "This is yours now, Murderer. Don't screw around and lose it."

"Why?" I shook my head. It made no sense. "That is, why, Father Krak?"

"Wherever you take this sword, the way will open. Men will be able to reach through to the gods again." Krak held up his fist—the one that destroyed twenty-five men at a time.

"And gods will be able to reach through from your side too, huh?"

"Of course." Krak smiled.

I almost spit in the river, but I held onto my temper. "To hell with it. I don't want it."

Krak shouted, "You'll take it and be happy with it!"

"Give it to Desh. He's young. He wouldn't know a shithouse full of scorpions if he saw one."

"Murderer, you could make a fence post burst a blood vessel!" Krak lifted his hands, and the river started rising. "All right, you grunting toenail, I offer you a trade."

I laughed at him. And laughed. I didn't stop until it was embarrassing for everybody.

Krak lifted the river until the water reached my neck. "You will carry the sword for us, and in exchange, I will give you knowledge."

"I'd laugh again, but I peed myself last time."

"You will carry the sword, or I will snap you in half like a bean! You have no choice!"

"Father of the Gods, you know what it's like with sorcerers. We always have choices, even if they're all bad."

The river water fell back down with a sucking splash. "Very well, smartass. I offer you this choice." Krak pointed across the valley. "If you don't want to trade with me, I will drop that hill on everybody here. But if you do agree to trade, I will give you the knowledge first. Then, if you think it was a good bargain, you will take the sword. If you think it was a bad bargain, you may go free without the sword."

I didn't see how I could lose, which meant I was almost certain to lose. But I'd never heard of any sorcerer getting a deal like this. I couldn't turn it down. "All right, give me this unfathomable knowledge."

"When you first assumed your debt with Harik, he did not

know that your daughter would die soon anyway."

"Did it matter? The pretentious twat would have done the same damn thing regardless."

"He would have. But since he didn't know, you could not have found out from him. No matter how clever or subtle you were, you couldn't have saved her. It was not your fault."

I looked down. Until that moment, I hadn't realized that I'd always known it was my fault. Not believed it, but known it. I was a sorcerer, so it had to have been. I must have missed some clue that Harik let slip, and it would have let me save her. I held out my hand to take the sword without looking up, because I sure wasn't going to let that sack-of-shit god see me cry.

I took the sword, and Krak returned to whatever birthday party or orgy he had planned next. Moris's remaining soldiers turned back for home in a somber mood. Pres, Ella, and I rode north into the Kingdom of Glass, and I avoided riding next to Ella.

On the second evening after the river tragedy with Krak, Ella looked at me across the campfire. "I accept your decision to take the sword. I understand why you didn't defy Krak. In fact, you were brave. Stupider than a bin of scrap iron, but very brave. And I apologize for your ear." She tossed a couple of sticks into the fire. "You're a terrible person, but I don't mind that. I understand why you ensured that Vintan was dead at the cost of leaving Pres mutilated. I understand, and I want to forgive you. But I cannot forgive you. That is the way I feel, and I can't help it."

"I don't know what to say. Again. My conversation skills have grown poor."

"I know what to say." Pres walked into the firelight carrying more wood. "Ella, your friend Bib didn't stab you in the heart like my friend did to me. That's a virtue."

"Pres..." Ella waved him away.

"Of course, he did save my life, so you have to be harsh with him for that. And he saved your life too, so you should be exceedingly harsh."

Ella glanced at Pres's arm. He had the firewood balanced tenderly since he lacked a hand.

Pres dropped the wood and raised his stump. "I could rule the kingdom holding this arm behind my back, if that would make a difference."

"Or wear a puppet on it," I said.

"Yes, a horse puppet."

Ella stared at us.

Pres said, "If you don't have to look at my stump, will you forgive him?"

Ella opened her mouth, closed it, and shook her head.

I said, "Who knows what may happen? After you get home and I leave again, it may be easier to change your mind. I'm told my company is more enjoyable in theory than in practice. More than one woman has fallen in love with me from a distance."

Ella smiled and tossed a stick at me. Then she lay down facing away from the fire.

A few days later, we reached Crossoak. All the citizens were hiding in their sturdy homes, and no one even peeked out. I wrote out directions for finding the coins I had hidden in the woods all around, and I left them under a rock in front of Sunflower's door.

Not far north of Crossoak, a column of riders came into sight, trotting downhill toward us under the Glass banner. We rode at an easy pace to meet them. The lead man waved at us to stop, and we stopped right away. "Who are you, and what's your business on the king's road?" said a barrel-shaped man with a singer's voice.

Before I said anything, Pres spoke up. "I am Crown Prince Prestwick. Since my father is dead, this is my road and I'm here on my own business."

Barrel Man leaned back and stared for a moment. "Well, pardon me for being a filth-scraping ass, Your Highness. Please forgive me, Your Highness. I don't want to get any red-hot barbed swords stuck up my bottom for being a scabby, disrespectful weasel. Am I forgiven?"

Pres glanced at me, but he had decided to snatch the reins for himself, so I shrugged. He said, "Yes, of course."

Barrel Man bellowed, "Shut it, you jerk-jawed oaf! A boy giving me orders. Corporal, disarm them."

"Bugger me with dried-up mackerel!" Stan walked up from the back of the column. "Here I figured you three was nothing but worm turds by now. Captain, this really is the prince. I swear, I saw him giving folks orders and everything. And his governess, a righteous woman, I didn't even try to lure her off for a quick roll. And—"

"Corporal, attention!"

Stan stood up just a little straighter but hung on to his normal air of disinterest.

"You will shut that rancid shit-canyon in your face until I tell you to puke out whatever limp thoughts you have fermented in that rotting horse turd you call a skull! Do you understand me?"

"Yes, Captain."

"You flogging well better, because you're nothing! You're like one of those little dogs with big ears and no balls. Now take their slut-rutting weapons before I have you sliced open and dragged all the way back to Glass!"

"Sorry," Stan muttered to me as he held out his hand for my sword. "I'd appreciate you handing it over and not cutting me in two, seeing as we're old friends and I shared my wine with you."

"Here you go, Stan. It's not your fault."

"Goddamn right it's not," he said. "To hell with this corporal bullshit. Thank you, miss, and you too, Your Highness. You try to save an officer from ruin, and it's nothing but insults. If Your Highness don't mind, could you see that the captain ends up dangling from the battlements by his tits, or something just as nasty? I'd count it a favor."

Captain Barrel Man called out to the soldiers behind him, "This far south is far enough. Reverse column! We're going home!"

The soldiers cheered while Stan carried away our weapons. I didn't even consider fighting. I wanted to be there when Captain Barrel Man got back to the capital and showed his bosses the fine prisoners he'd taken.

THIRTY-FOUR

Profanity is better than poetry in almost every way. Profanity is direct, easy to understand, and unambiguous. Poetry is evasive, obscure, and often confusing. I recall a poem that seemed to be about a boat, but I found out later it was about someone's grandmother remembering how she fell in love with a farmer. Those three stanzas about the boat were metaphorical.

I'm not opposed to metaphors, but I prefer them to have impact. When a poem talks about drifting among the scraping reeds at sunset, I have a good idea what that means, but I can't say that I care. I don't care who's drifting, I really don't care about the reeds, and if it's sunset, I just want to know where I can buy something to drink.

But when I say, "You slack-jawed, alarmist turd, gods damn you to the shriveled tits of your grandmother!" that is a metaphor with impact.

Captain Barrel Man and I found common ground in our love of profanity. His real name was Captain Baldir, and for eight days, he cursed everything in sight without once repeating himself. It was better than a concert. I came to understand that when he cursed, he meant no ill. Cursing was his way of recognizing that you were a living creature like him, so really it was an act of love, almost religious.

Ella wanted to cut Baldir's throat in his sleep, steal some horses, and race ahead to the capital. Pres never showed that the verbal abuse bothered him, or that he even noticed it. He preferred that we behave ourselves until he reached home. Even though Pres was just eleven years old, he was the prince, and this was his kingdom, so we did as he said.

We rode up through the mountains onto high plains full of tall, yellow-green grass to the horizon. The only trees we saw stood around occasional lakes and ponds. By the second day, we began passing ranches and farmhouses built of sod or mud-brick buildings, and the day after, we passed a few villages. My headache had become a flock of iron chickens pecking inside my skull. Every village must have had a few child-beaters or rapists for me to kill, but I respected Pres's commands. I let them live, and instead of killing, I just drank whenever Stan shared his wine ration with me.

The capital stood at the heart of the kingdom. As we rode toward it, we saw more timber and more people. Farms, villages, and towns lay closer together, and it was rare for us not to have some dwelling in sight. The prince's subjects didn't seem to care about forty soldiers and three captives riding straight through their towns, so they must have seen that sort of thing often.

Pres's ancestors had built the capital on high ground, with the castle at the summit. The city appeared bigger and busier than the community around the Eastern Gateway, but the castle looked dumpy and a little sad.

"Pres, what's this city called?" I asked.

"Glass."

"And that up there is..."

"Castle Glass."

"Why didn't your mother name you Glass? You could be the Crown Prince of Glass, future King of Glass, Ruler of the Glass Kingdom, who lives in Castle Glass and buys his shoes in Glass City."

"I could have you beheaded. You know, if you weren't the most dangerous man in the world."

"I could have said that you buy your gloves there."

He and I laughed hard, which we needed. Ella didn't laugh. She kept adjusting and readjusting the reins and brushing dirt off her sleeve when she wasn't staring at the castle.

Baldir halted the column in the castle yard beside a large and finely crafted wooden building. It turned out to be the First Barracks. Stan led us inside, almost giggling. "Shh! Listen for it. That whale-assed Baldir is going to get his narblies torn off and fed to the pigs."

Twenty seconds later, the screaming started.

An orderly debriefing had been underway, until Ella ran to an older man, grabbed his sleeve, and started shouting at Baldir, who screamed right back at her, but with a lot more bad words. The older man looked powerful for his age, with an aggressively bristly moustache, and he was trying to get one or the other of them to shut up. I watched from the side until Pres stepped in the middle of all this. The shouting faded and died.

I bowed. "I'll be the first one to show you reverence, Your Highness. Remember that it was me when it's time to start throwing people in the dungeon."

That started a few minutes of bowing, apologizing, accusing, explaining, and pleading. In the middle of all this, Stan scurried around returning our weapons and cackling like a nasty-smelling witch. Ella waved at me and pointed at the older fellow, who was hurrying away. "Follow Sir Linkan!"

I followed the man, while she and Pres followed me. We jogged out of the barracks, into the keep, and upstairs to a fancy sitting room. Linkan bowed to Pres and hugged Ella before leaving us in the hallway.

"Is this Linkan your father?" I asked Ella. She laughed at me over her shoulder as she walked into the room.

Linkan had brought us to the queen, a small, pale, stoop-shouldered woman in a blue dress that cost enough to feed Crossoak for six months. She embraced Pres, who said, "Bib, this is my mother, Queen Dall. Mother, this is Bib, the man who rescued me."

The queen glanced down at my left claw for a moment, and then she crinkled her eyes at me but didn't quite smile. "You have done us such a service, sir. I wish I could better reward you. For now, some refreshment." She pointed at a side table, and I missed the next minute of the conversation while I drank three glasses of wine.

When I caught up, Ella was saying, "Who remains loyal?"

The queen said, "Difficult to say. The other cousins support Duke Lundt on promise of titles and rewards. He has announced that Prestwick has been killed, so everyone is uncertain about the state of affairs."

I said, "Pres, who's the biggest pain in your ass? Let's just kill them."

The queen's face thought about smiling. "It's a little more complicated than that, sir... Bib?"

Pres said, "Yes, Bib saved my life."

"You have my deep gratitude. But it is more complicated. Prestwick, we must find a place for you outside the city. You're in danger here."

Ella said, "Flax Manor—"

The door swung open and a hard-faced young man entered, followed by more guards than I thought would be possible to pack into that room. The young man bowed. "Your Majesty. Your Highness. Governess, and... guest. His Grace invites you to join him in the Music Room."

I think the queen grew paler. It was hard to tell since she was already the color of an onion. No one tried to disarm us. Maybe it would be seen as insulting the prince or something like that. Or, maybe they thought outnumbering us four-to-one would keep them safe. In any case, they took us, and we went.

The Music Room didn't have so much as a tin flute in it. A pale, intelligent-looking young man in regular working clothes stood behind a spotless table. Four chairs had been shoved aside, and small couches and tables were arranged around the walls. A beautiful, multicolor tapestry of a coronation hung on the far wall. It included a representation of the twelve gods looking down and blessing the new king.

"Pres, is that your ancestor?" I asked.

He nodded. "Yes, it was."

I glanced at the young man by the table. "Is that his ancestor too?"

Pres nodded again.

"He looks like an asshole. At least I know you can take a joke."

By the time everyone who was going to enter the room had entered, we had His Grace and his two guards, Pres, Ella, the queen, sixteen more guards, and me. The room had only one door and no windows.

Lundt said, "Cousin Prestwick, I'm overjoyed that you're alive. Welcome home."

Pres said, "Thank you. How did my father die? I've heard rumors."

"A terrible accident with his horse. It was so sad. My condolences."

"Thank you again, and thank you for helping the queen keep things running. Now that I've returned, I'd like to schedule the coronation."

"Considering your grief... and your youth... perhaps that discussion should wait."

Pres crossed his arms. "I won't be getting any sadder, or any younger. It's time I was crowned."

"You certainly are your father's son." Lundt smiled and leaned toward Pres, hands on the table. "Yet I would feel irresponsible if I handed the throne to someone not yet prepared for the burden."

Pres said, "I certainly am—"

The queen interrupted her son. "His Highness is prepared—"

Pres held up his hand. "Mother, stop. I certainly am my father's son. To whom the throne should be handed is not your decision, because the throne does not belong to you. Murdering my father does not convey rightful ownership of the throne."

Lundt clenched his teeth. No one said anything or moved. Then I saw Lundt touch his thumb to his sword's hilt as he showed his teeth.

I said, "Hey, Your Grace, did you know your tapestry is wrong?"

Lundt squinted at me. "What?"

"It's wrong. It only has twelve gods. Not everybody knows this, but there are thirteen gods."

Lundt looked at the queen. "Who is this man?"

"My name's Bib. Nobody prays to the thirteenth god, She-Who-Must-Not-Be-Named. And we'll all agree that if you can't name her, then it's hard to pray to her. But I'll tell you a secret." I leaned in toward him. "I actually know what her name is."

I ran toward them. Part of their minds didn't quite believe I was coming, and that part paralyzed them. I drew my sword in the first two steps, lunged toward His Grace as he stood across the table from me, and opened his throat with a neat little slice. I slashed the right-hand guard across the skull and face. He'd live but might lose his eye. The left-hand guard stopped short and backed away from me toward the wall.

"Does anybody want to fight for this dead man?" I asked, facing the rest of the guards while Lundt's blood dripped down the side of the table. "No? Not when you have the true King of Glass right here, eh?"

Nobody had any fight left in them. I bowed to Pres, and everybody else did too. I gave the queen an extra little bow and smiled my most woman-stealing smile at her. "See, Your Majesty? You just kill them."

I stayed at Glass for two weeks before I'd begun annoying everybody around me. Pres was the exception, and I attribute that to youth and inexperience. He tried hard to get me to stay, offering me various positions and rewards. He offered me an earldom, a barony, or a knighthood. When I didn't bite, he tried to hire me as captain of the guard, weapons master, or enforcer of the king's justice. He followed up with tavern owner, brothel owner, beer inspector, or just walk around, do what I want, and let him clean up the mess. I turned it all down. I had places to take the stupid god-named sword, and I was counting on the fact that sometimes people like me better when I've been away for a while.

The queen didn't offer me any incentives to stay. She wasn't rude, but she acted as if I had dog shit on my boot, and it would be a relief when I took it outside.

I said to Ella, "Damn! How could you show such devotion to that dried-up horse apple of a woman?" My going-away feast had ended two hours ago, and just a few hardy fools were still talking.

Ella smiled but at the floor instead of me. "She gave me her only child to love and protect."

"Krak's teeth, I guess if she gave me something to love and protect, I'd feel differently."

"Where will you go tomorrow?" She didn't sound too interested.

"North, to Grollen. They're rumored to have bandit problems. What will you do once Pres is crowned?" I couldn't help sounding as interested as hell.

"He won't require a governess any longer. Perhaps I will

tutor." Ella stuck a big knife into the oak table. I barely saw her draw the thing. "Or not. I'm undecided."

I laughed as I pulled the knife free and handed it to her. "Ask Pres for a tavern, or a brothel. I'm not using mine."

"Ah? Brothel. Definitely a brothel." She started to smile but caught herself. "Some circumstances find men at their most childish. I am strikingly qualified."

"Keep it running until I get back. If you're not turning a profit by then, I'll save you. I'll be your star customer."

"You intend to return?"

"Of course! You can't fall in love with me from a distance if I'm right here in front of you."

"That's a foolish hope."

"But not impossible. Although that's not a barrier. I've seen shit happen that was not in any way possible."

"You're right, the hope is not impossible. But exceedingly foolish."

"If I wasn't being foolish, you wouldn't recognize me."

We embraced, and I wandered away to my chamber. The next morning, I rode north.

Grollen's bandit problem surprised me. Half the country's barons were the bandits. They had run the regular, honest bandits off into the countryside. Then they stole everything that their appalling reptile of a king had stolen from them. The only people who really got hurt were the ones not stealing anything from anybody.

It made me want to unleash lightning and call plagues on everybody rich enough to wear clothes without holes in them. I even tried to bargain with Harik for some power, but he and all the other gods ignored me. I ended up killing the seven worst barons and their loyal advisors, and then I had a sword-point conversation with the king from the foot of his bed at midnight.

I don't think any of it helped a bit.

I rode back into the City of Glass two months after I left. I went a little crazy and looked around for any new whorehouses Ella might have opened, but of course there weren't any. King Prestwick received me right away.

"Sorry I missed the coronation, Your Majesty."

I'd been away only two months, but Pres looked taller to me. He also ordered his people around with such determination that I figured someday he'd be a bastard to work for. Not yet, though. He sat me in a cushioned chair and poured wine. "It's good to see you. Will you stay?"

"Maybe. Where's Ella?" I ignored the wine.

Pres chewed his lip.

"Damn it to dog shit, you're a king and you can't even tell me? Is she alive?"

"She left."

"Left where?"

"I don't know. She didn't say anything. She was just gone."

I spent the night at the castle, but I turned down Pres's offers of feasts and banquets. The next day, I rode out of the city before dawn, still thinking about whether to search for her. If you declare love for somebody, and then they run away without warning, I suppose that's about the worst response you can get, short of bloodshed. The gods know I am not above doing stupid things, but at some point, stupid just becomes cruel.

I turned east toward the frontier. I hadn't journeyed that way in years, and I didn't think there was a single person out there that I liked. I should have some fine opportunities to kill people.

THIRTY-FIVE

Sometimes I daydream about finding a relaxed and comfortable situation in which people need to be killed. I'd appreciate living at a well-stocked inn, if a bunch of traitors and kidnappers would line up in the street every day no earlier than noon, so I could execute them. I wouldn't mind if they fought back or tried to escape. Hell, they might even kill me, but at least I wouldn't be dirty, soaked, tired, or freezing like I was today.

The far south frontier is a dark, barren, sharp land on the sweetest day of spring. Today was late autumn, and it was wet, blustery, and shatteringly cold. I was riding to the port of Deephold for no damn good reason. I didn't know anybody there, and I had nothing in particular to accomplish. I was just looking for people to kill. I told myself I was looking for the right kind of people to kill, the ones who really deserved it. But once in a while, when I was really drunk and harsh, I admitted I had grown less particular lately.

It was just a fact, and I wasn't whining about it. Nobody grabbed my hand and made me murder people.

When I had met Ella at Crossoak, I told her I liked to kill people. She told me to come with her, and we'd see whether there was anything to be done about it. We had done something about it, I remembered that for sure. I had since become a little unclear on what that was.

Today, Deephold lay two days of hard riding ahead on a clear road, and my horse had been killed five minutes ago. Some Hill Man I didn't see had thrown a javelin through her neck. That left me squatting behind the best cover I could find, a rock as stubby and frigid as Lutigan's heart.

I had gotten distracted by some unexplained smoke from just over the rise, and I left the road to investigate. I found two wagons and a few broken barrels on fire, along with four mules, three dead traders, and three Hill Men congratulating each other on how happy their wives were going to be with all the goods they'd just taken.

I had no argument with these men. Since I didn't speak their language, and they were the most dangerous fighters in the world, I wheeled my mare and rode like hell for seven or eight seconds until from somewhere a fourth one of the bastards killed my mare.

Charging them would just get me poked full of javelins, so I waited. If I were four Hill Men and had trapped a cowardly foreigner behind a rock, I'd feel fairly comfortable about just walking up and stabbing him to death. Before a minute had passed, I heard a boot scrape on the other side of my hiding spot.

I jumped out and startled one of them, stabbed him in the chest, and jumped the other way as a javelin whipped past me. Two more were running at me. They looked imposing in all their furs, but they were half a head shorter than me. They came at me from two sides, and I tried to dodge out from between them while blocking, cursing, and wondering where the last one was. At last, I slipped past one, hamstrung him, and flung him at his friend. The friend jumped out of the way, but I sliced his throat while he was still off-balance, and then I killed the hamstrung one from behind.

The fourth man appeared behind me, ready to ram his javelin

all the way through me. Something odd warned me, maybe the sound of his breathing, or the faintest of shadows on that gray day. I twisted so that the blade scraped my ribs instead of my liver. My foot slipped on a wet rock and I fell sideways. Then I heard a loud pop, and the Hill Man flopped over limp as laundry.

A man waved at me from forty paces away. "Are you still alive?"

"Desh?"

"I've been following you for weeks. If you're about to die, then this has been a disappointing trip." The young man walked up to me, leading his horse. He opened his cloak and groaned as he wrapped his sling around his waist. "Why didn't you go some place warm?"

"I didn't invite you along, so you did this to yourself. You look well, though. I don't have much to offer you. We could cook my horse."

He shook his head. "I need your help."

"Well, that seems abrupt, but I can't deny that I owe you. How's Limnad by the way?"

"Mystifying. I may require years to become an expert on spirits. I may never get there."

"I need to bind up my ribs, and those wagons are making a nice fire. Let's go over there." I disrobed just enough to get at my wound. "Who do you need killed?"

"No one. I don't need that kind of help."

"If you need advice on love, you came to a dry well. Sorcery troubles?"

"I need help paying a debt. A debt to Pres." He opened a satchel and brought out an intricate false hand crafted of pale wood and bronze.

"That's beautiful work. Assuming that it actually does something."

"It does. Just tell Pres that it's from me."

"Hell, his land is thirty days back the way you came! Why do you want me to do it?"

"There are two reasons. First, I have business that takes me north, not west toward Glass. Second, he knows you better than he knows me. Trust and confidence make these sorts of things work best."

I nodded. "All right, I said I'd help. I look forward to when you owe me a favor. There are a couple of toy boats I lost when I was a boy in Ir. I'd sure like to get those back."

"I'll watch for them in my travels." He pulled out a rough leather bottle, smaller than my palm. The stopper was sealed with thick wax. "Open this before you show Pres the hand."

"Could you ask me to do something a little less suspicious, like throw a snake down his shirt?"

"You don't need to make him drink out of it. Just open it. It will release enough power for you to properly fit the hand."

I took the bottle and examined it. "This seems awfully useful. Like stashing away a few extra arrows for an emergency. I've never seen anything like it. How does it work?"

"It's magic." Desh smiled. "Don't look at me that way. I don't ask you to explain how you make insects do tricks."

"I'd like to make one of these mules unsaddle my horse and strap the saddle onto himself, but I guess we'll have to do it the regular way."

An hour later, Desh said goodbye and rode off north. My new mule and I pushed on to Deephold, where I boarded a ship and sailed west. A week later, I bought a new horse in Garhalt, and three weeks after that, I rode up through the city of Glass on a dim morning in knee-deep snow.

Pres received me without any waiting around. He threw out his current company, two fancy-dressed buckets of bacon fat asking for some kind of favors, and he looked happy to do it. We wandered off to his library to chat.

Dark bookshelves covered two walls, filling the room with the smells of leather and wax. A charming array of hand weapons hung on the other two walls. "Pres, I assumed you could spell out a few words, but you seem to be a scholar. I see at least three books I've never heard of."

He finished pouring wine. "That's only because bars and brothels have much smaller libraries."

"Yes, Your Majesty. I'll pay respects to your mother soon, but before we get interrupted, I have something from Desh."

"Wait, I'll send for Ella."

"What?" I turned as if she might be standing behind me. She wasn't, but my elbow knocked over the wine.

Pres chuckled and waved to a servant. "Ella's here. If fact, Desh sent her here. He said I'd need somebody I trust when you arrived. If being cryptic is a quality of good sorcerers, Desh must be one of the best."

I started breathing. "Well... sure, why don't you ask Ella to come on in?"

Pres spoke to the guard at the door and sent him off. A few minutes later, Ella walked in and gave me a little smile. "You've arrived at last. I've enjoyed visiting with His Majesty, but I do not care to spend the entire winter here."

"I love you, and I missed you too."

She flinched and stared at me.

I laughed. "For once, you don't know what to say."

She and Pres both laughed with me, and she said, "I have missed your robust sense of mirth."

"I've missed it too. Sit over here. Desh sent me to do something, but he might have bumbled it. It could convince Pres he's as powerful as a god. Or make him want to farm melons. Either way, having people he trusts around him will help."

I showed them the false hand that I intended to fit onto Pres's arm. However, I couldn't answer a single one of their questions since Desh hadn't told me a damned thing about it. Ella demanded that the entire procedure be abandoned until Desh came to explain himself. Pres thanked her for her concern, told me to go ahead, and rolled up his sleeve.

I broke the wax on the bottle. The trapped power flowed out, and I pulled a green band before starting to work. I had to begin shaping the stump just as if I were building a new hand out of flesh.

"Is it supposed to look like that?" Ella asked.

"Hush. If I go too fast, he won't be able to make obscene gestures with it," I said.

"We wouldn't have this problem now if you—" She looked away.

I tried not to finish that sentence in my head.

"Go ahead," Pres said. "It's not your fault."

I couldn't help laughing at how foolish that statement was, especially for somebody who's supposed to be wise, like a king. I paused, thinking that if I had more power, I could restore his real hand.

Why didn't Desh do this procedure himself? His explanation about trust was bullshit. Ella didn't trust me worth a damn where Pres was concerned, and that poisoned all the trust in the room. Desh was a careful sorcerer. Everything he did had a reason. For some reason, he wanted me to fit this hand, and the most logical reason was that he'd made some sort of trade. The sort that he couldn't tell me about, because part of the deal was that I couldn't be told what I was supposed to do. The gods loved that kind of idiotic crap.

Preparing Pres for the false hand was a bit like healing, and that meant Gorlana was probably involved. What had Gorlana told me or given me that I might use in some way now?

"Is there a problem?" Pres asked.

"Just stop right now if there is!" Ella said.

"No, everything is fine. Just thought a sneeze was coming on."

I stood up and walked to the weapons on the wall, grabbed a short ax, and sat back at the table. I swung the weapon and chopped the claw off my left arm, right at the wrist. Blood splattered on all three of us. It hurt like a son of a bitch, and I cursed like one. I knew what to expect, and it still shocked me. Ella screamed and snatched the ax away. I guess she thought I'd chop off my other hand while I was holding the ax with it. Pres was on his feet and shouting something.

I didn't care. Gorlana had traded me the power I used to make that claw, and when I severed it, the power seeped back into me. Normally, power would never return when destroying something, so this must have been the deal Desh had made with her.

"Sit down, son!"

Pres said, "You ass-hopping whore!" Pres had benefited from his time with Baldir. He sat down.

I breathed deep and pulled some more green bands while my wrist bled on the table. Within five minutes, I had restored Pres's hand. I leaned back and sighed, wiping off sweat. Ella was bandaging my wrist with something, I didn't much care what. Pres paid no attention to his new hand. Instead, he yelled something at the guard, and then they ran out of the room together. I wasn't following the details around me with much care.

"That was insane!" Ella said, wrapping the bandage fast, like she was churning butter.

"I expect it was. Running all over the country killing people is insane, but I do that too."

"You didn't need to maim yourself to impress me!"

"I didn't do it for you. But I'm flattered you think I'm romantic enough to. I figured you'd love me just for being me. And because I've been away a long time." I shrugged, and I winced when the shrug bumped my wrist against the table.

Ella looked confused, which was understandable. She'd been

caught up in one deal with the gods, and maybe more than one. Right now, her view of the world might be changing in a hurry. She sat next to me and held my remaining hand with her two bloody ones. "You should not make such statements about love."

"I know. I thought maybe you wouldn't blame me so much for Pres's hand now."

"I have forgiven you. Forgiven you entirely, long before you returned today."

"So..." I stopped myself from shrugging and raised my eyebrows instead.

"Bib, I married Sir Linkan last summer."

That shouldn't be a problem, because even with one hand, I could kill that fart seven times before lunch. I almost said that, and the thought of his head rolling across the floor gave me a pleasant tingle. But she was gazing at me, patient and kind of wary, and I couldn't quite promise to make her a widow by the afternoon.

I had expected way too much from Ella. She wasn't what I'd call my ideal woman, but I couldn't think of anything I'd change about her. Now that I looked hard at it, though, there must be a thousand things about me that needed changing.

But Linkan, that mincing old mustache that walked like a man? By Harik, Fingit, and Krak, I'd never understand that.

I felt hollowed out, like there wasn't enough stuff inside me to fill out my skin. I had done a mountain of foolish things in my life, and I could pile this one on top with the rest.

Ella patted my hand, and I realized I'd left her alone in the conversation while I contemplated murder and woe.

"I can't say I'm happy about it, but I hope you are. Linkan... well, I won't say anything about him." I smiled. "What do you want for a wedding present? A whorehouse?"

Ella leaned over and kissed me hard and long. When we paused, I asked her to clarify her behavior, but she kissed me again before I finished the first word.

At last, I said, "So you won't object when I stab your husband in the heart?"

"Husband! I would never marry that man! Not even if he were made of gold and his mustache made of rubies. How can you consider such a thing?"

"Mainly because you said, 'I married Sir Linkan.'"

"Bah! Can you imagine me confined every day to his sad manor, directing servants, drinking tea, sewing? For the sake of all the gods, playing the spinet?"

"I suppose not."

"Raising his children?"

Or bearing his children, which she couldn't do. I didn't intend to mention that, but we both knew she was saying it. "Why in the name of the king's drawers did you say you were married? I could have killed him."

"But you didn't kill him. You composed yourself and offered congratulations as would any civilized man who is merely thinking about murder. I'm proud of you."

"So, it was a test? If I kill Linkan, then I'm still a murdering animal, but if I don't, then I may be worthy of walking within ten feet of your radiant self?" I was mad and trying to make her mad too. It's one of the reasons I'm hard to live with.

"No, your actions didn't matter a sliver. Well, I would have prevented you from killing Linkan. But I love you regardless of your decision. I simply enjoyed seeing you squirm."

I looked at the ceiling for a moment. It was an abrupt change of attitude, true, but I didn't think it was false. Gorlana had undoubtedly veiled me in Ella's sight when I agreed to let the goddess take her, and today's bizarre events had lifted that veil.

I sighed. "It's a ridiculous thing to say, but all of this was almost fun."

The next time we stopped kissing, the physician had arrived and was standing back against the wall. He was blushing and looked like he wanted to go find some other patient anywhere else in the castle but here.

Smiling, Pres clapped his hands. "Come on, stop that! You've bled enough on the rug already. It's an heirloom."

I watched Ella chat with Pres while the physician dealt with my wrist. Ella looked over at me. "What about the false hand? Can you wear it?"

"It would be awkward. Desh made it for Pres's right hand, and I'm missing a left. I'd knock my steak on the floor every time I tried to cut a bite."

"Can't you do something? Something sorcerer-like?"

"Of course I can. I can shut up and not whine about it. What I'd like to point out is the fact that you did fall in love with me from a distance, so my plan worked after all. You've got to admit now that I am a superior planner. So, where are we going?"

Ella stepped back and peered like I was some new kind of creature. "What do you mean, where?"

"Where do you want to go?" I pointed at two walls, and then at the other two. "What do you want to do? What are your ambitions?" I grabbed her hand.

"Do you want to travel with me? I didn't believe that you would." She stepped away but didn't let go of my hand. "I thought that either I must go with you, or we'd go different ways. And I'm not one to simply go along." She said it the way she'd state an indisputable fact, the same way she'd state that the sun will burn you red.

I laughed hard, the way I'd needed to for years. "And I wouldn't change that about you, not for a horse that flies and pisses whiskey. I will stay for as long as you can stand me. Go where you want. I don't need much, as long as I can bring this stupid sword along. Besides, any place we go will have people that need to get killed."

READ DEATH'S BABY SISTER

SEQUEL TO DEATH'S COLLECTOR

THE GODS HATE THEM, SO THEY CAN'T AFFORD TO HATE EACH OTHER.

Bib the sorcerer, the most accomplished murderer of his time, finds his simple, gently-alcoholic retirement crushed when an untrained sorcerer girl plops onto his doorstep.

The girl, Manon, is as unpredictable and deadly as a volcano, but otherwise like any twelve-year-old—she hates everybody and refuses to do as she's told.

Bib fumes but agrees to take Manon someplace safe where she can learn not to turn people into sand or make it rain whales.

They flee from a crusade of sorcerer-killing zealots, who burn and mutilate their way across the countryside. The cruel Goddess of the Unknowable reaches out to claim Manon and destroy Bib. The petty God of Death demands that Bib kill the girl, and Bib calls him an eyeball-scraping nugget of filth, which means no —for now.

An overworked, intra-planar monster, a mad, city-burning sorcerer, and some pretentious flunkies called "Death's Riders" enter the chase. Bib and Manon both run from multiple murderous threats—including each other.

As paths of escape become fewer and narrower, Bib and Manon must each decide what they're willing to sacrifice to vanquish their enemies and save themselves.

And if they can't both be saved, decide which one of them will die.

READ WEE PIGGIES OF RADIANT MIGHT

COMPANION NOVEL TO DEATH'S COLLECTOR

GODHOOD ISN'T AS MUCH FUN AS IT USED TO BE.

The idiot gods are being driven into feckless insanity—and they weren't all that stable to start with. An unexplained force severs the gods from a worshipful mankind, leaving them dim, flabby, and decidedly less immortal. Their eternal enemy now chases them in and out of other realities as if they were frantic bunnies.

The Blacksmith of the Gods, Fingit, has been mocked by his fellow gods since the beginning of time. But now only he is still lucid enough to conceive a scheme to save them and maybe reality itself.

Fingit contrives a plan so clever that if anyone dies it won't be him. But the most deranged being in the universe, his sister Sakaj, drags him into her own lunatic scheme.

Fingit must outwit Sakaj, defeat their incomprehensibly powerful foes, overcome the force thrusting them into oblivion, and grapple with the most singular problem of all—while the gods have been gone, has mankind cared?

In fact, has mankind even noticed?

CONNECT WITH THE AUTHOR

Visit his website at bill-mccurry.com
or on Social Media:

- facebook.com/bill.mccurry3
- twitter.com/BillMcCurry
- instagram.com/bfmccurry
- goodreads.com/billmccurry
- amazon.com/author/billmccurry

ABOUT THE AUTHOR

Bill McCurry holds a Bachelor of Arts in Sociology and a Master of Arts in Sociology from the University of Texas in Arlington. He is one of seven people known to have received a non-academic job using a sociology degree. Bill's short story "The Santa Fix" was published by Open Heart Publishing's anthology *An Honest Lie: Volume* 3. He has performed and taught improv and interactive theater for over twenty years. During his career, Bill has owned a small construction company, run market research projects, managed customer service groups, and developed computer systems as a contractor for the National Cancer Institute. He is currently writing his seventh novel, *Death's Least Favorite Toy*. Bill grew up in Fort Worth, Texas, and now lives in Carrollton, Texas, with his wife, Kathleen, an independent court reporter who is so keenly determined that she would always be able to kill him if it came to a knife fight.

CPSIA information can be obtained
at www.ICGtesting.com
Printed in the USA
LVHW041541280623
751013LV00002B/299